"I think he wanted Carla to know that he didn't kill her sister," Susan said.

"But why?"

"Because if a copycat killed Lisa, he's probably angry about it. He wants people to know that it wasn't him. And he'll probably strike again just to prove it."

Bannerman nodded. But Susan saw his eyes cloud over as if to say, "That's interesting, but I don't really care about him, or his six other victims, except to the extent that he endangers Carla. Or Susan. Or any of my people." Mama's Boy takes care of his own.

"You know, we just might have a shot at catching him," she said.

"That's not why we're here, Susan."

But she could see that he was intrigued by the idea. He wouldn't mind catching Claude. If the opportunity offered itself. If it could be done cleanly and quietly. Lots of *ifs*. But he would never use the police. Paul would never do that. Claude, if that was his name, would simply be found somewhere, maybe with a note in his mouth.

Mama's Boy doesn't do courts.

Other books by John R. Maxim

Novels
PLATFORMS
ABEL BAKER CHARLIE
TIME OUT OF MIND
THE BANNERMAN SOLUTION
THE BANNERMAN EFFECT

Non-Fiction
DARK STAR

BANNERMAN'S LAW

John R. Maxim

BANTAM BOOKS
NEW YORK • TORONTO • LONDON • SYDNEY • AUCKLAND

BANNERMAN'S LAW
A Bantam Book / October 1991

ISBN 0-553-29326-5

Published simultaneously in the United States and Canada

Bantam Books are published by Bantam Books, a division of Bantam
Doubleday Dell Publishing Group, Inc. Its trademark, consisting of
the words "Bantam Books" and the portrayal of a rooster, is
Registered in U.S. Patent and Trademark Office and in other
countries. Marca Registrada. Bantam Books, 666 Fifth Avenue, New
York, New York 10103.

PRINTED IN THE UNITED STATES OF AMERICA

RAD   0 9 8 7 6 5 4 3 2 1

For Christine
           . . . who makes the sun come up.

1

On a cool and perfect California morning, on the last day of her short life, Lisa Benedict parked her Fiero in a quiet residential area several streets away from the gate house of Sur La Mer.

She had come by a different route this time, using only back roads and residential streets. She avoided Tower Road, which ringed the grounds on all but the ocean side. It had been tempting to make a quick pass of it, to see that all was quiet, but that would have meant driving past the surveillance cameras. Better, she decided, not to let them see her car again. The car was white, with a USC Trojans decal across the rear window, a student parking sticker on the windshield, and a crumpled left front fender. They were likely to remember it from the previous Sunday. But without the car, she felt sure, they would not recognize her at all.

On that first Sunday she had worn a skirt and blue blazer, and a pair of heels, which she'd ended up ruining. This time she was better equipped. She wore a borrowed running suit, dark green and hooded—to hide the shine of her auburn hair—and she had muted her new white Reeboks with a bottle of Kitchen Bouquet which, she hoped, would wash out. The suit was three sizes too large and shapeless, all the better for camouflage. She would blend nicely into the thick forest of sugar pines that ringed the asylum.

She locked the car, then strapped a bulky tote around her waist, adjusting it so that her Nikon and recorder would not chafe her spine. She began jogging. Upon reaching Tower Road, where it bordered Sur La Mer to the south, she turned right, away from the gates, and paced herself with another runner some fifty yards ahead of her. *That's good,* she thought. *Not being the only one out here.* The other jogger, a man, faded red sweatshirt and shorts, visored tennis hat, glanced back over his shoulder but kept on.

He'd seen her. It meant she would have to keep this up for a while. She couldn't very well have him look back again and see that she'd vanished. But now he was turning, reversing his direction, heading back toward her. As he drew near, he nodded. A brief, polite smile, a flicker of eye contact. He was a man in his forties, well tanned but fleshy, not very fit.

That face. Did it seem familiar? No. Just a face. Don't get paranoid. She bobbed her head in response, then continued on, keeping the Sur La Mer estate to her left. She counted off two hundred paces and then pretended to trip as if over a shoelace. She stopped, pretending to tie it. Glancing the way she'd come, she saw the other jogger was gone.

Rats, she thought. She'd prefer to have seen him peel off toward his home. Or at least to be sure that he wasn't from Sur La Mer. Not that it should matter necessarily. She wondered what her sister would do in this situation. Better to make sure, she decided. She turned in the direction he had taken.

Keeping a steady pace, she approached the main gate, the only gate, and its video camera. The camera's stare remained fixed, not tilting or turning as she went by. Morning dew still covered the driveway. It showed one set of tire tracks but no footprints. Satisfied, she slowed to a walk, then reversed her field once more.

All was quiet now. No people in sight. She heard no sound but the distant yap of a small dog.

She reached the place where, seven days earlier, in heels, she had struggled over the low fence and scurried for the cover of the trees that formed a living moat around Sur La Mer. She did it again, this time smoothly vaulting the fence and promptly blending, green against green, into the forest. Just inside the tree line, she lowered herself into a squat so that it would seem, if anyone came, that she had paused to relieve herself. She waited for five minutes, listening, then she checked her watch. The climb to the main grounds, she estimated, would take twenty minutes. Last Sunday it had taken nearly an hour. But this time she was dressed for it. And she had a map. She knew where the trip wires were. She would not have to feel her way.

Not bad, she told herself, for someone who'd never done anything like this before. Her sister, Carla, would be proud of her. Well . . . maybe, after bawling her out first. Lisa had asked herself, all that week, how Carla would have gone about it. Careful preparation, came the answer. Slow and easy. Except Carla, being Carla, would probably have brought a weapon of some kind. And her heart would not be pounding this hard.

"Who am I kidding?" she muttered aloud.

Carla wouldn't have done this at all. She would have thought the whole thing was dumb. Seen too many movies.

On the other hand, Carla never cared much about her grades. She had never even finished college, let alone earned a masters at the toughest film school in the country. Let alone graduating third in her class, if she could lock in an A for Mecklenberg's course.

And if Nellie Dameon, up there, isn't worth an A . . . heck, an A *plus* once Mecklenberg learns that she, Lisa Benedict, actually got her voice on tape, then nothing is.

Lisa took a breath and began her climb.

2

She had gone to Sur La Mer, on that other Sunday, with no thought of trespassing. Her intention was merely to photograph the main gate and, if she could, to sweet-talk the gatekeeper into letting her walk up the entrance road for a shot of Sur La Mer itself.

Not that doing so seemed terribly important at the time. There were plenty of file photographs of the main house and gardens. But most were fifty or sixty years old. The only recent ones, and the only color shots, were all taken from the air. And not that her thesis would suffer for want of a current shot at ground level. Nor, for that matter, were photographs even required of her assignment. But they were a nice touch. And she'd be glad to have them if she ever wanted to try selling the finished product to a magazine. Maybe, someday, even expanding it into a book. Or a documentary.

More immediately, the name of the game was impress the professor. He'd told her that permission to visit was almost never granted. Not to the press, not to film historians, and certainly not to graduate students. She would dearly love to show him that she'd actually talked her way onto the grounds.

But there was no gatekeeper on whom to bestow her most melting sweet-young-thing smile. Only the camera and a tinny male voice from a box. She tried nonetheless. She promised the voice that she would not bother the patients. She would not talk to them or photograph them. The voice was friendly enough, in a lecherous sort of way—she could tell that its owner enjoyed looking at her—but, in the end, it was firm. The

4

rules were strict. No photographs, no admittance, no exceptions, sorry. The voice clicked off. The camera stared. She stared back. She tried looking sad. She even tried looking sexy, rubbing a hand over her breasts, head back, lips parted, her tongue running over them.

Nothing. No response.

This annoyed her. She tried to imagine that the man behind that camera was up there drooling over his monitor but she knew, more likely, that he was probably laughing and calling the other guards to come look. Lisa flushed. Glaring at the silent lens, she raised her Nikon to her eye and pressed the shutter, three times, out of spite.

This small act of defiance, while satisfying, was pointless. Lisa realized that. The inmates at Sur La Mer, the very existence of the place, were only the smallest part of her project, which dealt with the transitional period between the Hollywood silent film era and the sound era. Professor Mecklenberg called it a classic case study of corporate resilience in response to a revolution in technology. *"Imagine the gasoline engine becoming obsolete practically overnight. It was almost on that scale,"* he had said.

Lisa was doubtful at first. But Mecklenberg had lent her a few books on the subject and the more she read, the more fascinated she became. Back in 1927 many studio executives had dismissed "talkies" as a fad or, at most, a development that would be no more than an occasional novelty for years to come. As myopic as that thinking seemed in retrospect, the reasoning behind it was solid. To begin with, the prospective cost of converting thousands of theaters to sound was staggering. The amount would exceed the industry's entire income—not profit, *income*—for the whole preceding year.

Further, all earnings from European distribution would be lost; silent films were international, but Hollywood movies would now have to be recorded strictly in English. Dubbing was unknown. Even worse, the talkies would be of dreadful quality because of the limitations of the soundstage. They would be little more than set piece stage plays on film and the actors would be allowed almost no freedom of movement. The camera, enclosed in a soundproof box, would have to be stationary. The vacuum tube microphones of the day, sensitive in only one direction, would have to be concealed in lamps and in floral arrangements and actors would have to speak directly into them without moving their heads. Location films, outdoor adventures, battle scenes and chariot races, all that contributed to the sweep and grandeur of the silver screen, were now impossible. "Why the hell," asked one studio head, reasonably, "would the public give all that up just to hear an actor talk to a potted plant?"

What struck Lisa the most, in doing her research, was the human cost of the transition. Careers of long standing were shattered overnight. Actors and actresses who were household names in 1927 could find no work at all in 1928. Some failed because their voices were totally unsuited to their screen images. Virile leading men had high-pitched voices or pronounced lisps. Clara Bow had a Bronx honk and the Talmadge sisters spoke Brooklynese. Others could talk perfectly well but not in English. One western hero, a former Texas Ranger according to studio publicists, was actually from Sweden and could barely order from an American menu. Most actors, the studios realized to their horror, had virtually no concept of good diction. Almost all, except those few with stage training, would need voice testing and diction coaches. Elocution experts, many with invented credentials, flocked to Hollywood where they were promptly enriched by frightened, desperate actors.

The studio heads, meanwhile, began importing stage actors in great numbers. In effect, this left them with a double payroll because many film actors with unproven voices still had expensive contracts. More than a few studio executives conspired to break those contracts through intimidation, blackmail, invoking morals clauses, and even deliberately sabotaging the sound tracks of these actors' first talkies.

Gods and goddesses one day, unemployable the next. Many had come from nothing; some were little more than hoboes, lured to the film colony by the promise of work as extras. Others had been ranch hands or cowboys, runaways or prostitutes. A few found success, money, and adulation beyond their wildest dreams. Then, in a twinkling, they were nothing again. They lost their homes, their cars, and, quickest of all, their friends. Some became suicides. Some died of broken hearts. A few retreated into madness.

Clara Bow was one example. Nellie Dameon was another. Nellie, it was said, had been so traumatized by the sniggers that greeted her two attempts at talkies that she never spoke again. She became a recluse, entombing herself in her Benedict Canyon home until, abandoned by her one remaining servant when there was nothing left to steal, the Motion Picture Association quietly arranged for her care at a private asylum known as Sur La Mer. More than sixty years later, Lisa Benedict was astonished to learn, Nellie Dameon was still there. And there were others. No one seemed to know how many.

Sur La Mer, according to one of Mecklenberg's books, was located on the crest of a wooded hill high above the Santa Barbara shoreline. She was well into her thesis, in which this place appeared as no more than a single footnote, and had no real need, and certainly not the time, to attempt a visit. But she found herself haunted by visions of a frail old woman, silent, eyes glazed and distant, still clinging to those brief champagne years before her mind and heart were broken. And so, on a Sunday morning, dressed nicely as if for church, Lisa drove north to Santa Barbara. She wanted to see the place. Feel it. Perhaps have a photograph or two to show for the trip.

A shot of the entrance, thanks to the voice from the gate house box, was all she was going to get. At least it was something. And it was rather a good one. There was a heavy mist that morning. The road, beyond the gate, faded into it. A nice touch. Eerie.

But she was no less annoyed. A place such as Sur La Mer, she felt, surely had nothing to hide. Why, then, deny her a shot of the main house? And she was also tempted. What, she wondered, was the worst that could happen if she were caught climbing up through the trees? How much of a fine could there be for trespassing? It was done all the time by the paparazzi, even by legitimate journalists. More likely, the most it would cost her would be a dry cleaning bill for her skirt and the scarring of a pair of shoes that hurt her feet anyway. It seemed worth it. She decided to try.

Lisa climbed back into her Fiero, fastened her seat belt, and, after consulting a road map for the benefit of the surveillance camera, drove away, looking for a street on which to conceal her car. That done, she returned on foot to Tower Road. At one point, well up from the main gate, she caught a glint of metal in a tree that extended over the sidewalk. She moved closer, looking up. She saw two more cameras there. They were fastened in fixed positions, unable to scan, and they pointed in opposite directions. She was, she realized, in a blind spot that extended for perhaps twenty yards. She had approached them nearly at right angles. She would not have been seen. Convinced of that, grateful for her luck, she climbed the four-foot fence that ringed the property.

The fence, she soon learned, was the least of the obstacles preventing easy access to Sur La Mer. First there were the pines themselves, thickly planted and rising like steps. In places, the climb was nearly vertical. Trees that might have helped her seemed to have been deliberately cut away. Rock faces had been greased, then covered with peat moss so that any touch would leave evidence of an intruder. Peat moss, she was fairly sure, did not belong in a pine forest. Someone had definitely put it there. She paused, wondering whether this was such a good idea. As she rested, and as the rising sun began filtering through the pines, her eye caught another reflection off metal, this time on the forest floor. Carefully, she moved toward its source. She knelt.

It was a trip wire. Mostly hidden by moss. A two-foot section of it had been exposed, probably by rain, and now glistened with dew. What was this, she wondered? Why trip wires? She thought again about retreating. But now she was more than curious. Why, she asked, should a place like Sur La Mer need such a security system? Who was up there? Just a few old actors and actresses. Who would want to harm them?

She climbed, all the more slowly, gently probing the sphagnum with her fingertips. A few yards further on, she found a second wire. She would have missed the third, or she might have touched it, had not a sharp spit of flame erupted inches from her face. She blinked, waiting for the afterimage to fade and for her heart to be still. Now she saw it. The limp remains of a field mouse, eyes wide, face scorched. This wire, if not the others as well, was electrified. Composing herself, she pressed on. Just above, through the trees, she could see what seemed to be a clearing. She raised her head. Now she could see the outline of a roof. Another twenty yards.

And another twenty minutes to cover them. She moved, one step at a time, looking for more cameras, more wires, more dead animals. She found none. The climb, which might have taken ten minutes with the right shoes and without the obstacle course, had taken more than fifty. But now she knew the way. Going down would be easier. And she was there, inside, looking at a manor house so vast that it seemed to fill half the sky.

The house, built in the French château style, stood glistening as the morning sun burned through the mist and reflected off a million flakes of mica set in granite. She knew its history. Built in the 1890s, railroad money, owner ruined during the panic of 1907, couldn't find a buyer, gave it to the state in lieu of back taxes. The state kept it in reasonable repair by leasing it for use in location shooting to the new film industry down in

Hollywood and eventually leased it to the Motion Picture Relief Fund for use as a rest home.

The grounds were lovely. She had found a place behind a long low hedge from which she could see nearly all of it. A flawless dichondra lawn sloped down from the main house in the direction of the Pacific Ocean. The ocean was a full half mile distant and perhaps two hundred feet below the crest of Sur La Mer. But the skill of some long ago landscaper had made the ocean, the sky, and this place seem all of a piece. There was a good-size beach community down below, a suburb of Santa Barbara, but nothing of it could be seen or even heard from the grounds. Lisa imagined, correctly, that even if she climbed to the highest window of the main house she would see nothing that was not part of the serene little world that had been created for the members.

Members.

They were never called patients, she had learned. Nor inmates. They were members.

But why, she wondered again, all the security? She understood, she supposed, why no interviews were permitted. They lived, said one old article, in a carefully controlled reality, in rooms without mirrors. Some had no idea that they'd grown old. They dressed every day. They read scripts of photoplays that would never be made. They placed telephone calls to agents, studio heads, and columnists long dead; calls that were actually taken and answered by staff.

All very sad, thought Lisa. Such a fragile existence. So dreamlike. She found herself wondering how Nellie Dameon spent her days if she never spoke. Endlessly watching her own films? Living only within them, forever young? It seemed an intrusion even to ask, let alone to write about it. Better to leave these people and their ruined lives in peace. Be satisfied with a few photos of the house and grounds.

Staying to the shadows and low behind the hedge, Lisa set her lens at its widest angle and took several establishing shots before zooming in on details of the architecture and landscaping. She used a full roll of film. It was enough. She was about to back away, into the sugar pines for her descent to Tower Road, when she saw movement at the far end of the château. Members, she thought. Two of them. They were in wheelchairs, being pushed to a place of shade at the edge of a flower garden. Two men. One wore an overcoat with a thick fur collar and a black Homburg on his head. The other wore a yachting cap and blazer. Winter and summer. She wondered where they thought they were. She reloaded the Nikon.

One of the men who had pushed them, casual clothing, no whites, glanced in her direction. Lisa ducked down, stepping back from the hedge. Her legs touched a marble bench. She sat.

She could see through the hedge, although not well. More people were moving about. A man, wearing a long white bathrobe stepped out onto the terrace. A towel covered his head. She pressed the zoom button of her camera and brought one knee under her, raising herself.

His body filled the viewfinder. He was stretching now, rolling his head over his shoulders, luxuriating in the morning sun. One side of the towel fell away. Lisa saw that the face, all of it, was thickly bandaged. There were holes in the bandages for his mouth and for one eye. The other was completely covered. Lisa, on impulse, snapped a picture.

The man reacted to something behind him. Lisa zoomed back to take in more of the terrace. A woman in a matching robe, her face also bandaged but not as fully, approached him holding two mugs. The woman was slender, and seemed rather tall. Her hair, ash blond, shoulder length, was brushed out. It had the look of having just been washed. Steam rose from the mugs. His held a straw. He took it from her, sipped, and nodded thanks. She rubbed his neck, affectionately.

Someone else approached. It was another man,

sport coat, sunglasses, balding, a double chin. He was
speaking to the couple, gesticulating. From his body
language, he seemed to be urging them . . . no, ordering them . . . to go back inside. The man with no
face turned away, ignoring him. He moved with his mug
to the flagstone steps. The woman joined him and, very
deliberately, they sat. The second man stood, hands on
his hips, glaring at their backs. He was saying something. They paid no attention. The man with the sunglasses, clearly angry, took a breath. He raised one hand
and, first glancing around him, extended his middle
finger. Lisa snapped him. He turned, his color rising,
and stalked back toward the double doors of the château.

Lisa zoomed in on the sitting pair. From what she
could see of their skin they were certainly not old. And
they had lowered themselves easily, she into a lotus
position. What's with the faces, she wondered? Auto
accident? Plastic surgery? And why here? This is supposed to be a rest home for batty old actors.

A shadow passed over the hedge, its source behind
her.

Her stomach tightened.

Too late, she heard footsteps on a gravel path. She
cringed, eyes closed, waiting.

"Good morning, Nellie," came a voice. "Fine day."

Not yet daring to breathe, she half turned on the
bench toward the man who had spoken. He was quite
old, easily eighty-five, but he stood tall and was walking
steadily. He carried a large easel case in one hand and a
folding stool in the other.

She hesitated. "Um . . . good morning," she said,
clearing her throat.

The tall man slowed, then stopped. He cocked an
ear as if Lisa's return of greeting was cause for disbelief.
Now he turned and stared. Past her. Through her.

"Nellie?" His voice was tentative, not much above a
whisper.

She saw that his eyes were clouded. She was
tempted not to speak. But he took a step nearer, one

hand raised as if feeling his way. "Nellie?" he said again. "Is that you?"

"Ah . . . no, sir. I'm just . . ."

The dull eyes found the voice. "You're not Nellie." The eyes blinked. The man frowned.

"No, sir."

"But you're sitting in her place, you know. That's Nellie's bench."

"Oh. I . . ."

"You mustn't make her think it's been taken away."

"I won't. I mean, I'm sorry. I didn't realize."

"Any of the other benches is all right except that and this." He felt with his hand for the second bench, finding it. "This one is reserved for Garbo when she comes."

"Garbo." Lisa repeated blankly.

"Although knowing her," he sniffed, "she'll probably want Nellie's."

"But Garbo is . . ." She stopped herself.

It didn't matter. The old man's mind was already elsewhere. "Well, I've got to be moving along," he said. He raised his folding stool and waggled it in lieu of a wave. "Don't want to lose the morning light."

"Sir," Lisa raised her camera. It whirred three times. "Aren't you. . . . Are you Jason Bellarmine by any chance? The director?" She recognized him now. She remembered watching the Academy Awards when she was still in high school. Gregory Peck had presented him with a special Oscar for lifetime achievement. Even then, he was functionally blind from diabetes. He had to be led to the podium.

"All casting is done through my office." He walked on. "Have your agent call."

"But I'm not . . . yes, sir."

She watched as he made his way down a path lined with geraniums toward a marble terrace, where he set up his stool and easel with practiced ease. He took a blank, two-foot canvas from his case and mounted it. He squeezed a tube of red paint directly onto the canvas and began spreading it with a palette knife, stopping now and then to inspect the horizon. There was nothing red out there. And whatever he was painting had no shape that she could see.

She had taken several photographs of the blind artist at work when the soft Pacific breeze shifted and Lisa caught a scent of jasmine in the air. She lifted her chin and sniffed, searching for its source. She looked behind her, toward Garbo's bench. She gasped, stifling a cry. An old woman, thin, even smaller than herself, was standing at her shoulder. Just standing. Waiting. Lisa recognized her at once. The vivid reddish hair, marcelled, was certainly a wig. Her cheeks heavily rouged, her enormous eyes the color of cobalt. They were shining, becoming liquid. Her lips moved but made no sound. The chin began to quiver. Lisa, recovering, bolted to her feet.

"Please," she stepped away from the bench, gesturing toward it with her hand. "I'm terribly sorry."

The tiny bosom heaved but Nellie Dameon made no move.

"It's just that I'm a fan of yours," Lisa said quickly. "I wanted to see your . . . where you sat. I wanted to touch it. I should have asked your permission." Lisa hoped that somewhere in there was the reassurance that would keep this woman from slipping over the edge.

The old woman blinked several times as if trying to comprehend what Lisa was saying. Then, suddenly, the eyes cleared. They glanced at the bench and then away. Dismissively, thought Lisa. Now, in those eyes, Lisa thought she saw the briefest flicker of amusement. She had a sense that whatever had caused Miss Dameon's breath to quicken, it had nothing to do with Lisa's use of her throne.

Nellie Dameon smiled. She raised one gloved hand toward Lisa who accepted it, tentatively, then wondered what she was to do with it. Kiss it? Curtsey? Or assist Nellie Dameon to her seat. She presumed the last.

Nellie settled daintily onto the marble bench and smoothed the folds of her robe so that the hem covered her shoes. It was not so much a robe, Lisa decided, as an evening coat, the sort one used to wear over long dresses. The style was at least fifty years out of date but it showed little sign of wear.

"May I sit?" she asked. She realized that, standing, she was exposed to view from the château. Other staffers were moving about the grounds. One man, youngish, dressed in a suit, was walking across the lawn toward Jason Bellarmine. He carried what looked like a medical bag. Lisa lowered herself and backed away toward the bench reserved for Garbo. She hesitated. "Is this one all right?" she asked.

Nellie Dameon nodded. Lisa sat.

"I've seen several of your films," she said. "I have two of them on tape. *Broadway* and *The Four Horsemen.*"

Lisa bit her lip. She probably should not have mentioned videotapes. They belonged to a world that Nellie Dameon no longer knew. But if the word sounded strange to her, she gave no sign. Rather, she took notice of the drying mud that covered Lisa's hands, legs, and much of her clothing. She raised a finger, pointing it first at Lisa and then at the château, frowning, her eyes narrowing. She was asking a question.

"Um . . . no." Lisa chose not to lie. "I don't work here. I snuck in through those woods."

Nellie Dameon's eyes asked why.

"To see the house," she said. "To see you, I guess. But I never really expected . . ."

The old woman raised a hand. Her head had turned in the direction of the young doctor. He was moving toward them. Nellie Dameon brought a finger to her lips and gestured, urgently, in the direction of the trees. Lisa understood. Crouched low, she backed away. She hid herself.

She watched, between the branches of a juniper, as the doctor approached, greeted the old woman pleasantly, and eased himself down on his heels beside her bench.

"Was someone here, Miss Dameon?" Lisa heard him ask. She crouched lower. But the doctor, oddly, did not look in her direction. He was looking toward the house.

The actress shook her head.

"Mr. Bellarmine said there was a woman. He heard her speak."

Nellie Dameon smiled. Slowly, she raised a finger to her temple, making a circular motion with it.

The doctor answered her smile, but his eyes were stern. "Nellie," he tapped the seat beside her, "the bench is still warm. I feel her."

She shook her head, stubbornly. She made another circular motion with her finger, this time pointing it at the young doctor.

His grin widened, his expression now a bit sheepish. Lisa could see that his bluff had been called and he knew it. She had not been sitting where he claimed to feel warmth. He had only the word of a blind old man who thought he was still a director and who painted scenes that only he could see.

Lisa watched as he took Nellie Dameon's hand, his fingers feeling for her pulse. His eyes dropped to his wristwatch. He counted for a few moments, then frowned. "Your heart's really cooking," he said, distantly. But he was no longer looking at the watch. He was studying the grass around the bench. There were footprints there. In the dew. Too many. Lisa's heart began to pound as well. The young doctor touched the folds of Nellie's coat. He moved them slightly, revealing her shoes. Lisa understood. He was looking to see if she was wearing heals. She was not

Nellie Dameon took his hand. She slapped it, lightly, reprovingly. She gave it an affectionate squeeze. He raised his free hand in surrender, then continued his examination although his attention, thought Lisa, kept turning toward the house.

"Are you sure," he said at last, "that none of those people have been bothering you?"

She nodded, patting his knee.

"If they ever do, any of them, do you promise you'll tell me?"

Another nod. A smile.

Lisa watched as he finished the examination. It was not much of one. He looked into her eyes, had them follow his finger. He tested her grip and, lightly, he scratched each of her hands to determine that she had sensation in them. With a stethoscope drawn from his bag, he listened at her chest, then, partially peeling her evening coat, he listened at her back.

Satisfied, he covered her. His hands lingered on her shoulders, giving them a gentle squeeze. "Stay well," he said. Lightly, he kissed the top of her head, then turned abruptly toward the château.

Nellie Dameon watched him go. Not looking at Lisa, she raised a staying hand in her direction. The young doctor had reached the broad stone terrace. He seemed to pause there momentarily, as if deciding whether to go inside or to visit the two old men on the far side of the lawn. He chose, apparently, to continue his rounds. He set off toward the one in the yachting costume. The old woman motioned Lisa forward.

"He seems very nice," said Lisa tentatively, drawing near.

Nellie Dameon nodded. ". . . . ss."

"Um . . . Did you just say something?"

The actress looked at her. The eyes were clear. Searching. But suddenly they closed. She shook her head.

"Miss Dameon . . ." Lisa knelt at her side. "I think you did. I think you just said *yes.*"

There was no response. Nellie Dameon looked away. But those eyes had told Lisa that she was not mistaken.

"Is it that," she tried again, "you don't want people to know? That you can talk, I mean?"

Slowly, the eyes returned to Lisa's face. Searching again. A parchment hand rose toward Lisa's face. It touched a long curl that had fallen across her cheekbone. Nellie Dameon rolled it between her fingers, feeling it, studying it. Then, slowly, the eyes rose to meet Lisa's. They looked deeply. An eyebrow flicked upward, questioningly.

Lisa thought she understood. "No," she said earnestly. "I wouldn't tell anyone. Not if you don't want me to."

The old woman's eyes narrowed. Her mouth curled upward at one corner. It was a look of . . . skepticism. It removed any doubt.

"Listen . . ." Lisa took Nellie's hand and held it against her cheek. "It will kill me not to be able to say anything." *Especially*, she thought, *to Professor Mecklenberg*. "But for what it's worth, I swear. I won't say a word unless you give me permission."

The hand squeezed her own, briefly, then freed itself. Gently, it caressed Lisa's hair, bringing it forward, framing her face with it.

". . . Auburn," she said.

Lisa held her breath.

"Like mine . . . once," she whispered, distantly.

"You *can*," Lisa gasped. "You can *talk*."

The fingers moved to Lisa's mouth, silencing her. Now they moved to her cheek, feeling the skin, as if studying it. The eyes drifted, slowly, over Lisa's body, the small bosom, narrow hips, slim waist. *Like mine once*, she said again, but this time only to herself. And yet Lisa could hear it.

"Are you my d . . ." The old woman stopped herself. She closed her eyes. She shook her head as if to show that she knew the question to be foolish.

And once more, Lisa heard, or sensed, the word that was not spoken. The word was *daughter*.

"I'm just . . . Lisa Benedict," she said. "I'm only twenty-four."

Nellie Dameon nodded. So sadly, thought Lisa.

The actress wet her lips. "You look . . . eighteen," she said.

"I know." Lisa took her hand. "It runs in the family. We're all built like boys."

"Your mother . . . looks like you?"

"She did once, I guess. She died when I was little."

The old woman's eyes became moist. She swallowed. "She had a . . . mark. A strawberry mark." She touched her own throat just above the right collar bone. "Here."

Once more, Lisa took her hand. "I'm sorry. She didn't." She's not your daughter either. Lisa said this last with her eyes.

"Would you tell me," Nellie Dameon wet her lips, "when she was born?"

"Um, nineteen thirty . . . two, I guess."

The huge eyes blinked. The lips parted.

"Miss Dameon," Lisa said gently, "my mother was born in Madison, Wisconsin, and she lived there until she was eighteen. My grandmother also lived there all her life. She only died five years ago. Same build, same coloring as the rest of us. As much as I'd like to believe it, I don't think you and I are related."

The old woman turned away, nodding distantly, sadly, seeming to accept what Lisa had told her. Suddenly, she straightened, peering over the hedge. The young doctor had caught her eye. He had finished with the man in the yachting costume, or he had changed his mind. He was striding, with apparent purpose, toward the great double doors of the main house. She squeezed Lisa Benedict's hand. "Go now," she whispered. "You'd best go."

Lisa hesitated, wondering. She remembered the look of distaste on the doctor's face when he referred to *those people* there.

"Is today Sunday?" the actress asked, her eyes still on the house.

"Um . . . yes. Yes, it is."

"Next Sunday. Will you come then?"

"I'd love to. Could I . . ." Lisa wrung her hands. She wanted to ask if she could bring a tape recorder but she was afraid that would be pushing it. "Could I bring you anything?" she asked instead.

Nellie chewed her lip. "Have they written about me?" she asked.

"You mean biographies and such. Sure."

"Do they say that I have children?"

"I'm not sure. I could look."

"I remember one daughter. The one with your hair. And I remember one son. There might have been others."

"Well . . . ah, what would their names be? Their last names."

The cobalt eyes glazed over. They were suddenly far away. Lisa had a sense that they had gone back in time, searching. At last, she came back. The eyes cleared. The shoulders fell.

"I don't know," she said sadly. "D'Arconte, perhaps." She spelled it. "Or perhaps Dunville. I don't know about the girls. Except that the one with the birthmark is the eldest."

"I'll, um . . . see what I can find. Can I say that you asked me to?"

"Oh, you mustn't. Not until . . ."

Nellie's head had turned. She craned her neck once more. There was activity on the terrace. Lisa peeked over the hedge. That man, sport jacket and sunglasses, had come back outside with the doctor. They seemed to be arguing. The two with bandaged faces turned their heads. The first two began walking in Nellie's direction.

"Go," Nellie said, pushing at Lisa. "They mustn't see you."

"Who are those two in the bathrobes?"

"Go now. Hurry."

"Next Sunday," Lisa whispered. She gave Nellie Dameon a final squeeze, then backed into the tree line.

3

Nellie Dameon.

Lisa Benedict had turned, during the intervening week, to the listing in her copy of *The Film Encyclopedia*.

Born Eleanor Demjanek, July 1903, Ames, Iowa. Toured 1916 to 1917 with the Baker Stock Company of Omaha. Arrived Hollywood, 1917, on her own. Bit parts for D. W. Griffith and Mack Sennett. First featured roles: *The Hun Within* with Dorothy Gish and *Six-Shooter Andy* with Tom Mix, in 1918.

On the road at thirteen, Lisa noted. Possibly a runaway. No mention of theatrical parents. Then, by fifteen, a featured film actress. But that was not, Lisa knew, all that unusual. The Gish sisters had made some seventy-five movies between them before they were out of their teens. Mae Marsh and Mary Pickford had made their first films at sixteen and Norma Talmadge at fourteen.

Youth was king in Hollywood back then. It had to do with the film quality and the lighting technology available at the time. Kliegl lights hadn't been invented yet, reflective lighting was still experimental, and the nitrate film stock then in use had trouble distinguishing between soft shading and dark shadow. The result was that any facial line was enhanced on the screen. Actors and actresses in their early twenties looked to be ten years older.

Nellie, like most of them, cranked out six or eight movies a year until she finally hit it big in *Broadway*. Married 1921, widowed 1923. Husband was a rancher

21

turned actor, killed doing a stunt in a western movie. But no children, apparently from that union. Nellie kept on making pictures right up through 1928. Two talkies. Then a series of nervous breakdowns. Her voice was said to be shrill, nasal, irritating.

Wait a second, thought Lisa Benedict. From the little she'd heard, it certainly had never been nasal. On the contrary, it was low, soft, throaty. Might even be called sexy. And she'd had two years with a stock company, probably performing twice a day in small towns all over the Midwest, which means she came to Hollywood knowing how to say lines and how to project.

She would ask Nellie about that. And for a few more details about these children she seemed to think she had. The daughter, apparently her mother's age, would be about sixty now. And she was the eldest.

Hmmm. Hold it.

These kids, if they existed, would have been born after Nellie had her first breakdown. In fact, probably well after she'd been committed to Sur La Mer. Which meant that they were very likely a delusion. But the son's name, or names, anyway, did not seem likely to have come out of thin air. Maybe there really is, or was, such a person. Named Dunville or D'Arconte. No mention of either in *The Film Encyclopedia* or in any of her other directories.

Wait a second. Dunville. The name rang a tiny bell.

In her files, under "miscellaneous," she found several xeroxed pages with references to Sur La Mer. And there it was. Dunville. It was the name of the executive director of Sur La Mer—Carleton Dunville—and of two of its senior staff as well. Administration—Carleton Dunville II. Admissions—Henry Dunville. Must be a family enterprise. Maybe Nellie had just given her the first familiar name that popped into her head. But then, where did D'Arconte come from?

She could ask Professor Mecklenberg to do a computer search. He had files on everyone, from 1907 on, who ever spent fifteen minutes near a Hollywood cam-

era. But he'd ask why she wanted to know, and where
she'd heard those names, and she would have to lie to
him. Or, worse, she'd have to break her promise to a
sad, sweet, dotty old woman who saw, in her, or in the
color of her hair, the daughter she probably never had.

It would keep. At least until Sunday. One more
meeting with Nellie. Ask her the dozen or so questions
she'd prepared. She would bring a recorder this time.
Get Nellie's voice on tape . . . but only if she agrees to
it . . . and if she even knows what a tape recorder is.

4

Lisa could see sky now through the sugar pines.
Quietly, but for her own labored breathing, she climbed
forward. She saw the roofline of the château.

It occurred to her that the greased rocks and the
trip wires she'd passed would be just as effective at
keeping people in as at keeping people out. Not that any
of the *members* could have managed that slope, trip
wires or no. She thought of the two, the younger ones,
with the bandaged faces who seemed to have been
breaking a rule by merely sitting on the terrace steps.
Could they have been prisoners here? Committed here?
Lisa doubted it. They seemed too . . . confident for
that. And that other man had seemed intimidated by
them.

She stopped, still inside the trees.

The old actress was on her bench, waiting, as if
she'd never moved. Same hooded coat, her back to her,
keeping an eye on any movement from the main house.
Lisa looked over the grounds. No sign of Jason Bellarmine. No one else in sight either. Seemed strange. She

was tempted to wait for another member or two to be wheeled out, some sign of business as usual, but Nellie, suddenly, raised a gloved hand. Must have heard her. Or sensed her. She was motioning her forward, signaling her to stay low beneath the hedge. Lisa, crouching, stepped from the trees. Her own eyes on the château, she followed the beckoning hand. She saw it open, as if to take her own hand in welcome. Lisa reached for it.

The old woman's grip, the strength of it, surprised her. Nellie's body half-turned. The other arm came up, reaching behind her neck as if to embrace her. No. Seizing her. The fingers were gripping the hood of her running suit, pulling it down over her eyes, jerking her forward. Now Nellie was rising, wrestling with her, driving her sideways until her legs struck Garbo's bench and her body slammed against it. Lisa cried out, more startled than afraid, but a hand, a third hand, now reached in from the side and clamped firmly over her mouth. She saw a flash of red. A sweatshirt. Her eyes widened. It was that man. The jogger from Tower Road. And the woman wasn't Nellie at all. The face was young, dark, the skin deeply pitted.

Suddenly all fear was gone. She felt a warmth. A heaviness. The marble bench began to soften. Her body was sinking into it as if it were a bed. She saw, or thought she saw, a syringe being drawn from the flesh of her forearm, now bare. She wondered, vaguely, what it might be doing there. Then, in seconds, she no longer cared.

It seemed to her that she was home in bed dreaming. Her dreams annoyed more than they frightened. She tried to wake up, to shake them, but she could not. She was in a white room, like an operating room, strapped to a table, and she felt no clothing against her body. It seemed that her nakedness should have bothered her more than it did.

There was a single bright light above the table. A doctor, an older one, was talking to her, asking her questions. Most were about school. The woman with the pitted face was there. And there were other people who came in, looked at her. The woman showed them her recorder and some things from her purse. That was funny. Lisa tried to think. It seemed to her that she'd locked the purse in her car.

The doctor asked if she had family in the area. Did she have a boyfriend? No? Then whose warm-up suit was that? She did not mind answering.

One of the men who came in held out his hand for her keys. She tried to see his face but she could not move her head. Then he stepped closer and she recognized him. It was the man in the red sweatshirt except that he had showered and changed into a sport jacket. It was also the man she'd seen the Sunday before, arguing with the bandaged man.

With his free hand he reached out to her and, his eyes becoming strange, began exploring her body, feeling the slight mound of her breasts, the flatness of her stomach, touching his fingers to her lips. The woman spoke sharply to him. He stepped back, sighing. Such a waste, she heard him say, as if from a great distance.

Time passed. Minutes . . . hours, she wasn't sure. The lights came on again. The dream continued. The man who had touched her was back. Asking more questions. Who was her professor? Had he seen any of her work? Had she spoken to him, or anyone, about Sur La Mer? Did she have a locker at school and what was its combination? As he asked these things, he sorted through notebooks and papers that Lisa thought she recognized. Yes. They were hers. From her apartment. He was scanning them, discarding some, selecting others and making a pile of them on her bare stomach. Next came two yellow Fotomat envelopes. He went through the photographs that she had taken seven days earlier. He selected several, laying them out across her thighs.

Her mind was clearing, slowly. This wasn't her bed. And she was not dreaming. The doctor came forward.

He held a syringe. But the man she'd seen jogging waved him back. No more, he said. Leave us alone now. The doctor seemed as if he might protest. But he didn't. He left the room.

"Go get Nellie," she heard him say. "Bring her down here."

"What good will that do?" The woman's voice.

"I want to be sure. I want to see her face when she sees that we have this girl."

"Henry . . ." she hesitated. "It's been a week. She probably won't even remember that the girl was here."

"She remembers more than all of you think. Bring her."

A pause. "The Weinbergs are with her. They are watching films."

"So?"

"Mr. Weinberg has . . . *asked* us . . . not to bother her."

Henry Dunville bared his teeth. He snatched at one of the photographs, his fingernails gouging the inside of Lisa's thigh. She cried out. He ignored her. He thrust the photograph toward the woman.

"Show this to him," he hissed, "and then ask him if he would rather be bothered himself. You might ask him, while you're at it, just who the hell he thinks he is."

More time passed. The waves washing over her brain were coming less frequently. She could feel her body. It ached in places and burned in others. Her thigh, she thought, was bleeding. The realization that she was naked—not just dream-naked—became more focused. They could at least have given her a sheet. Not just those papers. She heard voices. Two men. One was much deeper than the other and slightly muffled. Something else about it. She tried to listen but the voices stopped.

A white mass floated above her. She squinted at it. She saw an eye. Oh, yes. The man with the bandaged head. Same white robe. He was looking, closely, at her face. Then her body. The head stopped above her thighs.

"She took these pictures?" she heard him ask. Something about his voice. Muffled. A trace of an accent. German, maybe.

"They were in her apartment," the jogger answered. "All this, too." He gestured toward the many papers. "Even a map of our security system."

A snort.

"We caught her, didn't we?" came the icy reply, petulant.

A wave of the hand. Dismissive. "Who is she?"

"A film student, or so it seems. Apparently doing some sort of thesis."

The larger man straightened. "A student? That's all she is?"

"If she's anything more, she'll tell me. I'll especially find out what she wanted with pictures of you and your wife."

The man known as Weinberg was silent for a long moment. When he spoke, it was very quietly. "Why," he asked, "did you not simply take her to a room and question her, threaten her with arrest, as you would any other intruder?"

"Because she spoke to Nellie. More to the point, I think Nellie spoke to her."

"Nellie does not speak. I would know it if she could."

Dunville shifted some of the papers on Lisa's stomach, uncovering a pocket-size notepad, left open. He jabbed his finger, jarring her, at several lines written in her hand.

> D'Arconte?
> Dunville?
> Daughter/b. 1931–2/strawberry birthmark
> Who are "those people" in the house?

"Where," asked Henry Dunville, "would she have gotten that information if not from the old woman?"

The man called Weinberg closed his one eye. The bandaged head shook slowly, wearily. His hands reached for the papers and photographs that covered Lisa's body. He gathered them all, then stepped to a cabinet where he found a supply of linens. He shook out a light cotton blanket and covered her with it.

Next, taking a full five minutes, he scanned the notes and photographs, including those that Dunville had discarded into a separate pile. This, he noticed, seemed to make Dunville ill at ease. He soon discovered why. There, before him, was a shot of Henry Dunville, mouth forming a silent curse, his middle finger extended at the backs of Weinberg and his wife. He smiled beneath his bandages. The photograph, he sensed, was taken to no purpose other than a conviction that cowardice should not go unrecorded. He was beginning, he decided, to like this girl.

"Has it occurred to you," he spoke at last, tapping a finger against the open notepad, "that this is not information at all? That these are simply questions based on rumors, legend, which she came here hoping to have answered?"

It was Dunville's turn to snort. "Why, then, would she have taken your picture?"

"Because she had a camera," he answered patiently, his voice pained. "And because I was there. She photographed everything she saw, Henry, from the main gate, to old Mr. Bellarmine's red seascape, to your rude little gesture."

Dunville's jaw tightened but the chin came up, defiantly. "Well," he sniffed, "we'll know soon enough."

"What have you given her?"

"Heroin. Scopolamine."

"How long until her head clears?"

"Two hours. Maybe less."

"I'll question her then." He raised a hand to stay any objection. "Why is she naked, by the way?"

The other man shrugged.

"Is it because you've been playing with her, Henry? Or does that come later?"

His tan deepened but he said nothing.

Weinberg reached an arm around the smaller man's shoulder. He stiffened but did not pull away. Weinberg guided him toward the door. "Henry," he said, shaking his head, "I'm going to try to explain what you've done here . . ."

Lisa listened to the fading voice. The man who had covered her. She did not want him to leave.

"By the way . . ." The man called Weinberg paused in the corridor outside the surgery, "when your little assistant asked me who I think I am, she wasn't speaking for you, was she?"

No answer.

"Because if she was, I'll tell you. Or would you rather I showed you?"

"What you are," he managed, the chin rising again, "is a guest in this house. Kindly keep that in mind."

"A paying guest," Weinberg corrected him. "And wouldn't you say that all that money should entitle Mrs. Weinberg and myself to a measure of peace and quiet?"

"It does not entitle you to interfere . . ."

The bigger man squeezed his neck, silencing him. "A little college girl climbs up through the trees . . . making it past that wonderfully sophisticated security system of yours . . . because she's doing a term paper about old movie stars and, quite naturally, she thought she'd try to talk to one or two. She gets in here but she has only anecdotes to show for her trouble. She has spoken to a blind old man about marble benches and to a nice old lady who can't talk back and who, even if she could, is in another world. Are you with me so far, Henry? Just nod."

He nodded.

"Enter Henry Dunville. You learn that this little girl has been here, having bested you, and you overreact. You deprive poor Nellie of her bench so that you and

your little friend can . . ." Weinberg stopped himself.
"How did you know she was coming, by the way?"

Dunville's expression became smug. "Her license
plate was recorded when she first approached the gate
house. Her face and voice were recorded as well. Mr.
Bellarmine confirmed that the voice was that of the girl
who spoke to him from Nellie's bench. She's been under
surveillance for a week. When she left her apartment
this morning, heading this way, obviously outfitted for a
return visit, we were alerted. We were ready for her."

"And you got her, didn't you, Henry." Weinberg
punched his arm, lightly. "You jumped her, drugged
her, strapped her naked to a table and you burglarized
her apartment. In the end, Henry, do you feel that this
will make her less curious, or more curious, about Sur
La Mer?"

"We can't let her go. Not now."

"Tell me why."

"Because she's seen you. And for all the reasons you
just mentioned."

"What she has seen is gauze, Henry. And anything
she has seen or heard since you drugged her will have
been through a fog. She's not going to die for that."

"We can't take the chance. What if she . . ."

Weinberg squeezed him again, very hard, shutting
off his air. "In a little while," he said, "Mrs. Weinberg
will come down. She will rap that girl smartly across the
back of the head and then she will put her clothes back
on. Your surgeon will put a few stitches in her scalp.
When she revives, you will tell her that she hit her head
when you grabbed her, which you regret, and she's been
in the infirmary ever since. Whatever she seems to
remember, you and the doctor will assure her that no
such thing happened. I will then come in and, standing
behind a light, I will proceed to frighten the wits out of
her. I will tell her that Nellie Dameon suffered a stroke
immediately after her first visit and is now in a vegeta-
tive state. I will threaten her with arrest on a charge of
criminal trespass and with a lawsuit for the damage that

she has done. I will then send her home to await our wrath. With all that on her mind, Henry, she might not even report the burglary of her apartment."

"But if she does . . ."

"Let her. You know nothing about it."

"Sh . . . she's been injected," Dunville said, flustered. "What about the marks?"

"Give her a tetanus shot and a painkiller. Use the same holes."

Dunville appeared to consider it. Then his jaw tightened. He began to shake his head. The man called Weinberg reached for his right hand, forced it open, then wrapped his own fist around the offending middle finger. "Must I put it another way, Henry?" he asked, gently.

"N . . . no."

"My bandages come off in three days. One week after that, Bonnie and I . . ." He corrected himself. "Barbara and I . . . will be gone from here. Until then, promise me, Henry, that you will do nothing to disturb the serenity of our stay."

"Let go of me. Please."

"Promise?"

"Yes."

Weinberg patted his cheek. "Thank you, Henry."

Lisa heard banging. First a door, slamming. Then muttered curses. Then things being thrown.

A face came into view. Her eyes were slow to focus but she knew from the deep tan and the color of the shirt that it was the jogger.

"You little cunt," she heard him say. His fist was raised as if to strike her. But he did not. Instead, the hand lowered, slowly. She felt it on her hip. It moved to her stomach, her chest, feeling her through the cotton blanket. And the face was changing. The anger was gone. Something else in its place.

Henry Dunville had made a decision.

Now she felt him unstrapping her. First her ankles,

then her wrists, then, last, her head. It had been held in place with a belt wrapped in thick terry cloth. More rolled up towels had been packed against her temples. She was free now. She raised one arm. It felt so heavy. She let it fall. The fingers seemed to work but not the arm.

She felt his hands reaching under her, lifting her. The blanket fell away. She was out of the light now. She could see better. The ceiling turned and she felt herself being lowered onto something cold. She felt its texture. A leather couch. He stood over her. He was only a shadow now against the light but she could see that he was undoing his clothing. His trousers fell. His belt buckle struck the floor. He stepped out of them. The shadow lowered itself on her. She screamed, cursing him.

A door opened. A woman's voice. The pock-marked one. *No*, she shouted. *Don't do that*. He turned his head. *Get out*, he said. *Right now*. *Out*. The door slammed. Angry words from outside it.

She felt him trying to enter her. Roughly. Clumsily. She made herself relax so that it would not hurt so much. Yes. That was better. She felt herself becoming moist. He felt it as well. He entered her.

She listened, her face turned away, as his breathing became rapid. She felt him raise himself on his elbows. His hands, which had gripped her shoulders, now moved to her throat. It frightened her. She looked into his face, saw his eyes searching her own, and she knew what he intended. She closed her eyes, tightly.

Carla, she thought, desperately.

What would Carla do?

She would use her teeth. Tear at his face. Bite into his neck with a pit bull's death grip. Drive the heel of her hand against his nose. But she could do none of these. She still had no strength. Except . . . except in her fingers.

"Open your eyes," he gasped, softly. "Look at me."

She squeezed them harder. She felt one hand come free from her throat. It slapped her, viciously.

"Open them," he snarled. "Open them wide."

The eyes, she thought. *Yes*.

She obeyed. She let him peer into the light that he wanted to watch as it flickered and died. The hand that had slapped her returned to her throat, joining the other. His grip tightened. He quickened his thrust. He was coming.

She saw her own right hand. She willed it to stop floating, to make a fist, thumb extended, to strike at his eye.

He shrieked.

Drive deep, she said in her mind.

She watched, almost curiously, as her long thumbnail felt its way, sinking in to half its length. Blood spat from his eye. She felt it on her face.

More shrieking. His hand clawed at her arm. His other hand, now a fist, tried to hammer at her face but his body slipped on the wetness between them and the blow glanced off her forehead. He steadied himself. Again he seized her by the neck. She felt his thumbs pressing, digging, much deeper than before. Something ruptured inside her throat. She heard it. And now more sounds. The door again, slamming open.

She heard, through a wall of pain and flashing lights, a woman's voice. A different one. This new woman was shouting, kicking at the jogger's ribs. She was trying to help her.

Carla?

No. Not Carla. Through a red veil she caught a glimpse of blond hair, bandages, white robe. And this woman was calling a name. It sounded like *Alan*.

She heard it again. Farther away. It faded into a distant echo. Everything was fading but for the bursts of light inside her brain. They were the last thing she saw.

Henry Dunville was on his feet. Backing away. Sniffling. Moaning.

He was bent over sideways, his left elbow pressed tightly against his ribs where Barbara Weinberg had kicked him. The ribs were broken. Blood dripped from his face.

The blond woman stood before him, moving with him as he tried to circle her, blocking his path to the door. His left hand held the waistband of his trousers. He tried to tug them up but he could not. They barely covered his thighs, hobbling him. His right hand held a small brass lamp by its neck. He gestured with it, threatened with it, but the woman, her expression cold, almost lifeless, did not retreat.

The man known as Weinberg knelt at the leather sofa, his face against Lisa's, his chest heaving as he tried to breathe life into her. He straightened, watching. She showed no response. Now he pumped at her chest although he knew it was useless. After a while, he stopped. He reached to close her eyes. Slowly, he pushed to his feet. He turned to face Henry Dunville. Dunville raised the lamp.

"See this?" Dunville cried. He turned the left side of his face to the larger man. The eye was like a red prune, oozing, clotted. More blood smeared his cheek and had soaked through the collar of his shirt. "Do you see what she did to me?"

Weinberg didn't answer. "Please wait outside. Watch the door," he said to his wife.

She shook her head. She gestured toward his own face under the bandages. "If he hits you," she said, "he'll ruin it."

"He's not going to hit me. I'm going to hit him."

"No," she said firmly. "You can't see to the side. You wouldn't see it coming."

He hesitated.

"Touch me," Henry Dunville gasped, "and you're finished. Both of you."

"You wait outside," the blond woman said. "I'll finish this." She walked to a cabinet. She opened a drawer. He heard the metallic rattle of instruments.

"What do you have in mind?" Weinberg asked, turning to her.

"I'm going to take his other eye," she said.

5

The door to the surgery had muted the screams. A second door, leading upstairs, would block them entirely.

The man and woman named Weinberg waited there, not opening it, until Henry Dunville's screams became sobs and until the sounds of crashing furniture became less frequent.

That done, the Weinbergs fully realized that they had a problem. Given their condition, there could be no question of running from it. In any case, they had an investment to protect.

The surgery on their faces, the new documents, all the weeks of coaching to prepare them for their new lives as Alan and Barbara Weinberg . . . had already cost them nearly $400,000. Add to that the cost of two new homes—the house in Santa Fe, the apartment in France—which were part of their new identity and, therefore, could hardly be used if they ran. It would be a million-dollar write-off at least. And even then, where could they go, how far would they get, looking like this?

By any standard he knew, the punishment of Henry Dunville had been just. The man had committed a useless, stupid murder. The girl had posed no real threat. She had discovered nothing that could not have been explained, denied, or ignored. Worse, he'd had her followed to Sur La Mer by someone who would soon conclude that she must have died there. That person might now have to be silenced as well. All because Henry Dunville enjoyed playing with helpless women.

He could only hope that the other Dunvilles would see the wisdom of cutting their losses. Keep Henry alive if they wished. As a new and permanent member. Let old Mr. Bellarmine teach him to paint. Or kill him and be done with it. He had nearly done that himself after Bonnie . . . Barbara . . . finished with him. But Barbara had said no. Let it sink in, she said, that he's done this to himself.

Weinberg doubted that allowing Henry time to reflect on his sins would lead to a spiritual awakening. Or to an insight for which he would thank her. It was really, truth be told, that Barbara tended to regard a quick death as a mercy rather than as retributive justice. And yet this is a woman, as he'd mused more than once, who will capture household moths and spiders alive and then release them out of doors. This is an unreconstructed romantic who thinks a woman should smell good and be sent flowers and have doors opened for her but should not be raped unless the rape was her idea.

He had yielded to his wife, letting Henry live, because she asked him to and because it might not be a bad idea to let the other Dunvilles learn of his stupidity from his own lips. But a bit of insurance would not be a bad idea either.

That in mind, he and Barbara proceeded through the second door and up to the main entrance hall, where they relieved two security guards of the pistols they wore under their blazers. They had the one who could still walk drag the other to a padded holding cell where they were invited to quietly pass the remainder of their shift. They returned to the administrative section and the office of Carleton Dunville, the younger. Both Carletons were away, hence Henry's temporary steward-ship. The father, semiretired, was in Palm Springs, cultivating the rich and powerful. The son, the smart one, was in Los Angeles participating in a fund-raiser for the Motion Picture Relief Association. He had long served on its board and had rotated, this year, into the chairmanship.

Their purpose in going to the younger Dunville's office was to get at his safe, which Barbara felt sure she could open given thirty minutes or so, and to get at the cabinet in which the heavier weapons were kept. Weinberg had seen them when, on arrival at Sur La Mer, he was required to surrender his own. A third purpose was to use the telephone.

But, on entering the richly paneled room, they found the phone in use. Henry's little friend—he'd only heard her called Ruiz—was standing at the desk, her back to them. Weinberg waited, listening. She was recounting certain of the day's events to, he assumed, the younger Dunville. Twice she used the word *idiot* in connection with Henry. She was clearly distressed. So, from her manner, was Carleton, though neither, as yet, knew the half of it.

Weinberg cleared his throat. She turned, startled. He made a "time-out" signal with his hands, using the guard's pistol to cross the tee. The woman with the bad skin blinked. Weinberg asked for the phone, but, upon realizing that it would not fit around his bandages, handed it to his wife.

Barbara Weinberg identified herself. Then, making herself comfortable, she explained to Carleton Dunville, the younger, why his half-brother had no eyes.

It was a comfortable office. The desk faced a couch and two chairs set around a low table in a conversational grouping. The door seemed sturdy enough. Two large windows looked out on the front lawn and gave a clear view of the driveway. The office had its own washroom. While Carleton Dunville made up his mind, it would do nicely.

As his wife busied herself with the safe, he had the woman, Ruiz, order a plate of sandwiches and two pots of coffee from the kitchen. He told her exactly what to say. He listened on an extension, satisfying himself that no alarm had been given. Still, it was only a matter of time until Henry found his voice again, or managed to unlock the door and come groping his way up from the basement.

Weinberg opened a narrow coat closet that was built into the paneling. Inside, hidden, was the cabinet that contained the guns.

"Do you have a key, by chance?" he asked the woman named Ruiz.

She shook her head, her expression sullen.

Barbara Weinberg looked up from the safe. Rising, she stepped to the coat closet and glanced inside. "Just kick it in," she said.

Weinberg, under his bandages, made a face. He had expected a measure of artistry. He braced himself, raising one leg.

"Wait." Ruiz winced. She reached into her pocket, producing a ring of keys. "I'll open it," she said. "But you won't need guns."

"We share that hope," he said. "Open it all the same."

It was, he thought, a rather odd collection. A dozen or so pistols, including his own, all different models. One Heckler & Koch MP-5 submachine gun with a sound suppressor, two Ingrams, two Uzis. He took the MP-5 for himself and one of the Ingrams for his wife because these two had extra clips while the others had, in some cases, no ammunition at all. And they'd been dumped into the cabinet carelessly and at random. Ruiz appeared to read his mind.

"He doesn't like guns," she said.

Weinberg said nothing. He checked the action of his weapon.

"He doesn't like Henry either. Vengeance will not interest him."

"What will?"

"Containing this."

"What will he do about Henry?"

"He might ask me to . . . give him something for the pain."

Weinberg looked at her. He found that he believed her. He saw no hint of pity concerning Henry. The concept of filial devotion was equally foreign to her and, therefore, perhaps to young Carleton. Still . . . the matter of insurance.

He asked Ruiz to take a seat on the sofa. He sat at the desk. There was a Canon fax machine behind it. He moved it onto the desk. He found a blank sheet of paper and began writing on it in large block letters.

"What's your first name?" he asked.

"Luisa. What are you doing?"

He fed the paper into the machine and punched a series of numbers. The machine hummed. He caught the sheet as it cleared the stylus and held it up for her to see. It read . . .

BOX 617

IF NO MESSAGE, MY VOICE, AT WEEKLY
INTERVALS, PLEASE ASSUME WORST. ASSUME C. DUNVILLE, JR.,
AND ASSOCIATE L. RUIZ, SUR LA MER,
SANTA BARBARA, RESPONSIBLE.
KILL THEM. PAYMENT GUARANTEED, CJP VIA THIS NOTE.
REGARDS, STREICHER

Luisa Ruiz bit her lip. "You made an agreement," she said darkly.

"It included leaving here alive." He turned to his wife. "How's it coming?" he asked.

"Got it," she answered. The safe door swung open.

The former Bonnie Streicher sorted through several piles of documents, discarding most of them. There were bundles of cash as well. Old bills. She made a rough estimate of the amount, then pushed the money aside. Beneath it, she found a locked leather folder. She broke it open and pulled out three manila folders. She knew at once that she'd found what she was looking for. "Wow,"

she said softly at one point. She began handing the
papers to Weinberg.

"He won't forgive this," Luisa said, sucking in a
breath. "He can't."

"No harm to me," Weinberg answered absently.
"No harm to him." His mind was on the documents.
They were single-sheet biographies, clipped together in
pairs. One sheet a true history of an individual, the other
an invented history. There were dozens, his own among
them. Axel Streicher—Alan Weinberg. Some went back
thirty, even fifty years. He removed the clips that held
them together and, after writing out a cover sheet,
began feeding them into the fax machine, although not
his own or that of his wife. The cover note said

BOX 617

HOLD FOR ME. NO ACTION UNLESS NO CONTACT.

STREICHER

That, too, he held up for Ruiz to see.

"Do you have any idea what you've done?" she
asked quietly.

"I certainly hope so," he said with a grunt. He had
unplugged the machine and turned it onto its back. With
a silver letter opener he began prying off bits of plastic,
tearing at its circuitry. "Would you mind calling again
about those sandwiches?"

Two hours passed. Weinberg heard a car. He
motioned his wife to the window where, carefully, she
moved one slat of the blinds. A white Mercedes. A man
in a dark suit climbed out of it.

"It's Carleton," she said. She watched as two men in
blazers came out to meet him. One was limping badly.
"Someone released those guards. Which means they
must have found Henry."

The guard with the limp was gesturing in her
direction. He was agitated. Now he was cocking his head
vaguely in the direction of the surgery. His hands came

up to his eyes. He made a gouging motion toward one of them and a ripping motion toward the other.

Carleton Dunville the younger winced, possibly for effect. His half-brother's overall condition was no longer news to him although Barbara had omitted certain details. He raised his own hands, waggling his fingers in a calming manner. No, the guards would not be blamed. She watched as he asked several questions, once checking his watch, twice glancing down the driveway in the direction from which he'd come. Then, as if on signal, another car appeared. A white Fiero, dented front left fender. It squealed to a stop behind Carleton's Mercedes. The driver, a squat, coarse-looking man, long hair bunched behind his head, started to get out but Carleton waved him back and, with words and gestures, seemed to be sending him to the rear of the building.

"Who is this?" She motioned Luisa Ruiz forward.

Ruiz reached the window in time to see the car drive off. "His name's Hickey," she said. "Henry uses him for this and that."

"Such as burglaries?" Barbara asked.

Ruiz shrugged, then nodded.

"And disposing of bodies?"

"Not until now," she lied.

Another hour passed. The phone rang. Ruiz, upon Weinberg's nod, picked it up.

"It's Mr. Dunville," she said. "He's outside. May he come in?"

"Certainly. It's his office."

Weinberg, standing behind Ruiz, leveled his weapon at the door. His wife, her back to it, covered the two windows. Carleton Dunville knocked, then entered.

He was an elegant man. Mid-thirties, slender, erect, dark hair going prematurely gray. His features showed little resemblance to those of his half-brother. If he were an actor he would have been cast in sophisticated drawing room comedies. A touch of David Niven, a little Tony Randall, even down to the black double-breasted suits he favored. Were it not for the eyes, he might be dismissed as a fop. But the eyes were alert, intelligent, and their usual expression, in repose, was one of detached amusement. Now they were cold.

Ignoring the weapons, they fell first on the open safe, then on the ruined fax machine, then on the sprays of dried blood that stained Barbara Weinberg's white bathrobe.

Luisa Ruiz coughed. She had picked up the two cover sheets and the small stack of files that Weinberg had transmitted.

"May I?" she asked Weinberg, gesturing with them toward Dunville.

"By all means," Weinberg nodded.

Carleton Dunville's expression barely changed as he sorted through the pages. "Did you open the safe for them?" he asked Ruiz.

"I opened it." Barbara Weinberg said, her attention still on the windows.

Dunville found her biography at the bottom of the stack. Her credentials. "Ah, yes." he said. He tilted his chin in the direction of the fax machine. "And the point of that vandalism, I assume, is to keep me from printing out the number you dialed."

"Until you've had time to . . . regain your perspective. Yes."

Almost a smile. "About what was done to Henry, you mean?" A small shake of the head. "You over-estimate my attachment to him. This, however, is another matter entirely."

"Nothing will come of it," Weinberg said, "if no harm comes to us."

Dunville returned to the first cover sheet. "And if it does, I gather, a person named CJP is to hunt down and kill Miss Ruiz and myself."

"It's not necessarily one person. And CJP only picks up the tab."

"Ah, yes." Dunville read the message more carefully. "The *recipient* of these faxes will avenge you."

"That's the idea, yes."

Dunville counted the biographies that had been transmitted. There were more than fifty including those of the Streicher-Weinbergs. Fifty men, a few women. Who they were before, and who they are now. "May I ask," another deep sigh, "how you knew to look for these?"

"I didn't," Weinberg lied. "I was looking for anything at all that might compromise you."

Doubt flicked across Dunville's eyes. He put it aside. "This box number. Six One Seven. You didn't, by any chance, send these papers to one of those Mailbox USA franchises, did you? Where some clerk could read them?"

Weinberg shook his head. "They probably haven't been read yet at all. The machine on the other end has a confidential mailbox. My friend has to punch in a code before the machine prints them out. He will do so on Monday morning, first thing."

Dunville considered this. Weinberg could see his mind working. Could he possibly, Dunville was wondering, get the phone company to give him that fax number, arrange elsewhere to have it traced, get reliable people there in time to intercept Weinberg's mystery friend, take the printout from him, kill him, all within approximately eighteen hours? A long shot. And even then, what is to keep whoever he'd send from making his own use of those papers? And, of course, if he failed . . .

"Well," he shrugged, eyebrows up. "Consider me compromised. What now, Mr. Streicher?"

"It's Mr. Weinberg."

The eyebrows went higher. "Your hope, am I to assume, is to proceed as before?"

"It's more than a hope. We have a contract. All this is to make sure you honor it."

"Although," Dunville folded his arms, "at more favorable terms, I assume."

Weinberg shook his head. "We made a deal. I'll keep it if you will."

"All of it? To the letter?"

"Pretty much." Weinberg hefted the Ingram. "Except we'd hold on to these for a while. And we move into the Members' Wing where we won't be so isolated."

Dunville started to object. Barbara Weinberg interrupted him. "There's a car leaving," she said to her husband. "It's that Fiero."

Weinberg moved to the window, glanced out. He saw the USC sticker as it passed.

"Is that the girl's car?" he asked.

"And the girl."

In the trunk, Weinberg presumed, wrapped in plastic. He forced the vision from his mind. His wife could not.

"What will he do with her?" she asked, her jaw set.

Dunville hesitated. "I am . . . sorry about that. More than you know."

"Answer me. How will he dispose of her?" Her weapon swung toward his chest. But Weinberg said her name, gently, and she returned to her window.

"She'll get a proper burial," Dunville answered all the same. "She won't be dismembered or thrown in a hole if that's what you're asking. Please, for all our sakes, leave the matter in my hands."

"And Henry?" Weinberg asked, glad of another subject.

"That as well," Dunville said. "He will need . . . long-term care." He glanced at Ruiz, meeting her eyes. Ruiz answered with a tiny nod.

"What do you think?" Weinberg asked.

They had walked out onto the terrace. He stood facing the ocean, she with her back to it. Both held their weapons, thumbs on their safeties, within the folds of their robes.

"They'll dump her someplace," she said. "Make it look like something else."

He was silent for a long moment. "I meant . . ."

"I know what you meant." Still, she waited before answering. "Who is CJP?"

"Nobody. I made it up."

She thought so. "Will anyone see those pages?"

"No."

"If he suspects that, we're dead meat."

"You saw those names. He can't just suspect. He'd have to know."

"Then he'll try to track that machine."

"It's reached through a relay. He would have to find two. And the one in Santa Fe is wired with thermite."

She allowed herself a smile of appreciation. "Even so," she said, "he's got to try to get them back."

"Perhaps not. Surely, he'll look for a way in which he can safely kill us. I can't think of one. In the end, he will probably accept that we have as much to lose as he does if we try to go our own way. It's a standoff."

"What about Nellie?"

"What about her?"

"We can't just leave her here. Dunville already wonders how you knew to look for those records. He knows we've been spending time with her. And he knows she saw that girl."

"I'll . . . make it part of the deal. He doesn't touch her."

She shook her head. "That would remove any doubt. He'd give Nellie the same stuff Henry gave the girl and he'd find out not only that she can talk but what she knows. Then, one day soon, we'd hear that she died in her sleep."

"Bonnie . . ."

"Barbara. Stick with the program."

"She's a very old woman. We'll hear that soon no matter what."

"I like her."

"Well"—he shrugged,—"so do I, but . . ."

Barbara Weinberg turned, staring at him. He tried

not to look. She waited. He began to fidget. At last, she saw his chest rise and she heard the low growl she was waiting for.

"The things I do for love," he muttered.

6

The next afternoon. Westport, Connecticut.

Paul Bannerman, one hand resting on the shoulder of Carla Benedict, walked with her, slowly, along the road that ran parallel to the town's public beach.

They had it largely to themselves. At water's edge, a young woman dismantled a windsurfer, the late April breeze having faded to a whisper. One couple walked with a golden retriever. In a week, the beach would be closed to pets. Parks Department vehicles would begin combing the sand for their leavings and for the winter's flotsam.

The sun seemed to hover in the western sky. Carla, Bannerman saw, could not keep her eyes off it. He could only imagine what she must have been seeing there.

"Would you like me to go with you?" he asked.

She shook her head.

She was a small woman, no larger than her sister, of whom he had only seen snapshots. Same color hair, almost bronze, but worn in a pixie cut while Lisa wore her hair longer. Seen together, in flattering light, one would guess that Carla was no more than five or six years older. But he knew that Carla had turned forty barely a week before her sister was murdered.

She was crying softly. Bannerman had never seen Carla cry. Not once in more than fifteen years. Not even when she took the call from California. But here, arriving at this beach, she had collapsed, utterly, in unimagined pain. He had held her, tightly, against his chest, enduring the fingernails that dug into his flesh, feeling the deep, wracking sobs that welled from so far within her that he thought her lungs must surely burst. But she was better now. Not yet in control. But better.

He glanced at his watch. Her flight would leave in less than three hours. Molly Farrell had the tickets. They would meet her at Mario's, perhaps get Carla to try to eat something, then leave from there.

"I want you to stick with Molly," he said, squeezing her shoulder. "Except for private times, like seeing your father, I've asked her not to leave you alone."

"Seeing my father is when I'll need her," she said, swallowing. She gestured toward the horizon with her chin. "He's sitting out there, right now, wondering why it couldn't have been me."

Bannerman chewed his lip. "Don't talk that way," he said. "I'm sure it's not true."

She didn't argue. But she knew better.

"Paul?"

He waited.

"Lisa liked me."

"I'm sure she did. And so do we."

"No," Carla Benedict said firmly. "You *accept* me. You *tolerate* me. Lisa *liked* me."

Bannerman stopped walking. He turned her so that she had to look at him. "At least four of us, me included," he reminded her, "would be long dead if not for you. We do love you, Carla, each in our own way. There's not a thing in the world we wouldn't do for you."

She leaned her face into his chest. A shudder rose from deep inside her. He felt new tears soaking through his shirt.

"Will you . . ." She swallowed. "Will you help me find the son of a bitch?"

She had asked him that before, within an hour of the phone call from a neighbor of her father. He answered only that he would do what he could. Make some phone calls. In the meantime, see to her needs.

He wanted to help her. They all did. They would have liked nothing better than to find and slowly dismember the animal who had done this to her sister. Raped her. Strangled her. Left her body, nude, spread-eagled near an off-ramp of the Ventura Freeway in Los Angeles, a grotesque smile cut into her face, just as he'd done to six other young women, all college students, over the past two years.

But this was a police matter. The police had a task force, organized after the third of these murders. The FBI had one of its own. Between them they had the experience and the tools. They had the psychological profiles of past serial killers, their behavior patterns, they had all the accumulated physical evidence, forensic data, the killer's DNA fingerprint from his semen, all on a computer. Bannerman's people had nothing. They would get in the way.

"I'll see what I can learn," he told her. "If we can help, we will."

"You could call Lesko," she said into his chest. "He probably knows about things like this."

"We'll see. I'll ask him."

No harm in asking, though he did not think it would do much good. Lesko had been a good street cop, but he'd mostly worked narcotics. New York, as far as Bannerman could recall, had never had a serial killer. Not that one would necessarily be noticed there. They all seemed to come from the West Coast. And Lesko, in any case, was now living in Zürich.

Still, Lesko had made a national reputation for himself. Bannerman had never met a policeman who hadn't heard a story or two about him. He might well have a connection or two on the Los Angeles force. Someone, at the very least, who could help keep an eye on Carla. Lesko would probably want to know in any case.

"Listen . . ." Carla fingered his lapels. "about Susan . . ."

Susan Lesko. Lesko's daughter.

"I'm sorry I gave you so much shit about her."

"Forget it." He shook his head. "That's in the past."

"She's been great about this. Everybody's been great."

It was Susan who'd made the flight reservations. And suggested that he send Molly with her. And had gone to Carla's house to help her pack the things she'd need. All this in spite of the fact that Carla made no secret of resenting her presence in Westport, telling him how foolish he'd been to take up with Susan, an outsider, unproven, untested, no skills. But Susan, over the past year, had more than proven herself. Everyone had acknowledged that but Carla. Until now.

"Maybe Susan's okay," she said.

"Thank you."

"Don't tell her I said so."

Bannerman made a face.

"I'll tell her myself. When I get back."

"That would be nice," he said. He steered her toward the parking lot where he'd left the car.

"Paul?"

"Umm?"

"Did you mean what you said?"

"About what?"

"That you love me. Except when I make you crazy, I mean."

"Even then." He leaned and kissed the top of her head.

"Don't take this wrong, but if Susan ever dumps you . . ."

"I'll come crawling," he said.

7

It was half past nine in the evening, California time, when the TWA 747 touched down at Los Angeles International Airport. Molly Farrell, a tall woman, lean, athletic, gentle eyes, a face that was more often described as good rather than pretty, left Carla to wait for the bags and went directly to the Avis desk where she signed the rental agreement on a blue midsize sedan.

Carla, left to that task, would have rented a Porsche or a Mercedes. There was no real reason not to, Molly supposed. No need to avoid attention. It was more force of habit. And Carla had argued, not without merit, that in this town a plain blue Chevrolet would stand out more than a Porsche. Most of the late-model Chevrolets, she said, were probably unmarked police cars.

Nor would Molly, given the choice, have reserved a bungalow at the Beverly Hills Hotel. Too much people-watching there. Too many eyes wondering who you are and whether you're famous. But Susan had made the reservations. Paul didn't correct her. He probably decided that there's no harm in that either. It's centrally located between Lisa's apartment and her father's house. And it's pleasant enough that it might take some of the edge off Carla's gloom.

Molly drove, heading north along the San Diego Freeway. Ten minutes later, approaching Santa Monica Boulevard, she signaled a right turn. She could see Century City, on the edge of Beverly Hills, still glowing red in reflection of the western horizon.

"No," Carla pointed. "Go straight."

Molly hesitated. "Sherman Oaks?" Where her father lived.

"And Woodland Hills," she said.

Where her sister was found. "Wouldn't you rather get some rest first? It's after midnight, our time."

Carla shook her head. "Let's get it over with."

Approaching the exit ramp for Sherman Oaks, Molly signaled again. And once more, Carla waved her forward. "Take the Ventura Freeway westbound," she said.

"It will only hurt you," Molly said gently. "And there won't be anything left to see."

Carla realized that. And that it would hurt. But she wanted, however irrationally, to feel the presence of her sister. Perhaps she was still alive when the killer brought her there. Perhaps there was still something of her in the air. "It's the third exit," she said.

Carla saw the place at once. A highway patrolman had been stationed there, with his car, hazard lights blinking. Farther down the slope she saw an area marked off with yellow tape. Amber utility lights blinked at either end. Molly pulled off the shoulder of the exit ramp, stopping behind the patrol car. She had barely placed the car in park when the young patrolman in his early twenties, stepped from his car and began to wave them on. Carla was out her door almost as quickly, her wallet in hand. Molly watched as the patrolman shined his light on her Connecticut driver's license and on a cropped snapshot that identified her as the sister of the Campus Killer's seventh victim.

The young patrolman did not know quite what to do. He seemed, to Molly, to be trying to reason with her, perhaps repeating what she herself had said, that it could only hurt. But in the end he turned with her, shining his light toward the crime scene, walking slowly. Molly watched.

The beam washed over a system of squares, marked off with string, where forensic specialists had done a grid search. It settled on a particular spot. There was nothing there now. No outline of a body. But Molly could see where an oblong ring had been flattened by the shoes of policemen, an ambulance crew, a photographer, a coroner. She could see the tire tracks of several vehicles.

They were coming back now, the patrolman's light marking Carla's path. Suddenly she stopped, looking down. She bent over, her fingers brushing something in the grass. She stayed, for a long moment, then stood erect and touched the young man's arm in thanks. He took her hand, gripping it as if to comfort her. He watched her go.

Seven victims, thought Molly. She wondered what the young man would have thought if he knew that the woman he was treating so gently had killed at least three times that number over the years. So had most of them, for that matter. Except that, as a rule, they never killed for pleasure. Satisfaction, now and then, but not pleasure. But in this case, any one of them, even Paul, she suspected, would make an exception.

Molly started the engine. "You okay?" she asked.

"I'm fine," Carla answered distantly.

"What did you find in the grass?"

"What?" Carla blinked. She was someplace else. "Oh. Those were footprints. They took casts of them."

Molly exited the ramp, then swung back onto the Freeway, going east.

"He wore rubbers," Carla told her. "Totes."

"You could see that? At night?"

"That kid told me. The cop."

"Oh."

"I could feel him, though. I could almost see him."

"Ah . . ." *Steady, Carla.* "What else did he say?"

It took a moment for the question to register. Carla shook her head as if to clear it. "They recovered her car today."

"Where?"

"Not far from here. In a parking lot at Pierce Junior College."

Another campus. Molly frowned. "Which means that's where the killer . . . found her?"

"I guess."

"Lisa was a grad student at USC. What was she doing at a little junior college? And on a Sunday."

"Maybe she wasn't there. Maybe he just left the car there."

The answer gave rise to more questions but Molly decided not to pursue them. The detectives, she knew, were asking them as well. Does this mean the campus killer forced his way into her car? Or asked for a lift? Why, afterward, would he go directly to another campus? Why that one? Had he left his own car there?

Whatever. Let the police and the FBI puzzle it out. Sooner or later, one piece at a time, they'll close in on him. Or he'll try to gray a decoy, a policewoman. And, if she's worth anything, she'll shoot his pecker off, and then his kneecaps, before her backup can move in.

"Which exit for your father's house?" she asked.

It was a small house, stucco, not much yard, neat, generally modest.

He met them at the door. He'd been sitting up, waiting, on the chance that Carla would come tonight. An average sort of man, thought Molly. Might have been nice looking once. Tall, almost her height but gone to flesh, hair more gray than brown. She could see some resemblance around the eyes and mouth but that was about all. Carla must have inherited her coloring and size six from her mother.

He leaned an inch or so toward his surviving daughter. And his hands reached up, just barely. He seemed to want to embrace her. That was Molly's impression. But for some reason, he could not.

Carla mumbled an introduction. Her father did not offer his hand. Rather, he stared at her for a long moment, a measure of surprise evident on his face. Molly was used it. She did not look like what she was. But then few of them did.

"I've . . . made a fresh pot of tea," he told them. It was not an invitation to enter. Not exactly. Nor did he step to one side. It was more like saying that if his daughter wished to come in, he would try not to make her feel unwelcome.

The living room was comfortable, very California, furniture that was a sort of Ethan Allan Spanish, fake beamed ceilings, lots of plants. There was a piano in one corner. Molly tried to imagine Carla, as a little girl, practicing on it.

Atop the piano there were several framed photographs. One frame was empty, its photo probably given to the police. There were three other pictures of Lisa, taken at various ages, one with her mother, now deceased. There were none of Carla.

Molly knew most of the story. Carla had gone to Europe nearly twenty years before, junior year in Paris, met a guy, an Algerian, who studied electrical engineering by day and made bombs at night. By the time Carla caught on, so had the French Secret Intelligence Service. She was given the choice to work for them or to go to prison, more likely to vanish. By then she was ready to get even with almost anyone. Stayed for four years until she hooked up with Bannerman—Mama's Boy— and he managed to get the French off her back. Nobody messed with Mama's Boy back then.

But for those four years, and the fifteen that followed, George Benedict had never seen her, had hardly heard from her. But he heard *about* her. Mostly from the CIA when they were building their file on her. They told him stories. Like the one about the Algerian engineer who she blinded with a ballpoint pen on a crowded street in Rome and then stood by watching as he staggered, screaming, into the path of a trolley. The Algerian's new address had been a gift from Mama's Boy.

"Miss Farrell," he said, awkwardly, as he poured her tea. "You are . . . ah . . . from Westport as well?"

She knew what he meant. "Yes. I am."

"And you've been back in this country how long? Almost four years?"

"Just about. Yes."

"Well," he sighed audibly, "it's nice that you took the time to come see me." He flicked a glance toward Carla, then quickly looked away. He filled her cup. The tea was yellow, Carla noted. Smelled more like straw.

"And when, Carla," he asked, still not looking at her, "did you last find time to call your sister?"

"A week ago Thursday," she said evenly.

He raised an eyebrow. His lip curled. Both doubt and scorn.

"And the week before that." Her eyes began to shine. "And almost every week, not counting visits, for the past ten years."

"That's a lie," he said through his teeth.

"And I sent her money," she hissed, "and paid her tuition, and I gave her that white car for her twenty-first birthday. Fuck you, George Benedict."

His color rose. He shook his head, slowly, still disbelieving. "She had a scholarship," he said firmly.

"That's right. I set it up."

His head shook again. His lips moved wordlessly. He seemed to be repeating what she said to him. "She would have told me," he said at last.

Carla leaned forward. "You told her you never wanted to hear my name again, George. You got your wish."

He closed his eyes. Molly saw moisture forming on the corner of the one farthest from Carla. He had turned his head so that Carla could not see it.

"Mr. Benedict," she said gently, "if there's anything we can do . . ."

"No . . . thank you."

"We can help with the arrangements. Make calls to friends and relatives."

"They all know. The newspapers, the . . ." He gestured toward his television set.

"Have you seen her?" Carla asked. Her manner had softened.

He nodded, shutting his eyes again.

"When will she be . . ." Carla rephrased. "When can we have her?"

"Tomorrow, I think. They were doing an autopsy today."

Carla became quiet. She had, she realized, hoped to see Lisa before the cutting began, having blocked from her mind the knowledge that the most terrible cutting had already been done. Abruptly, she reached for her purse and stood.

"We're staying at the Beverly Hills," she said to her father. Then, after a pause, "Will you be okay?"

"Some neighbors are coming over. They'll stay the night. Otherwise," he said, looking at his hands, "I'd ask you to . . ."

"I'll call you tomorrow," she said.

"Go ahead. Say it." They were back on the San Diego Freeway. Carla stared out the side window.

"It's none of my business," Molly said quietly.

"You think I was a shit, don't you?"

Molly shrugged. She said nothing.

"When I was twenty, I met this guy in Paris."

"I know. Paul told me."

"He told you what happened?"

"That one thing led to another, yes."

She was silent for a long moment. "They let me call my father. I told him I was in trouble. I asked him to come."

And he didn't, Molly gathered.

"He said I've made my bed. I should take my medicine. It's the chickens coming home to roost. He probably would have said that a stitch in time would have saved nine but I hung up on him."

Molly offered no comment.

"Christ." Carla let out a breath. "Have you ever met a man named George who wasn't a turkey?"

Molly said nothing.

"It wasn't the first time, either," Carla said.

"What wasn't?"

"That I got in trouble, and he changed the locks."

"What kind of trouble?"

"Nothing big. I beat up some girl who was giving me too much crap. And I got arrested a couple of times during demonstrations. Vietnam stuff. And I got pregnant twice by one of my professors. Had a bad abortion the second time. That was when I got shipped off to Paris."

"Um . . . in fairness, Carla . . ."

"I know. I was not every father's dream."

Molly steered for the exit ramp at Sunset Boulevard.

"Go straight." Carla touched her arm. "I want to see Lisa's apartment."

"Where is it?"

"Huntington Park, down past the USC campus. Twenty minutes, tops."

"You have a key?"

Carla patted her purse. "I've been out here a few times. I've stayed with her."

Molly swung onto the ramp. "I'm going to bed, Carla. We'll go in the morning."

Carla started to argue but a yawn stopped her.

"What does your father do?" Molly asked, to draw Carla off that subject.

Another yawn. "He's retired. He used to be with the water company." *Where they're probably all named George*, she thought.

Molly nodded. It sounded as if he'd made a living but not much more. A modest house. A widower on a pension and social security. Not likely that he could have put Lisa through USC and then graduate school. Lisa, probably at Carla's urging, had spared his pride by lying to him about a scholarship. He might never have learned otherwise if he hadn't started sticking pins into Carla.

"Molly?"

"Uh-huh?" Ahead, all pink and lit up, she saw the facade of the Beverly Hills Hotel.

"You're as tough as I am. How come nobody ever thinks you're a shit?"

"I'm not so tough. But there's tough and there's mean, Carla," she said, not unkindly. "There's a difference."

Carla dropped her eyes. She didn't speak for several moments. Then, "I wish you'd known Lisa. She didn't think I was mean."

"I'm sure that's true. And I do wish I'd known her."

Carla fumbled for a tissue. She turned her face as her father had. Molly reached for the back of her neck and squeezed it.

"I'm not always mean," she said, shuddering.

"I know."

"Do you like me? Even a little?"

"We've kept each other alive, Carla."

"So has penicillin. That's not what I asked."

Molly had to smile, although a bit sadly. Paul had told her about their talk on Compo Beach. That she felt she'd lost the only person who cared about her. And that she might be dangerously brittle for a while, and would need some hand-holding.

Paul had been tempted to come himself. But, he realized, every time he leaves Westport, someone, not least the U.S. intelligence community, begins to wonder what he's up to.

Anyway, she could handle it. She, and Paul, had dealt with this sort of thing, or something like it, a dozen times over the years. Contract agents are all a little crazy. And most of them had spent the better part of their lives doing unto others first. Retiring them, making new lives for them, trying to integrate them into a nice, laid-back community like Westport had taken some doing. Teaching them that you don't break some teen-ager's legs for throwing beer cans on your lawn or for trashing your mailbox, although maybe you torch his car if he makes a habit of it. But also teaching burglars, swindlers, and drug dealers that they'd be better off working some other town if they don't want to be found in a trunk just over the Westport town line.

Some of them had needed more teaching than others. Old Billy McHugh, for example, had always been a loner. They'd assigned him a job as a bartender at Mario's so he could get used to being around people. It had seemed like a good idea; he made a lot of friends. But then he had to be taught that just because you make friends, and you find out that your new friends have enemies, like divorce lawyers and such, who are treating them badly, you don't go out and solve their problems for them. Billy had solved eleven problems before Molly began to notice that the local suicide and accidental death rates were climbing well out of proportion to the population.

Carla hadn't done anything like that. But, once, she caught a young thief trying to steal her car radio and she did things to him that Dracula wouldn't do. Left his screwdriver sticking out his colon. Paul had to explain to her that, while he did not object in principle to the defense of her property, he was concerned that such total devastation of a burly male by a very small woman might attract undue attention.

And then, last year, there was that mission to Spain. To Marbella. Carla had done her job. Neutralizing a team of shooters who had ambushed Elena Brugg's car and killed Doc Russo. No arguing that. But the *way* she'd done it, carving up that Englishman, taking her time, had even made Billy McHugh wince. Not that anyone should have been surprised. She and Doc Russo had been close. But afterward, she had withdrawn from the rest of them more than ever. And they, in turn, avoided her as if she were a live grenade. It was months, after Marbella, before any of them asked her to dinner, or to play bridge, or take in a movie. Even Paul thought it best to give her time, leave her alone. And that was wrong. It wasn't what she needed at all.

"I trust you," Molly said, pulling into the driveway

of the hotel's main building. She took Carla's hand. "And I care about you. I know that's not everything you want to hear but . . ."

"Never mind," Carla shook her head. "It's okay."

Molly tried again. "Maybe we're overdue for a talk."

"About what?"

"I don't know. Things. Nothing serious. Isn't that how people get to know each other?"

"I guess."

"We'll order up some wine. We'll talk until we fall asleep."

No answer.

Molly tugged at her. "Want to try something? Let's pretend we're fourteen again. At a pajama party."

Carla rolled her eyes. "Give me a break."

"We'll call out for a pizza. Or some Roy Rogers chicken."

Carla chewed her lip. "Could we . . ."

"Whatever you'd like. What?"

"Could we . . . stay in the same room?" Carla's voice became small. "Just for tonight. I'll take the floor if you want."

Molly squeezed her hand. Then, the doorman approaching, Carla withdrew it. A little shmoozing was one thing, she thought. Looking like a couple of dikes to this putz was another.

8

That same evening, Monday, marked the passage of twelve long weeks since Barbara Weinberg came to Sur La Mer as Bonnie Streicher. And one week since the night when Nellie Dameon spoke to her.

The three months had been a time of study, of

surgical procedures on her face and body, and of boredom. For several hours each day, she and Axel . . . Alan . . . attended classes, listened to tapes, watched films, learned to be Jewish.

Soon, during the fourth month if all went well, they would emerge as Barbara and Alan Weinberg. Their features, their patterns of speech, would be vaguely Jewish. There had also been a two-week attempt to alter Alan's accent, make it a bit less German, more continental, like her own. But he had lapsed almost immediately. The accent was not terribly pronounced in any case.

They would not be religious Jews.

To be religious, to be active in their faith, might have required additional months of training. It would be enough that they could pass as people who had lived their lives on the edge of Jewish culture and tradition.

It was Carleton Dunville, the younger, who had recommended this option from among the several identity packages available to them. It was highly unusual, he pointed out, for a Christian to use a Jewish alias. And, therefore, an advantage. Most people, he said, tend to stereotype those they meet, at first meeting, as long as they are provided with a category. When you meet a divorce lawyer, a politician, or an Englishman, for example, you promptly apply certain preconceptions to him. If you think twice about him, wonder about him, you tend to do so within that context. Accordingly, he said, the category in which you place yourselves provides instant protective coloration. A Jew was a good thing to be.

If they insisted on remaining Protestants, he said, they could do so provided they choose some denomination other than their own and provided that it, again, carried certain stereotypes. The born-again variety, for example. Or the southern Baptist. But these, he felt, would tend to limit their circle of friends because many who did not share those faiths would judge them to be potentially tiresome and they, Axel and Bonnie, would find their new soul mates even more so.

Better to be nonreligious Jews, he said. Yes, your friends would tend to be other Jews . . . all the better for camouflage . . . but, presuming no latent anti-Semitism on your part, that will also have its own rewards. You will find them warmer, wittier, more well-read, and better conversationalists than most.

Your faces, he said, will be significantly altered but, never fear, you will not become caricatures. Axel's hair will be darkened and restyled, his lips somewhat thickened, and something will be done around the eyes. His nose will be made thicker across the bridge and slightly crooked, as if once broken. Facial moles will be removed and an interesting scar will be added. His jaw, now square and jutting, will be broken and reset and the chin reduced. The result will be a face that is oval in shape and a profile that is not at all reminiscent of Axel Streicher.

Mrs. Streicher, he said, will become a blond. Her nose would be fixed as well. It will be made not Jewish but almost too perfect, as if a Semitic feature had been surgically corrected. Her two most arresting features are her breasts and her eyes. The breasts are easily reduced. The eyes, violet in color, can be muted by tinted contact lenses and the lids can be made to conceal a bit more of them. All teeth, his and hers, will be newly crowned in order to render previous dental records useless for purposes of identification.

For both, new wardrobes will be selected with an eye toward their new coloring and toward the avoidance of any known preferences in dress. Virtually all habitual brand preferences—clothing, cosmetics, cigarettes—will change. Bonnie will learn new makeup techniques. Surgical alteration of vocal cords is a possibility but first, said Dunville, we will see if a therapist can effect a satisfactory change in the pitch and cadence of your voices.

The Streichers were impressed. No detail was too small for the Dunvilles and their staff. First names were chosen that began with the same letter as the names they replaced in order to minimize slips of the tongue. They were to use these names exclusively. There was no more Axel, no more Bonnie. They were Alan and Barbara Weinberg. Their training would begin at once. Moreover, their contract provided for refresher courses after their release. Two in the first year and one annually for four years after that. Attendance was mandatory. Dunville would even provide relatives. Alan Weinberg would have an aunt and uncle living in Fort Meyers, Florida. Barbara Weinberg would have parents who had moved to Israel and a cousin living in New York. A three-day briefing by their stateside "relatives" was scheduled for the second month of their stay at Sur La Mer. Upon graduation, they would fly to Tel Aviv for a two-week visit with Barbara's parents. These relatives, Bonnie presumed, were Sur La Mer alumni as well.

The Streichers, from the outset, felt no reluctance to become Jews. Axel rather liked the idea. It took him a full week to exhaust his recall of Jewish Princess jokes, all at Bonnie's expense. Their only shared misgiving had to do with the surgery. They liked each other's faces as they were and Bonnie's breasts held tender memories for Axel although she, secretly, had long planned to have them reduced well before she reached forty. This was, she thought, as good a time as any. They had come to Sur La Mer fully realizing that they would leave as different people.

So be it. She was now Barbara. He was now Alan.

The surgery, begun at once, went well except for a stubborn infection that threatened Alan Weinberg's right eye and the breaking of his nose, which caused him to snore. It was this snoring that, during the ninth week of their stay, caused Barbara Weinberg to take a midnight stroll through the lawn and gardens of Sur La Mer.

It was a pleasant night. The dew and the light of a crescent moon had turned the dichondra lawn to silver. Barbara, dressed in her long white robe, left footprints on it as she walked toward the smell of the ocean. A thick hedge halted her progress. A security guard saw her, turned a flashlight on her, but did not dare approach. Alan had crippled one of them during their second month. The man had poked at him when he did not respond quickly to a summons from Henry Dunville. And she had broken the fingers of another who had seized her by the arm when she wandered through a door that was forbidden to them.

And yet, barring the occasional lapse of good manners, she did not blame the guards. They were merely following the instructions of the officious Henry, who seemed to make rules just for the sake of having them. Not that she and Alan would have violated any sensible security measure or even any of the more arcane rules, provided someone had the courtesy to explain them. But Henry could be pointlessly authoritarian. And a *nudnik*. What was that other word Alan liked? A *shvontz*. A *feckuckhteh shvontz*. He was also a bully. A stupid one. He had foolishly thought that Henry Dunville was more to be feared than the former Axel Streicher.

Barbara stood, facing the lawn, admiring her ghostly footprints. She lifted her eyes to the house. Even from the distance of the hedge it took in most of her field of vision. It was only four stories high, not counting the basement and attic, but each floor had thirteen-foot ceilings. The Dunvilles, three of them, kept apartments on the top floor. Household and nursing staff lived on the third. The security guards, numbering at least ten, lived in what had once been a carriage house and barn. "Special guests," such as themselves, lived in suites on the second floor of the north wing, to her left. There were four such suites but she and Alan were alone there now. Below, on the first floor, were the administrative offices and some of the hospital facilities. The surgery and several classrooms, were in the basement.

The regular patients, so-called members, lived on the first and second floors of the south wing. They took their meals in a formal dining room just off the entrance hall. She had heard them through closed doors but she had seen them, thus far, only from her window. She had counted eleven of them, none younger than eighty or so. She and Alan were forbidden to speak to them or, to the extent possible, be seen by them. They were not to go out of doors during those exercise periods reserved for the members. Henry Dunville's rules.

Most of the windows were dark. In two of them she could see the flickering glow of television sets. Barbara yawned. She began walking, slowly, back toward the house. She had retraced her steps about halfway when she felt herself being drawn toward the dim light coming from one of the first-floor windows. It was, perhaps, curiosity. Or perhaps she felt the need for human contact other than that with staff and guards. In any case she resisted the pull, continuing on, reluctant to leave a diverging set of tracks. But by the time she reached the terrace, the pull, or need, had become stronger. She stepped out of her damp slippers and, barefoot, made her way to the window.

It was a casement window, opening to each side, very tall. Inside, heavy drapes had been drawn but one of them had snagged on a piece of furniture. She saw the television screen first. It was quite large and, oddly, it seemed built into the wall as if to resemble a movie screen complete with curtains and a valance. A silent film was being shown on it.

Barbara saw movement. A flitting hand. She hesitated, then stepped closer. It was that old actress, Nellie Dameon. Alan had heard of her although she had not. He said that she was once a famous star, known even in Europe. She sat, every morning, on one of those marble benches over near the trees, close to where the blind man painted. Each of the members seemed to have his or her private place. And private world. Now, Nellie Dameon seemed to be in another one. As she watched the silent film her hands and arms were moving, matching the gestures of the woman on the screen. Her face, from what Barbara could see, was matching the facial expressions as well. Barbara's first thought was that Nellie Dameon was watching one of her own films, reliving a time when she was young and lovely and famous. Before her mind had failed her. She began to back away, regretting having intruded.

But now the camera showed a close-up of the actress on the screen. It was not Nellie. The face was all wrong. Too round. No cheekbones. Beautiful, Barbara supposed, but in an icy sort of way. And the performance, she realized, was awful. A title card flashed on the screen.

"If you leave me, I will die," it said.

But from the young woman's expression, she might as well have been asking who left the toilet seat up. Barbara smiled. She heard a chuckle from inside. It was followed, very softly, by a voice repeating the words of the title, "If you leave me, I will die," and another chuckle. Then, in apology, trying not to laugh, "I'm sorry, Marion. Poor dear Marion." But she laughed all the same.

Barbara's smile widened but she was suddenly puzzled. Hadn't Alan said that Nellie Dameon never spoke? Perhaps someone else, possibly this Marion, was in there with her. She moved closer to the window and peeked in. No, she realized. The actress was alone. She was dressed in a feathery peignoir, seated in a high-backed chair of carved mahogany. The furnishings of the rest of the room were equally heavy. Oriental carpets on the floor. Paintings with gilt Italianate frames. Mementos crowding every surface. Once again, Barbara backed away. Her shoulder touched the casement window. It squeaked.

Barbara cursed herself even as she heard the gasp from within. She closed her eyes and made herself stay still. To run would pile rudeness on rudeness. She stood, just out of sight from inside, and said, "I'm sorry. I didn't mean to . . . I was just . . ." Oh . . . heck.

There was no answer. Only a rustling sound and the squeak of a chair. The rustle seemed to be approaching the window. Barbara waited, half-expecting hands to reach out and close it. Nothing happened. She moved closer, showing herself, hoping that the sight of her bandaged face would not startle the frail old woman.

It was Barbara who was startled. Nellie Dameon stood facing her but not seeing her. The eyes were glazed and they were focused, if anywhere, on a point just off Barbara's shoulder. The old woman's jaw was slack and she stood unblinking. She had withdrawn, totally, within herself. But, Barbara realized, she was also making sure that Barbara saw her that way. This was the same woman who, moments before, had laughed and spoken at the screen. Barbara knew what she was seeing here. It was another performance.

"Do you want me not to . . . say anything?"

No response. No reaction.

Barbara winced at her own question. What the old woman wanted, clearly, was that she go away, satisfied that she'd been mistaken. But Barbara wanted more than that. She wanted to see life in those eyes again.

Barbara sensed movement behind her. She turned. A patrolling guard had walked to the spot where she had stood at the hedge. He was studying the ground as if looking for spoor. He had not seen where she'd gone to and the plantings of the main house concealed her from his view. But he gave her an idea.

"Could I stay until he's gone?" she asked, tossing her head toward the guard. "I'll get in trouble." It was not quite a lie.

The eyes flickered. Nothing more.

Barbara tried a smile. "If you leave me, I will die," she said.

The light returned. The tiniest grin tugged at Nellie Dameon's mouth. But she forced it away.

"I'll go in two minutes. And I won't say anything that would hurt you. I promise."

Now, for the first time, the eyes looked into her own. Appraisingly. Intelligently. Her hand came up, nearly touching the bandages on Barbara's face. The eyes asked a question.

"I'm . . . uh . . . already in trouble, actually. So is my husband. We're trying to start fresh."

The patrolling guard had seen her footprints in the dichondra. He followed them with the beam of his flashlight, first to the terrace and then to the front door. He stood for a moment as if trying to remember. Had he heard it open and close? The old actress watched him as he pulled a radio from his hip and spoke into it. Then he started toward the house.

The actress wet her lips. A frown. A shake of the head. She held out a hand to Barbara Weinberg.

"You're in more trouble than you know," said Nellie Dameon.

9

Tuesday morning. Westport.

Susan Lesko, in a blue bath towel, her hair still wet from the shower, answered the phone while Bannerman was shaving.

She heard a brief pause, the hollow sound of an overseas call, then a sucking in of breath and her father's voice. "Um . . . Hi," he said simply.

Susan winced. She heard the disapproval. It was nothing overt. But she knew that he was seeing her, imagining her, in some state of less-than-proper dress. Bad enough, he'd be thinking, that she lived with the guy. She tugged the towel an inch or so higher, then realized what she was doing and that it was dumb.

Her father recovered first, clearing his throat. "How're you doing, sweetheart?"

"I miss you."

"Me too," he answered. "When are you coming over?"

"It depends." She smiled. "When's the wedding?"

A low grunt. "A week after yours."

The smile broadened. It pleased her that, for once, she'd managed to fire the first shot. She was living with Paul, her father was living with Elena. More than a year now. Both of them. She had not quite been able to persuade him that the two were the same. Nor could he persuade her that they were not.

Fathers.

"You heard anything from Carla?" he asked. "How she's doing?"

"Molly called late last night. She's having a tough time but she's holding up."

"Molly's with her? That's good." A thoughtful pause. "Listen, when you have an address, Elena wants to send flowers. Me, too."

"Is Elena there?" she asked. "Can I talk to her after you're finished with Paul?"

"It depends. You got any more cute little stories about me?"

"Nope. Just girl talk."

"Put Bannerman on. And you behave yourself."

"Love you, Daddy."

Bannerman dried his hands and took the phone. Acknowledging Lesko's strained greeting, he listened for several moments, then reached for a pad and pencil and asked Lesko to repeat a name.

"Andy Huff," Lesko told him. "Like Sam Huff of the Giants. He's heading the investigation for the LAPD and he's a friend of a friend. The FBI agent in charge is a guy named Jack Scholl."

"You spoke to Huff?"

"Yeah, but not Scholl. I got no leverage with the feds."

"What about Irwin Kaplan?"

"Irwin's DEA. What would he know about serial killers?"

"Nothing, but he's well connected. Maybe I'll call him myself."

"Better let me. You make him nervous."

"Thank you. What could Huff tell you?"

"Well . . ." Lesko hesitated. "He said the evidence, so far, points to the same guy who killed the other six. More or less the same pattern."

Bannerman thought he heard doubt. "More or less?"

"They think he snatched her Sunday morning, killed her, then waited till dark to dump her. The others were all snatched at night. This one also had heroin in her system. There was something funny about that but he wouldn't tell me what."

"Can you guess?"

More hesitation. "Probably none of the others did."

"Lesko," Bannerman frowned, "what's bothering you?"

"I'm not sure. Something."

"Would you do me a favor?"

"What?"

"Talk it over. Then call me back."

A pause. The voice dropped. "Bannerman . . . don't start that shit."

"Okay, then. *Think* it over. What could it hurt?"

An audible sigh. But no answer.

"This is for Carla. Maybe you owe her one. For Elena."

"Don't start that shit either," Lesko said quietly. "Whatever she did over in Spain, she enjoyed it."

"For me, then."

A long silence. "You being good to Susan?"

"I think so. I'm learning."

A grunt. It sounded, Bannerman thought, like *me too*. "You gonna be around?"

"At my office. I'll stay until you call."

"I didn't say I'll talk to him. What I'll do is think."

"Thank you." He saw Susan, blower in hand, asking with a gesture if he was through. "Hold on. Susan wants to talk to Elena."

"Me first," he said. "Let's see how much you're learning."

Bannerman stepped into the bedroom where he could finish dressing without appearing to listen. But he did. And he watched. •

Susan.

Even in the terry robe she now wore, her long brown hair plastered, still wet, against her face, Susan was the loveliest woman he'd ever known. So clean and fresh. Especially inside. And the way her body moved as she spoke. Animated, yet graceful, like a dancing cat. He loved to watch her at any time but especially in the morning. And especially before she woke up. When she slept, she almost always had this little smile. It was there when she made love as well. And also whenever she beat him at anything. Tennis. Scrabble. Doing the Sunday crossword.

Coming home in the evening, he still had trouble believing that she'd be there. That she wouldn't, one of these days, ask herself what she'd gotten herself into. But, as Molly had said, if she hadn't asked herself that a year ago, after he had, twice, almost got her killed, maybe she never would.

She was talking to Elena now. Whispering. Something private. Probably about Elena's efforts to have a child. Lesko had given up arguing against it but there had been two miscarriages already. Still, Bannerman had to smile at the image of this great brute of a man being called home every time Elena's temperature went up one degree.

Lesko, no doubt, had just as much trouble believing that he and Elena were still together after a year. That this elegant and very wealthy woman seemed to love him and admire him, and need him, all the more with each passing week. And that he'd been able to forget that it was Elena, in another world, another lifetime, who had ordered the death of his partner.

Except that the partner, David Katz, was not altogether dead. Lesko, in his mind, had clung to him.

Still talks to him. They all knew it. They understood it.

You spend ten years with one partner, day in and day out, and before long you're like Siamese twins. You finish each other's sentences, you think as a unit. One partner dies, leaving an empty seat, and you find yourself still talking to him, asking what he thinks. Except in Lesko's case they mostly argue because Lesko has never quite forgiven Katz for being dirty. Or himself for not realizing it in time.

It sounded crazy, Bannerman realized, but it's not so unusual. Widows do it all the time. People pray to dead saints.

None of this, however, had made Lesko any less sensitive about it. Even though Katz's presence had been useful on several occasions. Well . . . not Katz exactly. And certainly not his ghost. Katz had become, through years of habit, a sort of alter ego. Someone to bounce ideas off of. A subconscious, really, that occasionally saw and heard things that Lesko might otherwise have missed. That could be a considerable asset if not denied. Bannerman had tried to persuade him of that. So, in fact, had Elena. But listening to Katz was one thing and admitting it was something else. Bannerman's request, that Lesko *talk it over* with Katz, would have gotten his head bitten off were not the Atlantic Ocean between them. What it meant was . . . let your mind flow. Pretend he's still in that seat. Toss it around with him.

No, it doesn't, Bannerman muttered to himself. *It means ask him.*

"Paul?"

Susan, holding the phone toward him.

"For you. It's my dad again."

"I know what bothered me." Lesko's voice. A touch self-conscious. More than a touch defiant.

"What was it?"

"I thought about it. By myself."

"I know. That's what you said you'd do." Bannerman glanced at the ceiling.

"Just so we're clear on that."

"We are. Absolutely."

Lesko seemed to want to say more. Drive the point home a little harder. But all Bannerman heard was the sound of his breathing.

"When I talked to Huff," Lesko said at last, "he kept saying '*this* guy.' "

Bannerman shook his head. "I don't follow."

"*This* guy," Lesko repeated. "Huff only said it when he was talking about the guy who killed Carla's sister. Not when he was talking about the guy who killed the other six."

Bannerman frowned. "You're saying he doesn't think they're the same man?"

Lesko didn't answer.

"Is it just," Bannerman asked, "that the pattern is a little different this time? That it was done on a Sunday. And that heroin was involved?"

"Maybe."

"Lesko . . . what else?"

"I think it's not the same guy. And I think Andy Huff knows damned well it isn't."

Bannerman was silent for a long moment. "Why?"

"You're going to start with why?" Lesko sputtered. "First you ask me to talk to fucking Katz and now you want to get rational?"

Bannerman suppressed a smile. "What I want are your instincts," he said quietly.

"If I followed my instincts, you would have been in the hospital the first time you came within a mile of my daughter again."

"I know." Bannerman closed his eyes. Someday he'd have a conversation with Lesko in which he did not become homicidal on the subject of Susan becoming involved with Mama's Boy. God forbid that she should become pregnant. Which they'd been talking about. A little. He'd have to tie Lesko down, sit Billy McHugh on his chest, before he told him. "Lesko," he said patiently, "tell me what you think."

"Huff's sure. He *knows* it's not the same guy."

He was repeating himself. Bannerman waited.

"If that's right," Lesko finished his thought, "which is a big *if*, you tell me. How could he be that sure?"

Bannerman hesitated. "He must have a suspect. For the others, I mean."

"Keep going."

"They've had him under surveillance. When Lisa Benedict was killed, Huff's suspect wasn't anywhere near."

"You said it. I didn't."

"But you agree."

Lesko grunted. The equivalent of a shrug. "Or else the real killer called in to say he didn't do this one. That happens sometimes."

"So you think we're dealing with a copycat."

"Maybe. More or less."

"Why are you hedging?"

"There are three kinds of copycats," Lesko told him. "One is another psycho and the chances are he also picks a victim he doesn't know. The second is someone who reads the papers, has a specific victim in mind who fits the profile, and sees this as a way to pull it off. The third is your basic crime of passion. Guy loses his head, strangles a woman, then uses what he knows about the serial killer to cover his tracks. Except most times it doesn't work because the cops usually keep some of the details, like teeth marks or mutilation, for example, out of the press."

Bannerman nodded, thoughtfully. "But if it *was* a copycat," he asked, "the two task forces will look for him just as hard, won't they?"

"They'd say yes but they won't. Priorities."

"Would you?"

"Same way. First things first. The copycat will keep because the chances are he won't kill again and the other guy will.

Banner said nothing. But he understood.

"Bannerman?"

"Yes."

"What are you going to do with this?"

"I don't know. Maybe nothing. It's not . . ." Bannerman stopped himself. Too late.

"Not your field. Not your basic assassination or car bombing."

"Lesko . . ."

"Cheap shot. Sorry." Lesko tried to sound sincere. Nor did he wish to invite a rebuttal that asked how what he was doing for the Brugg family of Zürich differed from what Bannerman had done for a dozen or so governments.

"Bannerman?"

"I'm here."

"I think of anything else, hear anything else, I'll call you."

"I'd appreciate it."

"In the meantime, you want my advice, don't say anything to Carla. She's fucked up enough already. Me, I'd let her bury her sister and then get her back to Westport."

"I agree. But thanks."

"Later on, I'll call her. Tell her I'm sorry."

"That would be nice. Thank you."

"Meanwhile, you take care of Susan."

"Sure. Kiss Elena for me."

"Like hell I will." Lesko broke the connection.

10

One week earlier. Sur La Mer.

They talked for two hours that night. Haltingly, at first. There were many silences of five minutes or more. At times, the mind of the old woman seemed clear and sharp. At other times it wandered.

Marion, the wooden actress whom Nellie had mimicked, and then apologized for it, was Marion Davies. The film was *Beverly of Graustark* made in 1926, now on a cassette. Barbara read the label as Nellie Dameon poured her a sherry. Having set down the glass, Nellie took a framed photograph from an antique chiffonier and handed it to Barbara. In it, smiling for the camera, were Nellie herself, Marion Davies, William Randolph Hearst, and a very young Gary Cooper. The latter three had autographed it. Marion Davies had written, "Just found this. Popsy and Gary say get well. Love you." It was dated, in her hand, October 1931.

"She was Hearst's mistress, you know."

And protégé, Barbara nodded. She'd read about them somewhere.

"Marion didn't do much after sound came, either," Nellie said wistfully. "She had a stutter."

"Um . . . Miss Dameon?"

"Nellie will be fine."

"Thank you. Why do you pretend you're . . ." She searched for a word that would not offend.

"Crackers?" Nellie offered it. "Because I am. I think."

"Not that I can see. But, at the window, you tried to make me think you're catatonic. It would have worked if I hadn't heard you laugh."

The old actress glanced at the drapes, now fully drawn. "I'll keep those windows closed," she said.

"Nellie? Please tell me."

The eyes drifted. They glazed over. She was doing it again. But not for long. "It's a place I go," she said, as if upon waking. "It keeps me out of trouble."

That word again.

"Would somebody harm you? If they knew you could speak?"

She hesitated. "I don't know."

"Are you afraid of the Dunvilles? If you are, why don't you leave?"

She smiled, sadly. She shook her head.

"There are hundreds of places," Barbara told her. "You'd be with people your age. You could talk to them all you want."

The glaze returned. It hovered. It did not settle. "I went on a picnic this morning," she said, sitting back in her chair.

Barbara waited.

"Not here. At Malibu. Just girls. Me, Marion and Colleen Moore." She pointed to another old photograph. An actress with bangs.

Barbara looked but said nothing.

"We gossiped, and laughed, and ate everything we're not allowed." Nellie smiled at the memory. "We had horses there. We rode them, bareback, through the waves."

"You went . . . in your mind?"

The actress shook her head. She touched her fingers to the back of her hand. "I can still feel the salt."

Barbara understood. A little. "You're saying . . . you were really there."

"Yes."

"You can do that? Go off, be young again, anytime you like?"

She nodded slowly. "You learn. But everything has to be just so. It only works from this chair. And from my bench." She reached for her sherry and sipped from it.

The light flooded back into her eyes. "Of course," she said, smiling, "it helps to be crackers."

Barbara laughed aloud. She clamped a hand over her mouth as the old woman, still smiling, shushed her. She picked up her own glass and, with it, saluted Nellie Dameon.

"Nellie? Why did you say that I'm in more trouble than I know?"

The smile faded. "Is Barbara your real name?"

"It is now."

"Will you tell me who you were before?"

"I want to. But it's better if I don't."

"You don't seem . . ." She stopped herself.

"A bad person? I hope not. I like to think not."

Nellie wet her lips, deciding whether to speak. "Some never leave," she said at last.

Barbara stared. "Why would that be?"

"They break rules."

11

Tuesday morning. Los Angeles.

"Get off here," Carla Benedict pointed. "Go east on Slauson."

They were traveling southbound on the Harbor Freeway. Minutes earlier, they had passed the University of Southern California campus on their right, then the Los Angeles Coliseum.

Molly Farrell followed her directions, turning at last onto Alameda Street in the section called Huntington Park. There was nothing parklike about it, she thought. Not a good neighborhood at all. Seedy apartment buildings, most of them two or three stories, gratings over store fronts, the residents mostly black or Hispanic.

Carla pointed toward a row of apartments, wood frame, white, probably built just after World War II, in need of paint. Molly pulled up at the curb. Carla took a long breath, held it, then stepped from the car.

Lisa's apartment was on the far end, second floor, reached by an outside stairway. Two keys opened the two locks of the door. The hinges squeaked. Molly had half-expected some sort of police notice to be taped to it, sealing the apartment while the investigation proceeded, but there was nothing. She would have assumed that the police had been there, and a few reporters as well. Apparently they had not.

The apartment consisted of one good-size living room, a small bedroom, and a tiny bath. The living room had a kitchen at one end. Someone, long before Lisa, had removed the partition between kitchen and living room to give it a loft effect. Sparse furnishings made it seem larger than it was. It had a pullout couch. Carla had probably slept on it when she visited. There were framed posters on the walls, one Italian, one French, and a number of artifacts that were obviously European, probably sent by Carla over the years. Carla moved through the room, slowly, touching things.

Molly said nothing, reluctant to intrude, as she watched Carla's eyes. For the most part they were soft, unfocused, even lost. Now and then they would begin to melt as a memory passed behind them. But at other times they would narrow, and they would shine. Molly knew that they were seeing, trying to see, the man who had killed her sister. Trying to feel him, as she said she had where Lisa's body had been found.

It was strange, she thought. Like watching two different people. The Carla she'd known for years, and the Carla she was just getting to know as she'd finally stroked her to sleep in their bungalow at the Beverly Hills Hotel.

Molly had known, of course, that Carla and her sister had been born almost fifteen years apart. She'd presumed Lisa to have been an accident. Parents well into their forties by the time she was born. But the accident, it turned out, had been Carla. Mother, unwed, became pregnant. Father forced into marriage. Embittered by it. Resented Carla. Mother was much closer to her but became a drunk. Lisa born while Carla was in high school. Parents, especially the father, doted on Lisa, took her everywhere, bragged about her, rarely mentioned Carla except in terms of the scrapes she got into and the cars she wrecked, possibly to get their attention, although she'd deny that, possibly to hurt them back. And yet Carla, far from resenting Lisa, doted on her the most. She loved her, she had said last night . . . *"with the passion put to use in my old griefs . . . and with the love I seemed to lose with my lost saints."*

Molly had to shake her head. Carla Benedict, Calamity Carla, quoting sonnets from the Portuguese. The second bottle of wine had done it.

They moved toward the bedroom. Molly entered first.

A queen-size bed, no headboard, stacked with pillows. More poster art on the walls but these were of movies. Old movies. Some of them silent films. By the window, stood a scarred oak desk with a computer and printer on it. A telephone answering machine, not blinking. There was a two-drawer filing cabinet, and three shelves crammed with books.

Something was wrong here. She didn't know what, exactly. Perhaps it was the answering machine. After two days, there should have been a call on it. She reached for the switch and moved it to *Play*.

"Hi, gorgeous. It's Kevin."

The sound, a young man's voice, startled Carla. She stepped closer.

"Listen, I got a tape of Flesh and the Devil. *Gilbert and Garbo with a whole new score by the London Symphony. Great stuff. We're going to watch it at nine at DiDi Fenerty's. If you get this in time, just come over."*

Molly heard a TV in the background. The end of a

car commercial followed by a loud ticking sound. *"The mail this week was unusually . . ."* The caller disconnected. But the television show, she realized, was *60 Minutes.*

There was a second message. A woman's voice, no name but obviously a friend, asking if Lisa planned to run in the morning. The next message, an old one, had been partially taped over by the second. Two calls, thought Molly. Both on Sunday evening. But who had played them? Not Lisa. She was long dead by then.

"That wasn't flashing," Carla said quietly.

Molly nodded. "The police were probably here." But now her eyes were roaming the room. They fell on the surface of the desk. She sniffed it. It smelled of a cleanser. She felt it. It seemed to have been wiped clean. She leaned over the keyboard of Lisa's computer. Same odor there. And on the answering machine. But on the outer reaches of the desk she could see an accumulation of dust and soot. And on the bookcase.

She noticed something else. The bookcase had not been dusted, probably for a week or more. And in front of each book she saw tracks in the dust, fresh tracks, as if each of them had been examined. Why, she wondered, would the police look inside every book? The answer; they wouldn't. Not unless they had reason to believe that something had been hidden between the pages. Molly reached into her purse. From a zippered compartment she produced a pair of thin surgical gloves and slipped them over her hands.

She flipped the power switch of Lisa's computer. Molly knew the machine. It was a Leading Edge, an IBM clone, hard disk, fairly inexpensive. It hummed to life. At the C prompt, she typed in the access to Lisa's word processing software. The words . . . GENERAL FAILURE . . . appeared on the screen. She lifted the monitor and placed it to one side, then, carefully she raised the front end of the computer. Underneath, in the dust, many months of it, she saw what she was looking for. A pattern of marks and scuffs where there should have been none. Someone had moved the computer, roughly, probably banged it up and down until the hard disk crashed and everything on it was destroyed.

Molly turned to the bookcase. She'd noticed several computer manuals there. She looked through them, hoping to find that Lisa had owned and used a backup system that guarded against such a crash. There was none. Months of work, perhaps years of work, all gone. Personal records, correspondence . . . everything. Molly could not believe that a graduate student would risk so devastating a loss.

She searched through the drawers of the desk, looking for files of floppy disks. She found two sets. One, in a plastic case, contained a variety of utility programs and games but no duplicate files. The other, in a Maxell box, contained eighteen disks, each numbered in sequence. She took the first one, locked it into the computer, and booted it on the A prompt. The screen filled with symbols. They were scrambled. Hopelessly. She tried several more at random with the same result.

"What's wrong?" Carla asked. "What did you find?"

Molly shrugged. "I'm not sure." She tried to hide her concern. No use setting Carla off just when she'd calmed her down. But someone, for some reason, had deliberately destroyed all of Lisa's records and the contents of her soft disk file—which might or might not have been her backup disks—as well. She tried to imagine what it could have meant. That Lisa had known the killer? That she had written something about him on her computer? Stranger things had happened. Yet it hardly seemed likely.

"Molly?"

"Uh-huh?"

"Don't jerk me around," she said evenly. "I know what a crash looks like. And I know this place has been picked over."

Molly hesitated. "It could still have been the police. Or the FBI."

"Bullshit."

Then who else, she wanted to ask, but didn't. "Can you think of anything else that's missing?" she asked instead.

"She kept one of those month-at-a-glance calendars right here." Carla pointed to a nail hole in the wall by the desk. Even the nail was gone.

"How about an address book? Diaries, tape recorders, anything like that."

Carla scanned the room. Then, slowly, silently, she began opening drawers and closets. She moved into the living room. Molly could hear her. More drawers and now the hall closet. Molly waited, the Maxell box in her hand, thoughtfully tapping it against her chin. The light from the window caught some scratchings on the box's lid. Initials. Marked with a ballpoint pen. They read *DF/FB*.

Their possible meaning struck her at once. She was reaching for Lisa's telephone directory when she heard a sound coming from the front door. It was being opened. By someone who had a key. She sat still, listening. The hinges squeaked. Whoever it was, was hesitating. Now she heard feet, more than two, moving slowly over the thin carpet. Where was Carla? She took a pen from the desk, removed the top, and concealed it in her hand.

A man's face flicked into the doorway, then withdrew. Almost instantly, it returned, this time behind a revolver held in outstretched hands. A second man, also armed, stepped from behind the first. Both men, wearing suits, filled the doorway.

"Do you mind?" Molly asked quietly, nodding toward their weapons.

"On your feet," the older of the two ordered. "Slowly."

Molly made a face. "Identification, please."

"I said"—he gestured with his gun—"on your feet."

Suddenly, the second man collapsed. One knee shot forward, his head whipped back. He crashed heavily to the floor. The first man swung his revolver toward the man who was down. Too late. His head jerked back as well. Molly saw a flash of metal. A large bread knife. A hand attached. They appeared from nowhere. The serrated edge glistened at the throat of the man still standing.

"For Pete's sake, Carla," Molly said disgustedly.

Calamity Carla.

Irwin Kaplan, Drug Enforcement Administration, Washington, was eating breakfast with his daughters when he took Lesko's call. At the first mention of Bannerman's name, he told Lesko that he would get back to him in twenty minutes.

He returned the call from a Peoples Drug Store several blocks from his home.

It was not that he had reason to think his phone might be wired, except that this is Washington and you never know. What he didn't want was anyone in government, ever again, using his name and Bannerman's in the same sentence. *"Irwin . . . you know Bannerman, right? The guy trusts you, right? We have this problem and we wonder if you could . . ."*

"Absolutely not. Go away. Fuck off."

"Look. Hear us out. All we want is . . ."

"No, you look. I am an officer of the law. I am sworn to uphold the law. You ever hear of it? It's called the constitution. Nowhere does it say, if this doesn't work, try Bannerman's law."

"Yeah, well, we hear Bannerman's law worked for you, Irwin. Last year in New York. We hear about a Jamaican gang that's now mostly dead after you sent him a hit list. We hear you're also feeding names to Lesko and the Bruggs who are leaving bodies all over Zürich. We hear you're . . ."

"I don't know what you're talking about."

"Bullshit."

"Anyway, the New York thing was personal."

"But it was a win, Irwin. We need a win."

"Out. Leave me alone."

All this boiled in his mind as he drove to Peoples

Drug. He practiced saying no. No matter what it was.
Even if Bannerman just had something for him, no
strings. There were always strings.

It came as a relief, therefore, and it caught him
unaware, that all it was was the murder of Carla Benedict's younger sister. Thinking that way, in those terms,
also left him feeling guilty. Yes, he was sorry to hear it.
Yes, he'd make some calls to see what the FBI had. The
law's the law, but a creep who kills young women just to
see them die is something else. God should be so good
that Bannerman got his hands on the fucker and locked
him in a room with Carla. She'd take two days with him.

Bannerman's law.

Yes, he promised. He'd find out what he could.

12

"Nellie? How many, like me, have you seen here?"

"Like you? None, I think. You're very nice."

"I think you're nice, too. But I mean the special
guests. The ones in the north wing."

She thought for a moment. "Over the years . . .
hundreds, I suppose."

Barbara closed one eye, doubtfully.

"In the beginning, I was sick. I don't remember
much. But since then, yes. Hundreds."

Barbara made a mental note to ask Carleton Dunville. Claim idle curiosity, although he probably wouldn't
tell her. Nellie Dameon appeared to read her mind.

"Carleton, the young one, keeps lists of them. I
think they all send money and some come back. He kept
the lists in his desk, but not now."

Barbara leaned forward. "How would you know
that, Nellie?"

"We used to hear them arguing. Carleton found Henry looking at them. Now Carleton won't let him see them at all. He keeps them in his safe."

It was almost too much to absorb.

The numbers of people who had passed through Sur La Mer, going on to new lives. And how much this old woman knew.

Barbara was inclined to doubt much of what she said. Consider the source. And yet, in a crazy way, it made sense. The members, it seemed, were no more than props. They were kept there, to legitimize Sur La Mer. And they were, all of them, probably insane. Nellie as well, notwithstanding that Barbara was becoming fond of her. It seemed entirely likely that, over the years, many a careless remark was made in the hearing of one or more of these sick old men and women, part of the furniture, by people who saw only their vacant stares and eccentricities and assumed that nobody was home.

She would have assumed that as well.

They watched another film, *Polly of the Follies* with Constance Talmadge, made in 1922. Barbara inserted the cassette. The machine, she noted, was strictly a player. Unlike the one in her suite, it had no television function. Looking around the room, she saw no newspapers. Only a stack of old magazines in plastic covers. They were old fan magazines. *Photoplay*, *Silver Screen*, and a few vintage copies of *Time*.

"Nellie, what's today's date?"

"It's Monday."

"I mean, the exact date."

"I don't know."

"Do you know what year it is?"

"No."

"Don't you even wonder."

"Barbara, it doesn't matter here. Watch the movie."

*   *   *

"I'd better go," Barbara said. A Tiffany clock had just chimed two. She opened the curtains slightly, watching for the guard to pass on his rounds. "I'd like to come again," she said, turning.

"Do you like movies? We have shelves and shelves of them."

"Could we watch one of yours?"

Nellie blushed. "That's nice. Thank you."

"Could I bring my husband? You'd like him."

She hesitated. "Just you, I think, for now."

"May I tell him about you?"

Nellie smiled. The eyes were pleased that she had asked. "But no one else?"

"I promise." Barbara reached to ease the window open. She paused, suddenly frowning. A part of her could still barely believe that this visit had happened. "Nellie?" She turned again. "Does anyone else know you can talk?"

"The members do. Some of them. And a girl who came to see me."

"What girl?"

"She came yesterday. To my bench. She's going to help me find my children."

"Um . . . you have children?"

"Two that I remember. Harland says I have four but Harland says a lot of things that aren't so."

"Who is Harland?"

"You've seen him. In a yachting costume. He goes sailing every morning."

Barbara had seen him. On the far side of the lawn. The magic bench, in his case, must be his wheelchair. Barbara wanted to ask about these children Nellie seemed to think she had but an alarm, deep within her brain, had begun to buzz.

"This girl," she asked quietly, "is she one of the staff?"

Nellie shook her head. "Just a fan. She came up through the trees."

The alarm bleated. "Or a reporter? Could she have been a reporter?"

Nellie heard the low intensity behind the question and she seemed to understand Barbara's concern. She reached a reassuring hand. "I'm sure that she isn't. But I'll ask her when she visits again."

Alan, even more than she, could scarcely believe all that Barbara had learned from this old actress who was thought to be an hysterical mute and hopelessly insane. But, like Barbara, his most urgent concern was the girl who had come up through the trees. If she existed at all.

It appeared that she did. Nellie Dameon even got her name. Lisa something. Benson . . . Bickford. Nellie could not quite recall.

She remembered, however, that the girl had a camera. And Alan Weinberg had remembered that at the approximate time of this visit, he and his wife had been out on the terrace, sipping coffee, in defiance of Henry Dunville's rules. They soon went back inside but only because their coffee was cold and because the Ruiz woman came out to say that a doctor from the Motion Picture Relief Association had just entered the main gate. Still, this girl, this Lisa, could well have photographed them.

Alan now remembered an incident of that morning that had made no great impression on him at the time. The young doctor—his name was Feldman—came once each month to check medical records and give routine physicals. Alan had overheard him complaining to Henry, angrily, about Henry's "guests" bothering the members. Henry had seemed confused. He knew that his only guests were the Weinbergs and they had gone nowhere near the old actress or the blind painter. Although the two men clearly despised each other, Henry claimed innocence. He promised to look into it. Minutes later, he heard Henry shouting at his chief of security, a surly goon named Darby, who then rushed out of Henry's office.

Yes, he thought. Someone had apparently been there.

"They might have her already," he said to Barbara. "Darby might have grabbed her when she came down through the trees."

Barbara shook her head. "They'd want to know who she is first. They'd wait. Even Henry would know better than to grab a reporter . . . if that's what she is."

Alan frowned beneath his mask of bandages. He envisioned a grainy photograph of himself and his wife on the cover of some supermarket tabloid. *Alien Visitors at California Asylum?* or *Hitler Alive in Movie Madhouse.*

"I'd better ask Henry about her," he said.

"You can't say Nellie spoke to me."

"I won't have to." It was enough that he'd witnessed that scene with young Dr. Feldman.

It had taken some persuasion and the encounter had not improved their relationship. But Henry, in the end, acknowledged that there had been an intruder.

They know who she is, he said, and she's not a reporter. Merely a student. Her only interest seems to have been photographing the house and meeting Nellie Dameon. She is being attended to and Nellie Dameon is to be . . . examined.

"Examining that old woman," Weinberg told his wife, "will probably involve drugs. We don't want him finding out that she can talk, and especially the things she told you."

"How do we stop him? We can't move in with her."

"You might have to," he said. "For now, it's time that I met her. Henry has to know that we're her friends."

Barbara understood. Henry Dunville was afraid of them already. He might not risk forcing a confrontation without Carleton here to back him up. The flip side was that he would surely wonder about their sudden interest. But Barbara could handle that. She would simply tell him that there was nothing sudden about it. She had been sneaking into Nellie's suite for some time. Watching movies. Because Alan snored.

"What about that girl?" she asked. "What will they do to her?"

"What I'd do, I imagine. Give her something else to think about."

Barbara understood that as well. He would not hurt her. Not if she meant them no harm. But he would certainly frighten her.

That afternoon, the thug, Darby, sent by Henry to fetch Nellie Dameon found Barbara Weinberg with her, watching movies. Barbara told him to go away. He returned with the Ruiz woman but Barbara, by that time, had braced a chair against the door that locked only from the outside.

Ruiz returned with Henry Dunville, this time to the casement window. He demanded an explanation. Barbara confessed to having been coming there for weeks. She claimed to be a fan of silent films and of Nellie Dameon in particular. She said that, given time, she thinks she can get Nellie to speak.

Henry reacted as she had hoped. He ridiculed her presumption that she could succeed where psychiatrists had failed. He chastised her for breaking the rules. He said all that she had accomplished was the punishment of Nellie Dameon and a substantial fine for herself.

"Punishment?" In her mind, she thanked Henry Dunville for using that word. "I can't allow that, Henry," she said.

"Neither can I," said Alan Weinberg who appeared at the window behind Henry and Ruiz, and placed his arms around their shoulders.

All the rest of that week, they stayed close to Nellie Dameon. They attended no classes. They brought her, on the first night, to their suite in that part of the château she had never before seen. She seemed uncomfortable there. She would not speak, not even to Barbara.

A phone call came from Carleton, the younger, insisting that this foolishness stop at once. Henry had reached him, complained to him, threatened to use force. Carleton, aware that force would surely result in loss of life, forbade it but he did demand an explanation from Alan Weinberg.

Weinberg was ready for him. He told Carleton of Henry's reputation. That he had abused and mistreated members in the past. That he mocked them and played cruel tricks on them. That he, and the lesbian, Ruiz, were known to demand sexual favors of female staff.

He had heard no such things. They were strictly guesses, based on Weinberg's intuitive assessment of Henry, intended to persuade Carleton that his concern for Nellie's well-being had substance, if only in his own mind. But the long silence on Carleton's end, the lack of argument, convinced him that his intuition was at least in part correct. Carleton, disgust now evident in his voice, said that he would speak to his half-brother and that he would deal with this situation on his return ten days hence. He would instruct Henry, in the meantime, to avoid any escalation of tensions. He asked Weinberg to do the same. Weinberg said that he would as long as Henry and his guards kept their distance.

It was Weinberg's impression, after hanging up the phone, that Carleton had been told nothing of last Sunday's intruder.

The impasse went on. They returned Nellie to her quarters—to her world, they now realized—but still she did not speak. They watched movies with her, dined with her, and they took her each morning to her magic bench, retiring thereafter to a respectful distance. Nellie's passivity was such that Barbara almost began to wonder whether their conversation of the preceding Monday night had been a dream. Or, possibly, as Alan Weinberg suggested, the old woman's periods of lucidity were rare. That, he said, might serve to explain how she'd gone undetected so long. But on Friday afternoon, as Barbara selected a film, she spoke.

"What day is it?" she asked softly.

"Nellie?" Barbara, startled, rushed to her side.

"I've been away," she said.

"Are you . . . all right?"

She nodded, and smiled. "We went sailing," she said.

"Um . . . who did?" Weinberg asked.

The old woman turned at the sound of his voice. She saw the mask of bandages, the single eye. Her tiny chest heaved as if she might scream.

Barbara reached for her, taking her head, turning it so that Nellie looked into her eyes. "That's Alan," she told her. "He's been with us . . . since you left." Barbara threw a glance at her husband. Her expression said *I forgot to tell you this part.*

She stayed with them, in the present, all that evening. Alan did his best to put her at ease, a task made more difficult because she could not see his face. But she could hear his voice, kept low and soft with a slight German accent, and she could see the affectionate touching between her two visitors.

Mostly he listened, as Barbara, in bits and pieces, got her to repeat many of the things she had said before. Alan pressed her only once—on the subject of Carleton Dunville's safe—and she promptly withdrew. Thereafter, he resolved to say little lest he disturb what he thought to be the delicate thread of her sanity. Rather, he leafed through her scrapbooks, pretending interest in them at first but the interest quickly became genuine. He asked her, during a silence, if he might see one of her early films. He pointed to a publicity still from *The Hun Within*. Barbara had mentioned that title, joking that it could have been about him within his mask. Nellie Dameon seemed pleased that he knew it. She would try to find it for him, she said.

The next morning, seated on her bench, she was gone again. Barbara wondered where this time. Perhaps to a premiere in New York, going to Jack & Charley's 21

Club afterward, getting a standing ovation as she entered, meeting Dorothy Parker there. Perhaps even a weekend tryst with one of the great screen lovers. Valentino or John Gilbert.

They stayed with her all that day and through Saturday night. She ate, dressed and undressed without help but in the manner of a sleepwalker.

One Sunday morning, as they prepared to return with her to her bench, Henry Dunville appeared outside the door to Nellie's rooms. In place of his normal state of seething truculence, Henry appeared conciliatory and a bit breathless. He explained his behavior, through a door that remained closed, to a suspicious Alan Weinberg. Young Dr. Feldman, he said, was at the gate demanding to see another of the members and threatening a court order if he was denied entrance. He asked that Nellie be allowed to go to her bench as usual while they stayed out of sight. She would be returned to them as soon as the doctor departed.

Alan Weinberg, of course, refused. They would stay together, he said, but they would remain in her quarters. He could not see the smile that spread across Henry's face.

Nearly five hours passed before he learned the truth. There had been no visit from Dr. Feldman. But the young girl, Lisa, had come again. She had been captured, drugged, questioned, her apartment looted. Henry, pleased with himself, could not resist gloating. He sent Ruiz to get Weinberg.

Within an hour after that, the girl, Lisa Benedict, was dead. Henry Dunville had no eyes. Two guards had been taken. The safe had been entered. By late afternoon an accommodation, however tenuous, had been reached with Carleton Dunville the younger.

Thirty-six hours would pass before Alan Weinberg learned what had been done with the body of the young girl who had heard Nellie Dameon speak and who had wanted nothing more than to hear her speak again.

It was not a bad idea, he supposed. Deflecting

blame on Los Angeles's latest serial killer. Still, that man, Hickey, had butchered her. It sickened him. And he saw in his wife's eyes that one day, given a chance, she would gladly kill Hickey for what he had done, and Carleton Dunville as well, if the idea had been his.

13

His full name was Sumner Todd Dommerich. He liked having three last names. It made him feel special. What he didn't like was being called just Todd. It was too close to Toad. Toad is what his parents used to call him when they were drunk or high. Before he made them stop laughing.

Sumner Dommerich had been watching from his car when the two women arrived at Lisa Benedict's apartment house. He had been there since seven, parked near the Laundromat across the street and several buildings down on Alameda. On his passenger seat, he'd brought a load of wash and a bottle of Surf in case anyone noticed him and wondered. Not that he thought anyone would, especially. Most people looked right through him. Nor could he explain, even to himself, why he felt he should be there. All he knew was that he felt badly about Lisa Benedict.

His first thought, when the two women came in their blue Chevrolet, was that they were reporters. It was about time. The morning before, on Monday, he'd waited for three hours expecting to see policemen and film crews come swarming. It was that way for all the others. But here there was nobody. Nothing.

Now, two women, but they didn't act like reporters after all. No press card on their visor. Dressed in sweaters and jeans. No camera. And one of them had keys.

They were inside for perhaps twenty minutes when the two men in gray suits pulled up in a mustard-colored Oldsmobile. The men went first to the super's apartment, showed him their wallets, talked to him for a while, then climbed the stairs that the two women had taken. When they got to the door, Dommerich saw the older one raise a hand, silencing the other. They stood there, heads cocked, as if listening. Then the younger one snuck back down, carefully, no noise, and made a call on his radio. He crept back up and the older one opened the door, very slowly. They disappeared inside. Three minutes later the swarm finally started.

Two, then three police cruisers, lights, sirens, all from different directions. Screeching in. Cops running up the stairs. Dommerich wanted to run himself, but he didn't.

Two women, one in handcuffs, coming out. The little one yelling at one of the suits. Tries to kick him. Two uniformed cops pick her up, carry her down the stairs. Another cop car comes, this one unmarked, two detectives in it.

The tall woman is arguing with one of the gray suits. The younger suit is carrying two purses, going through them. A crowd gathering, mostly black, starting to boo the way they're treating the little one. Two of the uniforms are holding up their hands, trying to move them back.

Sumner Dommerich stepped from his car and moved closer, joining two white women with shopping carts who were watching from across the street. He could see better now but he couldn't hear. And the little one looked familiar. He crossed Alameda, pretending not to see the policeman who waved him back.

The detectives and the gray suits were in a huddle. The suits were angry but the detectives seemed almost amused. One of the uniforms said something to his partner and the partner had to stifle a laugh. Dommerich moved closer.

Now one of the suits, the older one, turned to the woman . . . who looked like Lisa, he realized . . . and, sure enough, he called her Miss Benedict. What he said was "Who are you, Miss Benedict?"

It struck Dommerich as a stupid question for anyone who had eyes, not to mention her purse, but then he overheard two of the uniforms.

". . . knocked the two feds on their asses," one said, smirking.

"That little one? The sister?"

The first uniform nodded toward the two agents. "They say they flashed. The sister and her friend say they didn't. So the sister takes them down and lays a bread knife across one of their throats until he yells he's FBI."

"No shit," said the other appreciatively and then, to Dommerich, "Would you move back, sir."

Dommerich melted into the crowd. He worked his way to a new point of vantage. Now, at the mustard-colored Oldsmobile, they were taking the handcuffs off Lisa Benedict's sister. Freed, she spun on them, cursing. They backed away. "Don't push your luck," he heard the older one say.

The taller woman, whom Dommerich heard them call Miss Farrell, pulled Lisa's sister toward the blue Chevrolet. Lisa's sister argued. She wasn't finished upstairs, she said. Another car pulled up. A sign on the visor said *Los Angeles Times*. The one named Farrell saw it. "Now," he hissed. "Right now."

They started their engine. Across the street, down a little, a second engine whirred and caught. Dommerich had not noticed, especially, but one of the uniforms did. He looked, squinting, at a silver Honda that was idling at the far curb a few yards up from his own Volkswagen hatchback.

"Isn't that Joe Hickey?" the uniform asked his partner.

"Oh. Yeah," the partner answered, frowning.

Dommerich thought he saw contempt on both their faces. Probably another reporter.

A police cruiser moved, allowing the blue Chevrolet to back out onto Alameda. Dommerich was sorry to see them go. He'd like to have told the little one that her sister was nice. That he'd seen her almost every morning, jogging down Alameda, two miles, almost to Watts, where she bought a bran muffin, sometimes a bagel with cream cheese, and then she'd run back. He saw that she smiled and waved at people while she ran and so, a lot of mornings, he would go for a walk where she'd have to pass him on the way.

She didn't smile at him the first time. That made him feel bad. But she did the time after that because he decided he'd try smiling first. It worked. After that, it worked every time. Even when he pretended to be looking the other way, she'd say "Hi!" and he'd say "Oh, hi!" right back.

And he'd feel good all the way home.

He'd like to have told her sister that. He'd like to have told her that he would never have hurt her. That it wasn't him.

Sumner Todd Dommerich walked back to his car.

"Smooth, Carla." Molly Farrell scowled as she straightened her wheels and pressed the accelerator. "So much for keeping a low profile."

"They could have identified themselves." The smaller woman folded her arms, muttering. Molly caught the word *assholes*.

Molly had to agree, although she was in no mood to admit it. Walking in, not knocking, pointing guns at a woman who was hardly likely to be the Campus Killer and was almost certain to be a friend or relative, ignoring her request for identification.

For all she knew, and all Carla knew, they could have been the ones who murdered Lisa, using the keys they'd taken from her, back for another search of the apartment.

Molly let out a sigh. Now who's kidding who?

She knew they were FBI the instant they showed in the doorway. Those suits, those haircuts, carrying those dumb little Detective Specials. Coming in, one high, one low. She could have, she supposed, let out a ladylike squeal so they wouldn't wonder why she wasn't afraid. Well . . . now they're wondering about a lot more than that. Such as who is this hundred-pound redhead who ducks into a closet when she hears them at the door and then, with a kick and a kitchen knife, takes two armed men from behind.

"You think they'll run a make on us?" Carla asked, looking ahead.

"Wouldn't you?"

Carla shrugged. "Maybe they'll be too embarrassed." A tiny smile.

"Trust me."

The older one, Scholl, is probably calling it in right now, she thought, while the other starts his search of Lisa's apartment. The first thing he'll do is check the messages on that machine. He'll assume that she must have played it but he'll have DiDi Fenerty's name. He'll look for her phone number in Lisa's address book and that's when he'll notice that the book, among other things, seems to be missing. He'll know they didn't take it, having searched their purses. But at least one question had been answered. The FBI had not been there before. Not them, not the police either.

"What else is missing?" she asked Carla.

"Birthday presents," she answered. Her manner became distant again. "A Nikon I gave her last year. A tape recorder from three years ago. Some jewelry."

"Jewelry? You're sure?"

"All her gold. Two chains, two bracelets, some earrings, and a pearl necklace. He didn't touch the junk."

Molly wasn't sure why she was surprised. She'd had

it in her head that Lisa might have known the killer. Or might have suspected him. Might even have been writing about him. Why else would someone come into that apartment and destroy or take everything that might have held notes? Even to the extent of looking through all her books. The recorder might have held oral notes. The Nikon, undeveloped film. But why the jewelry?

She'd read an article once about serial killers. She knew that they often kept souvenirs. Usually grisly ones such as fingers, ears, nipples. There was a man named Kemper, another Californian, who kept his mother's head for a week and used it as a dart board.

But they were not, as a rule, thieves. A piece of jewelry might serve for a souvenir but, she felt sure, it would probably be something the victim was wearing at the time he killed her. Not jewelry from her home. And not just the expensive pieces.

Better, she thought, not to ask these questions aloud just yet. Or to start Carla wondering who else might have wanted her sister dead. She's enough of a time bomb as it is.

Carla poked her. "You can't stay mad," she said.

"Yes, I can."

"Uh-uh." She shook her head. "We're best friends now."

No answer.

"Tonight we'll talk about boys and do each other's hair."

Molly looked away.

"You can tell me how it feels to get laid and I'll show you how to pop zits without leaving big red pimples."

Molly smiled, but she frowned inside. Carla Benedict, making jokes. This wasn't like her. Especially now. Ahead, on Alameda, she spotted a convenience store. She slowed, then pulled to the curb when she saw a sign indicating that it had a public phone. Carla followed her eyes.

"Who are you calling?" she asked.

"Not me. You. See if there's a listing for DiDi

Fenerty. If she answers, tell her you'd like to see her right away. If she doesn't, don't leave a message, but get the address."

"See her about what? Old movies? Lisa was dead for hours by then."

"I think DiDi has a copy of her computer files."

Carla blinked. "That someone wiped off her machine?"

"And heard the same message we did." Molly gestured toward the store front. "Go make the call."

Sumner Todd Dommerich had not intended to follow them. They were already out of sight by the time he started driving north on Alameda. He was not due at work until noon. He had time to drive over to the campus, have breakfast, read another newspaper. See what it said about Lisa. And what else it said about him. Maybe do his laundry there and listen to what the students were now saying about him. Or sit in on a lecture. There was no place he couldn't go at Southern Cal because (the thought always made him smile) he could make himself invisible.

Had it not been for the silver Honda, he might not have spotted the blue Chevrolet at all. The Honda, just ahead, had stopped at the curb again. That man, Hickey, was crouching behind the wheel. What made him especially easy to spot was that he was holding his arms up over his shoulders, his hands cupped around his temples as if he were looking through binoculars. Dommerich drove past him, not slowing.

Yes. That was him. Beefy. Thick lips. Thin hair, brushed straight back, not clean, curled and shaggy at his neck. And he was holding a video camera, not binoculars.

Dommerich followed its aim and he saw Lisa's sister. She was coming out of a convenience store. He saw a sheet of paper in her hand, a black stripe across the top like a page from the phone book. She held it aloft, waving it, and he followed her eyes to the blue Chevrolet and the woman named Farrell. Dommerich kept going.

He drove north for another long block and he pulled into the parking lot of a store selling cheap furniture.

Something was funny here, he thought. If the man, Hickey, was a reporter, why didn't he just go talk to them? Why was he sneaking around, following them, taking pictures? Why couldn't he just leave Lisa's sister alone? The policeman, back there, didn't seem to like this man very much. Dommerich was beginning to see why. He didn't like him very much either.

He waited until the blue Chevrolet went by, and then the silver Honda. He fell in behind them, memorizing the Honda's license plate as he drove. The Chevrolet turned west on Slauson. The Honda followed for two miles. Then, both cars climbed onto the Harbor Freeway, northbound, and got off again at the Vernon Avenue ramp. A little way farther, they turned north on Vermont.

This was really weird, thought Dommerich. They seemed headed toward the campus. They were going exactly the way he would have gone if he hadn't seen them first. If he didn't know better, he almost would have thought that they knew he would be there. But he wasn't. He was behind them.

He felt a tinge of relief, not unmixed with disappointment, when he saw that they were driving past the campus proper. But, suddenly, they turned left and he felt better. They were heading into the area, just north of the campus, where many of the students had apartments.

Lisa's sister and the older woman seemed lost. They kept turning, left and right, once making an illegal U-turn and doubling back. He could see that Lisa's sister was holding a map. They drove right past the silver Honda but they didn't seem to notice him. The Honda made the same turn but Dommerich couldn't. The light had changed. The Honda disappeared from his rearview mirror.

He began cruising the side streets in the hope of spotting them again. Five minutes later, crossing Menlo Avenue, he did. The Chevrolet was double-parked outside a big old Victorian, painted yellow. He knew that house. Number 2101. It had an antique popcorn wagon on the porch, chained down, and a park bench, probably stolen. Three or four graduate students lived there. Stained glass in the front door and in some of the windows. Lots of movie posters on living room wall and framed covers of old fan magazines in the foyer. That was as far inside as he'd ever been except he used the bathroom once.

Lisa's sister and the other woman were already on the porch, the taller one ringing the bell. The Honda was nowhere in sight.

Dommerich found a space halfway up the street. Recalling how he'd spotted the man named Hickey, he knew he couldn't just sit there. He stepped from his car and opened the hatch. He took out a peaked red and green cap with a pizza company logo on it and a large insulated pouch for keeping pizzas warm. The two made a wonderful disguise, he knew. No one ever looked twice at a pizza delivery boy.

He had no special plan in mind. Except to see Lisa's sister again. Get a better look. Maybe even hear her voice. Maybe pretend that he couldn't find an address. Get her to help him. Be nice to him.

He approached the blue Chevrolet. The street map, he saw, was still on the dashboard. Good. That would be a reason for speaking to her. Also, on the console, there was a parking stub from the Beverly Hills Hotel and the page he'd seen in her hand. He was right. It was from a phone book. Page 332. All the listings started with *F*.

A flash of silver caught the corner of his eye. The Honda. It was slowly rounding the next corner. Dommerich's heart rose to his throat but then he remembered. He was invisible. He stood erect, pretending to look around for the address that ordered a pizza. He chose a house two doors up with no cars in its driveway. He went there and pretended to ring the bell.

The Honda, which had hesitated several houses farther up, now cruised by, slowly. The two women were no longer on the porch. The Honda went on to the far corner where the driver with the greasy hair pulled to the curb three cars forward of where Dommerich had parked. Dommerich, tugging his visor down over his eyes, returned to his car. Opening the hatch, he took out a three-sided plastic pizza sign that had a magnetic base. He centered it on his roof. Now even his car would be invisible.

14

At the storefront office of Luxury Travel Ltd. in Westport's Compo Shopping Plaza, Paul Bannerman was preparing to leave for lunch—joining Susan at Mario's—when the light flashed on his private line.

He closed the glass door, shutting out the buzz from the reservations desks, and picked up the receiver. He said his name, then sat when he heard Lesko's voice.

"I was wrong about them having a suspect," Lesko told him. "Kaplan says they got zilch."

Bannerman was surprised. "No lists of known sex offenders? No anonymous tips about possibles who fit the profile?"

"They've got those up the ass," Lesko answered. "Kaplan says they've all been checked out. . . . I'm talking more than five hundred here. . . . And about twenty were worth a few days' surveillance, mostly because they had the killer's blood type. Most of those have been eliminated, or at least they were someplace else when the last killing went down."

"Which one? Carla's sister?"

"No. The one before. Kaplan found out why they don't think the same guy did Lisa Benedict."

Bannerman waited.

"You gotta kept this quiet, okay? They keep it out of the papers for a reason."

"I understand."

"Four things," Lesko told him. "First, the guy took some hair from each of the first six but not from Carla's sister. And the others were all blond, by the way, so make that five things."

"They're sure? That no hair's missing, I mean?"

"Yeah. This guy takes a pretty good chunk and some scalp about the size of a half dollar. The shrinks call it a totem. Basically a souvenir. You wouldn't believe the things some of these guys cut off and keep."

Yes, he would. "What else?"

"The next thing is she was douched. She was douched real good."

Bannerman blinked. "You mean after she was . . ."

"Yeah. No semen. No blood samples. In fact, she was scrubbed all over. Even under her nails."

Bannerman's frown deepened. "Go on."

"Here's the big one. Someone tried to revive her after she was strangled. And they don't think it was the strangler."

A long silence. "How would they know that?"

"Hand prints," Lesko answered. "One size hand choked her. A bigger hand used CPR. He left marks on her chest where he tried to pump it and on her cheek where he held it like for mouth to mouth. They also think he closed her eyes because they should have been open like all the others. And that ear-to-ear smile was cut long after she was dead."

Bannerman rubbed his eyes, taking a moment to absorb all this. Lesko was patient.

"There's more," Lesko cleared his throat, "but it's all theory." Bannerman heard the sound of a page being turned.

"Go ahead. Please."

"First, about the smile . . ." Lesko took a breath. "The medical examiner thinks whoever cut it wasn't enjoying himself. He used words like *hesitant, uneven.* In other words, he made a mess of it. The six others showed more practice."

Bannerman tried to blink away the image that his mind seemed to insist on showing him. "Is that it?" he asked.

"Just about." Another sound, a new page being turned. "For what this is worth," he said, "the first victim also went to USC and she lived maybe a half mile from Lisa. Kaplan says, or the FBI says, that the first victim of a serial killer is usually fairly close to where he lives or works. The guy couldn't help himself. A sudden impulse. But after that, he tries to spread it around more. Kaplan says it's unusual to hit his own neighborhood a second time."

"And, apparently, he didn't."

"Looks that way."

"Who do you think did? I mean, if you were investigating Lisa's death, where would you start looking?"

Lesko hesitated. "The kid was straight, right? She wasn't anything like Carla."

"Not at all."

"Then I'd look at boyfriends. Neighbors. Most murder victims knew their killer. This sounds like one guy did it and someone else tried to cover it up but he also tried to help her. Me, I'd look for that second guy to crack sooner or later." A thoughtful pause. "Let the LA cops handle this, Bannerman."

"Just asking."

"You going out there?"

"I'll fly out for the service. Actually, most of our people want to go. I said I'd think about it."

"You know who's already out there? Your KGB pal from Bern."

"Leo Belkin?" Bannerman blinked. "What's he doing in California?"

"He's with this group from Mosfilm. They're like Russia's Hollywood. The story is they're studying special effects. Belkin's probably along to keep them from going over the hill."

Bannerman doubted it. That's a goon's job. "Do you know where he's staying?"

Lesko riffed through several pages. "Century Plaza," he answered. "Anyway, if you do go, leave Susan home, okay?"

"Um . . . actually, she's one of those who asked."

"Bannerman . . ."

He winced, bracing himself. But a click on the line interrupted a likely review of Bannerman's unhappy travel history with his daughter. "Hold it," Lesko growled. "This might be Elena."

Bannerman drummed his fingers. Then he began counting on them. There was Billy McHugh and Janet Herzog. They wanted to go. Anton Zivic felt that he, at the very least, should represent the rest. Five or six more felt badly about having given Carla a wide berth and didn't want to add insult to injury.

That was probably too many. On the other hand, it was hard to argue that Westport would be left poorly defended. Their numbers had more than doubled right after Marbella and other old friends kept turning up every few months as word got around Europe that they would be safe here. The State Department had not interfered. Barton Fuller was keeping his distance, save for an occasional peace feeler. The CIA, surely at Fuller's urging, had not pressed its claim for the return of the money and property he and his people had seized. But the detente would not last forever. The other shoe would eventually drop.

Bannerman glanced at his watch. He'd been on hold for three minutes. Lesko, he imagined, would be talking to Elena, telling her about the latest imperilment of his daughter and threatening to break his legs if he . . .

"Guess what?" Lesko clicked back on. "That wasn't Elena. It was Irwin again."

The voice sounded oddly pleasant. Almost gleeful. "How long did you say Carla's been in California?"

Bannerman closed one eye. "She got in late last night. Why?"

"So that's what? Maybe four hours, not counting sleep?"

"Lesko. What has she done?"

"How does decking two FBI guys sound? How about if one of them was Jack Scholl, the agent in charge? How about if she also went at him with a kitchen knife?"

Bannerman felt a headache coming on. "Was she arrested?" he asked.

"Andy Huff was there. He squared it. But that was because he thought Scholl was a schmuck and Carla was just some poor bereaved sister."

"But now he knows better."

"What he knows is that he now has two professional assassins prowling his town looking for a . . ."

"Intelligence operatives," Bannerman said quietly.

"What?"

"Operatives. Not assassins."

"Hey! This is me, remember? I could count seven bodies from the first month I knew them."

And two more of your own, Bannerman thought, but he chose not to argue. He took a breath. "I'd better get out there," he said.

"But no Susan, right? Now especially."

"I'll talk to her."

"You don't talk to her. You tell her. Where is she now?"

"Down at Mario's. Waiting for me."

"Give me the damned number. I'll tell her myself."

Good luck, thought Bannerman.

He broke the connection, then punched out the number of the Beverly Hills Hotel. No answer in the bungalow. He left a message.

He started for the door, then hesitated. He returned to his desk and reached for a copy of the hotel guide on the shelf behind it. He found the number of the Century Plaza Hotel.

15

A massive young man in a T-shirt and shorts, clearly a weight lifter, answered the door when Molly Farrell rang. He stood, blocking it, his expression uninviting, as she asked for DiDi Fenerty.

She's not seeing anyone, he said. Not today. He began to close the door when he reacted to a touch behind him. A young woman appeared, easing him slightly to one side. Her eyes, swollen, haunted, passed quickly over Molly and settled on the smaller of the two visitors.

"You're Carla," she said. The eyes became moist again.

She offered them coffee, seating them in the high-ceilinged living room as she went to the kitchen for it. Molly looked around the room. The carpet, the furnishings, seemed expensive for a student residence. Well used, although not shabby. A large-screen television sat at one end. Movie memorabilia on the walls. Unlike Lisa's, these posters were originals and had been carefully framed and mounted. Two other young women, housemates probably, had excused themselves when she and Carla entered. The young man who had answered the door was now sitting, arms folded, on the bench outside.

DiDi Fenerty returned, holding a tray. She was a big girl, large boned, with a friendly open face that reminded Molly of an Aer Lingus commercial. She was dressed, unlike the others, as if for church or business. She wore a dark green suit, white blouse, no jewelry but for a gold crucifix at her throat and a Rolex on her wrist. She could not keep her eyes off Carla.

"I apologize for Kevin," she said, tilting her head toward the porch. "He lives two doors down. He's been sort of watching over me since . . ."

She stopped herself. She motioned toward the tray, urging her two visitors to help themselves. She watched as Carla sipped from her cup.

"You're . . . very much like her," she said. "She's talked about you a hundred times. Until now, I almost didn't believe you were real."

Molly was watching her, listening. Her sorrow, her own sense of loss, was profound and genuine. There was no question that she and Lisa had been close. She was saying now that they had been friends since high school. That she knew Carla's father. She said this almost apologetically, clearly aware that he and Carla had been estranged. She was about to go out and visit him. It was why she was dressed. Kevin was going to drive her.

Carla was listening, responding, putting her at ease. It was necessary to do so because, with all the other emotions DiDi Fenerty was displaying, there was also an unmistakable sense of awe. Molly could only imagine the sort of stories Lisa had told her. But Lisa would have heard them from her father, not from Carla.

"I . . . have some of her things here," the young woman was saying. "Just a Hermès scarf she lent me. A few videotapes. And those Majorica pearls you sent her from Spain last year. The police wanted everything but I wouldn't let them touch them."

"Um . . ." Molly leaned forward. "What police?"

"An FBI agent called yesterday morning. It was just after we heard about Lisa on the news. I don't know how much sense I made. And then a detective came by yesterday afternoon."

"Just one? By himself?"

"Yes."

"What was he looking for?"

DiDi Fenerty turned, meeting Carla's eyes as if to

ask if she really wanted to hear all this. Carla nodded encouragement.

"They both wanted pretty much the same thing," she answered. "The one who called asked if I could help them reconstruct her movements over the past week or so. How much had I seen of her and what did we talk about. Did I notice anything unusual in her behavior. Especially, did she say where she was going on Sunday. The detective asked basically the same questions and he wanted to see anything I had that belonged to her."

"What did you give him?"

"Nothing. He was a sleaze. I didn't want him touching her things. Kevin told him to go get a warrant. He said he would."

"That FBI agent who called," Molly asked, "What did you tell him?"

The young woman eyed Molly curiously but answered as best she could recall. They'd attended classes all week as usual. Both were going for the same master's degree. Film and television. They'd talked, but not about anything special. Mostly about Hollywood during the silent era. The last time she saw Lisa was at noon on Saturday. Lisa stopped by after their morning class to borrow her warm-up suit. Then she left for work. Lisa worked Friday and Saturday nights for a catering firm in Westwood, making hors d'oeuvres at parties, sometimes tending bar. DiDi went to Malibu for the weekend, to her parents' house there. She returned Sunday night at about ten.

"Wasn't there a . . ." Molly interrupted herself. "She borrowed *your* running suit?"

The young woman glanced down at her own body, acknowledging its size. "I know," she said. "I asked. She said she'd tell me later."

Molly returned to her train of thought, tossing her head toward the large-screen television. "Wasn't there a movie being shown here Sunday at nine? *Flesh and the Devil?*"

DiDi blinked, then realized how Molly must have

known that. "Kevin," she nodded toward the porch, "brought some friends over. They use my TV because it's the biggest one around. He told me he invited Lisa. He said he left word on her machine but she never . . . I mean, by that time . . ." She didn't finish.

Molly shifted gears. "Do you have a word processor, DiDi? With a hard disk?"

"Yes."

"Do you have backup software for it?"

"Sure. FastBack Plus."

"Did Lisa?"

"Lisa copied mine. We'd each do full backups once a week and swap the backup disks after our Saturday morning class."

Molly almost smiled. She'd guessed correctly. The *DF/FB* she'd found scratched on a box in Lisa's desk was shorthand for DiDi Fenerty/FastBack. Backup software was expensive. The student who owned it, and DiDi seemed to have more money than most, would share it with others. The makers of backup software usually recommended that copies of hard disk files be stored at a different location, ideally a safe deposit box, to guard against loss due to fire or theft.

Carla put down her cup. "Does that mean you have a copy of everything that was on Lisa's computer through Saturday morning?"

DiDi nodded. "And she has everything that was on mine."

Molly shook her head. "I'm afraid yours were damaged. Someone was careless with them."

The younger woman looked at her, oddly again, then shrugged. The loss was not important to her. She could quickly run another set. But now she was wondering how a full box of disks could have been ruined accidentally. And what could be on Lisa's disks that could possibly shed any light on her murder. The newspapers said she was a random victim. Same as the other six.

"This detective who came," Molly asked, "did he know that you had copies of Lisa's files?"

"He didn't seem to. He asked for notebooks, diaries, things like that. I didn't mention her computer files because her personal correspondence, maybe letters to you"—she looked at Carla—"is probably on them."

"Thank you," Molly said to her. "And this detective never asked for them?"

"No."

"What was his name, by the way?"

"He didn't say. He waved a badge and an ID card but I couldn't read it."

"Can you describe him?"

"Medium height, stocky, maybe forty, needed a haircut. A slob."

"How about the one who called? Could it have been the same man?"

"No. The FBI agent was polite, well-spoken. His name was Harris. He said there was an outside chance that Lisa might have known her killer and that's why it was so important that they know every place she might have been, who she talked to, during the past week."

Molly nodded, thoughtfully. "Do you know where these parties were? The ones Lisa worked?"

DiDi's shrug said it was just a job. Probably not worth mentioning.

Molly tended to agree, although there was always the chance that she met her killer at one of them. "What's the name of the catering firm?"

"Um . . ." The young woman tried to think. "Let me look in the yellow pages. I'd recognize it if I saw it."

Molly raised an eyebrow. "The FBI agent didn't ask? Or the detective?"

"I don't think so. No."

Molly resisted a glance at Carla. "Can you boot up Lisa's disks for me?" she asked.

The young woman hesitated. She looked at Carla as if for permission. Carla gave it. Still, she waited. "Could I ask you something?"

"Sure."

"What's going on here?"

"We don't know," Molly answered. "Someone got into Lisa's apartment and took some things. We think he also destroyed her computer files. It's possible that the FBI agent was right."

"That she knew the Campus Killer?"

"It's possible."

"I don't think so."

"Why?" Molly asked.

"Just from the way she was acting all week. She was on to something and excited about it but it had to do with her master's thesis and it wasn't anything scary. Besides, anything on those disks was probably already there before she went to work Friday evening."

"She never told you what she was on to?"

"I'm not sure she knew, exactly. She wanted everything I had on a silent film star named Nellie Dameon and someone named D'Arconte. Him, I never heard of. If I had to guess, I'd say she learned something about Nellie that's never been published. If that's true, it would have helped her grade."

DiDi Fenerty heard her own use of the past tense. She fell silent for a long moment.

"Molly? Are you . . ." She paused, searching for the proper words. "I don't know exactly what I'm asking but are you . . . like the CIA? Like Carla here?"

"We're not CIA."

"I meant, sort of."

"Not even a little."

The young woman sipped from a cup gone cold. "Let me ask in another way," she said, her voice at the edge of choking. "If you were to find the piece of shit who killed Lisa, would you hand him over to the police?"

Molly would rather have not answered that question. An answer would amount to a promise that, in all likelihood, she would be unable to keep. And which, otherwise, might one day be incriminating. Still . . .

"Eventually," she said at last. "We'd hand him over eventually."

Joseph Hickey, formerly of the LAPD, badly needed to relieve himself. There was always the curb. College kids did it all the time. The problem was that kid sitting on the porch, showing off his muscles. That kid, he thought darkly, was becoming a pain in the ass.

First he says no, you can't come in, go get a warrant. "I'll give you a warrant," he muttered. "Size twelve, right in your balls."

Yesterday, for two hours, Hickey had waited up the street for the weight lifter to leave so he could give it one more shot. Lean on the Fenerty girl. Threaten to bust her for interfering with an investigation. But the big kid stayed there. So did half the kids in this neighborhood at one time or another. Coming in groups. Bringing food. Half of them crying. With that crowd there was no chance of going in through a window either. But if he did, then what? What does he look for? Even Dunville couldn't tell him.

All Dunville knew, from the calendar on the dead girl's wall, was that they were friends. Tennis with DiDi. Party at DiDi's. DiDi's birthday. Fenertys' thirtieth anniversary. *"These aren't just friends,"* Dunville had said. *"These are best friends and best friends talk, especially when they're both into movies. Find out what she knows. Earn your money."*

"I've earned my fucking money," Hickey said aloud. "And you're going to be paying it for fucking ever."

The Fenerty girl didn't know shit. He was sure of that even before he rang her bell because he'd listened in when Dunville called her, pretending he was FBI. After the call, Dunville gets real pleased with himself until he's reminded that the real FBI will probably drop around sooner or later once they hear her name on the answering machine, not because they think it means anything but because it's something to do. When that happens, Hickey said to Dunville, don't you think they'll get curious about who this Agent Harris was? You don't think they'll wonder why anyone would care what Lisa Benedict was doing for the whole week before a serial killer was supposed to have picked her out, totally spur of the moment?

Go talk to her, Dunville says. See what she knows, Dunville says. And he did. And she didn't know shit. Then Dunville says *make sure*.

Hickey knew what he meant. But he wasn't about to do it. It probably would be next weekend, if then, before he could catch her without a crowd around her anyway.

He had started out for Sur La Mer that morning, to meet with Dunville, to try to make him see that enough was enough, when he picked up the police call on his radio, *Federal agents need assistance*, giving the Benedict girl's address, which he knew because he'd just cleaned it out two nights before. He sees two women, one in handcuffs . . . she could be the dead girl's sister . . . still dumping all over the two federal agents. This now looks interesting. Now maybe he has something to tell Dunville after all. He follows them and, sure as shit, they make a beeline for the Fenerty girl's house. He'd better stay with them. See who they are, where they're going.

But in the meantime, he really had to piss.

Hickey had to chance it. The risk was that muscles up there would spot him, maybe get curious enough to write down his license plate.

Ahead of him was the intersection. He couldn't go there, or even around the corner because a bunch of kids there were tossing a Frisbee. In the yard to his right, two old ladies were planting a bush. He'd like to have whizzed into the hole they dug, or at least stepped behind his car but they'd be looking right at him. They'd probably turn their hose on him, the way things have been going lately, or shoot off their mouths at him. Better, he decided, to walk back a few cars to where a hedge blocked their view. Hickey opened his door and eased himself out of his seat. The pressure from his bladder made him waddle and his reluctance to be seen made him crouch.

He spotted the plastic pizza sign, Italian colors, on top of a Volkswagen three cars back. All he had to do, he realized, was keep that sign lined up between him and muscles. Joe Hickey minced to the front of the Volkswagen. He opened his fly. He released without aiming.

The amber stream hit asphalt, then changed its pitch as it gathered force and snaked up over the front bumper and grill of the Volkswagen. A voice came from somewhere. Sounded like *Hey*.

Shit.

Some kid, sitting in the Volkswagen, a pizza hat down across his nose. Hickey tried to ignore him, aiming down, mostly, keeping his eyes on the porch where one of the women, the little one, had just come back out. Muscles standing up, saying something to her, shaking her hand. The tall one must be staying. Hickey's stream wandered again. Droplets of urine splashed high in the morning sun, arcing onto the Volkswagen's hood.

"That's my *car*."

Pizza hat's voice. *Shut up, kid*.

Kid taps his horn. *Hey. Shithead. Don't do that.* Hickey tries shaking a fist. But the kid taps again.

"Shut the fuck up," he hissed through his teeth. Hickey cut off the stream. Hot liquid ran down the inside of his trouser leg. He took two quick steps to the driver's window. With his open hand, fingers wet, he slapped the face of the kid in the pizza hat and then seized his shirt by the neck. He did this by feel. His eyes were on the porch. That one woman was leaving now, keys in her hand, walking toward the Chevrolet.

"You gonna be nice? Or do I piss in your face?" Hickey twisted the collar, jerking it, still by feel. A choked little squeak from inside. Hickey took it to mean yes.

He released his grip and hurried to the silver Honda. Climbing in, he flipped his trunk release, which sprang open. Then he stretched low across his front seat, pretending to busy himself at the glove box. He stayed that way until he heard the sound of the Chevrolet driving past.

There was no doubt in Molly's mind that the man who called was not an FBI agent and that the one who visited was no detective.

The FBI, she knew, would never conduct an interview on so serious a matter by telephone. Nor did police detectives work alone except in routine interviews such as door-to-door canvassing. Furthermore, if their purpose was indeed to reconstruct Lisa's activities, they had asked all the wrong questions and few of the right ones, especially the name of the catering firm and the location of the party, which might well have been the last place Lisa had been seen alive.

It seemed to Molly that they were more interested in finding out what, if anything, DiDi Fenerty knew about whatever it was that Lisa was working on. It also seemed clear that whoever had searched Lisa's apartment had found enough references to DiDi to conclude that they were close and were likely to have discussed it. If Lisa died because of some discovery she'd made, that would seem to put DiDi Fenerty in danger as well.

Still, Molly was not yet prepared to assume that someone other than this serial killer was responsible for Lisa's death. She herself had once executed three men by means of explosive darts. Their bodies hadn't even cooled before other people were busy looting their files. Those killings and the subsequent looting were unrelated. Lisa's death, in the same way, might simply have been a convenience to someone else.

The burglar, in any case, who was probably that false detective, would be a good deal easier to track down than a serial killer. Lisa's files, she felt sure, would point the way.

"You're all set," DiDi Fenerty told her, looking up from the IBM workstation in her study. "You'd better make yourself comfortable."

Molly looked at the screen. It showed a list of files. She touched a key and the list scrolled upward. There were some sixty files, overall about thirty megabytes worth of data. Even concentrating on the most recent entries, she might be here for hours.

She sat. Carla reached for another chair. DiDi Fenerty excused herself.

"Are you sure you're ready for this?" Molly asked her.

"I'm okay," she answered.

Molly doubted it. Carla's color had already begun to rise in anticipation of seeing words her sister had written. Molly called up a file labeled "Personal." She did so deliberately. It consisted of letters, mostly. Some to friends, many to Carla. Here and there, she had used her word processor as a sort of diary. She would share her thoughts with it, especially whenever she felt sad, or overwhelmed by her studies, or had been hurt by some slight.

She recorded wish lists. She wanted to travel, especially to Italy, taking a whole summer to see it top to bottom. She wanted Carla to go with her but only if and when Lisa was able to pay her own way. Enough was enough, she wrote.

If Carla wanted to give her a graduation present, however, and asked what she'd like, what she really wanted was an invitation to visit Westport. To meet Carla's friends. The famous Mama's Boy. Billy McHugh. Anton Zivic. Molly Farrell. Especially Dr. Russo. To see them all in the flesh. If they're Carla's friends, Lisa mused, how bad could they be? Molly, reading these thoughts, had the impression that Lisa had heard about the Westport group from someone other than Carla. Perhaps from her father, perhaps from federal investigators.

Above all, Lisa wanted to be like her big sister. Carla, she wrote, had seen and done so much. Been everywhere. She was so confident. So smart. And yet so kind. Lisa wondered if Dr. Russo realizes how lucky he is that Carla is even thinking about saying yes.

Molly blinked. The date of the entry was last August fifth. Doc Russo had been dead six months by then. Carla was apparently still talking about him as if he were alive, and her suitor.

Molly, embarrassed, turned to look at her. But Carla had turned away from the machine, perhaps in time. She was taking deep breaths, one tiny fist against her mouth.

"Carla," Molly said softly. "I wish I knew what not to read. But I don't."

"I know."

"Why don't you go back to the hotel. Call your father. Check in with Paul."

"No," she shook her head. "I'm all right."

Molly turned in her seat, took Carla's hand. "You know, don't you," she asked, "that I'll never tell another soul about anything I might read here. Not if it's private. And not unless you tell me I can."

Carla looked away. "I didn't lie to her," she said. "Not exactly."

"You protected her. I would have done the same thing."

Carla took a breath and exhaled. Her shoulders sagged. "You know what I used to do? When I was with Lisa?"

Molly waited.

"I'd try to be like you. Never a bad word about anybody. Not even my fuck-head father."

Molly smiled but said nothing.

"And Gary Russo did ask me once. He really did."

"I know. Or at least I knew he was thinking about it."

"Goddamn him."

For dying. Yes. Molly squeezed her hand. "Go back to the hotel," she said gently. "I'll be along. I'll take a cab."

"All that," Carla gestured toward the IBM monitor. "You won't leave it on the machine?"

"Not a word. I'll give you the disks when I'm finished."

"Maybe I'll lie by the pool for a while. Get some lunch."

"Good idea." Molly, relieved, stood up with her. Maybe now she'd get some work done.

Carla saw this last in her eyes.

And maybe, thought Carla, she would make herself useful. Maybe she would see if a silver Honda happened to turn up behind her again as she drove back toward the Beverly Hills Hotel.

Sumner Todd Dommerich, biting one of his hands, rolled up his window with the other so that he could scream. He did do, covering his face. He kicked at his brake and clutch pedals until the tops of his feet bled through his socks. He screamed so hard, starving his brain, that he nearly fainted. He did not see the Chevrolet until it was past him.

And now he saw the silver Honda pulling out to follow. His father was behind the wheel.

Dommerich watched, gathering himself, as it began to turn the corner, then stopped. A boy, maneuvering under a floating Frisbee, blocked his path. Dommerich's father pounded his steering wheel but he did not sound his horn for fear of being noticed by the driver of the Chevrolet.

Dommerich scrambled out of his seat. He seized the pizza sign, stripping it from his roof and throwing it onto his passenger seat and the hat that had been swiped from his head. He slipped once more behind the wheel and started his engine. The pizza sign, he knew, could work both ways.

Sumner Dommerich was invisible again.

He understood, calming himself, that the man who had soiled his car, slapped him, humiliated him, could not really be his father. His father was in hell. With his mother. His father who beat him. And did much worse to him. His mother who laughed at him. He had sent them both to hell. But they did not stay there. They kept coming back.

They came in his dreams and they came in daylight. Sometimes they took over the bodies of other people. Not for long. Sometimes only for a minute. Long enough to insult him, to laugh at him.

Dommerich eased his car around the corner. The Chevrolet was well ahead. It almost seemed to Dommerich that no one was driving and that there was no one in the passenger seat either. But then it signaled a right turn on Western Avenue and he could see that there was only Lisa's sister, chin high, peering over the dashboard. The silver Honda hung back but followed.

The Chevrolet turned left onto Wilshire. The woman's driving began to seem erratic. She was varying her speed as if she were a tourist. Once, at the La Brea Tar Pits, she seemed about to enter the parking lot but she changed her mind. Dommerich wondered about this. It did not seem that Lisa's sister should have much interest in sight-seeing.

A sign said they were entering Beverly Hills. After a while, the Chevrolet signaled a right turn onto Rodeo Drive. The street and sidewalks were crowded along the two-block stretch where the most expensive stores were located. There were many people on foot, window shoppers mostly, tourists, but there were many expensive cars parked along both sides, some with chauffeurs waiting.

The Chevrolet, suddenly, swung to the curb near the Georgio Armani store. Lisa's sister climbed from it and stepped to the meter where she searched her purse for change. The Honda, two cars ahead of Dommerich, hesitated but it could not stop. Other cars pressed behind it, Dommerich's among them. One driver tapped his horn. Dommerich gleefully pressed his own. Abruptly, as if angrily, the Honda cut its wheels and squealed into

a U-turn. Dommerich watched the driver as he went by.
He was looking at his rearview mirror, cursing.

Lisa's sister stepped quickly back to the door of her
car. Dommerich's smile broadened. He understood now
what she'd been doing. She had seen the Honda all
along. She had picked this street to stop, forcing him to
commit. He'd broken off but at least she'd had a closer
look at him. She might have even read his license
number if her eyes were real good.

The traffic moved forward. Dommerich pulled up
behind the Chevrolet as if waiting for the space. Lisa's
sister did not look at him. Her attention was focused on
the retreating Honda. At last, frowning, she reentered
her car and continued northward. Dommerich took the
space but immediately pulled out again as soon as a few
more cars had moved between them.

Four blocks later, a traffic light changed, stopping
Dommerich. Ahead, the Chevrolet was turning out of
sight. He waited, anxiously, although he was fairly sure
that he knew where Lisa's sister was heading. Once
again, a flash of silver caught the corner of his eye. Afraid
to look, but afraid not to, he glanced to his right and
froze. The Honda was there, alongside him. The driver,
thick lips, double chin, oily, even looked like his father.
Dommerich fought panic. Look away, he told himself.
Make no move that would catch his eye, cause him to
look this way, notice the rooftop sign on the front seat
and remember when he had last seen one like it.

The light changed, mercifully. The Honda surged
ahead. Dommerich could breathe again.

A part of him wanted to break off and drive directly
to the Beverly Hills Hotel. Lisa's sister, he felt sure,
would turn up there eventually. He had seen that
parking stub on the Chevrolet's console.

He could leave a message for her there. He could
leave her the license number of the silver Honda in case
she missed it back on Rodeo Drive. He would sign the
note "A friend."

But it would be so much better, he decided, if he

were able to tell her where that man lived. Where he
went next. What his name is. That way she would be
able to tell the police about him. That he'd been
following her all morning, bothering her. And if they did
nothing about it, he thought, maybe Sumner Todd
Dommerich would. He followed the Honda.

They called him the Campus Killer, he thought,
driving. They wrote about him, interviewed psychiatrists about him, said disgusting things about him.
Almost nothing they said was right, except some of the
things they thought had happened to him when he was
a child. The things his father had done to him. They
were right about that. But they also said that he was
afraid of women. That he could not confront the act of
sex with a live frightening woman, which was why they
had to be bound or dead first. That wasn't true. He
would not have been afraid of Lisa. If they never had sex
it would have been because they wanted it that way.
Because it's easier to be friends that way.

The dumbest thing they said was that he only hurts
young women.

Oh, yeah?

Ask his father about that. Or his mother. Ask the
doorman at The Grotto last year who grabbed him by the
collar, the way that man in the Honda did, when all he
wanted to do was go to Molly Ringwald's table and show
her a poem he wrote.

Ask that drunken bully from Arizona State who
tried to make him drink a beer glass full of urine and
then poured it on him when he wouldn't. Ask the girl
who was with him. The one who thought it was funny.
The one who called him *Toad*.

Molly Ringwald would have liked his poem. She
would have invited him to sit with her. And she would
have told that doorman what she thought of him. He
would have apologized. He would have said I'm sorry,
Mr. Dommerich. I didn't know that you and Miss

Ringwald were friends. If he had, maybe he would still
have hands.

Ahead, the Honda had stopped. The man was
pounding his wheel again. He had lost Lisa's sister.

Yes, thought Dommerich, that's what he would do.
Stay with him. See where he goes, see where he lives.
That man, when he grabbed him, slapped him, had
never even looked at him. He was invisible then, he was
invisible now.

Maybe Sumner Dommerich would bring him a
pizza.

16

At Mario's, a restaurant and bar facing the Westport
commuter station, Susan Lesko toyed with a bread stick
as she waited for Paul Bannerman. It did not seem that
this would be the uneventful lunch she'd intended.

Her first indication of that had been the phone call
from her father. The second was the arrival of several
members of the council, which managed, loosely, the
lives of the thirty or more men and women from Europe
who lived there now. Even Susan was not sure of their
exact number, or of the true names of several. Some,
Paul told her, had prices on their heads, others were
simply out of work. Some would move on, some would
stay. The council would decide.

The largest influx had come during the past twelve
months, since the events at Marbella. Word had spread
that Mama's Boy was still alive and was coming to Spain.
Dozens, from all over Europe, had converged there.
Some to back him up, to repay old debts, to see old
friends, some just to enjoy the show.

Quite a few followed when he returned to Westport where Anton Zivic, Billy McHugh, Carla, Molly, John Waldo, and six or seven others had long since settled. They too had been presumed dead for the three years before Marbella.

She was used to them now, she supposed. She liked most of them. Even Carla, lately. Several had become friends. Still, sometimes, she would wake up in the night half-believing that it all must be a dream. Susan Lesko, the daughter of a Polish Catholic cop from Queens, hanging out with mercenaries, bombers, arsonists, killers. All led by the man who loved her.

Sometimes, like now, she would look at the people sitting at the other tables—locals, townies—wondering what they would think if they knew. They were certainly better off for it, so far, because they were definitely safer. Criminals, burglars, drug dealers simply did not last long in Westport. And if they did know, if she told them, they would never believe it anyway. These people looked just like them.

Anton Zivic had entered Mario's alone. A dapper little man, cultivated, Italian suits, silver hair worn long, an utter charmer, although he told jokes badly. He very much looked the part of a high-priced art dealer, which he was, and not at all the part of a colonel in the Soviet Military Intelligence, which he had been. Zivic waved to her, one finger aloft, indicating that he would join her presently. He blew an affectionate kiss, then turned and huddled with Billy McHugh who stood behind the bar polishing glasses and with John Waldo who sat on a stool munching one of Uncle Billy's bacon cheeseburgers.

She watched the rolling motion of Billy's shoulders as he polished. He still seemed to be favoring the right one although he insisted that it was fine, no lasting damage where her father had shot him that day in Spain. Shot through him, actually, killing that maniac Tucker.

"Listen. You got to stop," he had said to her the last time she asked about his shoulder. "I'm running out of ways to tell you your father did okay."

"I was asking about you."

"No, you weren't. You're not asking if I still hurt. You're asking if what he did still hurts. You can't do that here."

It had taken her a while but she understood what he meant. No looking back. No regrets. Paul had said much the same thing. Regrets make you think too much. They can paralyze you. If her father had hesitated, Billy would have been dead. Nor did Paul mention, ever again, that her father had first shot him as well.

"If it makes you feel better," Billy had told her, "this summer I'm going to play tennis." He made, with the bad right arm, what he took to be a serving motion. It was more of a clubbing motion.

Susan could only blink. The picture of this great bear of a man thumping around a tennis court in shorts . . .

"Molly said she'd teach me. She's real good."

"I know." Former NCAA finalist. Radcliffe. Susan had played with her. Billy was saying that if Molly thought he could play tennis with that arm, everyone else should shut up about it.

"Anyway," he said, "I don't pester you about how you hardly eat anything."

"Yes, you do. All the time."

"Don't argue. Go sit."

He sent her a bacon cheeseburger.

Paul's car pulled up outside, and backed into a space. Someone walking by spoke to him. It was the woman who ran the bookstore up the street. He smiled at her, making small talk.

That shy smile. Soft voice. Gentle eyes. Even now, after almost a year and a half, she still found herself staring at him, trying to reconcile that face, that gentleness, with all that he'd done in his life. Looking at him, it was hard to imagine how anyone, anywhere, could be afraid of him. Living with him, knowing him, it was even harder.

Anton Zivic started toward her table but he saw Paul approaching the door and waited for him. They spoke for a few moments near the cigarette machine. She saw Anton close his eyes and shake his head, a weary grimace on his face. It was the sort of look parents have when told that their child has wrecked the family car. They approached the table, Zivic leaning to kiss her cheek. Paul squeezing her shoulder as he stepped around her.

"Did your father get you?" he asked, sitting.

"Ten minutes ago," she nodded. "He says if you take me to California you're dog meat. But he also says he and Elena might come. When's the service, by the way?"

"Molly will call when she knows. But I think Billy and I had better fly out tonight. Carla is . . . um, being Carla."

"She's trying to find the killer by herself?"

"Nothing like that. I'll tell you later." He turned to Zivic. "I've just put in a call to Leo Belkin. Did you know he was in the country?"

Zivic shook his head. His eyes asked a question.

"Lesko told me," Bannerman answered. "He and Yuri Rykov are in Los Angeles with a Mosfilm delegation. I spoke to Rykov. He said they'd look in on Carla today."

"*Our* Leo Belkin?" Susan wasn't sure she'd heard, especially because Anton Zivic's face showed no surprise. "What's the KGB doing with movie people?"

"Recruiting, I imagine," he said distractedly.

Susan made a face. Paul will have his little joke. And yet she saw no light of mischief in his eyes. "You're kidding, right?" she said to him.

Bannerman shrugged. "It's what he does, Susan. That's his job."

She closed one eye, still unsure of all this. "Recruiting spies? What's to spy on in Hollywood?"

Paul's expression told her that he had little interest in this subject except to the extent that Colonel Belkin or his aide, Yuri, could do him a favor. He answered nonetheless.

"I'm guessing," he said, "but film technology is pretty sophisticated. Some of it has strategic applications. He'll get someone to sell him whatever he's after."

"But how can you . . ." She stopped herself. She was about to ask how he could know that and do nothing about it. She knew what he'd say: "What is it you'd like me to do, Susan? Ask him to stop?"

They'd had such conversations before. He is one man, he would say. He cannot change the world. All he can do is protect his small piece of it. Fortress Westport. In any case, he is retired.

One recent talk had to do with the Cold War being over. No more Cold War, she had said, should mean no more spies, no more contract agents. Maybe he and his people will finally be left alone. He smiled, politely, and said, "Perhaps," but she could see that he did not believe it. She pressed him.

He explained, somewhat reluctantly, that the Cold War is not over. It has simply been redefined. The need to know the intentions of a potential enemy is as great as ever, especially one whose government may prove to be politically unstable. The need to "interdict" any force or faction seeking to destabilize an otherwise cooperative government is all the more critical. People will still be blackmailed, kidnapped, or killed. Espionage, if anything, will increase, particularly against Western industry because the need for economic intelligence . . . technology . . . is as vital to the restructuring of the Soviet economy as it was to that of Germany and Japan. Furthermore, because the Soviet Union is now seen in a somewhat more sympathetic light, their agents will have a much easier time recruiting American citizens as spies. What's the harm, the recruit would ask? Why not sell them something, make a few bucks at it, before Congress gives it to them for nothing?

What Paul said, she supposed, made a twisted kind of sense. But it was all so terribly cynical. So wearying.

"Not cynical," he would say, in that gentle way of his. "Realistic. But yes, it is wearying."

"Susan?"

Her mind had wandered.

Paul was discussing who should go to Los Angeles and when. And he was telling them both that Lisa Benedict had almost certainly been murdered by someone other than California's latest serial killer. He told them what her father had said. The killer could be anyone but he was more likely than not to have been an acquaintance, possibly a former boyfriend.

He had no expectation of finding the killer but they owed it to Carla to at least try to narrow the field. His first priority, however, was to keep Carla from drawing any further attention to herself, and, therefore, to the rest of them. If they should develop any leads, they will turn them over to the police, bury Lisa, and get out of there. He would not mind having her father there. He has a . . . talent . . . for this sort of thing and, if nothing else, he would be useful as a buffer against the authorities. As for Susan, she can come out for the service but, until then, although he anticipates no personal danger for anyone involved, he would prefer not to put her at risk.

"I'm coming," she said. "I'm coming with you."

He raised his hands. She ignored the gesture.

"I'm not just a mascot around here, Bannerman," she said quietly. "I was a reporter, remember? I know how to track leads."

"That was in New York. You've never been to Los Angeles. You wouldn't even know your way around."

She ignored that nonsense as well. They sell maps of Los Angeles. As for the question of possible danger, Paul's eyes said that he was telling the truth. He had no reason to expect any. And yet he was traveling with Billy. And if John Waldo was here, Waldo was probably being sent ahead separately. John had also gone to Spain separately. His job, she'd since learned, was to procure weapons, spare cars, and to prepare alternate evacuation routes. Paul had also asked Leo Belkin's help. Colonel Belkin, if nothing else, could be counted on to provide sanctuary, a safe house if needed, possibly within the Soviet consulate as he had in Lisbon. Even for Paul, who liked to be thorough, to hedge his bets, it seemed a lot of trouble to go to.

"What troubles you so much?" Anton Zivic asked the question before she could. "About this murder, I mean."

"I don't know," he answered, rubbing his chin.

"Do you have . . . an intuition of some sort?"

He shook his head. "Not even that. When a thing like this touches us," he said, "I'm probably just hesitant to assume that it's entirely unrelated to us. And yet I'm sure that it is."

"But it bothers you nonetheless. This is your reason for wanting Lesko there?"

A small shrug. He didn't answer. But Susan understood. She had heard the reference to her father's *talent*. Although he was reluctant to say it, for fear of seeming foolish, Paul wanted not only her father but he wanted David Katz. More rationally, he wanted that part of her father's mind that seemed to hear and feel things that were just out of reach for most other people. Anton Zivic seemed to know this as well.

"He'll come if I do," Susan said.

"And you'd be all he'll think about. That's not what I need."

"It's what *I* need," she said firmly. "I'm going with you."

17

Carleton Dunville the elder was not pleased. Although not yet sixty, he had hoped to pass the remainder of his life visiting Sur La Mer no more frequently than twice a year.

He had been born there, had grown up there, and he had sired, among others, two sons who had also remained there. But unlike his father, Count Victor, he was not content to die there. There was a whole world to enjoy, a world that he had helped create. There was power to enjoy. And there was fear. He saw it, all the time, in the eyes of those who owed all that they were to him and whose lives, fortunes, reputations depended, even now, on his continued goodwill.

He felt no such goodwill toward his sons today. There was Henry, still whimpering in the basement. One eye gone entirely, the other damaged, probably beyond repair; his usefulness, such as it was, at an end.

He would be no great loss. Henry had always been Henry, born with the genetic deficiencies of the alcoholic and drug addict who was his mother. What was her name? Famous once, during the forties. Frances something or other. Hard to remember. They came and they went.

He was doubly displeased with his namesake, young Carleton. Disappointed, as much as anything. Carleton had, since birth, been the apple of his eye. Carleton, much more than Henry, had grown to resemble him physically and intellectually. Even sartorially. Small wonder, of course. They had been groomed identically.

But the resemblance, sadly, did not extend to

decisiveness. Or to prudence. It was hardly prudent to keep copies of those biographies in his office safe. Or even on the grounds, for that matter. Worse, he had let Henry, and Ruiz, know they were there. But no one else, all three insisted.

And yet the German, Streicher, knew exactly what he was looking for and where to find it. Are we to believe Henry's blubbering fixation that Nellie Dameon is somehow behind this? He offers no evidence beyond a suspicion that the old actress has found her voice and the fact that the Streichers have been spending time with her. And would not let him question her.

Not that it matters, really. The damage is done. Now, it is a question of containment. In an orderly manner. One thing at a time.

The first order of business, in young Carleton's office, formerly his own, was the report from this thug, Hickey, who seemed to be the only one who had not made a hash of things.

"That's the one. The redhead," Hickey was saying.

Carleton, his son at his side, was watching a video-tape shot by Hickey. It showed two women, surrounded by police, one of them struggling while being carried down a flight of stairs, all the while kicking at a man dressed in a suit.

"Her name is Carla Benedict," Hickey told him. "She's the sister of the one I . . . the one you caught sneaking in here. The tall one's name is Molly Farrell. They're from back east."

Carleton the younger raised an eyebrow but said nothing. Hickey continued his narration.

"This is ten minutes later, up Alameda. They're stopping to get an address from a phone book. I stick with them because there's already something funny about them but I can't put my finger on it. After a while, I realize they're looking for the house where this girl, DiDi Fenerty, lives."

"Why? Do you know?"

Hickey spread his hands. "The only thing I can

figure is they heard her name on the answering machine. Anything else with her name on it, I already took out of the apartment."

"But that reference to Miss Fenerty, you said, was indirect at best. Why would they go to see her?"

Hickey shrugged. "To find out if the dead sister ever showed up there, I guess. Port in a storm."

Carleton the younger rubbed his chin. He wished now that he'd told Hickey to make it *look* like a burglary. Break the lock. Steal everything of value, including that machine. "What happened next?" he asked.

"They go to the Fenerty house. It's that white one with the porch. They're inside for about a half hour. The sister comes out but the other one stays. I followed the sister until I lost her . . . in traffic. I broke off, made a couple of phone calls, then I came straight here."

"How did you learn who they were?"

Hickey smiled, his expression smug. He reversed the tape and pressed *Pause*. "Look at the little one. Looks like the dead girl, right? Figures at least to be a relative. So before I come up here, I call the dead girl's father, say I'm LAPD, and tell him someone claiming to be a relative was at his daughter's apartment interfering with the investigation, and could he verify. The father doesn't sound surprised. He sounds disgusted. He says, 'That's Carla, all right.' He said she and her 'associate' are out here from Connecticut. I asked if they were staying with him. He said, '*No, they're at the Beverly Hills Hotel.*'"

"Associate?" asked Carleton the elder.

"I heard that too. And the way he said it. So I ask him if there's anything I should know about his daughter. There's this long silence. He tries to get off the phone. I remind him that this is a murder investigation and I ask him again. He says, 'I've told the government people everything I know, or care to know, about Carla.' I ask, 'Which government people?' But he hangs up."

Both Dunvilles were frowning. "What do you make of it?" asked Carleton the elder.

Hickey smirked. He hooked his thumbs inside his belt and patted his abdomen. "Like I told you," he said, "there was something about her. So I make one more call. There's this cop I know, I saved his ass once, who was one of the uniforms at the dead girl's apartment. I catch him coming off his shift and I tell him I'm working for the family of one of the other victims so he doesn't wonder why I was there."

He paused again, for effect. Carleton the younger, a chill smile on his face, nodded encouragement.

"Anyway," Hickey resumed, "I ask him what all the fuss was and he says the redhead almost carved up two FBI guys. He said they let her go because, sure enough, she's the sister and she had a right to be there. But then the feds do a computer make on her. She definitely has a sheet but I don't know what it says because the feds wouldn't even tell the LA cops on the task force. All they'd say is it's a federal matter and it has no connection with the case at hand. But my guy heard they turned white when the sheet came in and they spent the next hour on the phone to Washington."

"Well?" The young Carleton stared blankly. "What does it mean?"

Hickey was disappointed. He thought he'd been clear. "You need me to spell it out?" He leaned forward. "The FBI, not to mention the cops, are now paying special attention to a murder that was just one more slicing until the mystery sister shows up. That's not to mention these two women, either, who might just be pros and who are definitely not your basic grief-stricken relatives."

Carleton the younger watched the former policeman through hooded eyes. He began to feel pressure at his temples.

"Go on, please," he whispered.

"That's about it."

"We don't pay you to add to our worries, Mr. Hickey. We pay you to solve our problems."

Hickey's color rose. "What is this? Shoot the messenger? I thought I did pretty damned good."

"And you have," said Carleton the elder, raising one hand to silence his son. "You have been most resourceful."

Hickey's mouth twitched. He almost said thank you.

"Just one or two things more. You said the sister left the Fenerty house while the other one stayed. Why would that be?"

Hickey shrugged.

"Possibly because the Fenerty girl knows something of Lisa Benedict's activities after all?"

Hickey twisted his mouth, doubtfully. "If she does, it's hard to imagine the sister leaving. But she left pretty quick, probably headed back to her hotel. When I lost her she was heading right for it."

Carleton the younger turned toward his father. "We have no reason to think that the Fenerty girl knows anything. I spoke to her myself. Still, it would have been nice if Mr. Hickey made sure."

Hickey reddened. "That's all you'd need. Two girls, close friends, both dead. If you want every cop in town working on this, that would be the way to do it."

Young Carleton seemed stunned. "Dead?" he asked, straightening. "Who, for heaven's sake, said anything about killing her?"

"You said 'make sure.' You said it twice."

"I meant through detective work, Mr. Hickey. I certainly didn't mean . . ."

"Hey!" Hickey held up both hands. "Don't fuck with me." He gestured toward the basement room where he had first seen Lisa Benedict's body. "You didn't say carve up that girl's mouth, either. But it's what you meant."

Carleton the younger glared at him. He glanced at his father. Then, "Would you give us a few moments alone, Mr. Hickey?"

Hickey looked at the father. "I cleaned up this mess. I didn't make it."

"Mr. Hickey . . ."

"You want to talk, fine," he said. "While you're at it you can talk about my new job. It's here, full time. I want ten grand a month, effective now, and I'm your new chief of security. That guy, Darby, is a schmuck anyway."

Carleton the younger sputtered. He started to rise. His father put a hand on his arm.

"You deserve it," he said to Hickey.

Hickey, about to say more, only stared.

"There is no need to bluster, no need to threaten. You've done very well. The job is yours but I warn you, you're going to earn every dime of that salary."

Hickey nodded. "Sure. Yeah."

"I want you two to shake hands," he said, "and I want you to mean it. We cannot have friction here."

Carleton the younger made no move until he felt the bite of his father's nails. He extended his hand. Hickey took it. Carleton the elder clasped his own hand over theirs.

"Done," he said, releasing them. "Give us ten minutes," he said to Hickey. "No more."

"I have to piss anyway," Hickey said. He walked to the door.

"You're a good man, Mr. Hickey."

Carleton the elder heard the click of the door and leaned toward his son. "I want that man dead," he said quietly, "I want it done soon."

18

By the end of her first hour with Lisa's computer files, Molly Farrell had ruled out any personal involvement between Lisa and the Campus Killer. There was no mention of him anywhere, no sign of interest or concern. Nor, in her diary file, was there any suggestion of tension between Lisa and any of the several young men she saw socially.

Molly came on a reference to an abortion that Lisa had apparently undergone two years earlier. She had used the diary to sort out her feelings about it and her reasons for not telling the father, a law student who had subsequently graduated and moved to Sacramento. They still kept in touch, just friends, no romantic involvement. Molly erased the entire entry. Carla could live without knowing it.

Except for a few other letters to distant friends, virtually all entries made in the last three weeks of her life had to do with a master's thesis titled, "The Panic of 1927—A Study of the Film Industry's Transition from Silents to Sound—The Economic and Human Cost."

Molly scanned through it, stopping occasionally to read sections of it more carefully. She had no idea what she was looking for except, possibly, something new and interesting about an actress named Nellie Dameon. She tried to avoid becoming absorbed with the overall subject matter but, like Lisa, she found that she was especially struck by the human cost of the transition.

Lisa recognized that in any industry the loss of a livelihood can be frightening, even devastating. But there are always other jobs, no matter how humble, that can put bread on the table. What do you do, though, when you've been a star? Become a waitress? Pump gas?

In fact, some did. Molly found a reference file marked "Casualties." It listed more than a hundred actors and actresses who were adored by fans one month, unemployable the next. Louise Brooks, Zeigfeld star, film star, ended up homeless for a time, living on a bench in Central Park. Later a sales girl at Macy's. Karl Dane, once billed as "The Funniest Man in the Movies" until his thick accent did him in, was reduced to running a hot dog stand near the main gate of the studio where he'd been a star. People avoided it. They were embarrassed for him. Dane shot himself in 1934.

The file listed many more suicides of one kind or another. Some used alcohol, others speeding cars; many did it with drugs. Lisa had written a long section dealing with the widespread use of drugs, especially cocaine, in the Hollywood of the twenties. Molly was surprised. She had somehow thought that recreational drugs were a more modern phenomenon. But she forced herself to scan forward. The drug scene of the twenties had no apparent relevance to the question at hand. What could Lisa have found that might explain why anyone would feel the need to kill her? Or to destroy these files once she was conveniently dead by another means?

Lisa's first mention of an asylum called Sur La Mer had made no impression on her. It was on her "Casualties" list. A number of movie people had been sent either there, near Santa Barbara, or to the Motion Picture Country House and Hospital in Woodland Hills.

It did not appear again until Molly came to a file marked "Field Trips." Lisa had planned visits to both places and about a dozen others such as the archives at MGM/UA, Universal Studios, and the Hollywood Museum. She had apparently been welcomed at the Motion Picture Country House where she interviewed some of the very few survivors of the period but she was turned away by Sur La Mer. Her notes said that she would try again.

Suddenly, there it was. Lisa had typed the word-
PAYDIRT!!! Beneath it, NELLIE DAMEON TALKS. It
was followed by a remembered transcription of their
conversation. Molly read it and found it initially disap-
pointing. All Lisa had had, apparently, was a brief
conversation with an aged actress who seemed to think
Lisa was one of her children. She, and someone named
D'Arconte. There was another reference to an unnamed
woman, born 1931 or 1932, who had a strawberry
birthmark on her throat. This was followed by several
terse notes in question form. Among them, "Why barbed
wire and booby traps?" and "Per doctor, who are *these
people*?"

"DiDi?" Molly called Lisa's friend who had been in
the kitchen making phone calls. "Could you look at this?"
She made room for her at the screen.

Carleton Dunville the younger knew what was
coming. He had heard the same speech from his father
every year since his last in prep school, usually on the
occasion of his birthday. It would begin with the words,
You are a Dunville. It would last for six minutes. It
would end, in this case, with a patient explanation of
why Joseph Hickey had to die.

There was no need. Mr. Hickey was, and would
remain, a blackmailer. It made no difference that he had
committed at least two felonies in the process, he hoped,
of guaranteeing his future. In fact he had little to lose
and he knew it. If caught, he would strike a bargain. He
would suffer, at most, a few months' inconvenience and
the cost of a good lawyer. But his testimony would be a
disaster. It would destroy the work of three generations.
It might, in the end, ruin hundreds of lives.

Hickey had, in any case, sealed his own doom. Not
through his insolence. Not even through his venality. He
had done so when he allowed that unnamed policeman
to associate him, no matter how indirectly, with Lisa
Benedict, opening a possible avenue of investigation that
could, conceivably, lead to his association with Sur La

Mer. But he had also, bless him, identified the primary suspect in his own death and even suggested the means.

"What was Hickey working on, officer?"

"The search for the Campus Killer, he said."

"On whose behalf, unnamed officer?"

"For one of the families, he said. He didn't say which."

"We'll question them all. But he must have learned something. Got close."

"I guess. Too close."

"You are a Dunville," Carleton the elder began, interrupting his reverie. It was as he feared. His father was adhering strictly to the script. "It is not something you chose," he was saying. "Nor, God knows, did I."

"I understand that, Father. And I understand where my duty lies."

He said this last in the hope that his father might forgo the first minute or so of the speech in which he usually misquotes Emerson: "When Duty whispers low, *Thou must,*/The youth replies, *I will.*" Or, depending on the circumstance at hand, he would quote Longfellow's observation that, in this world, a man must either be an anvil or a hammer.

Whatever.

The middle part of the speech was similar to those heard by every young man of his acquaintance who happened to be born into a family of wealth, influence, and social standing . . . to say nothing of self-importance. It was an enlargement on the theme, *You are a Dunville,* as in, You are a Rockefeller, a Kennedy, or a Mellon; except that the burden of being a Dunville was infinitely greater and the advantages fewer.

A Mellon could choose to become, say, a marine biologist or a concert pianist. A Rockefeller could decide to be governor of any state in which he owned a house. A Kennedy could divorce. He might even marry a Protestant someday. A Dunville could do almost none of the above. He *could* marry—although none of them had. And he could breed children to his heart's content, as all

of them had. Sometimes on order, although there had
not been much of that lately. It had been almost two
years since Sur La Mer had a member of childbearing
age. The girl, Lisa Benedict, might have served. She was
certainly attractive enough although boyish in physique.
On the other hand, perhaps not. Narrow hips. And her
babies would probably have been redheads. There was
seldom much call for redheaded children. . . .

"Carleton . . . are you listening to me?" Carleton
the elder was frowning.

"Every word. Yes."

His father had been well into the third part of the
speech. It concerned riding the tiger. No way to dis-
mount. It had grown too big. What his grandfather,
Count Victor, had started as an accommodation for one
or two fugitives had grown over more than sixty years
into a network that defied the imagination. There were
hundreds of them out there. Thousands, if one counted
their progeny. Sons and daughters, most of them legitimate, some purchased. There were grandchildren. In-
laws. There were people out there who were four
generations removed from the founders of their families
and of their fortunes. Families that three generations of
Dunvilles had created. Not a one of which had existed
before 1931.

Carleton the younger loved to look at the names,
keep track of their lives, update their profiles. It was
astonishing to watch, really. There were, among the Sur
La Mer alumni, some thoroughly despicable people who
had, over time, become relatively decent and productive
human beings. Or who had produced second and third
generations who were relatively decent. Perhaps their
new environments had something to do with it. And
their training, with annual refresher courses, certainly
deserved much of the credit. And perhaps, over time,
the infusion of new and less predatory genes through
marriage. Carleton found that he took an honest pleasure in those who had done well. Some had built
financial empires. More than a few had entered public

life. There were, currently: one senator, two congressmen, two mayors, a federal judge, and assorted lesser officials still with bright futures ahead of them. Several had attended service academies and had risen steadily within the military. Some were educators. A few were even clergy.

These, the best of them, he rarely bothered. Only in the direst emergencies would their patriarchs be called on to do a service, as Don Corleone used to put it. For that, there were more than enough of the worst of them. For many who came to Sur La Mer as rotters continued to be rotters for generations to come. The Sniders of Philadelphia, for example. The Mareks of Los Angeles. Especially the Mareks.

From time to time, certain of these family trees needed pruning. Sometimes whole branches of them. But, as often, they were useful, if only to prune each other.

"It is the innocent," his father was saying, "who need . . . and deserve . . . our protection most of all."

Ah! Now we were getting to it.

"If Hickey brings us down, he could bring them down as well. All of them. No matter how innocent, no matter how blameless, they would be publicly humiliated, hounded by the . . ."

"Father, I understand. Hickey must go. For the sake of the innocent."

The older man's face showed mild annoyance. He searched his son's eyes for a sign of the sarcasm he thought he'd detected. He chose to believe that he saw none. Only an impatience to get on with the unpleasant duty that had been forced on them both.

"Use reliable people," he said. "Not anyone on staff."

"Of course."

"I will see to Henry myself. He knows that you've never liked him."

"That's decent of you, Father." *By all means,* he

thought. *Mustn't let Henry die sensing a lack of affection.*

"What are your plans for the Streichers? More important, how will you get those files back?"

"That . . . is a difficult issue."

He explained to his father that the fax number to which they had been sent had been traced. It was the number of a message service in Los Angeles. Ruiz had gone there this morning, before dawn. The machine at the message service had a relay function. It was set to route any transmissions from Streicher to a second number. The machine printed out that number. It was in New Mexico, Santa Fe specifically, where, as Alan Weinberg, Streicher now has a house. Ruiz is on her way there now, he said, but he doubts very much that she will return with the files.

"Why is that?" asked Carleton the elder.

"Because it's too easy. The second machine is somewhere within Streicher's Santa Fe exchange but it is unlikely to be in his house. Even if she finds it, it seems too much to hope that she'll find a hundred feet of fax paper dangling from it."

"She might find more than that. Knowing Streicher, that machine is likely to be booby-trapped."

Young Carleton blinked. He had not considered that.

"You think Streicher lied about having a confederate on the other end?"

"It seemed a bit pat, yes. There wasn't much point in coming to Sur La Mer in the first place if he hadn't broken off all contact with his past. Furthermore, Ruiz saw Bonnie Streicher's eyes when she saw his cover note asking for my death in retaliation for his. She is sure that she saw confusion in them. If so, either she knew nothing of an assassin sitting on the other end, which seems unlikely, or her husband was making it up as he wrote it."

Carleton the elder pursed his lips. "And yet he sent

the documents. Are there machines that will hold them? Unprinted, I mean?"

"Yes. Until a code is punched in."

The older man raised an eyebrow. "So, if Luisa does not return," he said, "We'll know that she found the machine and that the transmitted documents have probably been destroyed."

Young Carleton said nothing. He tried not to show his anger.

A small loss, thought the father. Ruiz. A disgusting creature really. Even if she did try to stop Henry from using the Benedict girl it was probably out of jealousy. "We have no one else," he asked, "who can trace that machine to its location?"

"We do. They're working on it. Streicher would expect no less. But there's still the matter of a booby trap. The point was to *know* that those files were destroyed unseen. *Probably* will not do. We cannot act on *probably*."

"Then what do you suggest?"

"Streicher has promised that he will abide by his contract in every particular. There's no question that he's tired of being hunted, for his wife's sake if not for his own. The only reason he did all this was out of concern that we would exact vengeance for Henry."

His father's hand made a flitting gesture.

"Like it or not," young Carleton continued, "short of finding that machine and standing there as it prints out those files to no eyes but our own, our hands are tied. My suggestion, failing that, is that we take him at his word."

"That is unacceptable."

"Why?" The son spread his palms. "There's no risk to us. The only risk is to those whose profiles he has and only then if he tries to blackmail them. If he doesn't, none of our clients will ever know they've been compromised. If he does, no place on earth will be safe for him."

Carleton the elder scowled. "Just chalk it off, you say. Go merrily on with our lives."

"Father, if you have an alternative . . ."

"Have you considered making him talk? Telling where that machine is? How to disarm it? Whether, in fact, anyone else has seen those files?"

"Yes, I have."

"And?"

"It crossed my mind to drug them. But they only eat what the members eat. We'd have to drug them all and it would probably kill half of them."

"What about during surgery? Is any more scheduled?"

The younger man shook his head. "Their bandages come off tomorrow. It's possible that Streicher will need more work on that eye but he will not, in any case, accept general anesthesia. Even if he would, his wife would be standing beside the table with an automatic weapon."

"You could . . . lull her. Overpower her."

Carleton the younger made a face. "That's Bonnie Streicher, Father. She does not *lull*."

The older man rose to his feet. He began pacing. On a sudden impulse, he stepped to the door and opened it, half-expecting to see Joseph Hickey's ear pressed against it. He did not. Hickey stood some fifty feet away, his back to him, smoking a cigarette near the main entrance. A security guard, the one who still limped, sat at a small desk in between. Hickey could not have listened. Hickey turned. Carleton the elder smiled and held up one finger. He closed the door.

"How soon can you see to him?" he asked his son.

"This evening, if all goes well. I'll use Marek's people."

"Have you considered that he might have left a diary, a tape recording . . . that sort of thing?"

Carleton the younger understood. Insurance. He shook his head. "That seldom happens in real life, Father," he said. "The risk of premature discovery is as great as any deterrent value. Nor is there any point to a deterrent unless he's told us it exists."

"Let's hope," his father sniffed, "that Mr. Hickey shares your . . ."

"I will see to it," he said, biting off the words. "There will be a search. I will deal with this."

His father, less than reassured, reached for a change of subject. "This business about Nellie," he said. "Is there anything to it?"

"That she can talk?" he shook his head. "It's hard to imagine that she kept silent for sixty years just to have a chat with the Streichers or with some college student who sneaked onto the grounds."

"How else could Streicher have known about the files?"

"He said he didn't. He feared for his safety after . . . Henry. He said he was looking for anything at all that might give him some leverage."

"And you believed him?"

Carleton the younger could no longer mask his annoyance. "Does it make more sense to believe," he snapped, "that Nellie Dameon, of all people, knew the contents of my safe and gave it to the first person who seemed to enjoy her movies?"

The father raised a placating hand. He tended to agree. Still . . . "I'd like to talk to him. Where is he now?"

"In Nellie's suite."

"Will he let me enter?"

The younger man shrugged. "With a gun at your chest. What do you hope to accomplish?"

Carleton the elder did not answer. He stepped behind his son's desk, formerly his own, and reached into the coat cabinet where the weapons were kept. He selected a large revolver, nickel plated, which he presumed to be of higher quality than the others. He took a small black one as well.

"You can't be serious," his son said, rising.

Carleton the elder understood. He smiled. "Hardly that," he said.

"Then what's the gun for?"

The smile faded. "First," he said, "it's time to say good-bye to Henry."

19

Nellie had gone away again.

Alan Weinberg was beginning to envy her.

"You need some time to yourselves," she had said. "I'll be back before tea."

"Any place in partic . . ."

She was gone before he could finish. Her eyes simply blinked out. It was as if a switch had been thrown.

On the day before, Monday, she had traveled in time to 1920. She was seventeen. Not yet a star. And she had a new beau. His name was Tom. He was ten years older than she was, a cattle rancher, or rather his family owned a ranch up in the San Joaquin Valley.

They had given him leave to try his hand at acting, get this movie business out of his system. After that, he was expected to return home and settle down. He had done fairly well. He had risen from extra to featured player when he met and fell in love with Nellie. He wanted to show her the ranch that would be his someday. Nellie took a rare break between pictures and went off with him to meet the family, and then go camping and canoeing on Tulare Lake.

She told the Weinbergs about it when she returned. She'd caught two big catfish, which he cleaned and she cooked for breakfast. Then they went swimming. Her blush, when she mentioned that activity, suggested that they had probably gone unclothed.

She married her rancher-actor a year later. He was

killed two years after that. He broke his neck in a
tumbling wagon during the filming of a chase by Indians.

Weinberg saw no sadness when she told him how
Tom died. He soon understood why. Tom was not dead
to Nellie. She could see him any time she wished. It was
more, much more, than the reliving of memories. She
could, almost literally, travel in time.

She could even, she told them, go back to Ames,
Iowa, and be a child again. She could relive the day
when the Baker Stock Company came to town and her
mother took her to see *A Winter's Tale* and she became
smitten with the boy who played the little lost prince.
The sweet misery of that unrequited crush faded away in
time, only to be replaced by a deeper love of all things
connected with the theater. She rarely missed a stage
performance in Ames, offering to hang posters or set
chairs in exchange for a pass, and always caught the
latest moving picture show at the nickelodeon, which
opened in the old Hopkins Dry Goods Store after Mr.
Hopkins sold out to Loew's Theatrical Enterprises. Three
years later, when her mother died, thirteen-year-old
Nellie ran off to Omaha to join the Baker troupe.

On Monday, while Nellie was away with Tom,
Barbara took her husband to the bedroom of Nellie's
suite and made love to him. Weinberg tried not to show
it but he was ill at ease. He kept expecting Nellie to
appear in the doorway, which they had left open so that
any attempt at entry could be heard. He wished that
they had Nellie's gift. He wished that he could throw
that same mental switch and go far away with Barbara.
To Salzburg. To the night of a party, during the Mozart
Festival, which he probably would not have attended
until he was told that Barbara would be there. She was
Bonnie Predd then. He had known her by reputation
but he had never imagined that she would be so . . .
feminine. So lovely. He was thoroughly intimidated by
her. It was she who approached him. Put him at ease.
And let him drive her home.

At her doorway he offered a handshake. She took

the hand and held it for a very long time as if deciding what to do with him. At last, with a smile, she offered him coffee. They sat together until dawn, fully clothed, only talking. They did not make love, not that time, and not for many days more. But by sunrise, he, the notorious Axel Streicher, had become her slave. If he had Nellie's gift, he knew that he would never tire of reliving that night, or any of the nights, or days, which they had shared since then.

Today, Tuesday, with the arrival of Carleton Dunville the elder, he had been unusually tense. It was not his habit to play a waiting game. He found himself becoming irritable. Nellie saw it. She saw Barbara take his hand. It was then that she announced that she would be gone until tea. Two hours. She seemed to be promising that they would indeed have that time to themselves. Now, looking at her, he believed her. There was no life in her eyes.

As much as he wanted to return to that bedroom with Barbara, he wanted to find a newspaper even more. If the girl, Lisa, had been found, or even reported missing, he wanted to know about it. He wanted to know what was said about her. There were no television sets in this wing, only more of those video machines made to look like movie theater screens. With Barbara covering him, he approached the main hall where he had often seen newspapers at the security guard's station.

The guards did not see him. They had stepped to the front entrance where that man, Hickey, was for some reason urinating into a bed of pachysandra. Weinberg saw a copy of the *Los Angeles Times* open on the desk. Making no sound, he took it. He stepped back into the Members' Wing.

It was on the front page. There was more inside. Barbara stood at his shoulder as he read. He could feel her growing anger.

"They cut her," she said in quiet fury.

"I know."

"They left her naked, with her legs spread apart. They promised they would . . ."

He reached for her hand, squeezing it. Even Weinberg winced at the mental picture of young Lisa, a bloody smile carved into her face, ear to ear. But while sympathetic to the girl, and especially to his wife, he could understand why it was done. It was sensible. This way, even if it were known that she had come to Sur La Mer on Sunday, it would be presumed that this lunatic, this Campus Killer, had found her well after she returned to Los Angeles. Her white Fiero had been located at a Junior College not far from where her body was found. Dunville was smart. Weinberg had to give him that. And all he had promised Barbara was that the body would be found so that it might have a decent burial.

"Make sure you hide this," Barbara said into his ear. "Don't let Nellie know."

Weinberg glanced at her. There was still no life.

"She was so young, so pretty," Barbara said sadly. She touched her fingers to the photograph in the newspaper as if to stroke Lisa's cheek.

"They all are," he nodded. There were six more faces across the bottom of the page. All fresh, bright, attractive young women, all dead. The photographs had come from high-school yearbooks. And these six victims were all blond. That bothered Weinberg. He raised his eyes to Lisa's photograph. In newsprint, her reddish hair seemed brown. It was not, in any case, blond.

There was something else.

He looked closer. "Does she look familiar to you?" he asked.

"You mean, other than . . ." She gestured toward the basement where they had first seen her.

"Yes."

Barbara shook her head slowly, then brightened. "She looks a little like Nellie did. When Nellie was young."

He nodded. "Yes. I suppose she does but that's not it. I've seen this girl before."

"Alan?"

"Yes, my love."

She took the paper from his hands. "I would like to be held, I think."

He smiled beneath his bandages. "We have until tea. Would you like to try something? Do you remember that night when we . . . ?"

"I think I just want to be held."

He understood. She wanted those faces gone from her mind. Perhaps she wanted to cry. He wanted them gone from his mind as well.

Still . . . the girl . . . Lisa. Something about that face.

Perhaps it would come to him.

DiDi Fenerty whistled softly.

"It's paydirt all right," she said to Molly. "Nellie Dameon's probably the only one on that casualties list who's still alive. If Lisa got her to talk she'll get more than a good grade. This might be worth a book contract."

"Why? Just for her recollections of the period?"

DiDi told her of the Nellie Dameon legend. That, the story was, her attempts to make it in talkies were a failure. That her studio forced her to make two terrible films and, even then, was rumored to have sabotaged the sound tracks in order to break a contract that was paying her $5,000 a week. That they got her on drugs, drove her to the edge. That she went to pieces, retreated into her self and had not, as far as anyone knew, said a single word since.

"This interview," Molly asked, choosing her woods, "or this book Lisa might have written. Is that something that anyone would want to keep from being published?"

"Like who?"

Molly shrugged. "I don't know. The studios? You said that they deliberately set out to destroy this woman."

DiDi shook her head. "They did that to a number of

actors. John Gilbert, for example. Even back then, studio heads like Louis B. Mayer and Harry Cohn wouldn't have cared who knew it. It would have helped them keep the others in line."

Molly had to agree. No one would care, certainly after all this time, except for film historians. "What if someone else, perhaps another student, knew that Lisa had spoken to Nellie Dameon? And then, soon afterward, Lisa was killed. The killing was unrelated but this person saw an opportunity to break into Lisa's apartment and steal her notes."

DiDi considered this, only briefly. "No chance," she said. "It wouldn't begin to be worth it. Anyway, at least a dozen people would recognize her work. We'd crucify anyone who tried to pass it off as theirs."

Molly knew she was fishing. But fishing was all she had. And the burglary of Lisa's apartment was a fact. She stared at the screen. There was that name again. D'Arconte. "You say you've never heard of him?"

She shook her head.

Molly gestured toward a wall of reference books, all film related. "Might he be in one of those?"

"I already looked. But I could make a phone call. Professor Mecklenberg might know." She hesitated. "Molly," she cocked her head toward the kitchen phone, "the police have been asking about you and Carla."

"When?" She hadn't heard it ring.

"I just called Mr. Benedict," she explained, "to ask about the service. I mentioned that you were here. He said a policeman who saw you at Lisa's apartment called to verify that Carla is her sister and they wanted your name, too. He gave it to them."

Molly was silent for a long moment.

"Are you . . . wanted for anything?"

"No. Why do you ask?"

"Because you got quiet, just like that, when I told you about the policeman who came yesterday."

"It's nothing." Molly tried a reassuring smile. "Given

what we . . . were, the authorities are concerned that we might interfere. That's all."

DiDi looked into her eyes. She saw them waver. "I'll help you any way I can," she said. "But I wish you'd be honest with me. That man who came yesterday. You don't think he was a policeman, do you."

Molly drummed her fingers. "No. I don't," she said finally. "And the man who called was not an FBI agent."

"And the one who called Mr. Benedict?"

"He wasn't a policeman either."

"How could you know that?"

"Because both the police and the FBI showed up this morning at Lisa's apartment. We had to produce identification. The police had no need to ask George Benedict who I am."

DiDi stared at her. "Molly . . . what's going on here?"

"I don't know. Truthfully."

"Am I in danger? Truthfully?"

Molly rocked her head sideways, a gesture of uncertainty. She flicked a finger toward the IBM machine. "Someone, not the police, seems very interested in how much you know. Whatever it is, I sure don't see anything in here that's worth . . ." Molly stopped herself.

"Killing for." DiDi completed the thought. "But you think someone did."

Molly grimaced, then shook her head slowly. "The two might still be unrelated," she said. "But just in case, I'd keep plenty of people around me if I were you. Don't go anywhere alone, not even to the Benedict house. When is the service, by the way?"

"This Thursday, ten o'clock, Saint Paul's Episcopal Church in Sherman Oaks. How can I help in the meantime?"

Molly picked up a yellow pad on which she'd listed three names. D'Arconte, Nellie Dameon, Sur La Mer. "Find out all you can about these. What's the name of that professor?"

"Stanley Mecklenberg. Or I could research it myself at the . . ."

Molly shook her head. "Do it by phone. Don't be seen looking up these names in a library. And if that same man or anyone else comes back asking you questions, say that you gave me a package Lisa left with you. Say that I asked if I could use your computer and then, afterward, acted very strangely but wouldn't tell you what was in the package. Say I took everything with me back to the Beverly Hills Hotel."

DiDi made a face. "In other words, I'm supposed to set you up."

Molly frowned. "If someone got in here," she asked, "past Kevin, and came at you with a knife, what do you think you'd do?"

"I . . . don't know. Scream, I guess. Try to run."

"What do you think I would do? What would Carla do?"

DiDi hesitated, only briefly. "Stick it up his ass?"

Molly blinked. "Why would you say that?"

"Lucky guess. But I hear you."

"Call your professor." Molly nodded toward the extension on DiDi's desk. "Is that on the same line?"

"No. It's mine. Private."

"May I make a long distance call? I'll pay for it."

"To Westport by any chance?"

Molly didn't answer.

"It's on the house," said DiDi Fenerty.

Nellie's gift to the Weinbergs—some time to themselves—was not entirely unselfish. She wanted to try, just once more, to go back to the day when her daughter was born.

But the scenes, as before, came in fragments. And they were always changing. Even the babies kept changing. One time it would be a son and the next it would be a daughter. Or one time she would be allowed to nurse the infant and the next it would be taken from her, forever, before she'd had a chance to hold it.

The yachtsman, Harland, had told her that there were four babies in all. She still had trouble believing that. She was reasonably sure of only two. There was the little girl with the strawberry birthmark. Nellie had kept her the longest. She had nursed her. She remembered the red hair, grown long enough to be tied with a little green bow. And then one day she was gone.

She was also quite sure of the boy. He was the first. His hair was dark. He cried a lot. And he hurt the most when he came. She seemed to remember that they thought she might die. She remembered a man's voice saying, *"I need that baby. Save her if you can, but I want that baby."* The voice, and the face peering down at her, was that of Vittorio D'Arconte.

She had dreamed of him before that and several times since. They were terrible dreams. It was dark, and he would be on top of her. She could taste his breath. It stank of wine and black cigars. She could feel him thrusting into her. Sometimes it was not D'Arconte at all. Sometimes, especially later, he would turn into Victor Dunville. But she soon learned that she could make either of them go away just by thinking of Tom. She could make Tom take their place. She could bear it that way.

It was, in any case, not really D'Arconte and certainly not Victor Dunville. The psychiatrist said that these were only dreams. They were the prank, he said, of a bedeviled mind.

This was later. Years later. She still could not speak but she could write. She could scribble questions and answers in her sessions with the staff psychiatrist. Her mind had begun to clear. The psychiatrist told her that she was making fine progress. There was no longer a need, he said, for quite so much medication.

It was true, he told her one year, that she had once borne a child and that it was, in fact, a difficult birth. The child did not survive it. The father was one of the other members, since deceased. She had wandered into his rooms one night. He had taken advantage of her. By the time the staff realized what must have happened, her pregnancy was too advanced to be terminated.

As for the other babies she thought she remembered, they were much the same as her memories of the actor who was known as "The Count." They seemed real to her, of course. But he assured her that they were not.

Vittorio D'Arconte, he told her, was also long dead. He had fled to Italy, a fugitive from the law, before Nellie had even been admitted to Sur La Mer. But justice had caught up with him. He was shot down, murdered, on a street in Naples. It was in all the papers, the psychiatrist said. Good riddance.

There was very little resemblance, he pointed out, between Vittorio D'Arconte and our own Victor Dunville. And no likeness at all in terms of character. Mr. Dunville is a humanitarian. A healer. He has devoted himself to restoring the minds of all who came, broken, to Sur La Mer. Making them whole again.

He has sat with you, the psychiatrist said, on many occasions. He has restrained you, gently, when you have become violent. He has comforted you. Because of your condition, however, you saw this caring restraint as an attack. You saw, through some trick of the mind, a resemblance between Victor Dunville and a man you despised for the ruin he brought on so many of your friends. To you, he was Vittorio D'Arconte.

For many years she believed him. In time she wondered how she could ever have thought that Vittorio D'Arconte and Victor Dunville were the same man. If there had ever been a resemblance, there was now scarcely a trace of it. Mr. Dunville was older and more portly. The eyes, the nose, even the jawline were very different. D'Arconte had a thin mustache and hair slicked with pomade. Mr. Dunville had been clean shaven and balding.

She had believed him about the children as well. Otherwise, where were they? he would ask. She had no answer. The only child she ever saw back then, older than a newborn, was Victor Dunville's little boy, Carleton. She saw him, from time to time, playing on the lawn. He had dark hair. And he cried a lot. He seemed very much like the baby she remembered. But it seemed to her that if that child had been her own, she would have some sort of feeling for him. She had none. She rather disliked him, especially after he had grown to adulthood and seemed to have been put in charge of things. If he tried to talk to her she would blink him off. Soon, she stopped even writing.

She never quite knew what had become of Victor Dunville. Harland said he died of an addiction to morphine but Harland was always saying things. He also said that the psychiatrist had been murdered after a quarrel with Carleton Dunville, and some agreed, but the new psychiatrist said he had retired to live in Hawaii. And then Carleton had a son. Or at least one appeared. No one even realized that the elder Carleton was married.

More years passed. Members came and went. Their overall number decreased steadily. Whole floors were given over to the Dunvilles' special guests. Harland said once that there had been a war and that some of them were German war criminals in hiding. That seemed especially silly to Nellie. She imagined that the last place where Germans would hide is in the country that defeated them.

Harland could be quite insistent about the things he claimed, especially where her supposed four children were concerned. He said that he heard them cry. Well? Where are they then? He said that they're probably Dunvilles now. Perhaps even D'Arcontes. You see? There you have it. She would have paid him no mind except for the dreams. They came less frequently but they never stopped. Especially about the little girl with the birthmark and the red hair tied in little green ribbons. The one she thought she saw again when that nice girl, Lisa, came to visit.

Perhaps Lisa would find her.

Perhaps Alan and Barbara would help.

20

Carla Benedict had stood for twenty minutes inside the front entrance of the Beverly Hills Hotel hoping that the silver Honda would appear.

There could be no doubt that it had been following her. It had made a U-turn on Rodeo Drive too quickly for her to get a clear look at the driver and another southbound car had immediately blocked her view of its license plate. She thought that she might have seen it once more, several blocks behind, as she approached Will Rogers Park but, if so, it had broken off once more. She could only proceed to the hotel, a logical destination given her heading, and see if it approached looking for a blue Chevrolet among the Lotuses and Lamborghinis.

She was reasonably sure that its solo occupant was not a policeman. He might have been a reporter who, having seen her at Lisa's apartment, decided to see where she was staying and try for an interview later, and then lost his nerve when he realized she'd spotted him. She hoped not. She wanted to believe it was someone who had reason to be wary of her. Someone who could answer a question or two about why Lisa's apartment had been burglarized. And he would have answered. One way or another, he would have answered. But she saw no sign of that car. She went to the front desk and asked for her messages.

"Miss Benedict?"

She turned at the sound of her name. A massive young man, late twenties, in an ugly sport jacket, shirt too tight, pale skin, bad haircut, stood grinning, nodding, in the manner of a shy schoolboy. Her eyes narrowed. At first she did not recognize him.

"It's Yuri," he said, tapping his chest. "Yuri Rykov."

If nothing else, she knew the voice. Slavic yet soft. Too high for his bulk. Still, it seemed impossible. Not in California. Certainly not in the Beverly Hills Hotel.

He saw the light come into her eyes. He bent closer. "You know who was here?" he whispered. "Jane Fonda."

Her head moved slowly sideways. He took it to suggest doubt.

"It is true. One hour ago. Look." He reached into his pocket and produced a book of matches which he held very carefully. "Here." The grin returned. "She wrote her name for me."

Carla began to weep.

His face fell. Lieutenant Yuri Rykov, aide to Colonel Leo Belkin of the First Chief Directorate, KGB, did not know what to do. She brought a hand to her mouth, her chest heaved. He stepped closer, placing his great hands around her shoulders, awkwardly, his eyes nervously scanning the lobby. He did not so much embrace her as attempt to conceal her. He would not have imagined that the famous Carla Benedict, whose autograph he also had and treasured, could so lose possession of herself.

He felt her trying to regain control. She was holding her breath, then breathing deeply. One hand, holding message slips, gripped his belt. The other crushed the lapel of his jacket. He did not mind. But people were looking. They would smile and look away, satisfied that there was no unpleasantness here, only, perhaps, an emotional encounter between loved ones. Still, he did not think it appropriate that Carla Benedict be seen like this.

Carla didn't care. Nor did it matter to her, for the moment, what the KGB was doing in Los Angeles or why Yuri had been there waiting for her. She knew only that his was the first friendly face she had seen in two days, not counting that of Molly Farrell. She had not seen him since their first meeting, more than a year now, when he wore the uniform of a limousine chauffeur and

had helped smuggle a wounded Paul Bannerman back
into Westport after the Marbella mission. No, there was
one other time. He and Belkin had come back to
Westport. They met with Paul and Anton. She was not
invited. But she saw him at Mario's afterward, devouring
bacon cheeseburgers and reveling in the presence of
Billy McHugh, John Waldo, Janet Herzog . . . names
he had known and regarded with awe since he was a
recruit.

Under a different teacher, she supposed, he might
have been taught to despise them. But Colonel Belkin
insisted otherwise. These are consummate professionals,
he said. The best of the best. Respect them, earn their
respect and, in time, their trust. Then much can be
accomplished. Belkin had freely admitted that this was
his goal although he expressed it with considerably more
reserve than his young aide who was, after two days in
Westport, hopelessly star struck. *And now, God help us*,
she thought, gathering herself, *he has even met Jane
Fonda*.

She took his hand, guiding him past the entrance to
the Polo Lounge—tugging at him when he strained to
look for celebrities inside—and toward the door leading
to the bungalow path outside. She needed to get to a
mirror, repair her face. He would not need to tell her
why he'd been there waiting for her because, as she
walked, she read the second of the two crushed message
slips—the first being from her father. "Stay by your
phone," said the second. "Wait for Belkin or Rykov. Do
not go out. Bannerman."

She blinked at it, curiously. It did not say *please*.
The message conveyed none of Paul's usual warmth or
politeness. He had instructed the operator to underline
not. Paul, for some reason, had shed his skin. He was
being Mama's Boy again. Which means, she assumed,
that he's either learned something about Lisa's murder
or, more likely, he's somehow heard about that mess at
Lisa's apartment.

Well, she shrugged, if she had to have a baby-sitter

she could do worse than Yuri. He was a good-looking kid, tough but no goon, and some of Belkin's polish was bound to have rubbed off on him. She would take him back to her bungalow, check in with her father, get weepy again and then, with any luck, have him fucking her brains out within thirty minutes.

Henry Dunville had been dozing. Hours had passed since Ruiz had last given him an injection for the pain.

He was sitting upright, knees drawn, his back against the padded wall on a cot that was the only furniture in the basement isolation room where they had left him. He could not lie down. When he tried, his broken ribs screamed and he felt as if all the blood in his body was trying to squeeze out through his eyes.

He heard the bolt being thrown. His head snapped up at the sound. The sudden motion made him cry out. "Who's there?" he choked. He tilted his head back as if he might see from beneath the bandages.

Carleton the elder winced at the sight. Over Henry's right eye, blood had soaked through and become caked. There was blood over the left eye as well but it was pinkish, still seeping. Pink tears flowed over his chin and onto his shirt. "It's your father, Henry," he said.

A great sob burst from his chest. More pink tears. "Father? Do you see? Do you see what that bitch did to me?"

"I see. Yes. I'm very sorry, Henry."

"That *cunt*. That fucking cunt."

The language caused Carleton the elder to stiffen. There was no excuse for it. "Henry . . . try to remember who you are," he said.

Henry's mouth fell open. Here he was, like this, and his fucking father is talking about manners. He bit his lip. "I've got to get to a hospital," he rasped. "A real one that knows about eyes."

"You know that's impossible," his father answered, not unkindly. "Even if they could help you, which they can't, how would we explain your condition?"

"But they *can* help," he cried. He tilted his head once more and pulled at the gauze covering his left cheek. "I can see light," he said. "I can even see movement."

Carleton the elder stepped toward him. He fished the cheaper revolver from his pocket and held it close to Henry's right eye. He waggled it. Henry gave no sign that he saw it. But the gun's mechanism made a faint clicking sound and Henry heard it.

"I saw that," Henry lied. "See? You tested me and I saw it."

"What, Henry? What did you see?"

"Listen," he pleaded, his voice becoming desperate. "You could say that I'm a patient here. That I see visions or something. That I went out of my head and tried to blind myself."

"Henry . . . they'd want your records. I can't help you that way. They can't help you at all. Please accept that."

A wail began low in Henry's chest.

"Oh, for heaven's sake," his father muttered.

Henry raised a hand. It said that he was gathering himself. He waited until his breath returned. "So what am I supposed to do?" he managed. "Stay here? Stay like this?"

"You might. But you might also want to end your pain. Don't you think that might be better, Henry, all things considered?"

"Wha . . . you mean . . . ?"

"Yes, Henry. I'm afraid I do."

"Oh. Oh, that's great. I'm like this and that's all you can think about? Henry the inconvenience. Henry who you never gave a shit about. You'd love that, wouldn't you, you bastard."

"No, Henry." Carleton the elder eased himself onto the cot beside his son. He shifted the black revolver to his left hand. He placed his right hand on Henry's shoulder. "What I'd prefer," he said, "is that none of this had happened. You do realize, don't you, that you brought it on yourself?"

"What? This?" Henry touched his bandaged eyes. "For fucking one girl, you say I deserve *this*?"

Carleton the elder sighed audibly. But there was no use, he supposed, in further attempting to correct Henry's language. Nor did it seem useful to make Henry realize that it was not *using* the girl that led to his present unhappy state. It was killing her. So uselessly. Young Carleton was quite right. The girl had seen nothing that could not have been explained or denied.

"Henry," he said, massaging the fleshy shoulder of the younger man, "I'm afraid it's time to make a decision. I came down here intending to make it for you but . . . perhaps a more honorable way . . ."

"What about that woman? The one who did this to me?"

"She . . . they . . . were not given the same choice, Henry. They died badly. They were cowards in the end."

The head came up. "You killed them?"

"I shot them, Henry. With the very pistol I'm holding in my hand. It should give you comfort to know that."

Henry Dunville was silent for a long moment. Then he nodded slowly.

"Your brother would be here . . . he wanted to come . . . but he could not bear to see you like this. He's never been as strong as you are, Henry."

"Father . . ." Henry Dunville held out his hand. "Leave the gun with me. Please."

Carleton the elder hesitated.

"It's all right, Father. I'm ready now."

"Would you . . . like me to stay here with you?"

"Yes. Very much. I would."

The hand gave his shoulder a final squeeze. Then it took his own hand. Henry felt the snub-nosed revolver being fitted into his fingers. He could smell the gun oil. Henry embraced it, bringing it slowly toward his mouth.

He parted his lips, tasting it. The cot creaked. He felt his father leaning away from him to avoid soiling his suit. He imagined the look on his father's face. There would be no respect there. No pity or regret. It would be the look he'd have if he'd stepped in vomit.

The gun, as he'd suspected, did not smell of being fired. His father, like his brother, knew nothing of guns. Axel Streicher would have taken it from him, rammed it down his throat. The Streichers were not dead. Why would they be? They were revenue. He was only Henry. Crop of 1955. Assigned to three different couples in ten years, each time returned when he was no longer needed. Or wanted.

"Be strong, Henry." His father's voice. A hint of impatience.

"Father?"

"I'm here, Henry."

"Fuck you, Father." He jammed the black handgun against the elder Carleton's chest and pulled the trigger.

Nothing.

Henry roared, an animal sound. He tried again. Again, the hammer fell on an empty chamber.

His father stood, breaking Henry's grip of his sleeve. Henry heard him sigh. Then he heard more sounds, a tugging against fabric and the double click of another handgun being cocked. Henry felt strangely calm.

"I'll wait for you in hell, Father," he said.

He heard an intake of breath as if his father was about to say something. Like . . . Good-bye, Henry. You've disappointed me again, Henry. More likely, he knew, it was simply a holding of breath. Like when something smelled bad.

"I'll have eyes then, Father. I'll be there waiting and I'll have two good—"

He never finished.

Yuri Rykov lay raised on one elbow, a sheet up to his hips, facing Carla. She was on her stomach. Her back, he noted, was finely muscled. No fat on her. No stretch marks or scars except for a thin line across her throat where someone long ago, she said, had tried to strangle her with wire.

"I want you to know," Yuri said to her, dreamily, "how special this is to me. You do me a very great honor."

She purred as his fingers traced lightly over her back and buttocks.

"Could I ask your permission . . ." He stopped himself. "No," he said. "Never mind."

"What?" she asked, stretching languidly. "Tell me."

His fingers wandered down her side, brushing her flattened breast. They continued down to her slender waist.

"You have an expression," he said. "Kiss and tell. There is one like it in Russian. It is a bad thing to do but . . ."

She chuckled.

"I think you know what I am asking. Is it so bad?"

Carla shivered as the fingers found a nerve. He withdrew them. "Don't stop," she said. "And yes, you have my permission."

She didn't mind. She thought it was rather sweet. This huge man, KGB, highly trained, certainly deadly when he has to be, but still, in many ways, a boy with a good heart. And like a boy, he wants to tell his friends that in Beverly Hills, California, he not only met Jane Fonda but boffed, twice so far, the famous Carla Benedict.

"They will not believe me," he said, wistfully, "but at least they will wonder. They did not even believe that Billy McHugh made a cheeseburger for me. He did, you know. With his own hands."

"I know. I was there."

"I had photographs. They took my picture with Billy on one side and Molly Farrell on the other. They had their arms around me. And another with Mama's Boy and Miss Lesko. But Colonel Belkin said I must show them to no one when we got back to Bern. Not everyone, he said, would understand."

"Good guess," she said. "Don't stop."

"He said also that it would be an insult to your hospitality to bring back recent photographs of such people. However I would not have let them be used in this way. It would be a point of honor."

She believed him. Belkin's influence. But she wondered how he'd feel if he knew that Billy, his idol, had twice gone into Russia, once alone, once with John Waldo, and had silenced two defectors. Not to mention several KGB border guards who tried to slam the barn door. On the other hand, she assumed that Belkin was not in California to see Disneyland. She wasn't about to pry. Belkin was doing Paul a favor, sending Yuri to watch out for her. *Wait'll he hears*, she thought, smiling, how big a favor. She wondered if she should ask Yuri's permission.

"Why did you cry?" he asked. "When you saw me, I mean."

"I had a bad day. Yesterday wasn't so hot either."

He nodded. He understood that much. Her sister's death, so terrible, and then the FBI, knowing who she is now, and even now going through all her sister's belongings, putting things in bags. He was glad that he could help her forget, if only for these past two hours.

He had read the message slips when she used the bathroom. Force of habit. One was from Mama's Boy telling her to stay, not to go out. The other was from her father. It gave the date and place of the church service for her sister. This seemed odd to Yuri. It was not a thing to be left written on a piece of paper in the hand of a stranger. It was a thing that a father ought to say to a daughter directly. And with kindness. Perhaps that, as much as anything, is what finally brought the tears.

"Yuri?"

"Yes?"

"What did you think of Susan?"

"Miss Lesko?"

"Yes."

"Colonel Belkin says she is very strong. Not strong like you are. But also soft."

"I'm not?"

"Your . . . skin is soft. Your touch is soft. At this moment, even your eyes. But you? No, you are not soft."

Carla said nothing. She waited, hoping that he would say more about her, what he liked about her. But Yuri did not realize that. He thought that the subject at hand was still Susan.

"In the beginning," he said, "Colonel Belkin thought that she would weaken Paul Bannerman, make him vulnerable. But now he says that she has made him more complete. I think this must be true. Last month, in Zürich, I met a young woman, a girl who . . ." Yuri realized his mistake. His hand stopped moving.

"It's okay." Carla poked him. "I won't be jealous."

"We are not . . . I mean, it's not that we have . . ."

"Yuri . . ."

He grinned, first sheepishly, then warmly. "Her name is Maria. I met her at the zoo. She had a little girl with her. The child was too small to see the bears so I put her on my shoulders. Maria thanked me. We walked together all that afternoon. It was a wonderful day for me. I think of it all the time."

Carla waited. "Well?" she prodded.

"I . . . investigated her. She is a cellist. My age. Quite a good family. She is widowed. Her husband was a reserve officer, Swiss Army. He died in a training accident. I went to see her perform. I sent flowers afterward. She called to thank me. We talked. She invited me to dinner at her parents' house but I did not go."

"Why not?"

"Because then I think, someday I will have to tell her I am KGB. I am afraid of what I might see in her eyes when I tell her this. And I will lose forever the way she has made me feel. But now, you talk of Susan Lesko. She did not run from Paul Bannerman when she learned about Mama's Boy. And it makes me think . . . perhaps Maria will not run from me."

"She might not. But Susan was already hooked on Paul Bannerman before she began to catch on. Take your time, Yuri. Don't tell her right away."

"Lying is bad. It is never forgotten."

"Paul didn't lie. He just left out a few things." Like fifteen years of his life. "Maria will leave out a few things, too. Mistakes. Old hurts. Old boyfriends. We all do that."

The Russian fell silent.

Carla turned to face him. She touched his cheek. She saw that his eyes were elsewhere. "Yuri . . . go for it," she said. "Stop moping."

"I was only . . ."

"Call her now. Tell Maria that you met Jane Fonda but all it did was make you miss her. Tell her you would like very much to meet her parents."

"Perhaps." The little boy smile returned. It became a blush. "Perhaps from my hotel I will . . ."

"Not later. Now. I'll give you some privacy." Carla rolled out of bed and picked up her bra from the floor. She would wait in the bathroom. She thought she needed to cry again anyway. She had a very large hunch that unless Maria blows him out of the water, she'd had her last good uncomplicated screw from Yuri Rykov.

The simple overseas call became a major production. Yuri decided that he certainly could not speak to Maria while naked, still damp with Carla, so he toweled himself off and dressed. Then, rehearsal time was needed and more coaching from Carla. What if she this? What if she that? Answers shouted through the bathroom door. At last, exasperated, Carla came back into the bedroom. She demanded Maria's number. She would dial it for him, ready or not, and hand him the phone.

The telephone rang as she was reaching for it.

She picked it up.

"Yes," she said, "this is Ms. Benedict. Who is this?"

Then she listened, her eyes widening, her mouth falling open, as a young male voice told her that he would never have hurt her sister. That she had always smiled at him.

21

Molly was thinking in circles and she knew it. The more she read of Lisa Benedict's files, the less motive she could find for anyone to want them destroyed. And none at all for murdering her.

Molly clung to the assumption that Lisa was the random victim of a serial killer. There was no reason to suppose otherwise. But there was still the phony detective and the equally bogus FBI agent, one of whom had almost certainly burglarized her apartment.

One thing that was clear, however, was that the situation involved potential danger. The phony detective had made a point of verifying Carla's name, and her own, and of finding out where they were staying. Weapons might possibly be needed. Just as possibly not. But better safe than sorry.

It was one in the afternoon when she placed her call to Anton Zivic's shop in Westport. Her intention was to ask that John Waldo fly out immediately to secure clean weapons, have them nearby, but stay out of sight as backup. All this would be communicated through the sentence, "I'm not having a nice time." The coded remark would also alert Anton that the phone she was using was not necessarily secure. He would answer, "Take the night off," or "Take tomorrow off," depending on when John Waldo could leave. He would ask no questions but he would expect her to brief him fully as soon as she could get to a phone she considered safe.

His response, however, was "Get off your feet. I will call you after you've rested." He broke the connection.

Molly stared at the phone, frowning. She understood the response and she didn't. Literally, it meant that she should get to her safe house because trouble is imminent. Because there was no safe house in this instance, she took it to mean the Beverly Hills Hotel. As for the trouble, she assumed that the FBI had identified her and Anton knew it. But that wasn't trouble. Only an annoyance.

Could there be trouble at the hotel? With Carla? Molly punched out the direct number to her bungalow. She heard a busy signal.

No, she decided. Anton would not have ordered her back to that hotel if he wasn't sure it was safe to go there. Carla was on the phone, probably talking to her father.

"Here's the scoop on Sur La Mer."

DiDi Fenerty, waving a yellow pad, entered the room where Molly still sat at the IBM console. DiDi pulled up a chair.

"Professor Mecklenberg, by the way, says he's going to graduate Lisa posthumously. I don't know whether it helps or hurts. But he says she's earned it and he wants to announce it at the graduation ceremony."

"I guess that's nice," Molly said, "but it should be the family's decision."

"He's going to ask." She riffled the pages of her pad. "There's a lot of stuff here. Also on Nellie Dameon and . . . there *was* a D'Arconte. First name, Victor. You probably can't read my writing."

Molly sneaked a look at her watch. When Anton says get off your feet, he means *now*. She was beginning to have bad feelings about Carla and what other trouble she might have got into. With DiDi waiting, she tried Carla one more time. Still busy. Then she called the hotel operator to confirm that the phone hadn't been left off the hook. It wasn't. A woman was using it. Molly decided that time was not critical.

Molly sat back. "What did you find out?" she asked.

She listened as DiDi read an oral history of the property, as a private estate and then as an institution. The institution was private although it technically fell under the supervision of the Motion Picture and Television Fund, formerly the Motion Picture Relief Fund, founded in 1921. Its patients, she said, were mostly loonies who were too far gone for the Motion Picture Country House. Originally, back in Nellie Dameon's day, many of them were actors and actresses who'd gone out of their head from drugs. DiDi gave the names of key medical and administrative officers, including three generations of Dunvilles.

Molly nodded frequently. She made few notes. The information DiDi had was pretty much what was shown in Lisa's files and in considerably less detail. No fault to DiDi. Lisa had been at this for months. Lisa had the names of fifty or more inmates—called members—dating back to 1926. It was not a very long list, given that length of time. Lisa, Molly assumed, had only listed actors. No production people or screen writers.

"Let's go on to Nellie Dameon," she said.

"One more thing." DiDi raised a finger. "If you care, I can get you a set of plans for Sur La Mer. I called my father. He's a developer. He said his Santa Barbara office can get them from the county clerk."

Molly's interest was slight. Her larger impression was that she now knew the source of DiDi's money. But because DiDi had taken the trouble . . . "Sure. Nice work. Can he messenger them, my attention, at the Beverly Hills?"

"No problem."

DiDi began on Nellie Dameon. Again, there was nothing new. Bad voice for sound. Career in ruins. Went over the edge. No record of children. The only jarring note was Lisa's observation that Nellie Dameon's voice was perfectly normal. But it meant nothing, necessarily. Maybe, as they'd discussed, she was sabotaged. Or maybe, over sixty years, she'd learned to enunciate. Molly listened with forced patience.

"Victor D'Arconte is an interesting character," DiDi said, flipping to another page. "Also a sleaze."

She began reading.

"According to Mecklenberg, Victor D'Arconte was an actor on the Sennett lot. Pretty well known but never a star. They called him "The Count" because he claimed he was the third son of some Italian prince or other. He made a few pictures over there. Also claimed to have been an aviator during World War One, said he shot down several Turkish planes before being shot in the hip by ground fire. Left him with a limp. Probably limited the roles he could take."

Molly nodded, not in agreement but trusting that this was somehow relevant.

"The story is," DiDi went on, "he showed up in Hollywood around 1920. A whole slew of Italian actors, directors, and technicians came here at about that time because the Italian film industry was collapsing. Everyone wanted American pictures, which was actually ironic."

"Um . . . why?"

Molly regretted the question almost instantly. She had blundered onto a theme that was DiDi Fenerty's passion.

"The Italians were the real pioneers," she proclaimed. "Not Hollywood. They *invented* the costume epic. Used enormous sets, thousands of extras. Used real lions in *Quo Vadis*, 1912. They made *El Cid*, *Macbeth*, and *The Last Days of Pompeii* while we were doing the Keystone Kops. They had a tremendous influence on DeMille and Griffith. If you want to be astonished, see *Cabiria*. Greatest film ever made up to that point. It had Hannibal's elephants crossing the Alps, the siege of Syracuse—"

"DiDi . . ." Molly raised a hand.

"Oh. Sorry."

"You said Victor D'Arconte was a sleaze."

"Oh, yeah," she nodded. "Big time. The Count was a drug pusher. People don't realize it but heroin and especially cocaine were just as common in early Hollywood as they are now. One story says that D'Arconte was already a morphine addict because of the hip and started dealing to support his own habit but Mecklenberg says he never touched it. Says he just saw more money in dealing than he did in acting."

DiDi flipped a page. "D'Arconte," she said, reading, "used to fly the cocaine in from Mexico himself. Heroin came from the Chinese but he had a piece of that action too. He used to deal in broad daylight on the corner of Fourth and Spring. The police never bothered him because they thought he provided a service. Kept the stars going, working twelve-hour days. Mecklenberg says you could stand on that corner and see half of the biggest names in Hollywood."

Molly was afraid she'd name them. "What happened to him?" she asked.

"Someone tried to shoot him. Once on his corner and once in his car. The police couldn't ignore it anymore so he was busted, and indicted. He dropped out of sight in 1930, maybe back to Italy. But in those ten years he ruined more lives than talkies. There was . . ."

Molly blinked so that her eyes would not glaze.

". . . Wallace Reid, Alma Rubens, Barbara La Marr. Big stars. His junk killed all three. La Marr was only twenty-nine. Reid died in a padded cell at thirty. It ended the careers of about a dozen more. Mabel Normand, Juanita Hansen . . ."

"Nellie Dameon?"

DiDi shook her head. "If she did drugs, I never heard it."

And yet, according to Lisa's notes, thought Molly, Nellie had mentioned his name. "Would she have known him otherwise?"

"Of him, at least. Sure."

"This man who died in a padded cell . . ."

"Wallace Reid."

"Might that have been at Sur La Mer?"

"I don't know. Maybe."

"You said Victor D'Arconte skipped in 1930. How old would he have been?"

DiDi looked at her notes. A flier in World War I. A working actor before that. "Around forty, I guess. What are you thinking?"

Molly took a long breath. "I don't know. Just fishing. Looking for a way that this might all tie together."

"As in Victor hiding out at Sur La Mer?"

"Something like that."

DiDi made a face. It suggested not so much doubt as indifference. "It's an interesting thought. But if he did, who would care now? The guy's got to be long dead."

Molly chewed her pencil, thoughtfully. "Let's play with that for a minute. How would he swing it?"

"Get some doctor to commit him, I guess. Say the doctor was a junkie. One of his customers."

"Doctors don't need dealers."

"They don't need to have their addictions made public, either. He could have blackmailed one."

"Okay," Molly nodded. "But how long could he have fooled the staff at Sur La Mer?"

A small shrug. "He was an actor. Maybe a good one."

"Fine. And, given the indictment, he would have changed his name. But the place was full of other actors, including Nellie Dameon. Wouldn't they have recognized him?"

"Nellie wasn't talking. The others were batty, or at least past caring. Which brings me back to my question. Who would care now?"

Molly sighed.

More circles.

DiDi, she felt sure, was almost certainly right. Let's say, she thought, that Victor D'Arconte did hide out at Sur La Mer. Let's say he bribed or blackmailed whoever was running the place. Let's even say he took the name *Dunville*.

Wait. Where did that come from?

Oh, yes. According to Lisa's notes, Nellie Dameon thought she had a son, last name possibly D'Arconte or possibly Dunville.

Okay. Let's say that she's not entirely crazy. Let's say that she had a son—not to mention a daughter with a strawberry mark and hair like Lisa's—and that the father was the drug-dealing actor D'Arconte.

Let's say all that's true, keeping in mind there's no sign that Lisa suspected any such thing. What have you got?

An interesting footnote to Hollywood history. That's all. Of interest solely to people like DiDi and her professor. No real scandal. No reputations to be ruined because all of the principals, except Nellie, are long dead. The kids, if they exist, would be in their sixties. If they're not at Sur La Mer, which they're obviously not if Nellie asked Lisa to find them, they were probably given up for adoption and would have no idea who their real parents were. And might not care.

Circles.

"I'd better get going," she said. "Carla really shouldn't be alone."

"Anything else I can do?"

Molly shook her head. She began erasing the copied files. "Just remember what I said about staying out of this. I took these disks. You have no idea what's on them. But let me know who asks."

"Will I see you again?"

"Sure. On Thursday. I assume you'll be there."

DiDi nodded. "Mr. Benedict asked me to speak. Molly?"

"Uh-huh?" The last of the files winked off.

"Why don't you just drive up to Sur La Mer? Ask them straight out."

"I might just do that."

With Molly gone, the house seemed suddenly empty. The computer even more so. One minute it had

Lisa in it—her words, her thoughts and dreams. The next it was blank.

DiDi wished she had been more help. It was hard to imagine Molly Farrell, no matter how good she was, going out and finding a killer that an army of police had been hunting for the better part of two years. But at least she might find the son of a bitch who robbed her afterward.

Maybe, thought DiDi, she'd do a little detective work herself. Make a call or two. Save Molly the trip.

The phone was right there.

She dialed Santa Barbara information.

22

"Wait. Don't hang up."

Sumner Dommerich heard the shouted plea from Lisa's sister as he lowered the phone. He hesitated.

"There's no way I can trace this," she called. "There's no risk to you."

He knew that. He was at a public phone on Victory Boulevard in Burbank. At an Exxon station. He didn't mind talking to her but there was always the chance that the man who had pissed on his car and slapped him would go out again. He had gone into a small mission-style apartment building just across the street. It had to be where he lived. He had taken mail from a box as he entered. The man, Hickey, had stopped just in time. Dommerich's gas gauge had hovered on empty most of the way back from Santa Barbara.

"I . . . don't know what else I can tell you," he said, returning the phone to his lips. He had told her he didn't do it. That Lisa had been nice to him. He had told her about the man in the silver Honda who had been following her and taking her picture with a video camera. He had given her his license number but not his name. Tracing the license would take time. Dommerich needed that time to decide how best to make him pay.

"I don't know either," Lisa's sister was saying. "But you must know something. You can help me find out who did it."

"I just know it wasn't me."

"You said you were her friend. I need a friend too."

Dommerich shook his head. He hadn't said that, exactly. All he said was that he liked Lisa and she liked him. Or at least she smiled at him. The one thing he hardly ever did was lie. Except for today. Today he had called in sick at work because he had to follow that man. They didn't even care that much.

"Did you read the papers?" he asked.

"You mean about Lisa?"

"About me. Almost none of what they said about me was right."

Dommerich could hear a change in the rhythm of her breathing. He heard, or sensed, movement on the other end. Probably the other woman. The tall one.

"Listen . . . Wait. My name is Carla. Give me something to call you."

He knew what she was doing. He saw on television once that serial killers mostly think of their victims as *things*. Not real people. It's the same with rapists. So if you're going to be raped or killed you should try to talk to the guy, tell him your name, try to tell him about any good things you do and try to get him talking about himself. They were wrong about that too. Once it started, he never even heard what they were saying. He'd hear a voice. A mean and hateful voice. But it wasn't theirs.

"How about Claude." Dommerich suggested. It had just popped into his head. Claude Rains. The Invisible Man. He had to smile.

"Claude, could you give me some kind of proof?" she asked.

"About what?"

"That you're really who you say you are. That this isn't some sick practical joke. Or that you're not just trying to blame someone else for what you did."

He thought about hanging up again. This one was not as nice as her sister. "I never once tried to blame someone else," he told her. "I always did it so they knew it was me."

"Did you always rob them?"

"I never robbed them," he said. The question offended him. The other thing he hardly ever did was steal.

"Someone robbed Lisa. There were things missing from her apartment."

"I didn't take them. All I ever took was hair."

A silence. Dommerich understood it. Lisa's sister didn't know he did that. It was never in the papers.

"You know who I bet did?" he asked.

"Who?"

"The man who was following you."

"Why do you think so?"

"I don't know. Because he's a pig." Dommerich was tempted to tell her about him urinating on his car. And smacking him with fingers that had piss on them. But the operator came on wanting another quarter. Lisa's sister said don't go. Please. He found one. It gonged and the line sounded clear again.

"I'm still here. But I do have to go."

"Claude . . . that man. Did you ever see him near her apartment before?"

"No." Dommerich chewed his lip. He had to be careful here, even if it meant telling a lie. "But I don't live around there."

"Does he?"

"No. But he was watching the place this morning. And then he was watching you. Maybe he was watching Lisa before that."

"Claude . . ." Her voice changed. It got very quiet. "Where is he right this minute?"

He didn't answer.

"You know where he lives, don't you, Claude. You're near there right now."

"No, I'm . . . hold on a minute." He held the telephone against his chest. He covered the mouthpiece. She was smart, he realized. She knew he'd been following that man. And she'd heard him say that the man didn't live near Lisa. He could only know that if . . . "I have to go." he said.

"Claude . . ." The same quiet voice. "He might be the one. He might have killed Lisa."

Dommerich took a breath. It made a whistling sound.

"Claude? Do you hear me? You liked Lisa and that man might have killed her. Tell me who he is and I promise you I'll make him talk. I'll carve the fucker up in ways you never dreamed of."

"I . . . have to go."

"Claude? Don't hang up. You owe it to . . ."

He missed the cradle twice, finally using his hand to break the connection. He saw Lisa in his mind. She was jogging toward him, up Alameda, carrying her breakfast muffin. He waved at her. Said hi. She waved back. Big smile. He watched her go. She had almost reached the wooden stairs to her apartment when something made her stop and look up. That man, Hickey, was coming down. He was carrying her television set and her cable box. Stealing them.

She looked around for help. She yelled. He dropped the television and grabbed her. He began choking her. Dommerich wanted to help but he couldn't. There was a glass wall, the wall of the phone booth, between them. She was on the sidewalk now, not moving. Hickey looked up. He saw Dommerich. He raised a hand as if to smack him again but there was the glass wall. Seeing Dommerich seemed to give him an idea. He pulled out a knife and bent over Lisa. He stuck one thumb in the corner of her mouth, pulling her cheek up. Then he stuck the knife under his thumb and he . . .

Dommerich screamed.

He screamed and he banged until the man from the gas pumps came, wide-eyed, and forced open the door. Dommerich ran to his car. He drove away. He drove almost a mile before the voice could be heard through the screams in his head. It was a mean voice. Hateful. But, as always, it began to calm him.

Dommerich slowed and stopped. His heart slowed as well. He saw his hat in the well of the passenger seat. He put it on.

He was all right now.

He was invisible again.

Dommerich drove back the way he came.

Nellie had returned in time for tea.

Barbara Weinberg, more than her husband, had become accustomed to Nellie's journeys into the past. She delighted in the stories Nellie would tell.

But it was different this time. Nellie had not gone to a party or a picnic, she had not gone camping with Tom, she had not gone dancing on the Venice pier. She had tried, this time, to go back to that part of her life that remained in shadows.

She told Barbara about her children. Two of them. Perhaps four. She told her what the psychiatrist had said. That she'd had only one, born dead. Still, she said, it was all very odd. There were other young members, over the years, who felt as she did. That they'd had children. The doctor's answer was always the same. These were dreams. Delusions. Not at all uncommon.

One of those members, she recalled, then asked the psychiatrist how it was that she had stretch marks on her breasts and on her belly. Then the doctor would admit, reluctantly, that another member, long deceased, had taken advantage of her. How very convenient, thought Nellie. Whenever pressed, the doctor always seemed able to produce a randy male patient who subsequently died but whom no one else seemed to remember.

She asked Barbara's help in learning the truth. Barbara promised it, but asked for patience. She could not very well ask Carleton Dunville. Doing so would reveal that Nellie was lucid. Perhaps, thought Barbara, she might get another chance at that office safe. She had seen that it contained records concerning the members but these had not interested her at the time.

Tea was served in a common room just down the hall from Nellie's suite. It was a formal affair, elegantly poured from a silver service into Wedgwood china cups. Cakes and scones were provided on Limoges platters with real Devonshire cream on the side. Alan saw little likelihood that the tea or the cakes had been drugged but, still, he and Barbara had chosen to partake of all meals on an alternate basis so that one might have a chance of remaining alert.

All of the members had gathered. A staff nurse, dressed as a maid for the occasion, served those unable to serve themselves. There were five men, the rest women, none under seventy. All wore glazed expressions. None seemed to notice the MP-5 submachine gun that Alan Weinberg held across his chest as his wife and Nellie sipped their tea. But the eyes, Barbara knew, would come alive when the nurse left the room. They would exchange smiles. They would whisper. The old man, Harland, would tip his yachting cap to Nellie and to Barbara in turn. But the nurse, this time, did not leave. She approached Alan, forcing a nervous smile. Nellie blinked away.

"There's nothing in the tea," she told him. "Mr. Dunville said you have his word on it."

Weinberg waited, saying nothing. He was aware of the uses of his bandaged face, only one eye showing. But the nurse did not look away or lower her eyes.

"It's true," she said. "I'd know it. And if anyone wanted to put you to sleep, we could have done it through your air-conditioner."

Weinberg understood that. He'd sealed it and the windows two days before. But he nodded, slowly.

"You're a real nurse?" he asked.

"An RN. Yes."

"What else are you?"

She hesitated. She did not answer. "Mr. Dunville . . . senior . . . would like to talk to you in private. He wants to end this."

"Where is he now?"

"Across the hall. In the office."

He glanced at Barbara's cup. She drained it, nodding. "Five minutes," he said. "Miss Dameon's suite."

They returned, with Nellie, to her rooms. She moved slowly, her eyes blank. Barbara asked her if she was there, pretending, or had she gone away again. She did not answer. Barbara steered her to her high-backed chair, then stepped into the corridor where she covered her husband's back as he trained his weapon on the double doors through which Carleton Dunville would come.

Dunville the elder opened them, wide, as if to show that no guards were lurking behind him. He stood there, holding his jacket open as well to show that he was unarmed. In one hand he held a cassette tape and what appeared to be a Polaroid snapshot. Weinberg waved him forward. Dunville closed the doors. He walked the thirty yards to Nellie's suite and entered it. He paused before Nellie's chair and looked into her eyes. She gave no sign that she knew he was there.

Dunville offered the snapshot to Weinberg. He examined it, then handed it to his wife who backed into the room and closed the door behind her. There seemed little point in covering the hall while Carleton Dunville was with them. Barbara looked at the snapshot. It was of a human head, eyes bandaged, blood soaked, badly misshapen. The rear right quadrant of the skull had been shot away. Still, she recognized Henry Dunville.

"Who did it?" she asked.

"I did."

"Why?"

"Because he deserved it," the elder Dunville answered. "And because I need you to know that he is no longer an issue between us."

"What is? Aside from the files."

Dunville shook his head, ruefully. "You needn't have taken them, you know. Young Carleton told the truth. You would not have been punished for what you did to Henry."

"You'll understand," Weinberg said, "why I chose not to bet out lives on that."

"Of course. Will you assure me that no eyes but yours have seen them?"

"No."

"Ah, yes. Your mystery assassin holds them in safekeeping."

Weinberg saw the doubt. It did not matter. "Mr. Dunville, let us save time. You have people out looking for the machine. If they found it, they are now as dead as poor Henry."

Dunville tried to study him, uselessly. "Will you return them?"

"No."

"Then how can I let you leave here?"

Weinberg glanced down at his MP-5, wondering if it had suddenly turned into a banana. He chose not to make an issue of it. "As I told your son," he said, "if there's no harm to me, there is none to you. If you kill us, those papers will be used because I will not be there to prevent it. Your son and Ruiz will die in the bargain."

"And if I let you go?"

"I will be Alan Weinberg. I will abide by our contract. The files will be safe while I live."

Dunville nodded slowly. He looked away lest Weinberg read his thoughts. Kill them both, he was thinking, and he would know, certainly within a week or two, whether that fax machine business was an elaborate bluff. Let them live and he might never know. And someday, weeks or years hence, the Weinbergs might die of other means. What then of the files? He did not relish living another thirty years with that over his head. Two weeks of doubt against a lifetime of it. His peace of mind seemed worth the risk.

Dunville, aware of that one eye trying to probe his brain, noticed the copy of the *Los Angeles Times*. He wondered how it came here. He picked it up. It was folded open to the page showing photographs of six young women.

"This was not as tidy as it might have been," he said. "There is a more immediate issue. One of containment."

One hand still held the videocassette he had brought. He leaned toward the actress, showing it. "Nellie? May I use your screen?" he asked. Her dead eyes stared ahead, unblinking.

Satisfied, he set the newspaper down and crossed to Nellie's player. He took out a movie and inserted the cassette. He turned once more to Weinberg.

"If you've healed properly," he said, "you can be out of here in a few days. But we have four Taiwanese arriving next week by way of Canada. Two Iranians are scheduled the week after that. All are illegals. They will pay fees, Mr. Weinberg, that will make yours seem a bargain. I cannot afford to have the police poking about while they're here."

"Why should they be?"

Dunville, cocking his head toward the newspaper, explained about Hickey. Hickey, he said, had done well on the whole but he had left a trail that might conceivably lead back to Sur La Mer. In addition, he had as much as threatened blackmail. He would have to go. Measures were already being taken.

Weinberg caught a glint of satisfaction in his wife's eye. She would gladly have seen to Hickey herself. Gratis. Still, he wondered why Dunville was telling him all this.

"He began leaving the trail this morning," Dunville told him. "Two women showed up at the girl's apartment, followed, in quick succession, by the FBI and the police. Hickey was there as well. Apparently, he was seen."

Dunville pressed the "play" button.

"There was a confrontation between the two women and the FBI agents. Why, I don't know. They had every right to be there. The smaller one is the girl's sister. Here you see the two women being led away . . . one of them struggling. Hickey will follow them to the residence of another student who . . ."

"Barbara," Weinberg interrupted. "Please watch the door."

She looked at him, puzzled.

"Please," he repeated.

She obeyed. She opened it and scanned the corridor. There was no one.

"Sorry. Go on."

Weinberg, once again, was glad of his bandages. His face would surely have shown that he knew those two women.

Dunville continued his narrative. He described the stop at a convenience store, clearly in search of an address. "There. She's holding a page from a phone book. Obviously she found something in the apartment, which Hickey was suppose to have cleaned, leading her to a source of possible information."

Weinberg dared not look at his wife. He could only hope that she would not consider her job done and return to view this tape. Her bandages did not hide her face. As it was, he could see a light beginning to flicker in the eyes of Nellie Dameon.

"The taller one stayed at this house for some time," Dunville told him. "We must assume that they learned something. It also appears that these women are professionals of some sort." Dunville told him of Hickey's call to one of the policeman who had been at that apartment and of Hickey's lie, ultimately transparent, about representing the family of another victim. He told him of the father's comment that suggested that the sister was well known by, but not a friend of, the federal authorities. "I wondered," he said, "if she just might be an agent. And if so, might Axel Streicher have crossed her path over the years."

Weinberg shrugged. He shook his head. But his one eye was burning. He knew now why the girls' photograph in the newspaper had looked so familiar. That face. The red hair. The name, Benedict. All of that should have been enough. No, he had never seen Lisa Benedict before. But he had certainly seen the woman she resembled so closely. He had seen Carla Benedict. And the tall one with the gentle face was Molly Farrell.

"What could the friend know?" Weinberg asked. "The one they visited." He was grasping for a change of subject. He hoped that it did not show.

"She knows, or believes, that the girl was here. She knows, or believes, that she came to see Nellie." Dunville stared, searchingly, at the old woman. "She telephoned a short time ago, asking. My son took the call. He denied any knowledge of a visit. But the girl asked . . . other questions. She knows too much."

"Do you intend to kill her?"

Dunville did not answer.

"If so, who will do it?"

"We have friends. Not here. Outside."

Weinberg stepped to the machine. He turned it off. "How will it be done?" he asked.

"Efficiently."

Weinberg, in no mood for this, felt an urge to slap the smugness from the face of the older man. He restrained himself, although he took a step closer.

"Do what you wish about Hickey," he said through his teeth. "But if you harm the girl who called, where will it end? With the two women who came to see her? With her close friends? Her roommates?"

Dunville blinked. "There is a good deal at stake here. More than you know."

Weinberg reached for Dunville's lapel. Again, he stopped himself. "None of this was necessary," he said.

"No part of it. Is it possible that you're as stupid as Henry?"

An odd blandness appeared in Dunville's eyes. Weinberg thought that he had glimpsed it before. But now he was sure. He knew that look. He had seen it on the day when he knew that he must get out of Europe. Dunville was looking at him as if he were already dead.

But now there was something new. A look of surprise. The eyes had drifted. Weinberg followed them. They were looking at Nellie.

Weinberg turned his head. There was Nellie. She was looking up at him. Tears had begun to well. In her hands she held the newspaper that Dunville had left at her side. She had turned it to the grainy yearbook photo of Lisa Benedict. Next to it, on the page, was the photograph of a body, covered with plastic.

"Did they do this?" she whispered.

Dunville could only stare.

Weinberg lowered himself to one knee. He took the newspaper. He put it aside. "We didn't know either," he said gently. "Not until it was too late."

He felt Carleton Dunville edging toward the door. It didn't matter. Barbara would stop him.

"Nellie?" He took her hand. "I swear to you. We would have stopped it."

"All she wanted was . . ."

"I know. To see you."

"I thought at first . . ." She removed one hand from his and reached to the newspaper. She touched Lisa Benedict's cheek as Weinberg had done. "I thought she might have been my daughter."

Carleton Dunville had reached the door. But now he was backing up. "Give me that one," said Barbara Weinberg. She took the sound-surpressed MP-5 from her husband's free hand and replaced it with her Ingram. Arms outstretched, she aimed the MP-5 at Dunville's face. "One move, one sound, you're dead." She mouthed the words.

"Nellie," Weinberg said, rising, "we have to leave

Sur La Mer. We would very much like you to come with us."

She looked at Carleton Dunville. "Make him . . ." She bit her lip.

"He'll come too. He'll get us out."

"Make him tell me where my children are."

"We'll need some things," said Barbara, backing Dunville to a wall. "Money. Medical supplies. Our files."

"Nellie? We're all going to walk down and visit young Carleton. We'll ask him. We'll see what else he has in his safe."

Joseph Hickey was on the toilet when his doorbell rang.

"Yeah?" he shouted. "Who's there?"

"Pizza," came the muffled answer.

"What?"

"Your pizza order. Mushroom and anchovy, large."

"I didn't order no pizza."

A short pause. "Apartment two-A?"

"Yeah but . . . it wasn't me."

A longer pause. The bell rang again.

"Did you hear me? It's not mine."

"You get three dollars off," called the voice through the door. "And you get a coupon."

"Look." Hickey began wiping himself. "I don't want your coupon and I didn't order your fucking pizza."

Another silence. The bell sounded.

"Jesus Chr—!" Hickey ground his teeth. "I come out there," he bellowed, "I'm gonna shove it up your ass."

"What?"

"I said . . ." Christ!

Hickey stood up. He flushed the bowl. The bell rang again. Hickey buckled his belt and stepped into his living room. He glanced out his window. There was the delivery car, parked at the curb. A dim signal tried to push through his anger. It was enough, just barely, to make him want to look through his peephole. He put his eye to it. Some kid in a windbreaker. Homely. Stupid face. Dumb little pizza hat. And he was reaching toward the bell again. Hickey flipped the chain. He jerked the door open.

"Two-A, right?" The kid looked up at him. "Pepperoni and sausage."

The blandness, the passivity of the young man's expression made him hesitate. Maybe the Special Olympics was going door to door.

"Less three dollars is six ninety-five," said Sumner Todd Dommerich. "And you get a coupon." He held a square insulated sleeve for keeping pizzas hot, one hand at its edge, the other beneath it.

"Kid . . . do you understand fucking English?" Hickey reached for the box, intending to throw it down the stairs and young man after it. Hickey seized it. He felt its weight. It seemed light. The signal came again, stronger this time. Something about this kid.

He belched.

For an instant, it felt like heartburn.

He blinked.

The pain stabbed at him again. He felt his legs go weak. His fingers became rubbery. He began losing his grip of the thermal sleeve. The pizza kid took command of it.

Hickey had no sense of what was happening. The kid's expression had not changed. Now he was offering the pizza again, pushing it to his chest, forcing him back from the door. Hickey staggered, turning. He grabbed the top of a chair to keep from falling.

Dommerich stepped in behind him. He now held the sleeve in one hand. A long thin knife was in the other. He thought of stabbing Hickey again. Perhaps in the kidneys where it would paralyze but it would not kill too quickly. It did not seem necessary.

There were Velcro fasteners on opposing ends of the insulated sleeve. Quickly, Dommerich opened them. He gripped the cardboard inner box and slid it out. He tossed it to one side.

Hickey saw it fall. It opened, partially, on impact. It was empty. His mind was fixed on that, and what it could mean, when he felt something soft and padded being pulled down over his head and shoulders. It was like a straightjacket. He raised one hand, feebly, to try to stop it. He was too late but the palm of that hand now touched his chest. It felt warm and wet. It was bubbling. Something hit his knees from behind. One, then the other. Bending them. He felt himself being jerked backward, falling. The chair came with him. Someone was catching him. Easing him to the floor.

Sumner Dommerich walked to the door. He listened there, and closed it. He examined his knife. It was a good one. A subhilt fighter with a dagger blade and a skull-crusher butt. He had ordered it from a catalog. There was very little blood on it. None on his hand. The thermal sleeve was another matter but that would clean easily. From his pocket he took a fresh packet of Kleenex. He broke the seal and pulled one sheet. He used it to clean the knife. He pulled all the rest and gathered them into a ball. With these, he walked to the fallen man and eased himself down across his chest. Hickey was gasping. Sumner Dommerich forced the ball of Kleenex between his teeth.

Dommerich felt the pulse at Hickey's throat. It seemed uneven but he was sure that the man was not yet dying. Dommerich had been careful to miss his heart but he must have hit a lung. The man's chest made little farting sounds inside the sleeve.

"Do you remember me?" he asked.

Hickey's eyes bulged under the weight. They showed more confusion than fear. Dommerich understood that. He still did not know what had happened to him. Or maybe, thought Dommerich, he just could not believe it. That happened a lot.

"I know. Wait." Dommerich pushed to his feet. He opened his pants and took out his penis. He couldn't go at first. He waited, straining. At last a stream of urine came, aimed at Hickey's forehead. Hickey bucked and kicked. Dommerich was careful not to wet his pizza sleeve.

"Do you remember now? This morning. When you followed Lisa's sister to"—he patted his pocket, then found a page torn from a telephone book, the same as the one he had seen in the blue Chevrolet—"to a girl named Fenerty's house. You pissed on my car there. You slapped me."

Hickey's eyes showed that he remembered. He squirmed hard, arching his back. Dommerich saw that one eye looked crazy but the other was beginning lose focus. It was time to finish.

Dommerich sat down again on the bigger man's stomach. A dull bang, more of a *whoomp*, startled him. The man gasped and went rigid. Dommerich smelled cordite and he realized what had happened. The man, Hickey, had a gun in his belt. He'd managed to get his fingers on it. Tried to free it. Shot himself in the ass. Served him right, thought Dommerich. But that was too close.

Dommerich reached into the pocket of his windbreaker. He pulled out a black leather case and from it he took another knife, a skinning knife, smaller. He opened it. Dommerich pressed the butt of his left hand against Hickey's forehead and put his weight behind it. With his right, he inserted the blade between Hickey's lips. Hickey bucked again. Dommerich slid the curving blade to the corner of his mouth, waited for Hickey to exhale, then ripped. Hickey's left cheek opened to the midpoint of his ear.

Hickey took more air. He tried to scream. Dommerich held the Kleenex in place with the flat of his skinning knife. Again, he waited for Hickey to exhale. Hickey did. Then Dommerich did the other cheek.

Hickey arched his back. He hammered the floor with his heels. Dommerich thought of the people below. He made a shushing sound. He brought a finger to his lips and the skinning knife to Hickey's eye. Hickey gurgled. He tried to be still.

"Have you guessed who I am?" Dommerich asked him.

Hickey's eyes said yes. He made a mewing sound through his nose and his brain screamed that this could not be happening. There was no way this kid, this maniac, could know that it was him who . . .

"It's never been just women," Dommerich told him. That flat voice. No emotion. "And I wouldn't have hurt Lisa. Did you know she was my friend?"

Hickey blinked and gurgled. His eyes were wide. He tried to focus them but he could not.

"You cut her, didn't you. You cut her, just like this, and then you stole from her."

Hickey tried to shake his head. His cheeks flapped sickeningly when he moved them.

"Why?" Dommerich asked. "What did she ever do to you?"

It ended too quickly. One moment Dommerich saw pain and terror. In the next, Hickey's other eye drifted and his mind went with it.

Dommerich could see that. He asked the question again, his knife probing deep into Hickey's nose but there was no reaction. There would be no more answers. Dommerich almost wished he hadn't pissed on him. It was satisfying. But it just used up time.

It was funny, thought Dommerich. The man really did look like his father. At least he did now.

Dommerich would like to have known why the man killed Lisa. But maybe it was just as well he didn't. Sometimes you find out things and you're sorry you did. What if Lisa was his . . .

Uh-uh.

No way. Lisa and a slob like this? No way. He didn't even want any of his hair. It was too greasy. And pissed on.

But he'd like to have known what this man stole from her. Dommerich glanced around the room. There was a television set but he could see from where he was that it had many days accumulation of dust on it. Same with the VCR. No cable box. His dream in the phone booth was wrong. He could see nothing there that Lisa would even want.

A few more bubbles. One long fart. Then Hickey was quiet.

Dommerich got up. He stepped around to Hickey's head and began pulling at the insulated sleeve. He dragged the corpse half way across the room before the sleeve came lose. The gun tumbled out first. Dommerich left it there.

He took the sleeve into Hickey's bathroom—filthy tub—and held it under the shower. He dried it inside and out. He turned to the sink where he washed his two knives and, with cold water, sponged off the blood that had splattered his knees and his windbreaker. That done, he peeked inside Hickey's medicine cabinet. He had no reason for doing so. He always did it when he used people's bathrooms. He suspected that most other people did that, too.

There was a tape recorder on the top of Hickey's bedroom dresser. It looked like a good one. Also a Nikon camera. He pressed the "play" button of the tape machine but it was blank. He took a fresh Kleenex and wiped the button. Then he began wiping everything else he could remember touching.

Time to go. Just one more thing.

He crossed to Hickey's telephone and dialed the number of the Beverly Hills Hotel.

23

The Members Wing nurse was still in the common room, cleaning up after tea. Weinberg beckoned to her with the Ingram. Several members looked up. They saw Carleton Dunville, his face flushed, being held by his collar. Nellie stepped into the doorway. She held a finger to her lips. Several grinned excitedly. The man in the yachting costume turned his wheelchair toward them, following the nurse. Nellie held up a hand.

"Not now, Harland," she said. "I'll be back to say good-bye."

The nurse was too astonished to speak.

Dunville and the nurse preceded them into the main hall. Weinberg, his wife covering, disarmed the two guards. He herded all four into Carleton the younger's office.

"Now what?" said the younger Dunville, spreading his hands. The question was asked with more weariness than alarm.

"One minute," said Weinberg. He pointed the two guards toward Dunville's washroom and suggested they make themselves comfortable. He shut the door behind them, promising to shoot through it if he saw the knob turn.

Dunville looked questioningly at his father, who only glowered. Weinberg stepped to the desk. Using the back of an envelope, he began making a list. He finished, then showed it to his wife who added several items while he covered the Dunvilles and the nurse. Barbara handed the list to the nurse.

"We'll want all our personal effects and our medical

files. All of Nellie's clothing, her scrapbooks, and cassettes of all her films." She turned to Nellie. "Is there anything else?"

She shook her head. "That's nice. Thank you."

Now Carleton the younger blinked.

"Also a full medical kit," Barbara told the nurse. "Anything we might need to remove sutures and some fresh dressings. Pack them in suitcases and have them here in one hour. If you're ten minutes late you'll find a dead guard in the hall. Twenty minutes and you'll find one of the Dunvilles. Do you in any way doubt that?"

The nurse glanced at Carleton the elder.

"Do it," said the son.

She hurried from the room. Barbara Weinberg locked the door behind her.

"Why, for God's sake?" asked Carleton the younger.

"Because," Weinberg bit off the words, "your father is either a fool or he's crazy. He wants to kill at least five more people including the three of us."

Dunville stared. His surprise seemed genuine. "Who are the other two?" he asked.

"Your man Hickey. And a girl named Fenerty. Where is Ruiz, by the way?"

"She is . . . out of town."

"If out of town is Santa Fe, you can make that six."

Dunville looked at his father. "The Fenerty girl? Is that true?"

"It was . . . a consideration. She can embarrass us."

The son closed his eyes. He rubbed them. He turned to Weinberg. "Hickey, yes. It's necessary and you know it. I've made the arrangements. But nothing, I repeat, *nothing*, was to have been done about that girl who called here."

The elder Dunville bristled. "I will decide . . ."

"Father. Shut up."

Carleton the elder strode to his son's desk. He slapped him. Dunville seized his father. They grappled.

Barbara Weinberg caught her husband's eye. She

motioned him toward her. He seated Nellie, then approached.

"Um . . . when do you tell me what's going on here?" she asked quietly.

"What? The family squabble?"

She shook her head. "Back in Nellie's room. Are we throwing four hundred thousand dollars away just because Dunville heard Nellie talk?"

"He made up his mind to kill us. I could see it."

"But we knew he might." She raised the MP-5. "That's why we have these."

"I'm afraid there's more. You remember that tape he showed?"

"I wondered. You didn't want me to see it."

"Guess who Lisa Benedict's big sister is. I'll give you a hint. Think of Mama's Boy."

Her mouth fell open. "Benedict . . . *Carla* Benedict?"

"The woman she's with is your height, long dark hair, athletic, plays a strong game of tennis."

"Oh, shit."

"Exactly."

"Molly Farrell was with the Fenerty girl. Then Fenerty called here. Which means . . ."

". . . that they both know Lisa Benedict came to Sur La Mer the day she died. But that Sur La Mer denied it. What would you do if you were Carla?"

"I'd come myself. Pick out a Dunville, stick a gun up his nose and ask him again."

"Say she gets shot for it. What then?"

Barbara nodded slowly. "Bannerman comes in force."

"Do you want to be here?"

"No. But where will we go?"

Weinberg checked his watch. "We'll leave after dark. That gives us a few hours to think about it. Meanwhile, I want another look in that safe."

Barbara nudged him. "Fight's over." She lifted her chin toward the Dunvilles. Young Carleton had his father in a headlock. The father was slowly sinking to one knee.

"It's not the closest family I've ever seen." He remembered the Polaroid of Henry.

"They don't think we're such hot guests, either. Don't count on being asked back."

"I won't. We're going to hit them for a refund."

Barbara turned thoughtful. "Alan . . . Are you still Alan, by the way?"

"For the time being. What is it?"

"Before we leave, we should warn that girl."

"The one who called?"

"Either that," she said, "or leave these two dead."

Thirty thousand feet over Colorado, Bannerman returned to his seat after taking an in-flight call from Anton Zivic. He was still shaking his head as he settled in next to Susan Lesko.

"Is there a problem?" she asked.

He took a breath. "Would you believe Carla talked to the serial killer?"

"You're kidding."

"It seems that he called her to say he didn't kill Lisa. His name is Claude, incidentally." Bannerman stirred the ice in his scotch. He wished he'd asked for a double.

"Well?" She turned in her seat. "Let's hear it."

"That's it." He tossed his hands. "Anton finally got through to her. He told her she'd been identified and that she should stay in her bungalow until we can arrange to stash her someplace else. Carla told him to stay off her phone because Claude might call her back and because she thinks she might have a line on the real killer. Anton insisted that she stay put. She hung up on him."

"She's been out there one day. How could she . . ." Susan stopped herself. Nothing about Carla should surprise her any more. "Isn't Molly with her?"

"Apparently not. She checked in with Anton an hour ago. He told her the same thing but she wasn't at the hotel. However, Yuri Rykov is. Belkin sent him right over when I called."

"I'd feel better if it was Colonel Belkin."

Bannerman shrugged. "Yuri's young but he's good. I don't think he'll let Carla do anything crazy. Certainly not without checking in with Leo."

He sipped his scotch. He hoped he sounded more sure than he was.

"Anyway, John Waldo's out there." Susan tried to ease his mind. "And we'll be down in an hour."

"He's out there somewhere," Paul answered. "But he's backing us up, not Carla. He's probably on his way to the airport right now."

She felt a tingle of satisfaction when he said *us*. She knew that he meant her, too. Not just himself and Billy.

Billy McHugh was in the back, flying coach. He didn't like first class, Paul had told her. He thinks it makes him stand out. He prefers to blend in. Susan believed that, more or less, until two hours into the flight when she decided she'd go back and visit him. Paul asked her not to. She wanted to know why. He was forced to tell her that Billy was afraid of flying. He always took an aisle seat, last row, where not so many people could see his white knuckles, and near the lavatory in case he felt faint.

It was hard to believe. Mama's Boy's monster, afraid to fly. This was the man who once made it out of Iran on foot, doing more damage along the way than Iraqi mines. She asked Paul what caused it, presuming that it must have been something horrendous that had happened to him. Something claustrophobic. Like being buried alive, with snakes, in some Third World dungeon. He said no. He's just afraid to fly.

"Oh." Bannerman remembered Anton's other message. "Your father's on his way. With Elena. They'll get in after midnight. He's going to just love hearing about Claude."

"How do you know he's not some crank? Claude, I mean."

Bannerman considered it. He shook his head. "Carla would have been the first to think so," he said. "He must have offered proof."

"Either way, how did he know Carla? How did he know where she was staying?"

Bannerman stared ahead. "Keep going," he said.

"The answer is he spotted her someplace, then followed her. He could have been watching her father's house last night but remember it was dark. More likely this morning at her sister's apartment."

"Why would he have gone to either place?"

"Curiosity," she guessed. "Compulsion. If a copycat killed Lisa, maybe he's angry about it. He wants people to know."

Bannerman rubbed his chin. "He wanted Carla to know. But again, how did he recognize her as Lisa's sister?"

"Wouldn't most people? You said they could almost be twins."

"Except they'd have to know what Lisa looked like first. When would Glaude have seen her?"

"In the newspapers, I suppose. But I think he knew her."

"Intuition?"

She made a face. "No. You just said it. He wanted Carla to know. To me, that suggests a relationship. Otherwise, all he had to do was call any reporter."

Bannerman nodded. He remembered what Lesko had said about the first of the serial killer's six victims being from Lisa's neighborhood. And that it's a pattern. The first one tends to be close to home, someone he knows, usually an act of impulse. After that the murders become more deliberate and the killer avoids soiling his own nest.

"That's very good," he said. "Nice going."

She knew that he meant it. She appreciated it. But she saw his eyes cloud over as if to say, that's interesting, but I don't really care about him, or his six other victims, except to the extent that he endangers Carla. Or her. Or any of his people. Mama's Boy takes care of his own.

"We might have a shot at catching him," she said.

"That's not why we're here, Susan."

See?

Bannerman sipped his drink. He put it down. "But why do you say that?"

Ah. Good. "This relationship," she said. "It sounds like it's now with Carla."

His expression showed doubt. "All he did was call her. He's not likely to let her get close to him."

"He followed her. He might do it again."

"He might."

"You could have Billy or John watching for him. Or me."

"Don't even think it."

"Or my father."

A vague shake of the head.

"Why not?" she asked.

"Huh? Oh." He waved a hand as if to show that he'd been thinking of something else. "Your father would be fine," he said.

Which, Susan knew, was a lie. She could see that he was intrigued by the idea. He wouldn't mind catching Claude. If the opportunity offered itself. If it could be done cleanly and quietly. Lots of *ifs*. But he would never use her father to do it because her father would . . . *might* . . . want to hand him to the police. Paul would never do that. Claude, if that's his name, would simply be found somewhere, maybe with a note in his mouth.

Mama's Boy doesn't do courts.

"It's me again."

Carla had been out the door, Yuri ahead of her, when the telephone rang and she rushed back to snatch it. The same voice, now oddly flat.

"Thank you," she said, waving Yuri back in. "Thank you for calling back." She mouthed Claude's name to the Russian.

"I didn't mean to hang up on you. I was getting upset."

"I know. I was upset, too. I'm sorry."

"That man who was following you? What stuff did he steal from Lisa?"

"Um . . . could I ask why you want to know, Claude?"

"I'm where he lives. I could see if it's here."

Carla's eyes widened. She fished a piece of notepaper from her pocket and held it up for Yuri to see. It showed an address in Burbank, written in the hand of the hotel manager. Yuri understood. He mimed a suggestion. Carla would keep this man on the phone. He would drive there. Carla tossed him her keys. Yuri tossed them back. He showed his own and left.

"Claude? Let's see. I'm thinking." She steadied her voice. "He took her college notebooks, her address book, her calendar . . ."

"How about a camera?"

"Yes. She had a Nikon Autofocus with a zoom lens. The strap is blue. Embroidered."

"That's here. There's a good tape recorder next to it."

"A Marantz?"

"I don't . . . oh, yeah. Marantz."

"Son of a bitch. Not you, Claude."

"I know. I told you it wasn't me."

"Claude what about the notebooks and things?"

"Hold on a second." She heard the phone touch a wooden surface, followed by a stillness and then the sounds of papers. Several drawers opened and closed. "No." His voice came back on. "He's got things like that but they're his. How about jewelry? He's got chains and bracelets here."

"Is there a chain with a real gold bar on it from a Swiss bank?"

"It says Credit Suisse. Is that it?"

"Yes." Carla took a breath. It stuttered. Dommerich thought he heard a sob.

"I could take Lisa's things if you want. I could leave them for you someplace. If I leave them for when the police come they'll probably keep them for a long time."

"The police? You're not going to call them, are you?"

"No. But they'll come. He'll start to smell."

"Claude . . . who will smell?"

"Joseph Hickey. I . . . got even for Lisa. And for you."

Carla closed her eyes. "Do you mean he's there, Claude? Right now?"

"He's here. He's dead."

"Look, Claude . . ." *Molly*, she thought, *will never understand this.* "I want you to do two things. Take her jewelry and get out fast. Right now. There's someone coming there. He's my friend but so are you. I don't want him to find you there."

A long pause. "Were you trying to catch me, Carla?"

"I wanted Hickey. Not you. Get out of there, Claude."

"Okay."

"Call me tomorrow about the jewelry. Tomorrow morning. Will you do that, Claude?"

"I guess."

She looked at her watch. "Claude?"

"That's not really my name."

"I know. But thank you. Now go."

Carla broke the connection. She looked up to see Molly Farrell standing in the doorway.

24

For the second time in two days, Barbara Weinberg covered the tall arched windows of Carleton Dunville's office. She had spotted four guards thus far, all armed with assault rifles and in varying degrees of concealment. There would be others at the main gate.

She was not greatly concerned. She had even considered releasing the two guards now held in the lavatory, if only to make that facility more accessible to the five who remained.

There would be no attempt to storm the office while both Dunvilles were there. The guards would wait for them to leave. They would probably try for two head shots as they approached one of the Dunville Mercedes. Until, that is, they saw Carleton the elder walking between them with the barrel of the Ingram in his mouth.

Her one disquieting thought was that Carleton the younger might, if left behind, order them to go ahead and shoot unless his relationship with his father improved markedly between now and then. They'd better bring both of them.

Her husband sat at Dunville's desk, sipping a cognac from a bottle he'd found in one of the drawers. He was studying the files. With greater care this time. As he finished each set he placed them in Carleton the younger's briefcase, the contents of which he had also studied and, for the most part, discarded. One item in the briefcase was a small cardboard wallet containing the key to a safety deposit box. He fingered it, curious as to the box's contents. No use asking, he supposed. And the key did him no good. He left it on the desk.

Weinberg had already packed the cash from the safe. It amounted to almost $40,000. Hardly a full refund. Barely ten cents on the dollar. But it would do until they could safely gain access to their own money.

He had tried, earlier, to send another message by fax. Carleton the younger had replaced the broken machine. The fax did not go through. He stared at the machine for a moment, then shrugged. Although he did not seem greatly troubled by its failure to send, Barbara knew what it probably meant. The machine in Santa Fe must have been found, probably destroyed, Ruiz—or whoever—along with it. He returned to Carleton's desk.

Two more hours until dark.

She understood her husband's desire to wait. Darkness makes escape easier and pursuit more difficult, but that was not the half of it. He did not want to ride around looking like a mummy in broad daylight. People would notice. He might frighten children. Nor did he want to remove his bandages in the presence of either Dunville because he preferred not to show them his new face. That was why, she realized, he'd asked for their medical files. They included *before* photographs and computer renderings of what they'd look like *after*. The renderings could probably be reconstructed from memory but, if so, there was at least a good chance that they would fall short of the real thing.

She glanced over to check on Nellie. The actress was seated in the far corner, out of the way of any possible crossfire or shattered glass. Barbara had half-expected her to wander off as was her habit when in the presence of staff. But she hadn't. She sat glaring at Carleton the elder. When her eyes did glaze over from time to time, Barbara imagined that she was seeing the face of young Lisa Benedict.

Both of the Dunvilles seemed to find her presence unsettling in the extreme. She wasn't sure why. Perhaps they were searching their minds for any remarks made within her hearing over the years. Or any deeds done within her sight.

The younger Dunville had tried to negotiate. He offered his word, his personal guarantee, that none of them would be harmed. He acknowledged that all of this had been the fault of his half-brother and now his father. He would do anything within reason to make amends provided that no further damage were done. He even pointed out the ludicrousness of two swollen-faced fugitives and a ninety-some-year-old movie queen in a stolen car hoping that they would not attract attention.

Barbara had to agree. And she tended to believe him. So did her husband. Young Carleton might even have been able to back up the guarantee because it was clear that a palace coup had taken place before their eyes. Several times now, he had angrily ordered his father to shut up, once threatening to shoot him himself. The father, for his part, could not get over the fact that his son had, once again, left those files in an office safe that, by now, might as well have been a box of chocolates for all that it deterred Barbara Weinberg. She had to agree with that as well. Still . . . gift horses . . .

But the question of an armistice was moot.

Carla Benedict was in town. She knew where her sister had spent the last day of her life. She would be coming.

True, the younger Dunville might simply insist that if the girl had come to Sur La Mer at all, the visit had to have been covert. She sneaked in. But he would not be able to explain why Lisa Benedict's apartment had been subsequently stripped of any reference to Sur La Mer. And, now, he would not be able to produce the woman she came to see. That, or he'd try to pass someone else off as Nellie.

"Want to see something?" Her husband spoke, rising from behind the desk.

She nodded, keeping one eye on the activity, or lack of it, outside, the other on the Dunvilles.

"Better close the drapes," he said, approaching. "We'll be backlit soon."

He was right. She saw that the shadow cast by a

jacaranda tree was already longer than its height. She'd allowed her mind to wander. Very dangerous. But she heard no reproach in his voice. He pulled the drawstrings himself and returned to her side.

"I think I've found the children," he said, whispering. There were several files in his hand.

"Nellie's?" she asked softly.

"Maybe. It's hard to tell." He separated one of the older files, dated 1943, into its *before* and *after* segments. Each showed a photograph. Although nothing so radical as plastic surgery had been done, the difference was striking. The man in the *before* photograph was about twenty pounds overweight, seemed in his late thirties and had a cruel, rather stupid face. The same man, months later, could have been a banker. The extra weight was gone, the hair fashionably cut; he had a trim mustache and conservative clothing. Even the expression had changed. It was, thought Barbara, like looking at an actor's composite. One actor playing two very different roles.

"This one," said Weinberg, "came here with a woman, apparently his mistress. By the time they left, six months later, they were not only 'married' but they had a child who was already a year old."

"Which means they got it here?"

Weinberg pointed to a notation at the bottom of the *after* file. It identified the baby's mother, although only initials were used. It described her coloring, her ancestry and the nature of her illness. The notation speculated that the illness was not likely to be hereditary.

"Whose initials are they?"

"A former member, I assume. Probably another actress. She's not here now so she's probably dead." He riffed through the papers he was holding. "I've found about twenty just like this," he said, "and I'm not even halfway through the files."

Barbara's expression darkened. "You're saying they used this place as a baby farm. To provide ready-made families?"

Weinberg nodded.

She could not quite believe it. "They never offered us one," she said.

"Dunville asked," he reminded her, "how we'd feel about having a child. He said that a family is an excellent cover. You wouldn't discuss it."

"Because I can't. My insides are . . ."

"I know," he said soothingly. "He saw that you had strong feelings. He backed off. But he was not talking about having your own."

She stared, remembering. Still, she was skeptical. "But where would they get a child now?" she asked. "The members . . . they're all old."

Weinberg only shrugged. But he could guess. Babies were stolen all the time. From maternity wards, from strollers outside supermarkets, from playgrounds. Also children, up to five or six years old. He had little doubt that if Barbara had shown interest, a child, even two, would have been found for them. Custom ordered. The right coloring. Probably from a nice young Jewish family.

But he chose not to say that to Barbara. Although she could no longer have a child of her own she was still very much a woman. It was the sort of thing that would eat at her. Distract her. She needed to keep her mind on how they might survive the night.

"Those initials," she asked. "Do any of them stand for Nellie Dameon?"

"Not that I've found," he lied.

"Ask Dunville. The father. Take him into the bathroom. Shove his face in the toilet and . . ."

"Darling . . ." He touched her with his elbow.

"Why not?" she asked.

"Nellie's children would be at least in their late fifties by now," he reminded her. "They might have children of their own, even grandchildren. All their lives of their own. All are innocent of this."

"I want to help her find them," she said stubbornly. "Ask Dunville."

He shook his head. "Then he'd know where you're going. He would be waiting."

She frowned. "Not if he's dead."

Alan Weinberg closed his one eye.

She felt it. "I know," she said. "Priorities."

He touched her again. He gestured toward the remaining files on Carleton the younger's desk. "I'll see what I can find," he said, turning toward them.

"Alan."

He stopped.

"We should warn that girl," she whispered. "If they've sent people after Hickey, they might send them after her as well."

"Warn her? What will I say?"

"You'll think of something. Call her."

Weinberg sighed inwardly. He obeyed.

A better solution, he thought afterward, would have been to make a clean sweep of the Dunvilles. It would certainly cover their own tracks. And it would keep them from bleating his name should Carla Benedict begin tickling their genitals with the point of a knife. But too many others knew. The guards, who were afraid of him, certainly knew that he was Axel Streicher. The instructors knew. And, probably, some of the medical staff. He couldn't get them all. Nor would he have the stomach for a slaughter on that scale unless they had done him a serious injury. Harmed his wife, for example.

Better to hope that they manage to convince Carla that they know nothing. Better to hope that they never learn who she is. That she buries her sister as quickly as possible and goes back to Connecticut, and to Mama's Boy . . . to that town he is said to own.

Regarding Nellie's children, he regretted lying to his wife. But it was not such a big lie. He would confess it later when she is less distracted.

He had found two of her children.

Before they left, he was sure, he would find two more.

But one of them was certainly Carleton Dunville the elder.

That knowledge would not bring a glow to Nellie Dameon's cheeks.

One afternoon.

Molly shook her head in wonder as she steered the Chevrolet, Carla navigating, through waning rush hour traffic.

Leave Carla alone for one afternoon and . . . she becomes chummy with a lunatic who denies killing Lisa . . . she decides that catching him just now would be unsporting . . . or ungrateful . . . she somehow gets the name and address of the man who apparently did kill Lisa . . . or at least was the one who robbed her apartment . . . and, from the look of her bed, also finds time to get laid by a Swiss-based KGB operative who just happens to be in Los Angeles.

"Go north," Carla pointed. "Hollywood Freeway."

Molly saw the entrance ramp. She signaled and turned onto it. Behind her, the sun had touched the horizon.

"This Claude . . ." Molly began.

"It's not his real name."

Molly made a face. She had been reasonably sure that a serial killer would not have provided references. "Whatever. You're saying he gave you this other man's address? This Hickey?"

"Just his license number. He's been following us all morning."

"Hickey?"

"And Claude."

"How did you get the address?"

"From the cops."

Molly blinked. "You didn't . . ."

"It's okay. They don't have my name."

Carla explained that she gone to the front desk, told the manager her car had been side-swiped by a hit and run silver Honda, gave him the license number, asked him to get her a name and address so that she could file a complaint. Anything for a bungalow guest, he said. He had the address in three minutes, courtesy of a sergeant with the ever-helpful Beverly Hills police.

Molly didn't like this at all. If Hickey was dead, as this loon had told Carla, Hickey's name would be all over tomorrow's newspapers. The man at the desk, to say nothing of the police sergeant, would remember telling Carla where he lived.

"Get off here," Carla pointed. "Olive Avenue. It hits Victory Boulevard in about three miles."

Molly signaled, then switched on her headlights. The sun was almost down. She turned right on Olive and then, abruptly, pulled into a Texaco station. "I need to make two calls," she said.

"Do it later. Yuri's alone and unarmed."

"This isn't just us, Carla. I need to call Anton."

"I talked to him. I told him about Claude. He just said be careful."

"Bullshit."

"Okay, he said stay put. But that was before Claude called back. We're almost there, damn it."

Molly ignored her. Anton, she supposed, could wait although he must be going crazy. But what bothered her even more was the knowledge that both Hickey and Claude had been on their tail all morning. That she'd been so deep in thought that she'd failed to spot them. That, not least, she'd led them both to DiDi Fenerty.

"Two seconds," said Molly. She shut off the engine, taking the keys. She snatched the torn page of the telephone book, bearing DiDi's number, and hurried to the public phone. DiDi answered on the second ring.

"It's Molly," she said. "Is Kevin still there with you?"

"There's a whole crowd here. Half the street and a couple of guys who work for my father. They're hoods, basically. Listen, I called . . ."

Molly cut her off. "That's good," she said. "Don't get nervous, but I want you to keep plenty of people around you. Tell them you'd had a death threat. Say the Campus Killer called to gloat about Lisa and that he said you're next. Don't go anyplace alone, and that includes with the police. Keep the lights on all night. If you sleep, make sure that at least two people stay awake, preferably your father's men."

"I know. That's what your friend said. Molly? I called Sur La Mer."

Her friend?

"They said Lisa was never there. But they were lying. I could tell from the way they . . ."

"DiDi . . . what friend are you talking about?"

"This guy. He said not to trust anyone I don't know except you and Carla. Keep the lights on, keep a crowd around, stay away from windows."

"Did he give a name?"

"No."

"What did he sound like?"

"Gee, I don't know. Um . . . Maximilian Schell, maybe?"

"The German actor?"

"*Judgment at Nurenberg, Topkapi, The Odessa File*," she answered typically. "Except he's Austrian. It was Bannerman, right? Paul Bannerman?"

"When did he call?"

"Ten minutes ago."

"When did you call Sur La Mer?"

"Just after you left."

"And this man specifically mentioned Carla and me?"

"By name, yes. Molly, what's going on?"

"It's okay. You're right," she lied. "That had to have been Paul."

"Oh, wow."

"Nice two seconds." Carla glared. "Start the god-damned car."

Molly did so, distractedly, and pulled onto Olive Avenue.

In her mind, she saw DiDi Fenerty dialing the number of Sur La Mer. Identifying herself. Asking questions about Lisa. Doing exactly what she'd told her not to do. Then she saw DiDi getting a call of her own, a man's voice, accented, telling her, warning her, to do exactly what Molly would have told her to do. Are the two calls related? They must be. Right?

"Who do we know," she asked, "a male . . . who has a German or Austrian accent?"

"Probably hundreds. Why?"

"No, I mean . . . this is someone who knows both of us by name, probably by sight, and that we're here in Los Angeles. He must be here too. And he might be a friend."

"That drops it to zero."

"We do have friends, Carla."

"I have one," she said, pointing. "But he's not German. Drive."

Molly brushed a hair from her mouth. That was Carla, she thought. All focus. One thing at a time. She was like a cat moving through tall grass. Eyes front. Oblivious to everything but dinner. Never thinking to watch her back. It was, Molly supposed, what made her so dangerous. It was also why Paul never let her work alone.

Molly noticed a large storefront, painted yellow. The sign said GUNS BOUGHT, SOLD & TRADED in three-foot letters. Speaking of which . . . "Did Anton say anything about sending John Waldo?"

"He's already here." She gestured vaguely. "Somewhere. Probably looting a store like that one."

Molly blinked. "Who asked for him?"

"Paul sent him. Paul and Billy are on their way." She looked at her watch. "They're landing about now. Half of Westport will be here by Thursday."

"Nice of you to share this with me, Carla."

No answer.

"Why this sudden decision to come. Do they know something we don't?"

Carla shook her head. She shrugged.

"And Anton said we should wait for them. Didn't he."

Again, no answer.

"Carla?"

Molly eased off the accelerator. Carla felt the car slowing.

"I like you, Molly," she said quietly. "I mean that."

"Well, I'm glad, but . . ."

"But this is about my sister. Don't fuck with me. I mean that, too."

Molly said nothing. She thought about turning back. Heading for the airport. But Carla, she knew, would probably fight her for the keys. Or take a cab.

What would Paul say?

Stay with her, probably. Keep her out of trouble.

And you can't leave Yuri hanging.

Take care of your own.

But later, he'd have Carla's ass for this.

He'd have to wait in line.

25

Yuri Rykov took his time.

He made two slow passes of the mission-style apartment house, keeping it in sight, ready to close on anyone—male, probably young—who stepped from its lobby.

He saw only one woman, going in, carrying groceries. A light flicked on in a first-floor apartment. In others he could see routine movement, kitchen activity, the glow of television sets. He parked Colonel Belkin's rented Ford in the lot of a store that sold hot tubs and made his way toward the entrance, memorizing the several cars parked at the curb.

There was a row of doorbells, about twelve. The second one from the top, 2-A, said *Hickey* in faded ink. He tried the front door. It opened. The lock, he saw, was long broken. He went in, tested the rubber clad stairs for squeaks, settled his full weight on them, and listened. A baby cried somewhere. Music played. A télevision audience laughed. He climbed the stairs.

One door on the second floor was well ajar. Rykov glanced at the pattern of letters on the others. The open door was 2-A. As he approached, slowly, he saw a glint of something that had been traced on the varnished wood of the door. It was, he realized, a face. A have-a-nice-day face. A smile. Except that the eyes were crosses instead of dots. He touched a finger to the smile. It came away stained red.

Silently, Yuri stepped inside, closing the door behind him. He saw the body at once but he ignored it. It was no threat to him. He waited, listening in the dim light. He sensed no other movement. He heard no sound of breathing. Rykov moved forward, crouching slightly, his thick arms crossed in front of him in readiness for sudden attack. If it came, he hoped for a knife. He did not fear knives.

The kitchen, the hall closet, were empty. The living room, though cluttered, offered no place of concealment. He checked the bedroom, all closets, the bathroom. He was alone, except for the man whose bloody smile matched the one on the door.

He knelt beside it. The eyes and mouth were open. The mouth had been stuffed with what looked like wadded tissue. The jowls flapped loose and open like those of a hound he owned as a boy. They had bled very greatly. The rear-most molars were visible. The cuts, he realized, had been made while the man still lived. He saw two puncture marks on the chest. These, he thought, had not killed him either. Not quickly, at least. Someone had wanted to watch this man die. The eyes, it struck him, were those of a madman. Or a man driven mad by the horror of what he must have watched being done to him. Tears, still damp, streaked over his cheekbones and made pools in his ears.

He noticed that the body had been dragged several feet. He saw marks made by heels and a trail of blood that seemed to have come from between this man's legs. He rolled the body onto its side and saw another wound. The flesh of his buttocks and thigh were torn, certainly by a bullet. The fabric of his trousers was scorched at its point of entry. The smell of cordite remained. It seemed to have been fired from this man's own gun. He saw the empty holster tucked inside the belt.

Now Yuri saw the gun. A revolver. It lay at the base of the dead man's couch as if it had been tossed or kicked aside. He picked it up. Blood on the barrel. One round had been fired.

Rykov shuddered in spite of himself. Carla had said that the man who called her, who said he had done this, had the voice of a boy. The voice, perhaps, but this was no boy. To seize a man like this, to pin his arms, to hold him down and butcher him so, great size and strength would be required. Even he would have had difficulty. The dead man was not so small.

Outside, close by, Yuri heard the sound of tires scuffing at a curb. Carla, perhaps. He approached the window from one side. It was not Carla.

He saw two men. They sat in a car, a white Lexus, making no move to step out of it. The one in the passenger seat was speaking into a telephone or radio. Both men were looking straight ahead. It seemed to Yuri that the car ahead of them, a silver Honda, was of special interest. The passenger nodded. He put down his phone. The driver stepped from behind the wheel. With gestures, he told the second man to stay. The passenger protested. The driver insisted. Now he closed the car door after him. He did so gently, as if to make no sound. He wore a raincoat. He reached under it, adjusted something at his belt, and walked toward the front entrance.

The second man stayed. He sat there, the engine running, looking up at Yuri's window. Yuri, unseen, stepped back.

The two, thought Yuri, had the look of policemen. But the car was wrong. It was too expensive. Also, they had separated. Policemen, on business, always stay together. He knew that from American television.

Yuri had a sense that the man in the raincoat was coming to this apartment. If so, he had no wish to be found there. True, he had diplomatic status. Of a sort. But it would not prevent publicity. Leo—Colonel Belkin—would be embarrassed, his mission compromised, and Captain Yuri Rykov, he thought, would be in very hot potatoes.

He wished now that the two had entered the building together. He could jump from the window. It was only four meters. Then he would stay, close by, to warn Carla when she comes. But he could not jump. If the man in the car was police, this would look very bad.

Yuri crept to the door. He listened for a moment, then carefully closed the bolt. The door had a chain as well. He chose not to use it. It would give evidence that someone was inside. The wood, in any case, was old and dry. The chain, even the bolt, would prevent nothing.

He put his eye to the peephole. His right hand still held the revolver. He thought of putting it back where he'd found it. But if this man now quietly climbing the stairs was indeed a policeman, and he was coming to this door, there would be time enough to put it down. If he was not a policeman, it might be good to have it ready.

The man, Yuri's age, well dressed, approached the door. He stopped. He seemed to be listening. Yuri, his fingers lightly touching the knob, felt it turn from the outside. Through the peephole, Yuri saw what seemed to be another move toward the man's waist. Yuri shifted his position, hoping to see whether the man held a gun.

The floor squeaked. The barrel of his own revolver tapped lightly against the door.

The man smiled.

It was a pleasant smile. Friendly. He took one step back and waved at the peephole with his fingers. Something large and black came into view. Yuri's brain screamed a warning. He ducked sideways.

He heard a dull crack, like a hammer against soft wood. Bits of the door exploded inward. Splinters gouged his cheekbone. A bullet fragment took part of his ear. Three more cracks stitched the door at the level of his chest. A bullet broke his right arm, another smashed his ribs. Yuri reeled backward, tripping on carpet, crashing to the floor.

He heard a new noise, much louder. A foot against the door. It flew open. The man in the raincoat ducked behind the frame and looked in. The smile, if anything, had broadened. Seeing Yuri down, he entered, both hands thrusting a pistol before him. The silencer was longer than the weapon itself and fully three inches wide. The man followed it through the door, training it on Yuri. He was about to shoot again, squarely into Yuri's chest when he hesitated, squinting. He was looking at Yuri's face. Confusion. The eyes drifted further. They saw the other set of feet, the body in line with Yuri's. They saw what was left of Joseph Hickey's face.

Yuri tried to raise his revolver. The arm that held it was useless. With the other, he snatched at the silencer, feeling its heat. He pulled hard. The man fell to one knee but he did not let go. Yuri's thumb found the hammer. He squeezed. The man could not fire. Yuri twisted it. The man squealed; his fingers were breaking. He turned his head toward the window and screamed a name. His mouth and his throat were now inches away from the powerful hand that gripped his weapon. The long silencer was bending. Yuri released it. He snatched at the man's throat. A squawk. He dug in his nails and ripped. Part of the throat tore free.

Footsteps on the stairs.

The man in the raincoat tried to crawl. Numbed fingers still held his weapon. Yuri rolled, swiftly, painfully, on his ribs. His left hand, wet with blood and tissue, clawed at the revolver held in his right. He fumbled for the trigger.

A second man appeared, framed in the doorway. He saw one man on his side, another on his back. He saw his partner on his knees, blood streaming down his raincoat, heard his wet choking cough, saw him trying to raise his weapon. His own pistol had no silencer. He had heard no doors opening, no shouts from other tenants. He chose to wait but he kept his sights on Yuri's chest.

The man in the raincoat saw Yuri rolling back toward him and now he saw the revolver held in a bloody hand. He swung his silenced weapon to Yuri's head and pulled the trigger. The bent silencer exploded. Thin shards of steel sprayed the room. The bullet, deflected, raised dust a foot from Yuri's head. The man in the raincoat cried out and fell backward. Yuri extended his left arm and fired twice. The noise was shocking. One bullet tugged at the flowing raincoat, missing the man. The second struck his armpit as he spun to avoid it. He fell against the window, smashing it.

Yuri swung his revolver toward the man in the doorway. The man fired first. He had aimed at Yuri's face but his shot struck Yuri's gun, slamming it back against his jaw. The room filled with flashing lights. Yuri was floating. He sensed, rather than saw, that the man from the doorway stepped into the room and rushed to his partner. He was pulling him to his feet. More gagging sounds. Dimly, he heard footsteps moving to the place where the man named Hickey lay. He heard words.

"Holy fucking Christ," is what Yuri thought was said. It struck him as an odd expression.

He remembered nothing after that.

Sumner Dommerich did not know what to do. Too much was happening.

He had been sitting in his car, watching to see who

would come, when the big man drove by twice, looking at the apartment, and then pulled in right next to him in the parking lot of the hot tub store. For a second there, he thought that the man knew.

Dommerich was wearing his hat. The sign was on his roof. He was invisible. Pretty much. Even so, that was too close. Wouldn't it be funny, he thought, if Carla came along after him and parked right next to him also. He'd probably blush or something. Maybe give himself away.

So, when the man walked down to the entrance of Hickey's building, Dommerich started his car and moved it across to the Exxon station where he pretended to be putting air in his tires.

He could see in his mind what was happening inside. The big man would have no trouble finding the right apartment. Dommerich had left the door open for him and he painted that face on the door with the dead man's blood. He'd never done that before. Maybe he would from now on.

The big man would go in. Real careful. And he'd find the body. He would be amazed. He'd say something like, whoever this Claude is, I really have to hand it to him. He'd say, Claude must be as big and strong as I am. Look at this. Hickey even had a gun and still he was no match for Claude.

Dommerich would like to have been that big. And have that nice square jaw and look like a jock. Except he would have found a better barber.

The arrival of the second car, the Lexus, interrupted his daydream. It pulled in right behind Hickey's car. One man went in. Real quiet. Maybe he was another friend of Carla's. Dommerich wondered why he wore a raincoat.

Nothing happened for a couple of minutes. Then there was this shout. It sounded like *Harry*. The voice was scared. Dommerich knew that the shout came from Hickey's window because the man who'd stayed in the Lexus jumped out and ran into the building. Dommerich smiled. It must have meant that the one in the raincoat saw Hickey's face.

But then there were shots. Two of them, real loud, then another one, not as loud. Even the man in the Exxon hat looked up from a car he was gassing but he couldn't tell where the noise came from. Then the window broke and the glass fell to the sidewalk. Now the Exxon man saw where. Dommerich waited.

In about ten seconds, the men from the Lexus came out. The one from the passenger seat—Harry?—was half-carrying, half-dragging, the one in the raincoat. One of the raincoat arms hung limp. It just dangled and flopped. The other was over the shoulder of the man who was helping him. There were big stains. Dommerich couldn't be sure in this light but they must have been blood.

They got to the Lexus. The man in the raincoat fell to the sidewalk, out of sight. The other man opened the door and bent down. Struggling. It looked, to Dommerich, as if the driver was heaving him into the back. Not on the seat. Down low in the well. The other man kicked at something, maybe feet, then slammed the door three times before it closed. He ran around the back and slid behind the wheel.

Dommerich was sure that the man in the back had been shot. And probably the first man, the big one, as well. Maybe he should go see. Try to help him. Say he was just delivering a pizza and he . . .

No. That was crazy. Carla would show up. She'd hear his voice and it would be all over.

He could just wait. Make sure she comes. Call the cops or something if she doesn't. But then tomorrow, when he calls her again, she'd want to know who the guys were in the Lexus, and where did they go, and why didn't he at least get their license number.

The Lexus pulled from the curb.

Dommerich ducked into his invisible car and followed.

26

It was half past seven, almost fully dark, time to think about leaving. Weinberg gathered one file folder, still unread, and the medical files of himself, his wife, and of Nellie Dameon. He was closing Dunville's briefcase on them when the telephone rang.

There had been only one other call since they had locked themselves in Carleton the younger's office. It was from Dunville's chief of security. Having discovered dead Henry in the basement, he wanted evidence that the remaining Dunvilles were still alive. Weinberg put young Carleton on the extension. The man asked if the Weinbergs were listening in. Weinberg touched a finger to his lips and shook his head. Young Carleton, obediently, said no.

Weinberg listened as the chief assured Dunville that the killers of his brother would never get off the grounds alive. Dunville did not bother to correct the first assumption. He asked the chief if his plan provided for the survival of himself and his father. The question was answered with silence. Dunville suggested that he give the matter more thought and hung up.

Weinberg presumed the second call to be from the same man with a more fine-tuned strategy. He placed a hand on the receiver and gestured for young Carleton to pick up the extension on signal.

"Dunville," said young Carleton, wearily.

"It's Harry," came the voice. "We have a problem."

"Um . . . this is not a good time. I'll . . ."

Weinberg shook his finger. Dunville glared at him, then took a breath.

"Is it done?" he asked.

"Yes, but not by us. Somebody ripped him apart. They did it like that psycho does . . . the one who kills college girls. We found him that way."

Dunville stared. He looked as if he'd been slapped. Weinberg heard a steady hum and highway sounds in the background. The call, he thought, was from a moving vehicle.

"It gets worse," said the voice. "There was a man there. It was like he was waiting for us. He damned near tore Marek's throat out, bare hands, and then he shot him. I finished him but I think Marek's had it."

Weinberg was on his feet. He scribbled a note. Carrying his phone, he passed it to Dunville.

Dunville ignored it. "What was Peter doing there?" he demanded.

"He . . . wanted the hit. I couldn't stop him."

Weinberg jabbed at the note he'd written.

"This other man . . ." Dunville squinted at Weinberg's scrawl. "What did he look like?"

"Real big. Tough looking. A pro, I think. Never said a word. Listen. I'm coming in. Have a doctor waiting."

"No. Don't. I've got a . . ."

Weinberg stopped him. He wrote another note, then held his pen ready.

"Where are you now?" Dunville asked.

"Just passing Ventura. Maybe thirty minutes."

Weinberg wrote again.

"This man," Dunville asked, "are you sure you killed him?"

"He took three hollow-points. Trust me."

Dunville squinted again, reading. "And this man cut up Hickey?"

"I don't think so. Hickey was already cold. And this guy would have had blood all over him."

Another scribble. Dunville read it. "Did you see anyone else there?"

"Like who?"

Weinberg canceled the question with a gesture.

"Look, I'm coming," said the man called Harry. "I don't think Marek will make it but your doctors better try or his father will want all our asses."

He broke the connection.

Carleton the younger groped blindly for the cradle. He stared up at Weinberg. All color had drained from his face.

"You're not surprised," he said accusingly. "You expected this."

"I was afraid of it," Weinberg acknowledged. "But not this soon."

In his mind he saw Carla Benedict. She was sitting on Hickey's chest. Hickey's hands were tied. She was asking him questions, sticking him, cutting him, each time he hesitated. How she found him, he had no idea. How she knew, this quickly, that it was he who mutilated Lisa's pretty face, left her naked at a roadside, he could not begin to imagine.

In his mind he also saw a big man, tough looking, a professional, who had taken three expanding bullets when one should have been enough, and who had the digital strength to rip out a man's throat. He saw a face. Although he could scarcely believe it, although he could not conceive of this Harry surviving an encounter with him, let alone besting him, the face in his mind was that of Billy McHugh.

"We're leaving. Right now," he said to his wife.

Barbara nodded, sighing. Once again, she must wait to be told what has just happened here. She handed the MP-5 to her husband, then stepped to the desk and picked up two Smith & Wesson Combat Magnums that he had taken from the hallway guards. They had four-inch barrels. With these she crossed to where the older Dunville sat and bent his head forward. He squealed in fear, certain that he was to be executed. She pulled at the collar of his suit jacket, then flipped up the collar of his shirt. She slid the barrel of one revolver under his exposed necktie and twisted it so that the necktie was now wound once around the barrel, the muzzle held firmly in place against the back of his neck.

She prodded him to his feet. Gagging, he rose stiffly, terrified. She steered him toward Carleton the younger's chair. Young Carleton understood what she was doing. He pulled up his own collar as she approached and, for the sake of his own comfort, loosened his tie at the knot. Barbara inserted the second Magnum with one hand and twisted it. It held securely. No need to choke him. She stood him up. She now had both Dunvilles, in front of her, each at arm's length. She pointed them toward the door where three suitcases waited. She nodded to Weinberg that she was ready. He was kneeling at Nellie's side.

"Nellie?" he asked softly. "Are you here?"

Her eyes had been glazed. But light returned to them. She touched Weinberg's arm. "It's hard," she whispered. "It's hard to believe."

"I know," he said.

"I'm old, Alan. And not very strong. I can't run long or far."

"We'll run," he said. "But then we'll stand. And in the meantime, I will show you things. Wonderful things."

Her eyes brushed over the open safe and onto the briefcase that sat waiting on Carleton's desk. "I did have children," she said. "Didn't I?"

"Yes."

A tiny fist gathered the fabric of her hooded robe. She looked at Carleton the elder. He, with his son, seemed to dangle like marionettes from the ends of Barbara's pistols.

"Is he one of them?" she asked. "I would like the truth."

Weinberg hesitated. "It . . . seems so."

She smiled, ruefully. "Then the others can't be bargains, can they?"

"You'd be surprised," he said, offering his arm. "Let's go see."

* * *

Molly heard sirens in the distance.

She approached the apartment house slowly, windows down, head cocked as if sniffing the air.

"There's his Honda," Carla said, pointing. "Pull in behind it."

"What was Yuri driving?"

"I didn't see."

"You're sure that's Hickey's?" Molly asked.

Carla squinted at the hotel notepaper on which she'd written the license number. "That's it."

Molly allowed the Chevrolet to coast. Then, almost abreast of Hickey's car, she cut the steering wheel and depressed the accelerator. The Chevrolet crunched into the Honda's side. It startled Carla but she understood at once. The car was now side-swiped. A reason for being here.

The sirens seemed nearer.

Molly passed the front entrance. She saw movement inside. A man in a T-shirt. He seemed agitated. She double-parked near a hydrant and stepped from the car. Carla followed.

Molly saw the blood. It left a weaving trail from the steps of the apartment house to the empty curb space in back of the Honda. She was afraid it was Yuri's. The man in the T-shirt stepped out through the door. He looked at them, then past them, as if waiting for someone else. He seemed in shock.

"Did something happen here?" Molly asked.

"Two guys," he managed. "Upstairs." He, too, noticed the blood. "I called the cops."

"I'm a nurse," said Carla. They pushed past him and took the stairs, following the sound of voices.

They saw the open door. Four holes through it, each the size of an egg. The peephole had been shot out. A knot of people stood near the door, some of them peering inside. A young black woman wearing shorts and a halter leaned against the frame, her fist to her mouth, hyperventilating. A black man, older, tried to soothe her. Carla slipped between them and into the apartment. She flipped on the lights. "Oh, my God," said another man behind her.

Molly entered. She recognized Yuri by his size. Carla was already at his side. Molly walked past. She looked down at the face of the second man, at the hideous grin, eyes staring. Her nose told her that his bowels had let go. She returned to Yuri.

"He's still alive," said Carla. Carefully, she opened his mouth. The jaw, broken, made a crunching sound. One cheek was gashed, one eye swollen shut, a bit of his ear had been shot away and a dozen splinters of blond oak peppered one side of his face. She blew into his mouth, hard, to clear his air passages. His chest bubbled. "Help me," she said. She reached for the broken right arm and, with Molly's aid, rolled him onto his shattered left rib. It did more damage there, but she hoped to keep the good right lung from filling.

Molly straightened his arm. She used her scarf to stop the blood flow. Carla, opposite, gently pried the revolver from the fingers of his left hand. At least two were broken but not cut. And yet, oddly, the thumb and fingertips were bloody. She saw flesh under the nails. She examined the gun. The cylinder was missing, the metal deeply gouged. It looked as if it had stopped a bullet. The shape of the gun, she saw, roughly matched the marks on Yuri's face. She found the cylinder on the rug nearby. Three chambers were empty.

The sirens stopped outside.

Strobing lights flashed through the room, some red, some blue, from several vehicles. Sounds of running feet.

"We live in the building," Molly whispered to Carla. "We don't know Yuri."

She stepped to the door where the tenants had gathered, still afraid to enter. She approached the black man. "What happened here?" she asked.

"I don't know," he sighed. "I heard someone yelling. Minute later, I heard three shots."

"Three? There are four holes in this door."

Two policemen bulled past, their hands on their weapons. Two paramedics, with satchels, followed. Then two more police, one a sergeant. Molly held the man's attention. She touched the door, noticing for the first time the smile traced in blood. She gripped a loose splinter and pulled it free.

"You didn't hear this?"

He shrugged. "I heard a little hammering, maybe, like someone hanging pictures. A little crashing around . . . like the man hanging pictures maybe fell off his chair. I didn't pay much attention till we heard the shots. My daughter poked one eye into the hall. There's two men, one could hardly walk, bleeding real bad from his throat. They ran out. My daughter here walks down, looks inside, starts screaming. I called the cops."

The policeman with sergeant's stripes approached. Even he seemed stunned. "Who called nine one one?" he asked.

"This man," Molly pointed. Suddenly, she sagged, gripping the black man's arm. "Oh, God. I'm going to be sick." She shouted it, almost hysterically.

Carla heard. She stepped around the paramedics. "I'm a nurse," she told the policeman. "We're just below. Let me take her downstairs."

The sergeant nodded. The black man raised an eyebrow, as much at Molly's sudden loss of composure as at the reference to the apartment downstairs. He said nothing. The sergeant asked the black man's name. Carla guided Molly to the stairs.

They reached the building's entrance, stepped out into the air. Another uniformed policeman approached. Molly began retching. The policeman hesitated. Molly lunged for the curb where spectators had gathered. They made room. Carla patted her back. A second ambulance came, distracting the policeman.

"Our car," Molly whispered. "It's blocked in.

"Screw it," said Carla, easing her toward the spectators. "I took Yuri's keys."

* * *

The moment of greatest danger, Weinberg felt, would come as they stepped through the main doors of the château and onto the terrace. There would be guards, braced and ready, on either side. They would try to snatch or tackle the Dunvilles, then others would cut down the rest.

He swung the doors wide as the tethered Dunville's waited. He sensed movement to his right. Weinberg tucked the MP-5 under his arm and slid the unsilenced Ingram—he wanted noise—between door and frame and fired a burst into a thick stand of acacia. He heard a squawk, more of fright than of pain. He turned the Ingram on Carleton the younger's white Mercedes and emptied the clip into its gas tank and rear tires. The Mercedes sagged like a sitting dog but the tank did not explode as he had hoped. Still, he had their attention.

"Here is what you will see," he said into the night, reloading. "Both Dunvilles will appear first, guns at their necks, my wife directly behind. The guns are tethered to them. A head shot will kill my wife but she cannot help but fire as she falls. Nellie Dameon will be directly behind. I will follow. I have two machine pistols. I will fire at anyone, armed or not, whose hands I cannot see."

A long silence.

"Mr. Dunville?" came a voice.

Barbara poked Dunville the younger. "You know your lines," she said.

"Don't shoot," he croaked.

"Say, get out where we can see you," she prompted.

"No guns," he improvised. "You'll kill us all."

That would have to do, she supposed. She jabbed them forward. The elder Dunville, eyes bulging, tried to raise the suitcase he carried so that it covered his chest. Barbara did not deny him that comfort.

She steered them toward Carleton the elder's car, also a Mercedes but black and, therefore, preferred. They stopped at the trunk. Dunville fumbled for his keys and opened it. Weinberg led Nellie to the front passenger seat. The Dunvilles loaded the trunk and closed it. Weinberg covered her as she herded them to the rear right door. He opened it, taking the keys from Dunville's fingers. His wife guided Carleton the elder in first and herself into the center. Young Carleton backed in last, Weinberg helping. Barbara straightened her arms, forcing their heads forward and against the opposing windows. She nodded to her husband.

Weinberg stepped around to the driver's door and placed the key in the ignition. Standing, he lowered all four windows, then straightened. He turned his one eye back toward the château. He spotted the Dunvilles' security chief, the goon named Darby, and waved him forward with the Ingram. Darby had an assault rifle in his hand but it was at his side. He stepped closer.

"Let it fall, please," Weinberg said. "Come talk to them if you wish."

Darby hesitated. Defiantly, he kept his weapon. But he walked to the Mercedes.

"I asked you to drop that and you didn't," Weinberg said quietly. "You're still alive because I'd prefer not to upset Miss Dameon. It is not an overwhelming preference."

Darby smiled. Contemptuously. He raised the rifle, slowly, and pressed the safety. Taking it by the barrel he held it out, at arm's length, pointing the stock toward the shadows of the château. He called a name. Another man, unarmed, came forward. He took the rifle from Darby and then retreated.

Weinberg grunted. A harmless show of bravado, he decided. For the good of the troops. He would forgive it.

"Down to cases," he said. "Do you see any way of killing us without killing them?"

"You won't get off the grounds," Darby answered. "The gate is blocked."

"Which means we drive down to it and just sit?"

"That's up to you."

Weinberg backed into the driver's seat. "You drive," he said to Darby. "I'll sit in the middle."

Darby folded his arms. That smile again.

Weinberg lowered his voice. "Three seconds, Mr. Darby, and you'll have no knees."

"Darby," Carleton the younger shouted. "Get in the damned car."

The security chief spat. But he obeyed.

At the foot of the long winding driveway, the Mercedes's headlights washed over a maintenance truck, parked sideways, that blocked the exit. Weinberg told Darby to stop. He could see most of the gate. Through it, he could see two expensive homes, well lit, on the other side of Tower Road. One seemed to be entertaining guests. Weinberg saw no guards near the gate but he knew there would be at least four, two on each side, hidden in the sugar pines.

"Do they have silenced weapons, Mr. Darby?" he asked.

No answer.

Weinberg turned to address Carleton the younger. "Tell him why I ask. Those houses should give you a clue."

"Darby," Dunville said through his teeth. "We cannot have shooting here."

Weinberg nodded. "Tell him what I'll do if they have silencers."

"He will fire at that house, Darby. The one giving a party. The people inside will notice. They will call the police."

Darby chewed his lip. Weinberg brought the Ingram to his ear. "Do you need more time to think?" he asked.

Darby closed his eyes. "Mr. Dunville?"

A sigh, behind him. "Move the truck, you ass."

"I let you pass," Darby protested, "you got no protection."

"Compared to what? This? Move the goddamned truck."

Darby sagged. He leaned out the window and called instructions. Two men appeared, moving cautiously. They carried assault rifles. No suppressors. One climbed into the truck and released the hand brake. The truck coasted backward. The rear wheels leapt a drainage culvert and became mired. The other guard, keeping one hand raised, touched a panel on one of the stone gateposts. A motor whined. The gates swung open.

On Weinberg's signal, Darby drove forward. On another, he turned left, past several houses, then stopped. Weinberg adjusted the rearview mirror. There was no sign of pursuit. He prodded Darby, forcing him from the car. He exited behind him.

"Go home now," he said. "Enjoy your life."

Darby glared, backing away. "Next time, wiseass, you won't have that . . ."

Weinberg ignored him. He leaned toward the rear window. "Gentlemen, remove your neckties, be comfortable. Barbara, if you would drive, please, I'll sit with our friends."

"If you hurt them . . ." Darby backed away farther.

Weinberg could only shake his head. The man was an embarrassment.

Ten minutes later, Barbara driving, the Mercedes picked up Route 101 at Montecito. They went one exit, doubled back, then doubled back again. Satisfied that they had not been followed, and that no one had waited to intercept them, Barbara left the highway at Carpinteria and began following signs pointing inland to the Casitas Reservoir. It was an area of rolling hills, few houses, frequent brush fires. Carleton the younger noticed the signs.

"Are we to be trussed and drowned?" he asked.

"You'll have a good walk, that's all. Try to relax."

The elder Dunville let out a breath. His hands were shaking.

"In fairness to Darby," said Weinberg, "there was not a great deal he could have done. But you might talk to him about all that silly posturing."

Darby was the least of young Carleton's concerns. "You're really going to let us go?" he asked.

"Yes."

Dunville drummed his fingers on his knee. "I would have let you go too, I think. But if you keep those files there are people I must . . . alert. They will want you hunted down."

"If they find me," said Weinberg, "I'll have something to trade. I will soon, however, be the least of your problems."

Dunville looked at him, thoughtfully. "You know who did that to Hickey, don't you."

A nod. "If I'm right, you'll never know what hit you."

"The girl's sister?" He seemed doubtful. "That little redhead on the videotape?"

That little redhead. Weinberg chewed on the phrase. He chose not to enlarge on Carla Benedict's credentials.

"Then who was the man?" Dunville asked. "The man found with Hickey."

If your man didn't kill him? Your worst nightmare. "No idea," he said. Nor was there any point in mentioning Bannerman. To do so might take away his edge. Weinberg had said just enough, he hoped, to have the Dunvilles looking over their shoulders.

Young Carleton became thoughtful again. "On another matter," he drummed his fingers, "Luisa Ruiz. Is she dead?"

"If she found my machine, very likely. Yes."

Dunville shook his head. He seemed saddened.

"She was born there, wasn't she?" Weinberg asked. "In your baby farm."

"Yes. By one of the guards."

"And none of your special guests wanted her?"

"One man took her. Treated her . . . very poorly. Then returned her. He asked for one with better skin. What he really wanted was a fresh one."

Weinberg heard anger not yet cooled. It was clearly genuine. "How long had he kept her?" he asked.

"Four years. Until she was eight." Dunville stared ahead. "He . . . damaged her," he said at last. "But she had good qualities. She was a better person than you know."

Weinberg glanced toward the rearview mirror. He saw Barbara's eyes looking back at him. He regretted raising the subject.

"Who is *he*?" his wife asked, her voice oddly flat.

"Barbara . . ."

"I want to know. Who damaged her?"

Dunville spread his hands. "It was twenty years ago. It was not the first time or the last. But, whatever you may think, nothing like it ever happened again. Not on my watch. Not until this thing with Henry. I would have destroyed anyone who harmed one of our children."

Weinberg found that he believed him. He nudged the father. "What about on *your* watch?" he asked.

Carleton the elder turned his head. His lips moved but he seemed unable to speak. Barbara looked into the mirror, first at him and then at his son. She felt, rather than saw, disgust on young Carleton's face. It answered her husband's question.

Weinberg leaned forward. "Take any of these dirt roads," he said. She took the next. Weinberg freed one hand of its weapon and, gently, massaged the shoulder of his wife. He looked down, and saw that her own hand was entwined with Nellie's. Weinberg squeezed Nellie as well. She turned her head and whispered something.

"I'm sorry," he said. "I couldn't hear."

She turned. She stared, clear-eyed, at Carleton the elder. "He'll hurt my friends," she said, her voice stronger. "Harland and the others. He'll hurt the ones who cheered."

"He won't," young Carleton promised. "I won't let him."

With a flashlight found in the glove box, Barbara led the Dunvilles from the car. She had taken the MP-5.

Her husband stayed with Nellie. He had taken the first aid kit from the trunk.

She walked behind them, her flashlight searching for a route that showed no sign of human traffic. They climbed a low hill to its crest. Barbara stopped. Below, she could see the Casitas Dam, marked by a necklace of lights and, well beyond, the glow from the city of Ventura. To her left, the leeward side of the hill sloped down into darkness. A sweep of her beam showed a dense thicket of chaparral. Low dwarf oaks and thorny brush. A body might lie there for years. She considered it. But her husband had told them they would not be harmed.

Carleton the younger read her mind. Or part of it. He trembled, hugging himself although the night was warm. He looked up at the stars. "May I have a minute?" he asked. He lowered himself. He sat.

The older Dunville turned ashen. "What? . . . Wait . . ." He stared at Barbara, then at his son. He backed away from both. "You don't have to hurt me," he sputtered. "You can be free. I can stop this."

"Can he?" she asked his son.

He looked at his father. With contempt. "I don't know," he answered.

"Can you?"

"I don't think so. Not now."

"He's wrong." The elder Dunville stepped toward her. "No one has to know you have those files. Give me your word that you won't use them and I'll see that . . ."

The son looked away.

"Can I believe him?" Barbara asked.

He shrugged.

"Tell me what you would do."

Carleton the younger spread his hands. "I'd like to let this go away, end here. But it can't. We don't know how much Hickey said before he died. Or to whom, really. Too many people are involved now. Outsiders. I think it's out of control."

"Then why don't you run? Choose a new life of your own."

A rueful smile. "I've made agreements. I'll try to protect them. But failing that . . . yes, I might run."

He sounded so tired, thought Barbara. It would almost be a mercy to shoot him. But it would serve no purpose otherwise. If these two men, and they alone, knew that Axel and Bonnie Streicher had been to Sur La Mer, that they'd taken those files, that they'd taken Nellie Dameon who had seen and heard so much, the two surviving Dunvilles would have been dead already. But the entire staff knew. The guards knew. They would tell that man who called . . . the one who had gone to kill Hickey . . . and who might even be an alumnus himself. He would have to warn the others. Even if the Dunvilles could not.

"I won't run," said Carleton the elder. "I can fix it. This was all Henry's fault. You know that. And you know I fixed him."

He had stepped nearer. Barbara swung the MP-5. He backed away.

"The files don't matter. They were only copies. No one saw you reading them. Only Ruiz and you say she's dead. No one saw you take them. Only that old woman. If you'll leave her, let me produce her, I can make them believe that you have nothing."

Carleton the younger sighed deeply.

"Can he?" she asked.

"Just take her. Take her and go."

"What would he do with her?"

"He . . . could not allow her to be questioned. Not Nellie. Not the other members. And, I expect, not me."

"But you're his son."

"So was Henry." Dunville picked up a stone and tossed it. He cocked his head toward his father. "Do I need to tell you who his mother is?"

Barbara stared.

From behind her, out of sight, came the impatient

tap of a horn. Her husband, she knew, would have his
bandages off by now. She was anxious to see. Her own
would go next.

Carleton the elder was talking again. Arguing. She
heard only bits of it. No denials about Nellie. A dismissal. That she, poor sick Nellie, had been used to
breed him was a detail of no consequence. Barbara
thought about mothers and their babies. She saw, in her
mind, the child she might have had once, but now could
not.

Barbara turned downhill. She took a few steps,
then slowed. She felt tears on her face. Her shoulders
straightened. Barbara looked at the sky.

She turned and fired.

She emptied half her clip.

"It looks . . . good," Nellie told him.

There was not much swelling. No angry lines of
sutures. The skin was pasty, damp to the touch, and the
thick stubble of beard made him look like a vagrant. But
these were nothing that a bit of sun and a razor could not
cure. She brushed at his flattened hair, arranging it with
her fingers.

The left eye was the last to be uncovered. The lid
and lashes were smeared with a yellow ointment but,
once wiped clean, its appearance was almost normal.

"Can you see with it?" she asked.

Weinberg dabbed at the eye with cotton. "It's
blurred. But I think it's clearing."

Nellie pulled back. "You don't look very Jewish,"
she said. "You look like George Bancroft."

He peered into the rearview mirror. "Who is George
Bancroft?"

"He plays gangsters, mostly. Or he did. That's what
you look like. A gangster."

"Wonderful," Weinberg grunted.

She ran a finger down the clip of the Ingram. "He
used tommy guns. Not these stubby little things."

Weinberg glanced down at the seat. The left eye, he

noticed, seemed to lag behind. He also noticed that his wife had taken the silenced MP-5. Just in case, he supposed. All she was to do was start them walking in a direction where they were not likely to find a telephone.

"Where we gonna hide out?" Nellie asked, affecting a gun moll accent.

Weinberg grinned. "For tonight we'll find a motel. Get some rest. After that, we'll see."

"I know a place. We could go to Tom's ranch. We could camp out by the lake."

"Um . . . maybe something a bit more comfortable," he suggested.

Nellie heard the hesitation. And she saw his eyes. "I know," she said, a bit sadly. "It's been a while."

But she had just been there. She was there, with Tom, because she didn't want to be in Carleton Dunville's office. And she could go there again, any time she wished.

"How about a boat?" she asked. "We lived on one for six weeks once. I was doing a movie about rumrunners."

Weinberg pursed his lips. "That's actually not a bad idea."

He was prone to seasickness. It was in his file. They would remember it, and probably not expect him to go anywhere near water. A cabin cruiser, well appointed, could probably be rented for cash with no questions asked. It was one of the benefits of the drug culture. Pay cash and you're presumed to be a dealer. And, therefore, left alone.

Nor is a boat, in a place like Marina Del Rey, all that easy to approach unobserved.

"Yes, Nellie," he said. "That might be an excellent idea."

27

It took only minutes to find Yuri's car.

The Hertz tag with his keys gave its description and the plate number. The two women waited for a break in the traffic. More police cars were arriving. Molly recognized the detective, Huff, whom they'd seen at Lisa's apartment. The two FBI agents might not be far behind. Molly eased into the street and turned in the direction of Beverly Hills and the telephone in their bungalow.

Twenty minutes later, nearing the parking lot of the Beverly Hills Hotel, she spotted a short, white-haired man in shirtsleeves, with powerful arms and the face of an unsuccessful boxer. He stood near a car with its hood up, as if waiting for road service. Molly pulled to the curb behind him. She blinked her lights.

John Waldo glanced up once, then again, noting the make of car she and Carla appeared in. Without a word, he closed his hood and started the engine. He made a U-turn. Molly followed. She knew that she was being led to where Bannerman was staying.

"Could he know?" she asked Carla.

Carla looked at the dashboard clock. Not quite an hour had passed since the first policemen appeared. "I don't think so," she answered. Not in time to have sent John Waldo for them. She flipped on the radio and found a news station.

Molly drove for another fifteen minutes, no bulletins from Burbank, until Waldo's car signaled a turn into the parking lot of a Holiday Inn in Brentwood, not far from the UCLA campus. She followed it to the rear of the inn where his headlights picked up the form of a much larger man in a red windbreaker who seemed to be strolling aimlessly.

Waldo swung around him and stopped. His trunk popped open. Molly watched as Billy McHugh reached into the trunk and lifted two suitcases from it. She could see that they were heavy. The bags, which she was sure contained clean weapons, strained at their handles. Billy closed the trunk. The car drove off. Neither Molly nor Carla bothered to memorize the plate number. Waldo never, while in the field, drove the same car two days in a row. Although he often slept in them.

Quickly parking Yuri's car, she and Carla followed Billy, who was now walking toward the back entrance of the Holiday Inn. He climbed one flight of inner stairs and proceeded down a corridor, rapping on a door as he passed it. He continued on. The door opened as Molly and Carla passed it.

They saw Bannerman's smile. Nice suit and tie. Just another traveling businessman. They saw those eyes, curiously gentle. But he also saw theirs and the smile faded.

"Come in," he said quietly. "What's new with Claude?"

By the time the Lexus passed Ventura, Sumner Dommerich was sure. It could not be coincidence. He knew where the two men were going.

They would get off at Santa Barbara, make two rights, follow the signs toward Montecito but then go left at the top of the hill. Dommerich had been there once today already.

For the most part, he could only see the driver. He was keeping to the middle lane, being careful not to go more than five miles over the limit even though the man in the back must have been bleeding all over seat. Dommerich didn't blame him. It would be really dumb to go shoot someone, which he was pretty sure he did, and then get stopped for speeding.

Dommerich never sped. Six different times he had

girls in his car and he had had to be just as careful. He would keep them in the well of his front passenger seat, all scrunched, covered with pizza boxes, because the well was easier to clean than seats. You could hose it out. But a Lexus probably had leather seats so that wasn't so bad. And another reason he never sped was that his company fired anyone who got a ticket while on a delivery.

At one point a Corvette with its high beams on passed both of them. Just then, the other man's hand had reached up, trying to grab the driver's shoulder, but it seemed to have no strength. It just sort of laid there, twitching a little, until the driver knocked it away with his elbow.

The driver, he now saw, was trying to talk on a cellular telephone. Dommerich moved closer, halving the distance between them. He knew he wouldn't be able to hear but it was fun to get closer anyway because he was pretty sure that the driver would be talking about him. Or about what he found back in Burbank. What Hickey looked like. Smiling up at him. All dead.

The only thing he still felt a little bad about was that they must have shot Carla's friend. The first one must have walked in on him—maybe the door was still open and he saw the smile drawn on it—and he saw Carla's friend standing over Hickey and he thought he must have done it. But Carla's friend must have heard him coming and shot him, too. In the throat. And in the shoulder, it looked like.

Dommerich shivered. He didn't like guns. They really bust you up. A knife is so cool and clean, and if you're careful, it doesn't kill until you're good and ready. And it's quiet.

Ahead, the man driving put the phone down. The Lexus sped up just a little. The sign said eight miles to Santa Barbara. Dommerich wondered how much cellular phones cost these days. He had a CB radio once but it got stolen. If he had one of those phones he could be calling Carla right now to ask if her friend is okay and to tell her he was following the two who walked in on him and that they must be friends of Hickey's because they're going to the same place Hickey went to before.

The Lexus signaled. Off the ramp. Two right turns. Dommerich smiled. He'd been right. But suddenly, on this dark part of the street, the Lexus pulled to the curb. The driver turned in his seat, on his knees, and reached down into the well behind him. Dommerich couldn't stop. The man was looking up at him. He went on past and kept going, around a bend and then, out of sight of the Lexus, he turned up the hill. The best thing to do, he decided, was to go right up near those gates, turn off his lights, and wait.

It was not so much that he noticed the black Mercedes coming down the hill. It was more of an afterimage. A woman, blond, had been driving and she had white tape across her nose and chin as if her face had been cut up and then put back together. And she'd looked at him.

Dommerich felt a thrill of fear. In the afterimage, she seemed all the more like a ghost. One of his college girls. And then in the back there was this other white ball, a face, totally covered with bandages, just like Claude Rains when he was invisible and couldn't make himself visible again. Dommerich remembered the way Claude Rains unwrapped his head, starting from the top, and there wasn't anything underneath.

Dommerich was scared. There were other shapes in the car but he couldn't make them out. If he had dreamed this, he would have thought that it was all six girls, their faces taped together, in this black car from hell, and they had him, the invisible man, in the backseat, wrapped up in bandages so he wasn't invisible anymore, and they all had knives, and . . .

He punched his head. It drove away the thought.

Ahead, on his right, were the gates. There was some activity there. He thought he'd better not get too close. On his left, almost across from them, was a big house and there must have been fifteen cars parked

outside it. He heard music. Sounds of a party. Dommerich swung off Tower Road and into the oval driveway of
the house. He got out of his car, gathered two empty
boxes, and pretended to be checking an order slip.

The gates were shut but just behind them he could
see men in gray uniforms struggling with a little truck
that seemed to have gone off the road. He could hear the
revving of the engine and the whirring of tires. Three or
four men were pushing it. Another man, who must have
been in charge, wasn't doing anything but yelling.

They had just heaved it back onto the road, sideways, blocking it, when the white Lexus appeared. It
pulled up to the gate. The driver stuck his head out,
shouted something. The man inside, in charge, held up
a hand telling him he should wait. They were still
maneuvering the truck, trying to straighten it. It stalled.
Dommerich could hear the engine grinding.

The man in the Lexus got out. He walked up to the
gate and stuck his arm through it. The man in charge
seemed surprised. Then angry. He raised his hands,
then said something over his shoulder. The guards
hesitated. He yelled at them. One shrugged. They
pushed the truck off the road again. Seconds later, the
gates swung open and the Lexus sped through. Dommerich watched the tail lights disappear.

Wait'll he tells Carla.

Wait'll she hears that he knows where she can find
the two men who walked in on her friend and shot him.
Probably. That they must be Hickey's partners. That
they probably know all about why he robbed her sister,
and killed her, and tried to blame him.

But Carla knew better. She was his friend. She said
so.

He still wasn't real sure she meant it. Not enough,
anyway, that he'd take a chance on meeting her someplace.

But after this, who knows? Maybe.

In her whole life, Sumner Dommerich would bet,
Carla never knew anyone who could do the things he

could. And already did. In her whole life, she never had a friend like him.

For thirty minutes, Bannerman listened about Yuri, and Sur La Mer, and especially about Claude, wishing, not for the first time, that he had never let Carla out of Westport. There was a soft rap at the door. Susan answered this time, greeting Leo Belkin with a handshake and a touch of both cheeks.

He was a man of middle-age, average height, balding, rumpled in dress. Tortoiseshell glasses, and a pipe Bannerman had never seen him light, added a scholarly appearance. His expression, normally one of detached amusement, was now grave.

Susan led him into the room. The television was on, the sound low. A network film had already been interrupted twice by fragmentary reports of the events in Burbank. Even now, a crawl came across the bottom of the screen suggesting that the Campus Killer had chosen a male for his eighth victim. Details at ten.

"Yuri is alive," said Belkin to no one in particular. "There is hope. He is very strong."

He touched Bannerman's arm in passing. The touch said that Paul should feel no guilt for asking the favor. He could not have known. There was no touch for Carla or for Molly. He looked longingly at a scotch bottle that sat unopened on a corner table. Bannerman fixed him a drink over ice. He took ice water for himself. Belkin noticed.

"Do you intend to take action?" he asked.

Bannerman's gesture was noncommittal. "We have a man," he said, "Joseph Hickey, who apparently burglarized Carla's sister's apartment and may also have murdered her. We have a maniac, known to us only as Claude, who is a serial killer being hunted by the police."

Standing, one foot on a chair, Bannerman outlined the events of the day as recounted by Molly and Carla. That this Claude, apparently, had known Lisa by sight.

That he resented being blamed for her death. That he had spotted Carla this morning, followed her, and later felt compelled to tell her that he was innocent of her sister's death. He told her that she was also being followed by another man who turned out to be Hickey.

"You keep saying *apparently*." Carla stared at the floor. "The man had Lisa's things. Everything else Claude told me turned out to be true."

Bannerman held up a hand. "For the record," he told Belkin, "the police don't believe that Claude killed Lisa either." He recounted how Hickey had been traced through his license number—provided by Claude— and how Yuri had rushed to that address while Carla tried to keep Claude on the phone.

Molly started to speak, as if to correct a detail. She thought better of it.

"Yuri found Hickey dead. Murdered, no doubt, by Claude, who by then was gone. Claude had mutilated Hickey. He did so in much the same way that Hickey, we think, mutilated Lisa. Two other men came to Hickey's apartment. One of them fired through the door, using a silenced pistol, which means he probably thought he was shooting at Hickey. Yuri, wounded by now, grappled with him. He had found a gun, apparently Hickey's. Yuri managed to injure one of the men . . ."

"He tore out his fucking throat," said Carla. "Half of it was still under his nails."

"All the same," Bannerman said patiently, "those two men were gone by the time Molly and Carla arrived. Yuri was unconscious. They did what they could for him. They stayed with him until an ambulance arrived."

Left unsaid, was that they didn't have to stay. If Yuri were not a friend, they would, and should, have left unseen. A flicker of appreciation on Belkin's face said that he understood this nonetheless.

"The complications are these," said Bannerman. "Molly and Carla had an encounter with the FBI this morning. They were subsequently identified as former contract agents. By now, two women matching their descriptions will have been placed at Hickey's apartment. The FBI will know that they arrived after the fact but they'll surely want them arrested and held as material witnesses."

"What do you intend?"

Bannerman looked at his watch. "Lesko should be here within two hours. The local police know him by reputation. I will ask him to act as intermediary. If I can, I'd like to keep Molly and Carla out of custody and certainly out of the media."

"What of the two men?" asked Colonel Belkin. "Why would they want to kill Hickey?"

Bannerman shrugged. He gestured toward the television set. "All we know about him is that he's a former cop, fired for cause. Lesko should be able to find out what he's been up to since then."

"Other than burglary. And murdering young girls."

"Yes."

Belkin sipped his drink. Doing so, he noticed that Molly Farrell was looking searchingly at Paul. He caught her eye. She looked away.

"What are you not telling me?" he asked Bannerman.

Bannerman had noticed the exchange.

"There is," he chose his words, "another element. Molly thinks that Lisa Benedict may have been killed because of something she learned about an institution called Sur La Mer. It's a rest home for movie people. She thinks that Hickey may have been in this institution's employ."

"And ordered to kill her?"

"I . . . find that hard to believe. Molly has been through all of Lisa's notes. Even she acknowledges that there was nothing in them worth killing for."

"Someone surely had a reason to kill Hickey. And surely you intend to look into it."

"I do," Bannerman nodded. "But through the police. Through Lesko."

"You will take no action on your own?"

Bannerman made a face. They had already argued this question. "Such as what?" he asked. "Carla wanted to go there tonight with John Waldo. Find someone in authority. Stick a knife against his eyes and begin asking questions. But that person, to say nothing of the institution, could be totally innocent of all this and John Waldo would probably have had to take out a guard or two on his way in."

Belkin had been watching Molly. He cocked his head toward her. "May I?" he asked Bannerman. Bannerman frowned, but nodded.

"Are they innocent?" he asked.

"I don't think so."

"You have reasoned, I take it, that because Hickey stole materials that pertained to this information, the institution must have sent him."

"Yes."

"And there is no doubt that Hickey stole them?"

"He had some of Lisa's things in his apartment. Claude described them to Carla. He has them now."

"This . . . maniac." Belkin seemed dubious. "This sequence killer."

"*Serial* killer. Yes."

"How do you know he didn't have them right along?"

Molly started to answer. She found that she could not.

"It's a very good question," Paul said to her.

Carla shook her head. "Then he would have volunteered that he found them. He didn't. I had to tell him what to look for."

"There's more," Molly said to Belkin. "There's this girl, DiDi Fenerty, who had copies of the stolen notes. Hickey followed us to her house so he knows we talked to her. After I left, she called Sur La Mer to ask if Lisa had been there the day she died. They said no. Soon after that, she got a call warning her to lay low, keep people around her, and not to trust anyone she doesn't know except Carla and me. The caller, a man, slight accent, probably Germanic, knew our names."

The KGB Colonel looked at Bannerman, one eyebrow raised. "Paul? You intended to keep this from me?"

Bannerman sighed. "What would you have concluded?"

"That you have an ally at Sur La Mer."

Bannerman shook his head. "Any number of policemen, FBI agents, perhaps even reporters, knew their names by that time. The Fenerty girl's name was left on Lisa's tape machine. They would have expected Carla to look her up. I don't know who would call with such a warning or why. But it's just as easy to believe that we have an ally among the authorities."

Belkin heard little conviction in these words. A Los Angeles policeman or a federal agent with a German accent? He knew that Mama's Boy himself did not believe it. "You were afraid, I take it, that I would send my own people to this place?"

"It crossed my mind."

Bannerman decided that he'd like a splash of Dewar's after all. "That's all we'd need," he said, pouring. "First we have Carla and Molly, both of whom have had a KGB price on their heads at one time or another, identified as former agents of Mama's Boy. Then we have a KGB captain, although not yet identified as such, found in a room where the possible killer of Carla Benedict's sister has himself been carved like a roast. We have Carla, who incidentally is known to work with a knife, placed at that scene. Next we have one faction or the other raiding an old folks home for actors, a place that may or may not have employed Hickey, and almost certainly leaving a few more bodies behind."

Bannerman sipped. "The media would notice, Leo. And given the players, a dozen intelligence services would start wondering what's going on here. Your mission would be blown. You'd be expelled within a day."

Susan, sitting on the bed, shook her head as if to clear it. Good point, she thought wryly. Can't let a Russian spy go home empty handed.

Belkin read her expression. He touched her shoulder in passing, patting it. The gesture was meant, variously, to say that he understood, that he was fond of her, and that his purpose here would not, in any case, result in nuclear winter.

"My suggestion," Bannerman was saying, "is that we proceed in this way. We'll let the police investigate Hickey's role in all this and any connection he might have with Sur La Mer. They will look for the two men who shot Yuri, and, given that one of them is badly hurt, they'll probably be successful. We will involve ourselves only if they fail but by then, through Lesko, I hope to know everything they've learned in the meantime."

The smaller man nodded. His expression said that this was sensible. He waited.

Bannerman's eyes met Susan's. They moved to Carla. "We're also going to try to take Claude," he said.

"Hey." Her chin came up. "Wait a minute."

Bannerman made a face. "What are you going to say, Carla? That he's on our side?"

"He's on Lisa's side. He gave us Hickey. Without him, Hickey would have been dead anyway and we wouldn't know shit."

"We'll know even more if we can question him," he said. "But that's not the point. If we take Claude we'll have something to trade. No publicity for us, none for Leo, Yuri is not detained and you two stay out of jail."

"He's been straight with me," Carla said quietly. "He didn't have to stick his neck out for me."

"For Pete's sake, Carla," Molly muttered.

"He didn't," Carla insisted. "He would have . . ."

"What he *did*," Molly said through her teeth, "was rape and butcher six other college girls just like Lisa. What he *will* do is rape and butcher at least six more if he isn't stopped. Tell Paul the rest of it."

"What rest?"

"Tell him what I heard while you were still on the phone with him."

"What? That I didn't want Yuri walking in on him and ending up like Hickey? Sure. I told him to get away from there."

"That's not the reason you gave Claude. Tell Paul what you said to him."

Carla stared at her, angrily though blankly. She seemed not to remember.

"You said he was your friend," Molly reminded her. She looked up at Paul. "She told Claude he was her friend."

28

It was not so much that Weinberg was angry with her.

Well, yes he was.

He had as much as given his word that neither of the Dunvilles would be harmed. Her answer was the father and son were at odds. To the son, killing seemed a last resort. To the father, it seemed a first principle. The father might well have prevailed. Better to leave the son unencumbered.

He could not deny the logic of her explanation. And he did, as always, trust in her judgment. She was there, after all. She'd heard them both. The son said that the father would leave no witnesses, perhaps not even himself. The father did not think to deny it. She made her decision.

Except that he did not believe her. Logic, he felt sure, had very little to do with her decision. He knew her. He had looked into her eyes as he listened to her words. He saw the remains of recent tears. They were hardly for Carleton Dunville the elder. Barbara wanted Carleton the elder dead. That was the long and the short of it. Still, he would like to have been consulted.

They had driven west, then south, from the Casitas Reservoir, crossing the San Gabriel Mountains, following the signs to Pasadena. Weinberg's reason for going there was that there was no reason. He knew nothing of Pasadena except that it was associated with an annual football game, a sport to which he was wholly indifferent, and a parade involving roses. Nothing in his background would have suggested that he might go there. Logic would have suggested that he drive through the night, far north or far west, putting as much distance as possible between himself and Sur La Mer, probably leaving the state.

Weinberg, like Bannerman, chose a Holiday Inn as their place of rest for the night. It was near a convention center. Large, busy, undistinguished, no bellboys, no need for anyone but Barbara to be seen. Barbara registered, paying cash in advance. She wrote that she was Mrs. Gabriella Cansino, traveling with her child, Maria, and would need a cot in their room.

Weinberg, with Nellie, waited in the bathroom while the cot was delivered and again while a room service tray was brought in. Alone at last, Weinberg sat with young Carleton's briefcase and opened it. Barbara took it from him. She told him to shower and shave.

Nellie, picking at a crabmeat salad, could not get enough of the television set in their room. There were thirty-one stations, or channels as Alan called them, and nearly all were in color. She could go forward, or backward, or jump from one to the other just by pressing little square buttons with arrows on them.

She had heard about television. She had even glimpsed it once through a window at Sur La Mer. But she had not imagined that there was so much to see. There were programs about nature, cooking, world

events, westerns . . . there was even Garbo doing
Anna Karenina again, as a talkie this time.

"Where you live," she asked Barbara, wide-eyed,
"do you have one of these?"

"Um . . . what's that?" Barbara glanced in from
the bathroom where she was cleaning a residue of
adhesive from her husband's face. "Oh," she said, smiling now. "Yes. Almost everybody has one."

"And it's free? All of it?"

"A lot of it. For what it's worth."

Nellie raised an eyebrow at the indifferent response. "But it's like having a theater right in your home.
Dozens of theaters. How could you bear to do anything
else?"

Another smile. Barbara checked her watch. "It's
almost ten, Nellie. Aren't you sleepy?"

She shook her head. "I'm too excited," she said,
squirming. "Thank you, Alan. This truly is wonderful."

Weinberg blinked. Then he remembered his promise. "I didn't mean television, Nellie. I meant . . ." He
stopped himself. Barbara was wiping his upper lip with
alcohol. Just as well.

He turned to the vanity mirror, examining the
result. "You haven't told me what you think," he said.

No, she hadn't.

She would have said that she liked his old face
better. But she wanted to hear him say that to her. First.
And also that it didn't matter. That to him she was still
beautiful. Even more so. She needed to hear that. "It
doesn't look very Jewish," she said.

He grunted. So I'm told. "It's sort of the Jewish
gangster look," he said. "Like George Bancroft."

"Who?"

"An actor," came Nellie's voice. "He was very
rugged. But a sweet man."

"Oh," Barbara muttered.

"Alan?" Nellie again. "A word with you, please."

Weinberg excused himself. He went into the bedroom and stood over Nellie. Her eyes not moving from

the screen, she reached for the flesh of his arm. She pinched him, hard, and he yipped. She reached for him a second time. He tried to back away but she seized his shirt, pulling him closer.

"Did you tell her she's beautiful?" Nellie whispered.

"I . . . ah, was going to," he said. "I thought we might take a quiet walk after you fall asleep."

She cocked her head toward the briefcase. "But not until you've played with those papers some more," she scolded.

"Well . . . actually," he said, stammering, "there's something in there that I need to discuss with her." That name . . . Marek, who the other one, Harry, said was injured, possibly dying. He had seen that name.

Nellie reached for the briefcase. She placed it on her lap, then put her salad on top of it. "It can wait," she said firmly.

At the Los Angeles airport, Molly Farrell waited among the relatives and limousine drivers as Lesko and Elena passed through customs and proceeded to the international arrivals gate.

She had called their aircraft in flight. She had told Lesko very little because, she suspected, ground to air communications on commercial flights were routinely monitored. But at least they would know that there were *difficulties*, and they would know to look for her.

She spotted them easily as they approached the heavy glass doors. Lesko pushing a cart. Elena helping to guide it. More than a year had passed since she last saw him. They both had changed. Remarkably.

Lesko had lost weight. It became him. His color was better, his taste in clothing had improved, and the expression on his face had noticeably softened. It was always a good face, very strong, but one that looked intimidating even in repose. He had perfect teeth. They flashed when he spoke and he had a habit of standing very close, developed, no doubt, during his years as a

New York City detective. Those he questioned must have thought that they were about to be eaten.

But now much of that menace seemed gone. Elena's influence, certainly. Molly had to smile. A kinder and gentler Lesko. God save us.

The change in Elena was equally striking. She had full use of her arms, for one thing. When last Molly saw her they were both in slings; machine gun bullets had shattered one arm and one shoulder and others would surely have killed her had they not been stopped by Gary Russo's body.

She was a small woman, not as small as Carla, but she seemed a child in contrast to Lesko's bulk. And yet there was something larger than life about her. She was dressed in a Chanel suit, very little jewelry, hair in a careless shag cut, trim figure. Quite attractive. And the money and breeding showed. But there was something else that made people take a second look, as other deplaning passengers were doing now. A certain serenity. A strength. Molly had not seen it before.

It seemed that more than her arms had healed. There had always been a certain sadness to Elena. It would be, on meeting her, one's first impression. Now, Molly saw no sign of it. Molly remembered the way she used to look at Lesko. It was a look which, for all her wealth and power, seemed to say, *I know that you can never love me. But perhaps you can forgive me*.

That too was gone. In its place was a look of utter trust and comfort. She adored him. And he did love her. Sometime in the past year, thought Molly, he must have even brought himself to say it.

Molly knew that look. She'd had it herself, she felt sure, during her early years with Paul. And probably still. Even after Susan.

Lesko spotted her and pointed.

Elena waved.

She came forward, her smile genuine, offering her cheek. Lesko waited his turn. When it came, he said that he was pleased to see her again. He bowed at the waist and shook her hand.

Lesko bowing?

A year ago, thought Molly, his greeting would have consisted of "How's Susan? What difficulties?" and he would have stepped closer, slowly baring his teeth, as she answered. About halfway through, one hand would have balled into a fist and he would have said, "Fucking Bannerman. Where is he?"

But this, it seemed, was a new Lesko. Housebroken. With some manners. Perhaps even eager to display them for Elena's benefit.

Count your blessings, thought Molly. Maybe the ride back to the hotel wouldn't be so dreadful after all.

She began briefing them as they approached Yuri's car.

Weinberg had taken Barbara's hand. She allowed it, not responding, saying little. They walked for a while through the hotel grounds, past the outdoor pool, through a garden. Weinberg saw the entrance to a hotel lounge called The Greenery. He led Barbara through the door. He ordered two cognacs.

It was, he realized, not the wisest thing to do. His face was not quite right. But the room, intimately lit, was further darkened by the shadows of giant tropical ferns and hanging plants. The waitress had hardly glanced at him. This was not unusual. People rarely noticed him when he walked through a door with Barbara. All eyes went to her. Women's eyes as well. Even women who were younger, prettier, men hovering about them.

But none were so elegant. None stood so tall, so graceful, so serenely confident. And, of course, none was so dangerous.

Weinberg shook his head, frowning. No, he thought. Danger had nothing to do with it. These people did not know that she was Bonnie Predd. Then Bonnie Streicher. She would have the same effect, no doubt, as Barbara

Weinberg. Surgery did nothing to mute the . . . electricity she gave off.

Nor, in fact, was she all that dangerous. Certainly not in the same sense as a Carla Benedict. Carla had always been a ticking bomb. Insult her, slight her, and your life could well be in danger. Not so with Barbara. Insult Barbara and you might very well hurt her, even move her to private tears, but you could not provoke her. In most cases. She was too self-possessed. Most of the time.

This, apparently, he thought, was not one of the times.

"I have met someone else," he told her, sipping his Hennessy. "I intend to have an affair with her."

She looked at him, lips parted, as if she had not heard correctly.

"There was a time," he said, "when I thought that Bonnie Predd was the loveliest, the most exciting woman I've ever met. It is no longer true."

A shy smile. Barbara hoped that she knew what was coming. "This other woman," she asked quietly. "Is her name Barbara, by chance?"

Weinberg made a show of considering the question. He waggled a hand, then gestured dismissively.

"Who, then?"

He did not answer.

"Would you like this cognac poured over your head?" she asked.

He ignored the threat. He looked away. "Her name," he said, "is Gabriella. Shall I tell you about her?"

The smile returned. "If you feel you must."

Weinberg held nothing back. Her full name, he said, was Gabriella Cansino, and she was staying in this very hotel. She was a married woman, or possibly divorced, not that it mattered to him either way because he was hopelessly enchanted by her. She was one of those passionate, fiery Latin types. Not at all like those cold Anglo-Saxon ice maidens and fatuous Jewish princesses he'd been accustomed to.

Latin or not, she had golden hair and soft blue eyes to die for and yet her skin was deeply bronzed, healthy, glowing—not the pale and pasty flesh one finds in northern climates. Her breasts were high and firm and perfect—unlike a certain buxom and pendulous Brunnhilde he once knew. Her body, thus far, was an unexplored treasure. It would have none of the markings that he knew so well and had wearied of. He hoped, he said, to explore it that evening, button by button, inch by inch, except that Gabriella was traveling with a daughter. Might Barbara, he wondered, have a suggestion?

"Passionate, you say. Is she athletic?"

"She . . . gave herself to an entire soccer team once."

"Adventurous?"

"They were scuba diving at the time."

Barbara was grinning. "Button by button, you said."

"And inch by inch."

"How does she feel about leather?"

"It depends. For wearing or whipping?"

"Backseat leather." She dangled the keys to the Dunville Mercedes. "Pay the check, Mr. Bancroft. I have fantasies of my own."

The grin stayed on her face as she led Weinberg through the doors of The Greenery, past the pool and, somewhat carelessly, across the open expanse of the parking lot.

She didn't care. She felt like a teenager again. Hot, eager, mischievous, that same dim thumping deep in her belly as glands opened and flowed. She felt his hand. It explored her hip, her waist, her back as they walked. His fingers closed over a button of the loose silk dress that she wore. It fell open. His hand moved on to the next.

She tried to shake it off. People would see. And it made her shiver. Her whole body tingled. Her new body.

That excited her. It would be like their first time. Certainly without bandages. Two new faces. No bathrobes. Clothing to remove. And she had lost weight. She had never been heavy but it had been at least ten years, well before they met, since her weight had dropped below 130 pounds. Those last few days at Sur La Mer had made the difference. Eating erratically, exercising doubly hard to keep mind and body alert. She was proud of this body. So firm and tight. Now, he was discovering that as well. She could almost feel his surprise, his pleasure, through his fingertips.

Reaching Dunville's car, he took the keys from her. He fumbled for the lock, awkwardly, once dropping them. Her grin widened.

As he bent to retrieve them, her eyes drifted across the second-floor level of the Holiday Inn. She picked out their room. The lights had been turned off. It was fully dark. But she thought she saw movement against the drapes. A shadow moved. Then it seemed to crouch.

Probably nothing, she thought. Nellie closing the curtains.

But she was troubled, even so.

It had been days, she realized, since they'd left Nellie alone.

"Do you think she's all right?" she asked.

"Nellie?" Weinberg followed her eyes. "The door is locked. She'll be fine."

"She's by herself. What if she's frightened?"

"No, she's . . ." He stopped himself. Barbara was already reaching behind her back, fastening buttons. He sighed deeply, deliberately. "We're going to go check, aren't we," he grumbled.

"Two minutes," she said, patting him.

Weinberg made a fist. He pounded the Mercedes, lightly. But he followed her.

Fucking Bannerman.

Lesko was mouthing the words at him even as he hugged his daughter. Susan embraced Elena in turn. Behind Lesko, Molly said with a nod that she'd told him all she knew. Bannerman had no need to ask how he reacted.

Lesko turned to Molly and gestured toward the door. "Why don't you get Elena checked in?" he asked. "Take Susan with you. They can get caught up while Paul and I have a talk."

Elena took his arm. She reached for Bannerman's hand. "We will all have a talk," she said firmly.

Lesko mumbled something into her ear. "I'm not going to . . ." was all that Bannerman heard but he could imagine the rest: "I'm not going to hit him . . . like he did the first time they met. I'm not going to shoot him . . . like he did in Marbella. I'm just going to ask, nicely, whether Bannerman ever goes anyplace where everyone is still alive by the time he leaves."

His next question would have been about Susan. Also asked nicely, Like: "Are you going to get Susan on the next plane out of California or do I crush your face the first time Elena gives us two minutes alone?"

"What's the latest on Yuri?" Lesko asked instead.

"Holding his own. Leo just left for the hospital."

"And where's Carla?"

"Down the hall with Billy. I told her to get some sleep. Why don't you and Elena do the same and we'll talk in the morning?"

Lesko shook his head. Two drinks and an ounce of NyQuil had put him to sleep by the time he was over Scotland. But for Molly's call, they would have slept through to Los Angeles. He reached into his pocket for a pad on which he'd jotted the outline of Molly's summary. It crossed his mind to insist that Susan take a walk. But a glance at her told him that she knew more than he did. The same eye contact told him that she would not leave in any case.

"Just so I have this straight," he said, reading, "you think this dead guy, Hickey, killed Carla's sister."

"It's a possibility."

"And you think he's connected with this loony bin up north?"

"We don't know that either. But if there's a connection, the police may well have established it by now."

"And you're willing to leave this strictly to the cops? Why doesn't that sound like you?"

Bannerman was tired. And he was becoming annoyed. "The memorial service is on Thursday morning," he said quietly. "By that afternoon, I want all of us on a flight back to Westport. In the meantime I want no trouble with the law and none of our names in the newspapers."

Lesko remained doubtful. He glanced at Molly. "What if, like Molly thinks, this Sur La Mer is behind everything?"

"In that case," Bannerman told him, "our council will discuss it and decide what action, if any, is appropriate. If there is no direct threat to us, and if the police have the situation in hand, we may well decide to do nothing."

It was, Lesko thought, what he'd wanted to hear. Still, he frowned in spite of himself. "Carla's sister gets carved up, and by you that's not a threat?"

"No," Bannerman said evenly. "It isn't."

Lesko understood, he supposed. Hit Bannerman or one of his people, on purpose, and Bannerman hits back fast and hard, always in a way that leaves the survivors scared shitless. He has to. It's his only protection. But Lisa Benedict did not die, apparently, because she was Carla Benedict's sister. And anyway, the guy who probably did it was dead.

"Council or no council," he asked, "how do you stop Carla?"

"For her own good, and ours," Bannerman answered, "we'll stop her."

How, Lesko wondered? Chain her to a bed? He chose not to ask. "This serial killer," he said—he could still hardly believe this part—"he's not a threat to you either, right? Would you still try to take him if you didn't need him for a trade?"

Bannerman hesitated. "Yes. But we would end it."

Elena touched Lesko's hand before he could speak. She was looking at Bannerman. Her eyes, and a nod, said that she would end it as well. There would be no media circus, no trial, no years of appeals.

"On the matter at hand," she said to Bannerman. "you realize that Lesko behaves in one way when his daughter is involved and in quite another when she is not."

Bannerman nodded. All too well.

"Susan has now lived with you for one year. Is that correct?"

"Just about."

"Is there anything of substance that she does not know about you?"

"Um . . . not of substance, no."

"She is accepted by all your people?"

Bannerman understood where she was headed. "She is accepted for the person she is and within the limits of what she can do. Otherwise, she is trusted without reservation."

"Then we can agree, perhaps, that she is not made of spun sugar."

"That would . . . shorten discussions, yes."

"Lesko?" Elena nudged him.

"Hey." He raised his hands. "I'm her father. I get protective."

"You are *my* protector. You are my lover. One day, please God, I will have your child. Your plate is full, Lesko."

It was more than a blush. Color exploded on his cheeks. Susan had to hide her face.

Lesko pushed to his feet. He looked at the door, longingly. Elena took his hand and held it.

"What do you want him to do?" she asked Bannerman.

"Call the detective in charge of the task force. Tell him we think that we can give him the serial killer but we will do so only on these conditions. No detainment of our people or of Leo's, no formal questioning, no surveillance, and none of our names are released to the media. Further, he agrees to tell us, through Lesko, everything he learns about Hickey and Sur La Mer."

"Can he make such an agreement?"

Bannerman shook his head. "He'll need the approval of his superiors and the cooperation of the FBI. That will take time so the call ought to be made tonight." He turned to Lesko. "They've identified Carla and Molly and by now they know that the KGB is involved so I think they'll take you seriously. I'll meet with them if necessary but I'd prefer not to. I'd like you to be the intermediary. You will deliver Claude if we catch him."

Lesko nodded slowly. "In one piece?" he asked.

Bannerman hesitated, only slightly. "We'll try," he said, "for Carla's sake."

29

Reaching their door by way of the inside corridor, Weinberg inserted a key of coded plastic and opened it quietly. The light from the hallway revealed a telephone notepad on the floor just inside. There was writing on it. His hand snaked to the Smith & Wesson in the small of his back. Barbara saw this but not the note. Her own hand reached into her purse. She covered the hallway as Weinberg stepped inside. Barbara followed, closing the door but not fully.

The sliver of light from the hallway showed no sign of Nellie. Or, oddly, of her cot. The heavy drapes were drawn across the picture window. Barbara saw that they bulged at the bottom. She approached the bulge, soundlessly, from the side.

Behind her, Weinberg now closed the door fully.

He flipped on the bathroom light. That surprised Barbara. He had left her backlit. But she did not turn.

"Hey," he said softly.

Barbara glanced back though only for an instant. She reached for the edge of the drapery but as she did, his brain registered an image that made no sense to her. It was that of her husband, the note in his hand, no weapon, silently kicking off his shoes. His jacket was already on the floor. Barbara shook it off.

She parted the drape where it met the window wall. She saw Nellie, on her side, her face lit by the moon. Someone had moved her cot flush against the window. Someone had drawn the drapes over it. Nellie's eyes were half open. They stared sightlessly. One arm rested on Dunville's briefcase.

Fabric rustled behind her. She crouched and turned. And she froze. She saw her husband, standing, framed in the light from the bathroom. His shirt had come off as well. He was twirling it, tossing it, in the manner of a strip tease dancer. He undid his belt.

"Alan . . ." It was more a gasp than a word. It was all she could say.

He was dancing now. Advancing on her. To music. His tongue made the sound of muted snare drums against his teeth.

Barbara rose, slowly. "Have . . . have you lost your mind?" she managed.

Still dancing, he held out the note. She took it. He reached for her gun hand, caressing it, kissing it as he eased the hammer into place. He took it from her, putting it aside, then led her toward the light while undoing her buttons for the second time.

Barbara held the note to the light, straining to read it. Weinberg made it difficult. The snare drums had stopped but he was now humming. *"A pretty girl . . . is like a melody . . . she haunts you night and . . ."* He slipped her dress from her shoulders, down over her arms, over her breasts. She wore no bra. It was no longer needed quite so much. Weinberg undid her belt.

The dress fell. He took her by the waist, lifting her, bringing the perfect new breasts to his lips. He made purring, groaning sounds. "Gabriella . . ." she heard, in a throaty whisper. She felt him swelling against her thighs.

She wrapped an arm around his head and steadied the notepad with the other. She was able to focus now. The note, in Nellie's hand, was addressed to him. It read:

> Would it shock you to learn that a sweet old lady still enjoys a good romp in the hay? Well, this one does. You might try it yourself. I have gone to the lake with Tom. Will return after breakfast. I have taken your silly briefcase with me.
>
> P. S. Have you told her yet that she's beautiful?

Bannerman was in bed.

Unlike Weinberg, he would have preferred to sleep while he could. It was not yet midnight, Pacific time, but almost three on his and Susan's biological clock. Molly and Elena had gone to their respective rooms. Lesko had driven off in Yuri Rykov's car.

When Susan emerged from their bathroom, leaving its light on, wearing nothing at all, a can of baby powder in one hand, Bannerman knew that sleep was not imminent.

She moved, gracefully, languidly, through the semi-darkened room, past their bed to the window where she parted the drapes. She stood there, in the light of the moon, looking up at it. She sprinkled baby powder into the palm of one hand and rubbed it, very slowly, along each arm in turn and then against her throat, working lower.

Bannerman watched through hooded eyes. Next, he knew, she would do her breasts. She would linger over them, far longer than necessary, one hand moving in circles, kneading, caressing. The hand would then move to the flatness of her stomach, then lower, over the tiny bulge of her abdomen, then lower still. Her back would arch. She would shudder as if chilled. She would pretend to have no idea that he was watching all this. No idea of its effect on him. He was about to be manipulated again.

Someday, he said in his mind, he ought to tell her that this routine of hers had worked him only once or twice, maybe three times. Certainly not the tenth time or the twentieth. But he would not. He enjoyed being vamped.

She'd wheedled him into letting Billy teach her to street-fight, and to shoot a few standard weapons, but not into giving her a gun of her own. He still could not bear the thought of it. He'd let Molly, not Carla, teach her how to defend against a knife. Carla would have taught her to use one. He'd had John Waldo show her a few things about driving. Spotting a surveillance. Foiling pursuit.

All of these were essentially defensive skills. When pressed, he could not justify saying no. But knowingly letting her get into a situation where she might have to use them was something else entirely. No, she was not made of spun sugar. But she was no Carla Benedict either.

The vamping process was picking up steam.

Susan, just about now, would turn and she would say, "Oh," or "Hi." She would stand there, totally unself-consciously, making no effort to cover herself. She would wait for an outstretched arm before coming toward him.

She would approach him, slowly peel the covers from him, and she would turn him onto his back. Carefully, barely touching, she would sit astride him. He would feel a cool sprinkling of powder or, first, the touch of her lips against his chest and the soft trickle of trailing hair.

"Oh," she said from the window. "Hi."

"Um . . . hi." In the darkness, Bannerman allowed himself a smirk. But he quickly made room for her.

She tossed back the covers and sat across his thighs. He reached to touch her, not with any real expectation of doing so but because this was where she would normally take both his hands and slide them under her knees, pinning them.

Her head came forward. The hair trailed. Her tongue, this time, explored his chest. It caused him to squirm. Several minutes passed before he felt the powder.

"Where did my father go?" she asked, in a soft murmur. "To meet that detective?"

"Ah . . . not yet, I don't think."

He did not enlarge on his reply. Susan had just eliminated her father as the subject at hand. She would ask several more questions, usually unrelated, before she eased into it. It would begin with the phrase, "By the way . . ."

"Then where did he go?"

"Who?"

"My father."

"Oh," Bannerman answered, stretching. "He wouldn't have called from here. He'll move from phone to phone for a while."

She sprinkled more powder onto his shoulders. She began massaging them.

"What were you two talking about? Just before he left, I mean?"

"Mmm? When was that?"

"You walked out into the hall with him. Were you talking about me?"

"Nope. Just some odds and ends."

He had asked Lesko to warn the police that any agreement, once made, must be kept. That once they agree to no surveillance, and bearing in mind that the two who shot Yuri were still unaccounted for, anyone caught following them will be presumed an enemy and might never get the chance to prove otherwise.

"Did you ask him to talk to Uncle David?"

Lesko's dead partner. "I . . . told him that if I had an extra mind, another set of eyes and ears, I'd certainly use them."

"You have mine. You have me. And I'm real."

"I know that."

"Do you?"

Bannerman chose not to rise to the bait just yet. He was having too nice a time.

He felt her hands pressing against his forearms. Holding them. The knees moved off. Her body backed away, her hair with it. He felt it trailing lightly over his stomach, his abdomen, then lower. He felt only the hair. She was teasing him with it.

"By the way . . ."

"Hmmph."

Her head came up. "Beg pardon?"

"Um . . . nothing. By the way, what?"

"Well, I was just thinking." The hair came back down. "Carla said she asked Claude to call her in the morning. He'd call the Beverly Hills Hotel, right? And Molly says the hotel is holding some maps of Sur La Mer for her by now."

"Uh-huh."

"But you told them they can't go back there. They can't even go get their things."

"They knew that. Their hotel would have been staked out within an hour of that mess in Burbank."

"They'd be arrested?"

"Unless we can make a deal, yes."

"Would I?"

"Probably not. They'd photograph you . . . try to find out who you are that way. One would follow you when you leave. But the others would sit tight and wait for Carla and Molly to show."

She sat erect, her head cocked to one side. "Bannerman?" she asked. "Does your mind really work that fast or have you already thought about this?"

"Sending you over there? I've thought about it."

"I could be there when he calls," she said quickly. "I'll tell him about Yuri and why Carla has to lay low. I could offer to meet him someplace and take him to her."

Bannerman felt himself go limp. "Not a chance, Susan."

She reached for the bedside light and switched it on. In almost the same motion, she vaulted into sitting position at his side, resting on her heels, her hands on her thighs. Sex must be over, he thought, grumbling.

"Listen," she said. "That phone call is our only chance of making contact with him. If Carla can't be there, someone else has to, right? And a man's voice would probably scare him off."

Bannerman realized that.

"Even if Carla *could* be there," Susan pressed, "your next problem is getting her to help you catch him. You heard her. She thinks this guy is her friend."

"I know," he said, frowning.

His initial thought, still taking shape, involved having Susan tell Claude that Carla wanted to meet with him. She would warn him not to say much over the phone. Someone might be listening in. Short of a court order, which did not seem likely this soon, Bannerman doubted that the Beverly Hills Hotel would permit eavesdropping on a guest. But better not to take the chance. And the warning might persuade him that this was no trap. She would tell Claude that Carla was in trouble. That she needed him. That Carla said she'd wait for him at the place where Hickey had turned his car around to avoid being spotted. He would know that she meant Rodeo Drive. Bannerman could have a dozen people there by early afternoon.

"Could Carla really be that . . . damaged?" Susan asked, not unkindly.

"That she'd think of Claude as a friend?"

Susan nodded.

"She could be that loyal."

Susan blinked. She started to speak but she fell silent.

Nor did Bannerman try to explain. Instead, he looked at her. That lovely face. So clean. That marvelous slender body. Hardly a mark on it. No scars, save the one through her eyebrow. A constant reminder that she'd once almost died because of him. But, unlike Carla, there were no deeper scars.

No, there was nothing fragile about her. She was very much Lesko's daughter. Smart. Honest. Strong but not tough. Never mean. She was exactly what he wanted . . . *needed* her to be.

But what Susan needed, or thought she did, was something else. She needed to be a part of it. An equal part. Like the others. He'd tried, more than once, to explain to her that it could never happen. People like Carla and Molly, all of them, were born with something extra or something missing. He was never sure which.

How could Susan possibly understand that what Claude had done to six young women would mean very little to Carla? Carla had seen too much death and many of those victims were just as innocent. On the other hand, he thought, how would he explain Molly? Good-hearted, warm, compassionate Molly who could sit up all night with a hurting friend, and who was Susan's admired buddy, but who was every bit as deadly when push came to shove.

"Susan," he said, reaching to touch her. "We'll see how your father makes out with the police. But in the meantime, I'm going to ask Elena to wait by Carla's phone."

"Good luck." She twisted her mouth. "My father will rip your face off."

"I'll talk to him. She won't be in danger."

"Then neither will I," she said firmly. "The difference is that my father doesn't have to know I'm there."

He started to speak . . . to shake his head . . .

to say that he didn't even want Claude to know that she
existed. But she put her hand to his lips.

"I'm not a child, Bannerman. And I'm not just
someone to fuck."

He winced.

"Okay. Make love to." She forgot. Mama's Boy
doesn't use bad words. He only shoots people.

"Paul." Her expression softened. But once again,
her fingers kept him from speaking. "You're going to tell
me that I'm much more to you than that. I already know
it. It's why I stay with you."

She held up a hand. "You're also going to tell me
that I'm not Carla. I know that, too. But you want me to
be less than I am. That has to stop. And so does this."

"So does what?"

"Me having to seduce you every time I want to take
a step forward. Besides, I'm a feminist. We're not
supposed to do this shit."

He was silent for a long moment. "Becoming more
like us . . ." he said slowly, "That's your idea of personal growth?"

"You're not listening. I don't need to be more. I just
won't be less."

Bannerman rubbed his chin. He rolled from the
bed, taking the can of baby powder, not knowing why.
He wandered, not speaking, to the window. Her back
was to him, She knelt, facing his empty pillow. She had
not moved.

"What if I say no? Will you leave me?"

"No."

He had expected a threat. At least a qualifier. *Not
unless . . . Only if . . .* But the answer was no, quiet
but firm.

It should have relieved him.

But all it did, together with the sight of her proud
straight back, head held high, that marvelous hair
gathered in one hand, pulled over her shoulder, was to
make his desire come surging back. And with it, a thrill
of fear.

For nearly all his adult life he had thought of those close to him, even those he had come to love, as acceptable losses. And they knew that. There was no other way. He could not have functioned otherwise. But he knew, all that time, that he was half-dead inside.

Since Susan, that had changed. Carla saw it even before he did. She had nothing against Susan, really. She simply knew the danger of caring too deeply. *"There are people who hate you,"* she said. *"It gives them a way to hurt you."* And she was right. They had tried.

"If anything happened to me," he asked, "what would you do?"

"I've . . . accepted that something could."

Left unsaid was that she, like Elena, had decided to have a child. Unlike Elena, she had not told the man who would father it.

"If you had died last year," his voice dropped to a murmur, "I think I would have gotten over it. I could have gone on."

She said nothing.

"But not now." He groped for words. "You've become . . . so entwined with me, such a part of me that . . . and it's not at all that I want to hold you back. The truth is I'm scared to death."

"Nothing scares you." She uncoiled, turning, rolling onto her side.

"You do. This conversation does."

"Come back to bed. Make love to me."

He hesitated, blinking.

"You've said some lovely things. Come to bed."

Bannerman sighed. Mostly in exasperation. The subject, somehow, had shifted. Just once, he thought, he would like her to stick with an argument to its conclusion. Just once, he would like to hear her acknowledge that he was right.

"He probably won't even call," Bannerman said.

She didn't answer.

"And I need Carla there if he does. He'd hang up as soon as he hears your voice."

"He might."

"Then what are we arguing about?"

"He might not."

Bannerman chewed his lip. "You'd talk to him. That's all. You'd give him no information about yourself."

"Paul . . ." she said wearily. "This is not like I'm parachuting into Beirut. It's just not that big a deal."

"I'll sleep on it."

"Not yet, you won't. Bring the powder."

30

Young Carleton was drained.

He was exhausted.

Three hours ago he had watched his father dance under the impact of a dozen bullets. It had been so odd. Surreal. He didn't fall at first. He staggered about drunkenly, taking little mincing steps. The shots didn't even sound like shots. More like a chain saw. Finally, he just sat. He sort of folded in half, legs straight, and crashed, seat first, to the earth. His upper body, arms trailing, slowly tilted forward as if taking a final bow. Toward Barbara. It was like ballet. Even to the final nod of his head. Then Barbara, tears on her cheeks, simply turned and walked away.

His own thoughts surprised him. He found, watching her disappear into the night, that he didn't blame her at all. It was as much a suicide as murder. His father's own words had killed him.

He had dragged the body into the chaparral, once he could move, once he stopped trembling. He had walked four miles by moonlight, back to the main road, and a mile after that before he found a bar sufficiently crowded that he would not be noticed or remembered. He had called Darby. Told him to bring the truck and something in which to wrap the body.

So, at last, he was an orphan. And an only child. Not counting, that is, the odd half-brother or sister still out there somewhere but he was certainly the last to carry the Dunville name. The use of it, for the first time in his life, required no adjective. No more young Carleton. No more Dunville the younger.

It felt strange. As if a weight had been lifted. He felt so free, in fact, that he now wondered anew whether that riddled mess in the basement had actually sired him. There had never been much of a resemblance. Even less to Henry.

He had asked his father about that once. His father brushed the question aside. He insisted that none of the special guests at the time would have dared go near the Dunville private stock of brood mares. Arrogance again. Young Carleton, now the only Carleton, had long rather hoped that one of them had.

There were two possible candidates. He'd spent hours, over the years, with their files. Both had the right coloring, the right bone structure and both had interests that were similar to his. One was still alive, quite successful, more or less behaving himself. Dunville had decided, or rather fantasized, that he was the one. He imagined himself calling on this man someday and asking, straight out, whether he remembers creeping into the Members' Wing sometime around March eighth of 1955.

But he knew he wouldn't ask. This man, now the father of a congressman, could hardly be expected to take him in his arms. Still, it would have been nice.

He would have been able to believe, once and for all, that he was untainted by the Dunville genes that also seemed to carry the curse of eventual madness. His *father* had shown increasing signs of imbalance in recent years. Henry was simply a bad seed. And his supposed grandfather, the Count, had died strapped to a bed, raving, in the very room where Henry now lay.

Count Vittorio D'Arconte. Bastard son of the duke of Parma. Italian war hero. Shot down six Turkish planes. Or eight. Or twelve, depending on the telling. These heroics, in any case, led the duke to recognize him, hence the title. Steered him into the Italian film industry, which was then controlled by the aristocracy. A new art form. Best not left to the Jews or Germans. Made his mark but was forced to defend the family honor when insulted by a Fascist rabble-rouser. His pistol against a shotgun. Dropped him in one shot, at thirty feet, although he was wounded himself. Thought it best to spend a year or two making American films. Stayed on.

Dunville did not believe a word of it. Except that he flew. The Count, according to his . . . father, had kept a little Ryan Seaplane at the Santa Barbara Marina with which he made regular 250-mile drug runs to Ensenada.

Among his customers was one Avery Johnson, then executive director of Sur La Mer. When relatives of some of his other customers began shooting at him on the streets of Los Angeles, he decided to blackmail Johnson into letting him lie low for a while at the asylum.

Once there, and safe, he was in no great hurry to leave. He had, at his disposal, at least four of the world's most beautiful women—although evidently they were all something of a wreck at the time. He insisted that they be kept bathed and beautified and costumed. And drugged, where necessary. He enjoyed them all, and shared them all. Except Nellie Dameon. He kept Nellie for himself. Although she probably never knew it.

Later that year, one of his Mexican suppliers got into trouble. He was sitting in a shore restaurant one night when his mistress and another man entered, nuzzling each other. The supplier crushed the other man's skull with a champagne bottle and slashed his mistress with the broken stem. Nothing might have come of it had there not been an American diplomat in the same restaurant that night. The authorities felt compelled to make a gesture.

The Count spirited his supplier out of Mexico in the tandem seat of the Ryan Seaplane and put him up at Sur La Mer. But the man was trouble from the start. Bad tempered, more so when drunk, would not obey the rules and he wanted the use of Nellie. Enough was enough. The Count put him to sleep with a dose of his own wares.

Months later, another Mexican associate, named Galinas, asked what became of him. The Count, unwilling to admit that his late guest was now nourishing the bougainvillea, ad-libbed that he was now living in another state, under a new identity, for which the Count had trained him during his stay. This new identity must, of course, remain a secret. He was honor bound.

Galinas, far from doubting this, decided that it was quite a good idea. He asked D'Arconte to begin creating a new identity for him as well. An entire life history such as, he suspected, the Count had already created for himself. This Mexican, in fact, would become an Italian. He was already more or less European in appearance and the Count could help him with his accent. Perhaps he, too, could have been an aviator. Or a race car driver. Disfigured in a crash. Undergoing a long series of reconstructive operations. That would explain a year or two of bandages and his eventual new face.

The Count was entirely willing to do this, for a price, but had no wish to be killed when the Mexican was ready to cut off the last link with his past. He would keep records. The Mexican would know it.

By 1933, Señor Galinas had not only moved into his new identity but into a new family. He was a widower with two handsome infant sons, both of whom resembled him because they were in fact his own, courtesy of another deranged but fertile inmate of Sur La Mer. He had also begun converting drug profits into California real estate, specifically vineyards. In less than a decade, with imported wines cut off by the war in Europe, his new name would be on the labels of half the cheap domestic wines sold in America.

Vittorio D'Arconte, meanwhile, knew a good thing when he saw it. His next move was to recreate himself. He became Victor Dunville and got himself named to the Board of Trustees—the only other trustee being Avery Johnson—and eventually became executive director when Johnson, who had argued against him once too often, electrocuted himself in a bathtub.

The vintner, by the middle 1930s, had become a life benefactor of Sur La Mer. A plaque in the main hall so honored him. He was the first but the list grew. Slowly, at first. In the beginning they were mostly drug traffickers who thought it prudent to plan for their retirement. Then, by word of mouth, other types of criminals appeared. The Count, now Victor Dunville, specialized in embezzlers for a while but avoided mafia types. The latter were far too family-oriented for his taste. Never willing to end all ties to their past.

Staff was not much of a problem. Quite a few had been stealing from the members for years or otherwise amusing themselves with them. For most, it was simply a matter of putting further temptation in their path, catching them in the act, and blackmailing them into continued loyalty. Money usually did the trick for surgical and psychiatric staff, most of whom had established practices on the outside, and saw a chance to earn handsome fees that need not be shared with their partners, their spouses, or the tax collector. All such transactions, of course, were recorded against the day when they might try to withdraw their services.

Several of these associations yielded unanticipated long-term benefits. One staff psychiatrist, whose duties included convincing female members that they'd only imagined having had children, himself had a son by one of them. The psychiatrist, Marcus Feldman, brought the son home to his barren wife, told her that he was the illegitimate issue of two famous movie stars—the mother was his patient—and suggested that they raise him as their own. They did, and the son grew up to be an internist. Quite a good one. Third in his class at Johns Hopkins. And, unaccountably, a rather decent young man. Named Michael.

When the Motion Picture Relief Fund decided that it really ought to assign one of its affiliated doctors as a liaison with Sur La Mer—a sort of inspector general—Carleton the elder rushed to nominate young Michael. Young Michael was flattered and pleased to accept. All went smoothly enough until the young doctor began hearing stories from the members, and noticing the occasional special guest. He questioned Carleton the elder who, after making an unsuccessful attempt to bribe him into minding his business, sat him down and laid his father's dossier before him.

His proposition was straightforward. Make your inspection visits, verify that the members are receiving good care, report back to that effect and keep your mouth shut on all matters that do not concern you. Say or do anything that might bring unwelcome scrutiny to Sur La Mer and the reputation of your late father will become the first casualty. Your dear mother's life will be the second. You, after a brief period of mourning, will be the third.

That arrangement, the surviving Dunville reflected, seemed to be working in spite of the fact that they had no real hold on the young doctor other than his sense of duty to a parent who had lied to him all his life. Still, young Dr. Feldman did more or less as he was told. Although not meekly. He visited his charges, saw to their needs, but insisted that they have no contact whatsoever with any of the special guests. He also saw to it that no new patient of child-bearing age was ever again institutionalized at Sur La Mer.

Not that it mattered much. No child had been born there for more than two decades. Stolen and brought there, yes, but not born there. What young women they did get these days were often so ravaged by drugs and disease that the act of impregnating them was repellant and the resulting child, if it survived, was often stunted.

Carleton Dunville the younger had never been at peace with the practice of breeding babies for use as props and he loathed the stealing of them. That was another thing. He had grown up in an environment where such activities were a perfectly routine part of the family business and yet they had always bothered him. He took it as one more reason to hope that he was unsullied by the genes of Vittorio D'Arconte and Carleton Dunville the elder. In any case, one of his first acts as chief executive of Sur La Mer was to put an end to the trafficking in children.

There were many things he'd intended to do differently. Being more selective for one. Attracting a better class of special guests. The Hong Kong Chinese, for example. Hong Kong is certain to be a gold mine as 1997 draws near. Dunville had already begun outlining special programs for all those Chinese who, having been denied legitimate British or American passports, will be dripping in dollars with no place to go.

Placing Orientals had its problems, of course, but it would at least be more morally satisfying than, for example, that crew that came through during the late 1940s.

They were the real boom years to hear Count Victor tell it. Sur La Mer's golden age, when its capacity was strained with fleeing war criminals, Nazis in particular, and several French and Dutch collaborators, all of whom had made their way to California with sizable fortunes in gold, gems, and stolen art.

But the greatest of the art thieves was in fact a Pole. One Tadeusz Ordynsky turned up in the early 1950s with a two-inch stack of canvasses by Rembrandt, Renoir, and Corot plus a Botticelli on wood. Most of the Corots turned out to be fakes but the others were genuine.

Tadeusz Ordynsky, after a ten-month stay, emerged as Theodore Marek and, that same year, created the art auctioning firm of Richardson-Marek, which then grew to become California's answer to Sotheby's. The real impetus behind the growth of Richardson-Marek was not so much art auctioning as art theft, which Marek brokered. That, and the sale of counterfeit art, including the Corots.

Marek had once remarked to Carleton the elder that Camille Corot painted eight hundred canvases in his lifetime, of which four thousand ended up in American collections.

During the 1980s, as art soared in value, Theodore Marek was among the first of the art auctioneers to appreciate the money-laundering potential of his chosen profession. He could sell a painting to a drug dealer for a suitcase full of cash. The federal authorities paid little attention to the cash flow within auction houses and none at all to the intrinsic value of the objects being sold because, in the art world, there was no such thing. A bit later, Marek would auction the drug dealer's painting for him, always at a profit, always for an unconscionable commission, and the drug dealer would then have clean money.

His association with drug dealers had other benefits. Foremost among them was the fact that he had, at his disposal and, therefore, at the disposal of the Dunvilles a small army of thugs who would resolve any unpleasantness that might arise in the course of their business dealings.

One such thug was Harry Bunce, who had been asked to resolve Mr. Hickey. Another, to whom hurting people was more of a hobby, was Theodore Marek's own son, Peter.

Well, not actually his son, thought Dunville. Peter was provided by Sur La Mer. His real father was Carleton the elder or, more accurately, the semen of Carleton the elder. No surprise, therefore, that the young man was psychotic. He had been born a handsome enough child, according to Dunville's father, but one had only to look into his eyes to see that something was awry.

Not that his subsequent environment was likely to

improve matters. Theodore Marek, for all his acquired polish and studied charm, was the single most execrable human being Dunville had ever met. Small wonder that the drug dealers sniffed him out so readily. He must give off a scent.

There was a certain irony to the fact that Carleton the elder and Peter Marek now lay, equally dead, in adjoining rooms in the basement of Sur La Mer. To say nothing of Henry. It was Carleton the . . . Carleton the *dead* . . . who had offered Peter as a replacement for Luisa Ruiz, whom Theodore Marek had virtually destroyed before trading her in for a newer model.

Marek was down there with his son. Dunville tried to imagine the scene. Was Theodore Marek capable of shedding a tear? Or was he looking at him in the way one looks at the ten-year-old clunker in his driveway when it will no longer start: Well, I got my money's worth. Time to check the ads.

Thoughts of cars led Dunville to recall that Harry Bunce had arrived driving a white Lexus. That, it seemed to him, was Peter Marek's car. He realized, with a shock, that Peter had used his own car. God knows how many bystanders had seen him being dragged back to it after the shots were fired.

Dunville sighed deeply.

Speaking of cars, he thought, it was getting to be just about time to borrow a car from one of the guards, drive down the hill, wait for the bank to open, and then begin a leisurely cross-country trip with nothing but the clothes on his back and the contents of a safe deposit box. Two new life histories, two sets of documents. His choice of a town house in New Orleans or a shore villa on Hilton Head. No Sur La Mer alumnus within a hundred miles of either. He would shave his head and grow a mustache. The Gordon Liddy look. He could even . . .

"Yuri Rykov."

The voice at Dunville's door yanked him back to the present.

"Rank of captain, KGB, almost certainly a trained assassin and, by the way, still very much alive."

Theodore Marek's face pink and unlined despite his age. Four face lifts . . . one day his ears will meet, thought Dunville. He stood reading from a sheet of notepaper. His tone was accusatory.

"Carla Benedict, contract agent, assassin, knife work a specialty. Molly Farrell, contract agent, assassin, electronics a specialty. And someone named Paul Bannerman, aka Mama's Boy, apparently their control." Marek looked up at him. "Quite a cast of characters."

Dunville chose not to reveal, just yet, that two of the names were familiar to him. He stared blankly at the mention of the third. Clearly, Marek had been on the telephone before arriving at Sur La Mer.

"Rykov, Benedict, Farrell," Marek ticked them off on his fingers. "All three have been positively identified by the FBI. All three were at Joseph Hickey's apartment this evening. First Benedict, apparently, with her knife. Then Rykov. Then Benedict and Farrell again. It was Benedict who killed Hickey." He jabbed one bony finger toward the basement. "It was the Russian who did that to my son."

Dunville was astonished. He tried not to show it. That young girl's sister again. And now a KGB agent? Hilton Head was emerging as his choice. It was farther away.

31

"Nothing's real here," David Katz muttered.

Lesko rolled his eyes. It was the fifth time Katz had said it.

Lesko had driven due west from the Brentwood

Holiday Inn. The signs said Santa Monica and the Pacific Coast Highway. Being this close, he thought, he might as well see the ocean. And Santa Monica was as good a place as any from which to make his first phone call to the LAPD.

The message he left was: This is Raymond Lesko from New York. Call Andy Huff, wake him up, get him down there. I'll call him in one hour, one A.M., on the nose. Tell him I got something hot.

He had killed the hour by first driving south as far as Venice. There was a road along the coast that seemed familiar to him. He asked Katz. Katz said that road was in a lot of movies. He said he'd seen it maybe ten times on the old *Dragnet* show alone.

Katz didn't think much of the Pacific. You can hardly see or hear a single wave, he said, and you can't even see the horizon because there's this dirty low haze that looks yellow even at night. Katz also thought it looked fake. Like it was painted. And the people roller-skating up and down this long boardwalk thing all looked like zombies. Just skating along, late at night, in bathing suits, faces blank, no smiles. Katz thought all their brains must be fried on drugs but Lesko said that druggies don't skate. Druggies don't do shit, he said. They just do drugs.

Lesko turned back north and found Sunset Boulevard again. The first part wound around through some dumb little mountains and it eventually leveled off to the section they called "The Strip." This was also familiar. Katz had seen it in movies and on TV all his life but it also reminded him of parts of Manhattan. Broadway in the seventies. Hookers and dealers on every other corner. Saloons, porn shops, fag movie houses, shit shops like in Times Square, and fast-food restaurants.

What was different was the people again. More zombies. People in New York were more . . . like . . . awake. On their toes. Lesko said it was just a different life-style. Out here they were just more relaxed. Katz thought it was more than that. New York, he said, had its share of people who walked real slow, and talked real slow, and called everybody "dude" and they were the same as these. Katz said he knew cows that could make better conversation.

"*You know what the real difference is?*" he asked. "*Look what they're wearing.*"

Lesko saw. More skin than back east. More weird outfits and junk jewelry. Clusters of punks with purple or green hair. Fags dressed like bikers. A few yuppie-type women but the men with them dressed like pimps. Girls not much older than twelve showing off their new tits. "*What about it?*" he asked.

"*They're in costume,*" Katz said.

"*So? People don't dress up in New York?*"

"*No, I mean real costumes. Like this was all a movie. And they all had parts.*"

Lesko shrugged off the observation. He checked his watch.

"*You don't get it,*" Katz pressed. "*These people all think they're actors. They don't think life is real. It's why you don't need brain cells to live out here. Or maybe it's like being in the Marines. Do you know why Marines only need one more brain cell than horses?*"

Lesko shook his head.

"*So they don't shit while they're marching.*"

Katz laughed at his own joke.

Lesko had to smile. For Katz, that wasn't bad. Then, when he realized he had never heard it before, he frowned.

This was the part that bothered him about Katz still being around. It was okay when he remembered jokes that Katz had told over the years. It was even okay when Katz noticed things he didn't or shot the breeze with him or even argued with him. Because these were the kind of things Katz *would* have said if Katz were still alive. Or *had* said before he got killed. And most of the time, Lesko knew, it was all in his own head. He'd held on to Katz because of all the memories and because Katz was better than nothing. And for a couple of years there, nothing was all he had. Except for Susan.

But when Katz starts telling him things he flat out never knew or, like now, tells him jokes he's sure he's never heard before, that, Lesko thought, has to make him wonder if he's got a full deck after all.

"*Hey, Lesko. You know why this town looks fake?*"

Lesko decided to ignore him.

"*I figured it out. I think.*"

His watch said five to one. He looked for a pay phone.

"*It's all those TV shows they shoot here. When you actually come see the place, everything looks like a set.*"

He saw a restaurant up ahead, well lit, in a lush tropical setting. Lesko flipped his turn signal.

"*Another thing,*" Katz pointed. "*You see all those plants? Where's the only other place you ever saw plants like them? Hotel lobbies, right? Fake plants in hotel lobbies. So when we see the same plants out here, and they're real, to us they look fake.*"

This last did not ease Lesko's concern. Either that was really Katz talking or that dumb-shit observation had come from his own mind.

It was useless to ask Katz about it. Katz thought he was still alive. Try asking a ghost if he's a ghost when the guy you're asking thinks he's your partner, still alive, riding with you like always. Try telling him you saw him when half his face was shot away. He'll look at you like you're nuts. "*I'm sitting here, right? I got a face, right? Lesko, what the fuck is wrong with you?*"

Screw it.

Lesko pulled into a slot and almost patted his pockets for some change before he stopped himself. All he needed was Katz reaching to fish out a quarter.

Andy Huff was waiting for his call. He asked Lesko for his old badge number and for a few other personal details. Huff had obviously called the NYPD in the meantime. Lesko answered his questions. He appreciated the caution.

In addition, however, Huff also wanted to know if Lesko had really once bitten a perp's finger off and swallowed it and whether, although he understood that Lesko couldn't answer, he had really blown away five greaseballs and the woman who had sent them to kill his partner.

It wasn't five. It was three. And he didn't shoot Elena. He left her standing there. And the finger thing was like fifteen years ago. Anyway, he didn't swallow it. That's how you get hemorrhoids.

Huff, in any case, lost interest in old war stories as soon as Lesko began to lay out Bannerman's proposition. He asked if he could get his partner on the line. Lesko appreciated that as well. Lesko took it from the top as soon as Huff cut off the partner who wanted to know if it's true that once this Brooklyn leg-breaker poked a finger against Lesko's chest and Lesko took the finger and . . .

The offer to deliver the Campus Killer had won Huff's full attention. Lesko explained, in as few words as possible, the relationship that had developed between Carla Benedict and this man . . . sounds like a kid . . . probably lives near USC, who was known to Carla as "Claude." That the carved ex-cop, Hickey, may well have killed Lisa Benedict. That Claude, not Carla, killed him. That two other shooters, connection unknown, had apparently also turned up at Hickey's with the intention of killing him. That Lesko has this friend, sort of, named Paul Bannerman who . . .

"Bannerman's here? In LA?"

"Maybe." Lesko hesitated. "What's your interest in him?"

"Until now? None," Huff answered. "But he scares the shit out of the feds."

"Tell them not to get nervous. All he wants to do is go to a funeral and then go home. In the meantime, he doesn't need any press and he doesn't want any of his people held."

"Will he talk to us?"

"If necessary, he says. And privately."

"And that's the whole deal? We leave him alone for a couple of days and he gives us this creep?"

"Pretty much." Lesko explained about the possible involvement of someone at a place called Sur La Mer. Carla's sister went there the day she died. Guy at Sur La Mer denies it. Bannerman would like Huff to run it down, tell Lesko what he finds out.

"How do I get back to you?"

"I'll call you. When?"

"I need two hours, maybe more. I'll have to get the feds in here, the DA, my own brass . . ."

"Two hours. I'll call you." Lesko broke the connection.

32

Theodore Marek waved his sheet of notepaper as if it were a list of charges.

"Do you feel," his eyes became hooded, his upper lip curled as he spoke, "that Peter was adequately briefed before he undertook this . . . housekeeping task for you?"

Dunville knew that look. He imagined that Marek probably practiced it in front of his bathroom mirror. He was in no mood for this.

"Peter," he twisted his own lip, "was not briefed at all. He was not briefed because he had no business being there. He involved himself because he saw a chance to inflict pain. He is dead because he made a mess of it."

Marek's nostrils flared but his eyes seemed to acknowledge the truth of it. He brushed that subject aside.

"Carla Benedict," said Marek, now as if speaking to

a child, "is the sister of one Lisa Benedict. Lisa Benedict
was raped and murdered two days ago. Her death,
according to my friends, was made to look like the work
of that serial killer. Do I gather that Hickey knew better?
Is that why you borrowed Harry Bunce?"

Truly amazing, thought Dunville. Take any situation, no matter how complex, and Theodore Marek will
plunge right to the sordid heart of it.

"Who, therefore, murdered the girl?" The bony
finger pointed through the floor again. "I leap to the
assumption that it was Henry."

Dunville hesitated, then nodded.

"And who poked out Henry's eyes? Certainly not
this same Carla Benedict."

Dunville told him, in broad terms, what had happened. He was not eager to get into a discussion of Alan
and Barbara Weinberg but there seemed to be no help
for it. His father's body, after all, lay in a bag right
next to Harry's. Marek would have unzipped it. And outside, Marek's driver and bodyguard—a Mexican named
Felix—would be passing time with the guards about
now, learning, at the very least, that the two Dunvilles
had been taken out at gunpoint by two of the special
guests. One of whom was said to have blinded Henry,
allowed him to suffer for a while, and then executed him.

Marek listened with what appeared to be growing
amusement. Dunville knew that it was nothing of the
sort. It was, rather, as if he were hearing a reading from
Alice in Wonderland.

"And these Weinbergs," asked Marek, the finger
signaling a question, "they were willing to throw away
their investment just for the sake of avenging a girl they
didn't know?"

"It was . . . an act of impulse. They feared retri-
bution. They decided to run." Dunville chose not to
mention the files. There were others he would warn. But
not this man.

"What is their background?" Marek asked. "Who
are they?"

"They were . . . agents. For the East Germans, primarily. Apparently they became an embarrassment."

Marek's brow shot up. "They were assassins? Like this Bannerman?"

Dunville shrugged. "I wouldn't know about Bannerman."

"Carleton . . ." Marek brought both hands to his cheeks, miming dismay. "Don't you suppose that the people in that line of work all know each other?"

"The Weinbergs recognized the two women," Dunville acknowledged. "They saw them on videotape. But there has been no contact between them if that's what you're thinking."

"On whose word? Theirs?"

"Yes."

"Then how did those women find Hickey?"

Dunville's lips parted but he said nothing. He had, somehow, in the rush of events, not thought to wonder.

That girl who called, Fenerty, was clearly convinced that Lisa Benedict had been to Sur La Mer on the day she died. She would have told the sister. But he could have handled that. He could still have denied knowledge of any such visit.

But Fenerty could not have known anything that would have led to Hickey. The only possibility he could imagine was that, when Hickey was following the two women this morning, they must have somehow turned the tables and followed him to his home. Hickey had, in the interim, been to Sur La Mer. Therefore, they would have to have followed him there as well.

Worse, Hickey had, by the sound of it, not died quickly. They must have questioned him. Tortured him.

Marek thought he saw the truth in Dunville's eyes. "If the Weinbergs have made contact with them," he said, "they'll be coming here next, won't they? After you."

Dunville nodded slowly but his mind was racing. He almost wished that Marek was right. That the Weinbergs would contact this Carla Benedict, explain to her what happened, tell her that there was no one left to punish. Except for that business with the Russian.

"Or after you," he said.

He scarcely knew, at first, why he had said that. It might have been wishful thinking. A desire to deflect any assault on Sur La Mer, perhaps even prevent it. But the lingering thought of Hickey being followed there had blended into the image of Peter Marek and his white Lexus.

"Peter's car," he said. "Is it registered to your address?"

The older man blinked. Dunville could see it dawning on him that his son had used his own car. Dunville could see him cursing Peter for that stupidity, and Harry Bunce for permitting it. At last, slowly, he shook his head. "I'd know by now," he said. "My . . . contacts would have warned me if the police had the license number."

"Not the police. Those two women. If they were on the scene when the police arrived, they must have been close by when Peter was shot. They would have seen Harry dragging him to the Lexus."

It was more wishful thinking. But if true, if they did turn their attention to the owner of that car, it would, at the very least, buy him time.

Marek stood for a long moment, averting his eyes, absently tapping his nose. Then he began pacing. Dunville had no trouble reading his thoughts. He knew the man. And he knew that Marek, right about now, was wishing that he had a bomb big enough to turn all of Sur La Mer into cinders. And everyone in it. End once and for all any possible connection with his past. Marek's eyes fell on Dunville's safe.

"My file," he said. "I don't suppose it's . . ." The bony finger pointed.

Dunville forced a smile "Hardly," he said.

Marek took the smile for smugness. He resumed pacing.

As he walked, he drew a piece of notepaper from his

pocket and stared thoughtfully at it. "We have two addresses for the Benedict woman," he said. "One is her hotel. The other is where her father lives. If she's gone to either, the police should have her by now."

Dunville said nothing. He watched as Marek stepped to his phone and dialed a number. The conversation was brief. Marek broke the connection. He glanced at Dunville and shook his head. He dialed again. Another brief exchange, instructions given. He replaced the phone.

"The police haven't found them," he said distractedly. "No activity at my house, either."

The night is young, thought Dunville. He resisted the urge to say it.

Marek stared at the phone. His finger ran down a list of Sur La Mer extensions. It stopped at one marked with the letters GH. "Is this the gate house?" he asked.

Dunville peered and nodded.

"If another car had followed Harry Bunce up here," Marek asked, "might your guards have been alert enough to notice?"

Dunville doubted it. They'd been busy with that stupid truck. But he was pleased to see that Marek's imagination was taking hold.

The video scanners, at least, had been in operation. Dunville called the gate house, confirmed his doubt, then led Marek to a small office at the rear of the main hall where the monitors were kept. He asked the guard on duty to replay the tapes from the Tower Road cameras.

There, on one monitor, was the Lexus, Harry Bunce driving, mouthing shouts at Darby to open the gates, Darby shouting soundlessly at someone else. Now, Harry Bunce, climbing out, pulling a pistol, thrusting it between the bars. In seconds, the gate swung open. The gate camera stayed with the Lexus until it disappeared from view, then returned to its sweep of Tower Road.

A second camera had recorded the approach of the Lexus. Dunville rewound that tape. No car had followed

the Lexus but, just before it appeared, another pair of
headlights came up Tower Road. That car seemed to
hesitate, then swing suddenly to the left. The camera did
not follow it. It continued its scan to the other end, then
returned, pausing on the activity at the large Tudor-style
house just across from the gates. A party was in full
progress. Many cars were parked on Tower Road and on
the side street. One, in the driveway, still had its
headlights on. That must be the car that turned left,
thought Dunville. He touched the pause button and
peered at the screen.

The car, a subcompact, was fairly well illuminated
by the lights of the house. He could make out the shape
of a triangular sign of some sort. It was strapped to the
car's roof. He recognized it. One of those pizza delivery
companies. He could see the driver, standing at the
open hatch, and he could see the flat square outline of
pizza boxes.

Marek, behind him, cleared his throat. Dunville
continued the slow scan of Tower Road. He saw nothing
out of the ordinary except, perhaps, that when the
camera scanned back to the left, the pizza car was gone.
Dunville frowned momentarily but decided he could
dismiss it. Delivery need not have taken more than a
minute or so. Still, he wondered. Not about the pizza car
but about what the driver may have thought about
all that shouting at the gates of Sur La Mer. The
answer . . . nothing. A disabled truck, an impatient
new arrival. He was too far away to have seen that Harry
Bunce had menaced Darby with a gun.

"No sign that Bunce was followed," he said to
Theodore Marek. "There's only that one car, delivering
pizza."

Marek stroked his porcelain nose. "Pizza to a dinner
party?"

"They have three children. Ages nine through
twelve," Dunville answered, although he could not
actually recall whether there were children in that house
or not.

Marek stared at the screen. "Still," he said, "that driver was there just as Harry arrived. Rather convenient, don't you think?"

Dunville affected a sigh. In his mind he could see Marek's thugs tearing the shirts off a dozen or so pizza delivery boys to see if one of them was Carla Benedict in disguise. "All that young man cared about was his next delivery," he said. "Harry was not followed to Sur La Mer. There is still, however, the possibility that the car will be traced to your home."

Marek nodded thoughtfully.

"I don't know about these two women," Dunville pressed, "but if it were Bonnie . . . Barbara Weinberg, you'd wake up with a knife at your throat and a quiet voice asking you where Peter is."

The older man sniffed. "They would never get past . . ."

"Then there's the KGB, of course," Dunville added. "They will want to know that as well. Especially if the one Harry shot is able to identify them both."

Dunville realized that he was pushing it. But his hope was that Theodore Marek would take the hint, go home, ring his Malibu estate with extra guards, and become a stationary target while he . . .

"Where else might they be?" Marek asked. "The two women."

Dunville shrugged. "They certainly wouldn't go near the Russian's hospital."

"Hardly. Where else?"

Dunville rubbed his chin. "They might surface for the sister's funeral. But that could be days from now. In the meantime, they could strike anywhere."

Marek said nothing. He was staring at the monitors, his eyes searching shadows. The predator, thought Dunville, had become the hunted.

"Speaking of funerals?" he asked, "what do you want done with Peter?"

Marek blinked as if distracted. Then he seemed to recall that his adopted son, now useless to him, was still in the basement. He made a vague gesture with those bony fingers. You see to it, it said. It was the sort of gesture made by a maître d' when he wishes a busboy to clean off a table.

Dunville felt a welling of disgust. Some of it toward himself. He had not, in fairness, shown much more compassion for either of his own namesakes. The redeeming difference, he hoped, was that he was capable of knowing it. He had made his decision. A voice inside him said, "*Good lad. It's about time.*"

He knew the voice. He had imagined conversations with it many times. It was that of the man whom he wished . . . or fantasized . . . to have been his real father.

"*I'm not so good. But you're right. It's time.*"

"*Go to Hilton Head, Son. Take up golf. Golf is soothing to the soul.*"

"*I'll see to the members first. And I'll try to protect you. You and most of the others.*"

"*I know you will.*"

"*But not this man. Not Marek.*"

"*I can't stand the son of a bitch either. What do you have in mind?*"

"*How does one dial the KGB? Any idea?*"

"*I doubt they're in the phone book. Anyway, I'd say those ladies deserve first dibs, wouldn't you?*"

"*I suppose I would. Thank you, Father.*"

"*Take care, Son.*"

. . . "What? Did you say something?" Marek hooked that finger behind his ear.

"Um . . . no."

"It sounded like 'Take care.' "

"I said I'd take care of Peter."

"Oh. Yes."

"I'll take care of everything, Mr. Marek. You sit tight. Leave those women to me."

Marek snorted. "If you have an idea, I want to hear it."

"Never fear. I'll settle this by noon tomorrow."

"You can keep this from my door?"

"Depend on it."

"If this touches me, Carleton, you'll see Harry Bunce one last time."

"Trust me, Mr. Marek."

Dunville watched from the flagstone terrace as Theodore Marek's taillights winked from sight. The Lexus, Harry Bunce driving, followed close behind.

He could see a soapy puddle where the Lexus had stood. Bunce must have hosed it out and scrubbed it. Marek, he imagined, would probably have him abandon it somewhere and claim not to have seen it for days. Or Peter either.

Poor Harry Bunce.

He'll now pass the rest of the night listening to Theodore Marek's analysis of every word that was said, every nuance, every conceivable scenario up to and including a KGB plot to drag him before a war crimes tribunal.

Just as well.

Perhaps it will keep them both out of trouble.

Carleton Dunville returned to his office and looked for the scrap of paper on which he'd noted the number of Miss DiDi Fenerty.

33

Lesko had two hours to kill.

On his map, Queen of Angels Medical Center looked fairly close. He could swing by the waiting room. Leo Belkin might still be there. But a better idea, he decided, might be to keep an eye on the restaurant from which he'd made his call.

Huff, he knew, could have had an address for that pay phone two minutes into their conversation. Lesko had no reason not to trust him. But someone, like Huff's boss, might have been tempted to set up a surveillance. So Lesko watched and waited. He sat in a darkened Mazda dealership just down Sunset Boulevard.

For an hour nothing happened. Traffic on Sunset was light. A car every five minutes or so. Then, suddenly, two cars pulled into the lot, two men in one, a couple in the other. The couple entered and took seats at the bar, heads together like love birds although they had not touched on their way in. One of the men entered two minutes later and sat at the far end. The other man never left the car.

"That took too long," said Katz.

Lesko understood. It should not have taken an hour. The cops, from the look of it, had already determined that he was not there. Probably called the manager. These four were probably waiting in case he came back to use the same phone.

"They got a third car, you think?"

"No." Katz pointed. *"The guy who stayed outside. He's their chase."*

Lesko waited, to be sure. After thirty minutes, he started his engine.

"Sit low. They're lookin' for a moose."

Lesko, crouching, swung onto Sunset, then made his first right turn toward the Hollywood hills. He saw no lights behind him. He continued on for a while, then stopped to check his map. He was almost in Burbank.

He had no special reason for going there. But he remembered that the reporter on Bannerman's TV said that Hickey, the slashing victim, lived there. Victory Boulevard. The camera had panned over a white apartment house that looked Mexican. It couldn't hurt to make a pass.

Lesko found it with no trouble because two patrol cars were still parked outside and a crime scene was lit up and taped off. Also an unmarked van with its rear door open. A man wearing an FBI vest was reaching inside. Lesko, approaching, saw him pull out a towel. He cruised by. As he passed, he saw another man, in coveralls, lying on his back under the rear bumper of a parked car. The agent with the towel began wiping it off. He seemed in a hurry.

Looked like a Chevy, thought Lesko. Must be Yuri Rykov's. The towel probably meant they had dusted it for prints and didn't want to leave powder all over it. The guy in the coveralls looked like he was rigging something. A bug? A tracking device? What for?

Lesko checked his watch. It was time to look for another phone and it probably shouldn't be in Burbank. He followed a sign that said Hollywood and stopped outside an all-night supermarket. At three sharp, he punched out Andy Huff's number. Huff picked up on the second ring.

"It's Lesko. What's the story?"

"Ah . . . we might have a deal. I have some questions first."

"Is this going to be a nice long chat, Detective?"

A brief silence. Then, "I'm just a cop, Lesko. You know what I mean?"

Lesko understood. "Yeah. I know. Tell them three minutes. After this, I don't call again."

Another silence. Lesko heard whispers.

"Why is Paul Bannerman here and whom else has he brought?" Huff asked. He actually said *whom*. That, and his tone, suggested that he was reading the question.

"I already told you."

"What is his interest in Sur La Mer?"

"I told you that, too."

More whispers.

"As far as we know," Huff was reading again, "Sur La Mer is a legitimate institution but we will check it out further. Do we have Bannerman's word that he will take no action on his own?"

"Tell them yes, Detective. As long as they're straight with him and they don't fuck with me."

Huff took a breath. "What is the KGB's interest in Sur La Mer?"

Lesko frowned. "Tell them you have one minute, Andy. You want this Campus Killer or don't you?"

"We . . . I want him. I want him bad."

"Do we have a deal? Yes or no."

"The . . . Los Angeles Police Department will not interfere with Bannerman or any of his people before midnight Thursday if he will promise us an interview, his place or ours, within forty-eight hours of that time."

"He can put that in the bank?"

"You have the word of the LAPD. You hear what I'm saying?"

"I hear you." Fucking FBI. "You all understand that there are other shooters involved, right? And that we don't know who they are?"

"We understand."

"So if I, or Bannerman, see anyone who looks funny, or we spot a tail, we're going to know these people must be them because you just gave me your word that they won't be LAPD, right?"

"Um . . . you got it, Lesko."

Lesko heard a smile.

"I'll be in touch," he said. He replaced the phone.

Sumner Dommerich was getting upset.

All he could think of, driving back from Santa Barbara, was how glad Carla would be that he had followed those men. And now he couldn't find her.

He had left the Pacific Coast Highway at Sunset Boulevard and stopped at the first bar that he knew to have a phone booth with a door on it. It was in Westwood, a beer and burger hangout for UCLA students. He would go there sometimes when he began to get those feelings. Almost always, he knew, he would see at least one girl there who was snooty and stuck-up and blond but he didn't care about that now. All he cared about was that phone.

He dialed the number of the Beverly Hills Hotel. But the man said there was no answer from Bungalow 6.

There was no use going home. He would only have to go out again to use a public phone that wasn't too close. Dommerich found a place at the bar where he ordered some potato skins and a glass of milk. He would try again in an hour.

There was no answer the second time either. But by then he had heard the kids at the bar talking about him. And what he'd done to Hickey. He asked them about it. They said it was on TV.

They said it was different this time because the victim was a guy and because there was also this big shoot-out but the police weren't saying much about it. One of the TV reporters, though, said that the dead man had been seen that morning near the apartment of the serial killer's seventh victim and so they began wondering if this man, Hickey, was actually the Campus Killer himself. Maybe the friends of one of his victims, or even the mob or somebody, tracked him down before the cops could.

The bartender said he heard that they blasted their way in but Hickey also had a gun and he hit a couple of them before they got him and carved him up.

Dommerich tried not to smile. "That's what I would have done," he said.

He was instantly sorry because he saw the way some of them looked at him. A big guy in a Grateful Dead shirt said. "Yeah. Right." A blond girl, half-stoned, put her chin on this guy's shoulder and giggled into his ear. He looked at Dommerich and smiled. A mean smile. He said, "You got milk on your upper lip there, killer."

Dommerich picked up his napkin. He pressed it, hard, against his mouth as he glared at these two. He would remember both of them.

He left his stool to try Carla again. She was still not in. This time he left a message that *Claude* called and it's important. He broke the connection, then slapped his forehead. *I know*, he thought. *She's probably at her father's house*. He remembered George Benedict, Sherman Oaks, from the newspapers. He called information, then tapped out the number.

Carla wasn't there either. Her father was still up. He sounded funny. He asked Dommerich if he was one of her friends from . . . it sounded like *Westport*.

Dommerich said, "No, just from here. Mostly I knew Lisa. I'm really sorry."

George Benedict mumbled a thank you. His voice dropped almost to a whisper. "Your name again?"

"Claude."

"How recently have you seen Carla?"

"A few hours ago." Sort of.

"What time, exactly?"

"About ten, I guess." Dommerich did not know why he lied. Except sometimes it's a good idea when people try to pin you down.

"She was okay then? She wasn't hurt?"

"She was fine."

Dommerich heard a long sigh. It sounded like relief. "Claude," he lowered his voice even further. "If you find her, tell her she'd better not come here. Or not to use the front door if she does."

"I'll tell her."

"Tell her . . . that I'll help her. Any way I can."

"So will I. Don't worry."

But now Dommerich *was* worried. If he'd seen Carla at ten, which he hadn't, that would have been long after she went to Hickey's apartment. If her father was relieved that she was still okay then, he must have been afraid that something happened to her earlier. Or that something might.

It occurred to him, for the first time, that maybe they thought she did Hickey. Maybe the men with guns were looking for her too. Maybe they already found her and that's why he couldn't.

Dommerich, his face flushed, hurried from the bar without stopping for his change.

Near the long-term parking lot of the Santa Monica Municipal Airport, Theodore Marek waited with his bodyguard, Felix, as Harry Bunce disposed of the Lexus. Or rather, parked it, first wiping it carefully.

Peter was in Mexico. With some woman. Felix had suggested the story. He'd been gone for a week. Felix would provide witnesses who had seen him there. That, if the question were asked, would be all that Marek knew.

That would be enough for the police if they inquired. That and a well-placed phone call if they persisted. But would it be enough for this Carla Benedict? To say nothing of the KGB.

He almost wished that Harry had disappeared as well. The Russian had seen his face. He might possibly identify him. A disappearance would be no more than Harry deserved. *The guy who killed Peter is dead. Mr. Marek. Trust me. He took three hollow points.*

Trust me indeed.

Except that he might need Harry.

And now, Marek brooded, *I am also to trust young Carleton. Who has already cost me a useful son. Who is entirely unrepentant of it.*

And who, come to think of it, seemed entirely too sure of himself. Almost smug. But on what basis? He had as much to fear as anyone. Sooner or later, Joseph Hickey would be traced to his doorstep. By trained assassins, no less, who were possibly in league with those two who ran off. What protection could Dunville have? Clearly, he had a course of action in mind. *I'll settle this by noon tomorrow.* Did he have something to offer in trade? The address of Harry Bunce? A dossier or two? The former Tadeusz Ordynsky in payment for the Russian?

Marek felt a chill.

Wouldn't the KGB love that, he thought. Wouldn't they love strapping him to a chair, electrodes on his testicles, taking their time as they asked for the location of every piece of art that the Nazis had looted during the final days of the siege of Leningrad, nearly all of which he had cataloged and dispersed, some of which remained buried near Pushkin, along with the Russian prisoners who dug the caves, and even the two SS sergeants who had executed them.

Wouldn't they love a stroll through his house, seeing, on the walls of his library, the splendid amber panels that had once graced the summer palace of Catherine the Great. And then a look at his vault.

No, he decided. Not possible.

Dunville knew nothing of these. No one who had seen those panels had the slightest idea where they'd come from and no one at all had seen his vault. And Dunville would not want him taken alive and questioned.

Much more likely, Dunville would try giving him to that Benedict woman and her friends. Marek fingered the piece of notepaper on which he'd written all that he'd learned about her. A dangerous woman. Made all the more dangerous, and possibly unstable, by her grief. In his mind, Marek now recalled how Dunville's expression had brightened when he realized that those women might well have seen Peter's car and might, by now, have the Marek address. He might even give it to them. Yes. That's exactly what he might do. Dunville had even made a point of telling him to go home and stay there.

The thought infuriated Marek. Here he was, totally innocent of any involvement in the death of this Carla Benedict's sister and he was to be offered in recompense. Or as a distraction. Hoping that the Benedict woman would not bother to question him, or to take him alive. Hoping that she would be content to kill him and go home.

"Mr. Marek? We're all set."

Harry Bunce had returned. Marek had barely noticed that his car door had opened and closed. Only that the interior light had flashed on the sheet of paper he'd been staring at in the darkness. He told the Mexican to proceed, then reached for the lamp at his left shoulder.

He read the names. Benedict, Farrell, Bannerman.

WASP names, basically.

The odd thing about such names, it struck him, is that they always seem distinctly nonmenacing. More like a student roster at an eastern prep school. And the nickname, code name, whatever, of this Paul Bannerman hardly could have been chosen for its intimidation value. What had his source said? Oh, yes. Bannerman's mother had been an agent of note before him. Hence, Mama's Boy. Still . . .

Marek's eye worked back to Molly Farrell's name. It suggested little to him. Not as WASP as the others. A Molly Farrell could be anything from a washerwoman to a socialite. Carla Benedict could be almost anyone as well were it not for the notation—likes to work with a knife.

There was a line drawn from her name to another notation below. Marek followed it. Ah, yes. The father. George Benedict. Sherman Oaks.

Marek looked at his watch.

The FBI, he knew, had been there looking for the daughter. He wondered, aloud, if they might still be watching the house.

"Round the clock?" Bunce asked. "I doubt it."

"Would they not expect her to go there?"

Bunce shrugged. "Not if she has any sense. She'd lay low. Anyway, she'd probably spot them first."

"You're saying that no one is protecting the father."

Bunce frowned. "From what?"

"From you and Felix here," He gestured toward his driver, "if you were to pay him a visit."

"And whack him? What good is that?"

Marek raised a staying hand. That had not been his thought but he considered it nonetheless. No, he decided. The father's death might have some value as a distraction but in the end it would only escalate matters. Borrowing him would be better. The great advantage of kidnapping over murder is that it's an even greater distraction, lasting longer, and, in the end, one is left with something to trade.

Why should Carleton Dunville hold all the cards?

34

Sumner Dommerich had to get out of there. He would have gone to pieces if he stayed. And they all would have seen it.

He knew that the more he thought about Carla, the more he worried about her, his face would have started turning red and he would be biting his knuckles so he wouldn't scream.

He screamed in the car.

He climbed into the passenger seat so that he could hold his knees up under his chin, balling himself tight so he wouldn't break things, and he screamed through his teeth until he couldn't breathe. No one heard or saw. In five minutes, he was himself again. He felt able to think.

Dommerich wished he wouldn't get like that. Especially when it was for nothing. Carla was probably okay. But if she wasn't, maybe it would be on the radio.

He switched it on and pressed the scan button, waiting as it searched for a news broadcast. He found none. His dashboard clock showed seven minutes after the hour. He'd probably just missed the news. He left it on scan and put his car in gear. He drove toward the Beverly Hills Hotel.

There was always a chance, he realized, that Carla just wasn't answering her phone. One thing he could do was go knock on her door. Bungalow 6. But what if she answered? Then she'd know what he looked like. She wouldn't turn him in, he was pretty sure. Not after he told her where those men went.

He would also tell her that the man at the desk had given out her room number. They're not supposed to do that. That's how rooms get robbed. Anyway, maybe he'd just listen at her door. Maybe leave a note under it. And leave Lisa's jewelry in the bushes where Carla could find it.

He could see as he approached the hotel that something was going on. Some big party, just breaking up. Valets bringing up cars. That was good. They'd be too busy to notice that he was delivering a pizza to one of the bungalows. You weren't supposed to do that either. Dommerich had delivered plenty of pizzas to hotels in the middle of the night but the fancy ones usually made you wait in the lobby to get paid while their own bellboys took the pizza to the room. Half the time, the bellboys would say there wasn't any tip but you'd know from their eyes that they kept it.

Dommerich put on his hat and slipped an empty box into his thermal sleeve. He scribbled an order on his pad and tucked his knife into his belt. The main entrance suddenly lit up. Someone with a video camera and floodlights. They made the doorman blink. Good. Dommerich moved toward the path leading to the bungalows.

The bungalow area, he thought, was like being in the woods. Lots of thick bushes and trees, dark except for foot-high lamps along the winding path. A phone was ringing someplace. As he drew near, the sound seemed to come from Bungalow 6 but he couldn't be sure. The ringing stopped. There was a light on somewhere inside, dim, like from a bathroom. Suddenly, he was afraid. What if someone was there but it was the other woman, Farrell? She was definitely on Carla's side but that didn't mean she'd be on his.

He stood still for a long moment, pretending to squint at his order sheet, trying to decide. Better, he thought, to try to look in the window first. Most of the windows were around the side.

Dommerich had just turned the corner when he heard a spit of static. It was like the sound a bug zapper made except he hadn't seen one and except the noise seemed to have come from where he'd been standing. He froze and listened. He heard a man's voice, speaking quietly but clearly.

"Just some kid. . . . Delivering pizza."

Dommerich's heart began pounding. He eased the knife from his belt.

Another spit. Another voice, very dim. He couldn't hear what it said but the first voice asked *"Who said?"* then, *"Fine with me. I could use some sleep."*

Dommerich eased into a deep shadow at the corner of Carla's bungalow. He heard a rustling of bushes and the scrape of shoes reaching the path. He risked a peek. He saw a man, dressed in a suit and tie, something in his hand. Dommerich could see a bent antenna on it. A walkie-talkie. The man, he realized, had been waiting for Carla.

Suddenly he was more angry than afraid. He saw himself walking up to that man, asking him which way to Bungalow 10, then sliding the knife into his chest as the man told him to get lost. He could drag him back into the bushes and leave him there. He could tell Carla, later, to go look.

Except the man was now walking away. Dommerich waited a few seconds, then followed. The man left the bungalow area and stopped at the driveway. A car pulled up, another suit and tie driving. The headlights washed over the man with the walkie-talkie. The man got in. The car drove off.

Dommerich knew who he was. He had seen him outside Lisa's apartment. He was one of the two from the FBI who had dragged Carla down the stairs in handcuffs and now it looked like he was trying to do it again. Dommerich almost wished that the man hadn't left.

He knew a stakeout when he saw one. And from the way the man from the bushes said *Fine with me*, it didn't sound as if they'd found Carla someplace else. It sounded like they'd just decided to give up.

Dommerich went back to the side windows and peered through them. He could see two bedrooms. One bed was made, one wasn't. Carla was definitely not there unless she was hiding under her bed. He couldn't imagine her doing that. He also saw pieces of luggage, and toiletries were visible on the bathroom counter. This meant she'd be back. The phone rang again. It made him jump. It seemed to ring a long time before it stopped.

He tore a blank sheet from his order book and wrote her a note. He tucked it under her door. From his pocket he took the handkerchief in which he'd wrapped Lisa's jewelry. He concealed it behind a shrub near the edge of the door and covered it with green leaves. Dommerich returned to his car.

Where to now? he wondered. He turned up his radio. It was still on scan.

He could drive up to Sherman Oaks, he supposed. The FBI was probably watching that house as well—which must be why her father said she should come in the back way. But if the two at the hotel gave up, the ones at the house were probably gone by now too. Still, it was a long way to go for nothing. He'd call again instead. At least tell her father about the note and the . . .

Dommerich jabbed a finger to stop the scan. Too late. It had played part of a news broadcast. He'd heard, "*. . . former policeman, Joseph Hickey . . . the wounded man . . . identity withheld . . . spokesman at the Queen of Angels Medical Center told reporters that . . .*"

Dommerich brightened.

That's where she'd be.

Maybe.

Staying with her friend. Anyway, Queen of Angels was on Vermont Avenue, which was on his way home. It was worth a look. After that, he could use some sleep himself.

"*What do you think?*" Lesko asked this question of his empty passenger seat.

"The feds want the collar for themselves," Katz said, shrugging. *"What else is new?"*

Lesko nodded slowly, then shook his head. *"It's more than that."*

"Like what?"

"Like they got this whole task force that's spent at least a year looking for this Claude creep but suddenly all they care about is Bannerman bothering those nice people up at some movie nut house."

"So? Ask why."

Lesko rolled his eyes. *"Why didn't I think of that?"*

"Not them, you putz. Call Kaplan."

Lesko blinked. Right. The feds here would have called Washington. Their bosses, once Bannerman's name was mentioned, would probably have called Irwin. He looked at his watch. A quarter after six, Washington time. Irwin would be trying to get back to sleep.

"Say you're sorry."

"All night, you had one idea. Don't make a big deal."

"You're so smart? Tell me why they'd be rigging Yuri Rykov's car back there."

Lesko had wondered. But mostly about them doing it at three in the morning. And whether his call to Andy Huff had anything to do with it. *"I don't know. Why?"*

"The answer is they wouldn't. Think about it, wise ass."

Lesko nodded slowly. *"You're saying it's not Yuri's car? Then whose?"* But he knew the answer. Someone who they hope will come get it. Carla? She wouldn't be that dumb. But if they're rigging it, they can't intend to take her. Probably follow her to Claude. Or maybe Bannerman.

"There's the hospital," Katz pointed.

Lesko saw it off to his right. Big place. The only building in the area still fairly well lit. Nothing looks quite so lonely, he thought, as a hospital at night.

"We could check it out. See what the reporters are saying."

Not a bad idea, thought Lesko. The press would still be hanging around in case Yuri dies, meanwhile schmoozing with orderlies to see what else they could learn. He also wouldn't mind talking to Belkin. And it was as good a place as any from which to call Irwin.

Lesko flipped his turn signal.

35

Molly Farrell counted ten rings before the night operator confirmed that no one was answering. Molly, her eyes on Carla's empty bed, cursed under her breath.

She looked at her watch, uselessly. It was almost four. But she had no idea how long Carla had been gone.

Molly identified herself as the other guest staying in Bungalow 6. She listened for any strangeness in the operator's voice and, hearing none, left a message asking Carla to call her the moment she gets in. Ms. Benedict, she said, knows where to reach her.

"There's another message for you, Ms. Farrell. A Ms. Fenerty called a short while ago. She says it's urgent and you have the number."

Molly snatched at her purse and found the torn page from the telephone book, hopeful that Carla might have gone to DiDi's house. And was there now. She could only guess why. Perhaps to feel closer to Lisa. Or perhaps someone had tried to get to DiDi.

It would be better, she realized, not to make these calls from her hotel. But Molly had no car with which to get to a distant phone. And please God, come to think of it, don't let Carla have gone to get that Chevrolet.

No. She would have had to take a taxi all the way to Burbank. She could just as easily have taken the taxi to

DiDi's house. Molly punched out the number. DiDi answered on the second ring.

"It's me," Molly said. "Is everything okay?"

"Hi, M . . ." DiDi stopped herself. "Can I talk on the phone?"

Molly appreciated her discretion. But she'd decided that a wiretap was unlikely. "It's all right. Is Carla there, by chance?"

"Ah . . . should she be? I haven't seen her since she left."

"Just wondered. She went out a while ago. What's urgent, DiDi?"

"I had a phone call you won't believe. Were you and Carla . . . ah, up in Burbank last evening?"

"Tell me about the call."

"It was this man. He said to tell Carla that the Russian was shot by a man named . . ."

"Hold it," Molly snapped. She thought quickly. "Are your father's men still there with you?"

"They're right here."

"Is there a neighbor's phone you can use? Not one of your house mates'."

"Kevin's place. He's still sacked out on the porch."

Molly asked for the number. She said she'd call it in ten minutes. DiDi's bodyguards were to go first and make sure the street was clear. She broke the connection, grabbed a pocket recorder, then hurried downstairs to the lobby phone. It would have to do. The remaining minutes passed slowly. She rang Kevin's number. DiDi picked up.

"Can the bodyguards hear you?" she asked.

"They're waiting outside. But I'm afraid I already told them."

"No sweat." But she grimaced. "Start from the beginning."

"That man, Hickey, who was cut up last night? He's the one who came here claiming to be a cop."

"I know."

"He killed Lisa."

"He might have. Tell me about the call."

"And another man was shot there. A Russian named Rykov?"

"How did you know that name?"

"The man who called knew it. He said Rykov was shot by two men driving a white Lexus. Its license number is. . . . Do you have a pen?"

"I'm getting this. Go ahead."

DiDi read the tag number from her notes. "The two men were Harry Bunce and Peter Marek." She paused to spell both names. "Peter Marek, if you're ready for this, is the son of Theodore Marek. The art dealer? Richardson-Marek?"

The firm name was vaguely familiar. Perhaps she'd seen a catalog in Anton Zivic's shop.

"Except," DiDi paused for effect, "Theodore Marek's real name is Tadeusz Ordynsky." She spelled that name as well. "Ordynsky was, and is, a fugitive war criminal and an art thief. Somehow Lisa found that out. He had her killed by that man, Hickey, who was cut up last night in Burbank. Then he sent these other two to silence Hickey but Carla beat them to it . . . says this guy . . . and they ran into this Rykov who is, by the way, a KGB agent. Do you believe this?"

"Parts of it," she said thoughtfully. "Carla didn't kill Hickey."

DiDi hesitated. "I guess I'm sorry to hear that," she said.

"This man," Molly asked. "Was he the same one who called before? The German accent?"

"You mean Paul Bannerman?"

"Um . . . yes."

"No," she said. "This one sounded like that FBI agent, Harris, who you said was a phony. Two real ones have been here, by the way. They seemed more interested in you two than in Lisa."

"How much did you tell them?"

"Almost nothing. That you picked up some of her things and left."

"Nothing about Sur La Mer?"

"They never asked. They just . . ." DiDi fell silent, as if she'd remembered something else.

"They just what?"

"Not them. The man who called. You know who else he sounded like?"

Molly waited.

"He also sounded like the man I spoke to at Sur La Mer. The one who said Lisa was never there."

For a time, in the chill of the night, Nellie thought she was still at the lake.

Her eyelids flicked open, sleepily, as she felt her arm being raised. Far to the east she could see the first gray sliver in the predawn sky and, near the window, the dark branches of a tree waving as if to greet it. She felt the covers being brought up over her shoulder. Tom's hand brushed against her cheek. She murmured softly, and smiled. In seconds, she was dozing deliciously.

She did not sleep for long. The murmur of a cool lake breeze had begun to take on a mechanical sound. More like that of an air-conditioner. In the distance, she could hear the throaty growl of passing trucks. Her eyes snapped open.

The glow in the east was lighter than before, although far from blue. She knew that she was back.

Nellie turned one ear toward the heavy curtain that she'd drawn across her cot and listened for Alan and Barbara. She was prepared, if she'd heard them stirring, to try to go away again. To allow them another hour or two of privacy. She wouldn't mind another toss with Tom herself. Besides, she wanted to be sure that she could do it. Go away, that is. At will. Without benefit of her bench or her chair.

She heard other sounds now, soft whispers, but they did not seem to be coming from the bed on the other side of the curtain. They were farther away and muted. Nellie frowned. She slipped one arm from under her blanket and felt for the briefcase which she'd taken to bed with her. It was gone. She realized at once that it wasn't Tom who had lifted her arm. It was Alan, wanting those silly papers again. He had taken them into the bathroom and closed the door. She heard Barbara in there with him.

Nellie eased herself out of bed and cleared her throat, loudly, in a way that would tell Alan and Barbara that she was awake and that they were about to be scolded.

Sumner Dommerich knew a Pizza Hut on Sunset that practically never closed. He stopped to buy two large pies, one pepperoni, one sausage.

It bothered him to buy from a competitor, especially because his company and Pizza Hut had been in this big race to see who opened the first franchise in Moscow and Pizza Hut had won. But it was not his fault that none of his own stores were open. Anyway, no one would know the difference now that he'd taken them out of the Pizza Hut boxes and written them up on his own order form.

It said that someone named Jackson had ordered them. There wouldn't be any Jackson at the hospital, probably, but there was a good chance that someone else would take them if he gave them a deal. Someone is always hungry for a pizza. And this way no one would wonder why he was there. Dommerich put his hat back on and drove to Queen of Angels.

There were two men with cameras and one security guard at the entrance to the emergency room. All three were smoking. We didn't order any pizza, they said. Try the waiting room.

At least a dozen people were sitting or pacing there. Two cops were questioning a black man with a bandaged cheek. A doctor was talking to a young couple who looked worried. The woman was holding a teddy bear. A big, tough-looking man, probably a detective, was talking on a wall phone. A much smaller man stood near him, sucking on a pipe that wasn't lit. There was no sign

of Carla. But she might be with her friend, he thought.
Or in the ladies room or the chapel. Dommerich decided
to wait a few minutes. Then he would roam the hallways
looking for a room with a policeman standing guard. He
hoped they didn't only do that on TV.

"We were, um . . . trying not to wake you."

Alan Weinberg looked up at Nellie from the edge of
the tub. Barbara sat at his side. She, like her husband,
had papers in her hands. More were spread over the tile
floor at their feet. Alan's expression, thought Nellie, was
that of a boy caught reading a girlie magazine.

Hands on hips, Nellie shook her head in theatrical
dismay. Alan was more like George Bancroft than he
knew. George used to save his most salacious fan letters,
the ones making indecent proposals, and tuck them into
scripts he was supposed to be studying. She was about to
instruct Weinberg on the proper use of a lazy morning
by two people who love each other but Nellie saw the
grin that now split Barbara's face. The grin said that
giving them a few hours to themselves had been, by no
means, a wasted gesture.

"So," Weinberg shifted uncomfortably, "How did it
go at the lake?"

Nellie did not look at him. Her eyes were on
Barbara. "None of your beeswax," she told him.

Weinberg, now ignored, glanced from one face to
the other. He watched as the brow of one would rise
slightly and the lips of the other would purse in response. A subtle eye movement here, an answering
twitch there. He was witnessing one of those maddening
telepathic conversations of which only women are capable and from which all men are excluded. He felt his
color rising. The flare of a nostril, for all he knew, could
be describing the length of his penis. Weinberg crossed
his legs. The women locked eyes and laughed. Weinberg
threw up his hands. Barbara seized his sleeve to keep
him from leaving the room.

"I'm sorry," she said, but she had to bite her lip. She

reached for one of the dossiers that her husband had been holding and told Nellie, telepathically again, that there was a need to be serious for a moment. "Nellie," she asked, "what do you know about a man named *Marek*?"

Nellie's mouth formed an expression of distaste. Sur La Mer had begun to seem far away. She was reluctant to go back there, even in her thoughts.

"We have to ask," said Barbara, gesturing with the Marek file. "This sounds as if the Dunvilles use him for their dirty work. Is that right?"

She didn't know. Not at first. But she allowed her mind to drift. It wandered across the years, sorting through a hundred snippets of gossip and dozens of eavesdropped conversations. She remembered something that Harland had told her.

"Was there really another war with the Germans?" she asked.

"Ah . . . quite a while ago, yes."

"Harland said that the father used to work for them. But I don't think he was German."

Barbara shook her head. "He was Polish, but a war criminal. What about the son?"

"Little Peter," she nodded. More distaste. "Peter's not really his son. They gave him Peter after he brought Luisa back. We were glad to see him go. He would stick thumb tacks in Harland's legs while he was sleeping. Harland had no feeling in them but all the same . . ."

"Theodore Marek . . ." Barbara's eyes narrowed. "Is this the man Dunville was talking about last night in the car?"

"The one who ruined Luisa. Yes."

Weinberg squeezed his wife's knee. His touch urged a measure of detachment on the issue of child abuse, especially because Weinberg himself had probably blown her to pieces. "It seemed to me," he said to Nellie, "that young Carleton despised him. If his father were . . . out of the picture, would he continue to use him?"

Nellie considered the question. Something in Alan's eyes hinted that it was not an academic inquiry. And something else was odd. She had trouble remembering what Carleton the elder looked like. Or caring. Whether she'd borne him or not. "He might have to," she answered at last. "Harland says the guards all really work for Marek."

"Why would that be?"

She shrugged. "When new guards come, he always brings them. Harland thinks they're all on the lam. That's gangster talk for fugitives."

Weinberg thanked her for the clarification. "Did he supply Hickey, by chance?"

She nodded. "But Hickey wasn't a criminal. They say he was a policeman once. Several of them were."

"Nellie . . . are you aware that Hickey is dead? And that Peter Marek may be dead as well?"

As for Peter, she was not a bit surprised. Nasty child. And she had assumed as much about Hickey from what was said in the car. And later, she told Weinberg, it was discussed on the television receiver.

"Ah, yes." Weinberg had forgotten that she might see the news. He would have watched for it himself had he not been preoccupied with Barbara. "Did that report mention anyone else?"

"Another man was shot but he's alive. One station said he was rumored to be a diplomat of some sort."

Weinberg blinked. "A diplomat?"

"From the Soviet Union."

Perhaps Nellie had misunderstood. "It wasn't an American? A man named McHugh?"

"The reporter was quite emphatic that he was Russian. He seemed very pleased with himself."

"Did he name a suspect?"

"He talked about the killer of all those young girls mostly. But he didn't seem to think he did this."

"Any mention of Carla Benedict?"

Nellie shook her head. "Just of poor Lisa. Along with the others."

Weinberg pushed to his feet. For a long moment he stared thoughtfully into space and then into the bathroom mirror. The new face seemed better this morning although he still looked as if he'd been in a fight. "I think I'll walk down and get a newspaper," he said to his wife. His eyes said Come with me. She answered with a nod.

The private exchange did not escape Nellie. She made no move to let them pass. She watched as they stepped into their shoes and as Alan slid a revolver into the small of his back. Barbara slung her purse to her shoulder and placed her hand inside it.

"Just a newspaper?" she asked.

Barbara followed Nellie's eyes to her purse. "And perhaps to make a call from a public phone," she said. "There won't be any trouble."

"Does this phone call involve Mr. Marek?"

Barbara glanced at her husband, and then Nellie. "We might try to . . . distract him if we can."

"Couldn't we . . ." Nellie looked away. "Couldn't we all just go and find a boat? Is that so selfish?"

"We will." Barbara gathered the files. "And no, it isn't."

That assurance, Nellie decided, was probably no less sincere for being curt. She backed away from the bathroom, watching Alan and Barbara as they unlatched the door and stepped into the corridor, one at a time as always, cautiously as always. Telling her not to open it for anyone but them.

They were a fascinating study, really. Quite nice people. They were certainly kind. But it was astonishing to watch the way they could, in the wink of an eye, step out of one character and into another. Rather like actors. Except that with an actor one usually knew which character was real and which was pretend.

She could get used to it, she supposed. She could get used to the guns as well but she disliked the thought of having to. It was so much fun escaping. And her first night of freedom was wonderful. There would be plenty of time to see what the world has come to. All she

wanted now was to feel wind and salt spray on her face.
And not have a care.

Except about Harland and the others.

Which gave her an idea.

She couldn't imagine why the Weinbergs went out
to make their call when there was a perfectly good
telephone right here with instructions printed next to
the buttons. There was even a directory.

She opened it and found the number of young Dr.
Feldman.

36

"Irwin . . . Shit head . . ."

Lesko was getting aggravated.

The more he tried to assure Kaplan that Bannerman
wasn't there on a hit, the less Kaplan believed him.

"You're telling me," Kaplan challenged, "that Leo
Belkin just happened to be in Los Angeles and Rykov
just happened to run into Carla. Who the fuck would
buy that, Lesko? And you wonder why people are
nervous."

Those nervous people, Kaplan had told him, began
calling at half past four in the morning, his time. The
calls began, in other words, thirty minutes after Lesko
had laid out his proposition to Andy Huff. And the calls
were from heavy hitters. Two were sitting members of
the National Security Council. The last one was from
Roger Clew, an undersecretary of state who had built his
career on being Bannerman's control until Clew tried
this scam to lure him back out of retirement. It got a
bunch of people killed.

Why all this interest? Kaplan says they wouldn't say.

They would cite the usual need-to-know and national security bullshit but they still expected Kaplan to tell them whether Bannerman and/or the KGB was planning a hit on Sur La Mer.

"For the last time, Irwin," Lesko showed his teeth, "Bannerman didn't know Leo was out here until I told him. Then all he asked Leo was to keep Carla out of trouble until he got here himself."

"Why is the KGB there in the first place?"

"Spy shit, probably. You want to ask Leo? He's right here."

"Forget I asked. I would hate knowing."

"Also for the last time, Bannerman doesn't care squat about Sur La Mer. He only . . . Hold on a second."

A kid with a quilted pizza box had wandered over and was staring at him. Lesko covered the mouthpiece. "What?" he asked.

"Mr. Jackson?"

"No."

"Did you order two pizzas?"

"No."

"There's a pepperoni and a sausage. If I can't find who ordered them, you want one for half price?"

"Kid . . . I'm on the phone here."

"Sorry." Sumner Dommerich turned to Leo Belkin. "They're still hot. Want to see?"

Belkin eased him away from the phone.

"Wait." Lesko snapped his fingers toward the KGB colonel. "You got any money? Get us the pepperoni, okay?" He hadn't eaten since his flight.

"Lesko! Will you stop with the fucking pizza?" Kaplan shouted into his ear.

Oh yeah. "Here's what you tell them, Irwin. There's no hit, no nothing, as long as they leave us alone. In two days we bury Lisa and we all go home."

"And Bannerman delivers this serial killer?"

"He gives it a shot but the FBI has to give Carla some room. Otherwise we keep her stashed."

"How about if he calls Roger Clew on this himself. So I'm not in the middle."

"He won't. He's finished with Clew."

"Better yet," Kaplan dropped his voice, "he should call Bart Fuller."

Clew's boss. The secretary of state. Same thing, probably. Same reasons. "I doubt it. But I'll ask."

"Lesko," Kaplan sounded weary. "Does Bannerman want to keep that bug up his ass or does he want answers?"

"Those two almost got Susan killed, Irwin. And they got Elena shot. They're lucky I didn't . . ." He stopped himself. "Answers to what?" he asked.

"Think about it. Go eat your pizza."

Sumner Dommerich waited in his car. He thought, not for the first time, that he should have been a spy.

He'd read about them.

The good ones, he knew, were nothing at all like James Bond. They were just average looking people like himself. No one ever gave them a second look. And they liked it that way. It never hurt their feelings.

Dommerich knew that he could sit for hours, at a bar, for example, and the people around him could be having really private conversations and it would be like his stool was empty.

He didn't mind that. He liked being invisible. But now and then, if they were just joking around or talking about baseball or something, he would make a comment on what they were saying. Not butting in or anything. Just telling them something he knew, or what he thought. That's when, most times, his feelings got hurt. They'd look at him, they'd say "Oh . . . right," and then they'd move their heads closer together so he couldn't hear anymore. Sometimes they'd tell him to buzz off. Sometimes they'd laugh.

It was the girls, mostly, who laughed. They'd either roll their eyes or they'd give him that somebody-must-have-farted look and then they'd put their heads together and cover their mouths. Girls must practice that.

Lisa wouldn't have laughed. Not Carla either.

And soon he would know where Carla was. That man with the mean face would lead him to her. Dommerich even knew which car he was driving. Or he was pretty sure. There was a Ford parked in the circle that looked just like the one that pulled up next to him at that hot tub store except that the one who got shot was driving it then.

Now Lesko had it.

Lesko.

Dommerich heard his name when the man on the other end, named Irwin, yelled it. Lesko . . . stop with the fucking pizza. The third man, the one who bought the pizza, full price, was named Leo.

Lesko was a little brusque but Dommerich was not offended. He just needed to finish with Irwin. Dommerich would not have interrupted him except that he needed to get closer when he thought he heard Carla's name.

He'd heard it, all right. That and a lot more.

Lesko is here for Lisa's funeral. That means he's a friend. Someone named Bannerman, another friend, is here to watch over Carla. Everybody seems to know about Sur La Mer, maybe even that Hickey and those other two came from there, and nobody wants to do anything about it.

But maybe Carla still doesn't know.

Maybe Lesko and Bannerman aren't telling her.

Or maybe they *would* tell her, and go *do* something, if only the FBI would leave them alone.

That's it, thought Dommerich.

Lesko said they'd "give it a shot but the FBI has to give Carla some room" and maybe the FBI already did because they're not watching her hotel anymore.

That's one more thing he had to tell her.

Dommerich held his order pad up to the light. More names and notes.

Somebody named "Crew" or "Clue"
"Susan—almost killed."
"Elena—shot."
By "those two."

Those two might be the killers in the Lexus, he
thought, yawning. Maybe they also shot two women
named Susan and Elena.
Carla would tell him.
He yawned again.
He wished he'd thought to buy some coffee.

37

Jack Scholl, special agent in charge of the Campus
Killer Task Force, had argued, pleaded, even threatened
in his effort to duck that assignment. He was told to take
it or retire.

Scholl's duties, for the five years preceding the
discovery of the second victim, had essentially been
limited to public relations. He had become the unofficial
spokesman of the Los Angeles field office because he,
unlike his boss, was comfortable in front of cameras and
because he looked and sounded a bit like Efrem Zim-
balist, Jr., of the old FBI television series.

That resemblance, a measure of celebrity, and the
fact that he was, by bureau standards, independently
wealthy, caused him to be a frequent guest at civic and
social functions. Scholl seemed to know everyone. Pol-
iticians whispered into his ear. Filmmakers sought his
technical advice. Religious leaders sought his moral
voice.

His fellow agents were less than impressed. They

regarded Scholl as living proof that it was better to be lucky than smart.

They remembered a time when he was considered a marginal agent, just good enough to be allowed to put in his twenty and retire. His run of luck had begun with a weekend trip to Las Vegas. Scholl announced on returning that he had won almost $10,000 at blackjack. That windfall served to explain how Scholl managed to live better than most, drive a nicer car, take better vacations.

At about that time, he also began enjoying a series of well-publicized successes as a federal agent. He led several major drug raids and found two aging Nazi fugitives who were living in Los Angeles. Although Scholl's boss was inclined to count his blessings, he could not help wishing that some of Scholl's were more the result of competent investigative procedure—teamwork—and less the result of anonymous tips.

Scholl's most extraordinary piece of luck came soon after the death of his father. The father, a widower, had died some six years ago, leaving Scholl his Pasadena home and everything in it. Everything, as it turned out, included an attic trunk containing his father's World War II memorabilia. It also contained three rolled-up canvasses by Corot and one Delacroix self-portrait. The paintings were authenticated by the reputable firm of Richardson-Marek, which also determined through the International Institute for Art Research that they had never been reported stolen and had no claims against them. Richardson-Marek sold them to a Japanese auto parts manufacturer for more than $2 million.

Scholl's boss was surprised that he stayed with the bureau. His fitness reports, for all Scholl's luck, did not auger promotion. The pension would be nice but no longer essential. Scholl, however, not only stayed but thrived. His pool of informants seemed to grow in proportion to his social and media contacts. Scholl's boss could only shake his head.

After the second victim was found, and the FBI was

called in, Jack Scholl was his boss's choice to head the bureau's end of the task force, primarily because no one else wanted the job. Serial killer cases often dragged on for years and were, in the end, usually solved by dumb luck. The real job involved persuading the media that progress was being made. In the event of an arrest, Scholl would be there, in front of the cameras, elbowing his way past whoever made it. That's what he was best at. In the meantime, better him than to waste an agent who had genuine talent.

Scholl could not have refused. The retirement option was unattractive because retirement would mean the end of his usefulness to Theodore Marek. And Marek, as he'd often pointed out, could always suddenly discover that the Corots and the Delacroix were worthless forgeries and urge a lawsuit by the Japanese buyer. There could be no defense. A charge that Marek had provided them in the first place would be equally ruinous. Scholl would be disgraced. He would lose his pension as well.

But now, for the first time in his ten-year relationship with Theodore Marek, providing him with files, doctoring others, protecting Marek's friends and harassing his enemies, Jack Scholl began to feel that he might have the upper hand.

By the time he'd made his visit to the apartment of the Benedict girl, largely for the sake of procedure, he was already satisfied that she was almost certainly the victim of a copycat. When told by the superintendent that someone was already inside, he presumed the intruder to be a relative but possibly a reporter. If the latter, his own entry, gun drawn, all business, might lead to a very respectful interview. Instead, those two women had humiliated him.

He knew all about them within the hour. Professional assassins, both of them. He was astonished. Washington was in an uproar. Why, they asked, had he not held them?

He would have. Had he known. Or had that

Detective Huff and those other smirking policemen not intervened.

Never mind, said Washington. Say nothing to the media. Not even to the others on the task force. Await further instructions.

Washington, he thought at the time, was overreacting. More than anything else, he decided, they were probably afraid of two female vigilantes stirring up a media circus. Avenging angels, going around executing suspects, that sort of thing.

He had traced them, that afternoon, to the house of the Fenerty girl. She was their only lead, a name on the dead girl's answering machine. But Fenerty claimed that she knew nothing, had told them nothing. The two women stayed only a few minutes, then left.

Scholl was sure that she was lying. For one thing, she referred to them as Molly and Carla. The reference smacked of familiarity. For another, there was that beefy young man on the porch who obviously gave an alarm when he pulled up and there were two other men, swarthy, hard-eyed, loitering inside. Unless Fenerty knew more than she was saying, why should she feel the need for bodyguards? Scholl returned to his office where he arranged, without benefit of court order, for a monitoring of Miss Fenerty's telephone.

The shocks, that evening, came in rapid succession. Joe Hickey, a corrupt policeman now on Marek's payroll, slashed to death in the manner of the serial killer. Another man, shown to be a KGB captain, shot. Two men, one bleeding, seen stumbling from Hickey's apartment and rushing off in a white Lexus.

Marek's son had a new white Lexus.

The two women, Benedict and Farrell, positively identified as being on the scene. Benedict—*works with a knife*—almost certainly the killer of Hickey. Theodore Marek, calling, clearly shaken, demanding details on the people involved, asking if the two who drove off had been identified. Marek, according to Scholl's readout, had called from Sur La Mer.

Scholl knew little about Sur La Mer. Only that he was to respect, misdirect, or quash any inquiries that came through his office. He presumed it to be either the center of Marek's drug operations or a sort of convention center for art forgers. Maybe Marek's son was the bleeder. Maybe he's hiding out there.

The final shock, or series of them, came late that night. A call from someone named Lesko, denying that the woman killed Hickey, claiming that the Campus Killer did it, offering to catch and deliver him in return for certain guarantees. Also asking about Sur La Mer. And acknowledging that this man, Bannerman, was in town.

Scholl had never heard of Bannerman—Mama's Boy—before that morning. But Washington certainly knew him. A renegade contract agent, apparently. And very possibly a traitor judging by his involvement with the KGB. But one with "friends" in the State Department. Probably people he's compromised.

As for that nonsense about the Campus Killer, thought Scholl, it was absurd on its face. Too many inconsistencies. For one thing, no hair was taken. For another, Hickey was hardly a college girl. He was a tough, even brutal ex–police officer with a gun on his hip and yet he had been subdued and tortured. Scholl could see no way in the world that the Campus Killer, thought to be a young man of less than average height, could have done that by himself. Those women did it. Probably with the help of their hulking KGB friend.

And yet that moron, Huff, bought Lesko's story.

Washington was also buying it although their main concern seemed to be this Bannerman's possible intentions toward Sur La Mer. Marek, no doubt, had friends of his own in government.

What, Scholl wondered, was really going on here?

His best guess was that Marek had ordered the Benedict girl killed. He had no idea why. Perhaps she was one of his couriers. Tried to steal from him. Perhaps the Fenerty girl was another. That would make sense.

She might know, therefore, who was likely to be given the job of killing Lisa Benedict.

Marek, in any case, gave the job to Hickey. The girl's sister returned the favor. Peter Marek and another man—Harry Bunce, like as not—apparently walked in on her. Perhaps Hickey had phoned them for help. Perhaps he spotted Carla Benedict and the Russian as they pulled up in that Chevrolet. Or perhaps Peter merely blundered onto the scene as the Russian was ransacking Hickey's apartment.

Regardless.

The key, from his point of view, was that Theodore Marek had, in a rare lapse, left a trail leading back to himself. This Campus Killer business was a ruse aimed at giving Carla Benedict and friends an unimpeded shot at him.

So be it.

Scholl would cooperate with Huff. Up to a point. He had lifted his surveillance of the Beverly Hills Hotel and of the Benedict house in Sherman Oaks. He'd had a tracking device wired to that woman's rented Chevrolet in case she was foolish enough to recover it. He would give those people all the slack they needed until he was sure where they were holed up.

He was almost sure already. Thanks to the Fenerty girl.

Then he would tell Marek. And sit back and watch. While they slaughtered each other.

38

The clock at his bedside read a quarter past four.

Bannerman, wrapped in a bed sheet, his expression grim, made notes on a telephone pad as he played, for the second time, Molly's recording of her conversation with DiDi Fenerty.

Susan had slipped into Bannerman's shirt when Molly knocked. Now, listening to the tape, she searched his garment bag for a fresh one so that he could dress. They would not be going back to bed. Not with Carla missing.

Her ring raked across something hard within the folds of the hanging bag. She traced her fingers over it, instantly recognizing the shape of an automatic pistol in a belt-clip holster. She was withdrawing her hand when she felt a second weapon, smaller than the first, no holster.

Billy, she realized, must have quietly stashed them when he stopped by earlier. It surprised her that there were two. She wondered if Billy had taken it on himself to see that she was armed as well. She doubted it. Paul might have finally decided to treat her as a grown-up. But it was not the time to ask. He was concerned about Carla. And he had just been given the name of the man who'd ordered the murder of her sister.

"You called her from this hotel?" Bannerman asked Molly.

"I . . . made several calls. Yes."

Bannerman chewed his lip.

"A wire," Molly told him, "didn't seem likely. Not this soon and not on DiDi's phone." She pointed to her tape machine. "That conversation, at least, was on a clean line."

Bannerman arched one eye.

"I know," she said. "It wasn't smart."

Susan thought she understood. If DiDi's phone had been wired, the call from the man who gave her those names would have already been intercepted. Having DiDi repeat them over a clean line had been of little use. A part of Susan was glad to see that Molly was human.

Bannerman chose not to press the point in front of Susan. He gestured as if to say that the damage, if any, was already done. He tapped his notepad. "Could Carla have these names?"

"How?" Molly tossed her hands. "DiDi hasn't heard from her. And I've been with her all this time."

"Where else might she have gone?"

A shrug. "I called the Beverly Hills. If she's there, she's not answering. I just tried her father. He hasn't seen her either but Claude, if you believe it, called him a couple of hours ago. Claude's looking for her too."

Bannerman stared. "Carla's father knows about Claude?"

She shook her head. "He thinks it was just some friend of Lisa's. But he's worried about Carla. He thinks she killed Hickey and he's been seeing cars with men in them."

Probably detectives, thought Bannerman, although they should have been pulled by now if Lesko made the deal. His eye fell to the names on his notepad. It was obvious, he realized, that someone, possibly at Sur La Mer, wanted Carla to bloody the names on that list. Perhaps that same someone had played it both ways . . . told those names that she'd be coming. He was getting a bad feeling about this.

"How did Carla leave here? Did she take Yuri's car?"

Molly shook her head. "Lesko has it. He's still not back."

Bannerman checked his watch. He was beginning

to get a bad feeling about that as well when Molly saw a wash of headlights in the parking lot outside. She stepped to the window. "Here he is now," she said.

Bannerman waited until he heard the slam of a car door. He flicked his lamp on and off three times. "He sees us." said Molly.

Susan tossed clean socks and a laundered shirt to Bannerman. She stripped off his old one and dressed quickly, choosing tan slacks and a green blouse. Bannerman, finding his trousers, asked Molly to go and wake Billy.

"Tell him I want him outside with John Waldo," he said. "We just might have visitors. But you go back to your room. Sit tight in case Carla shows. Call the Fenerty girl. You might as well give her your number in case she has any more mystery callers."

Bannerman picked up the phone and dialed. He turned his head. As good a time as any, thought Susan. She reached into his garment bag and found the smaller of the two automatics. She dropped it into her purse. She moved to the bed, straightening it, hiding the baby powder. Her father was funny about such things.

Bannerman was talking to Anton Zivic. He read the names from his notepad, then listened in silence for a minute or two. He thanked Zivic and replaced the phone.

Molly had left the door ajar. Susan could hear her father in the corridor, in muffled conversation with Molly. She heard him say, "In a minute." He walked past in the direction of his own room. Susan ran a quick brush through her hair.

"Anton's heard of Marek," Bannerman said behind her. "There are rumors that he deals in stolen art. He'll see what else he can find out. In the meantime," Bannerman made a face, "Roger Clew has been trying to reach me."

Susan turned. "After a year?"

Bannerman nodded.

"In connection with this?"

Bannerman shrugged. "One wonders. But he wouldn't say."

She saw that his eyes, normally soft, had taken a curious shine. They were going back in time, she imagined, over the years of his relationship with an increasingly cynical Roger who had, in the end, played one game too many. But those eyes, right now, seemed to be lingering on her purse. She searched them for any sign that he had seen her take the gun. She considered mentioning it. She would when they were alone again.

He noticed that she was studying him. The eyes narrowed slightly and he cocked his head. She had a guilty feeling that he was trying to read her mind.

"Nothing," she shrugged dismissively. "I just like watching you."

That made him self-conscious. It always did.

"You're so controlled," she said. "I admire that."

She didn't really. Women never did. But the flattery distracted him.

"I'm in control?" He slipped into his shoes. "You mean now?"

"You're not exactly flipping out."

Bannerman almost laughed. He began counting on his fingers. "We have Carla, who is *not* in control, missing. We have her pal, the serial killer, out looking for her and even having a chat with her father. We have Molly, who should know better, having compromised our location. We have two different anonymous callers, one of whom wants us to go kill an art dealer. We have two shooters who . . ."

The telephone rang.

Control.

Not to mention Sur La Mer, an angry KGB colonel and what, if anything, Roger Clew has to do with all this.

Bannerman picked up the phone and listened. Susan thought she heard a soft groan.

"Okay," he told Molly. "Go find John Waldo. See what he knows. Then call that girl." He replaced the receiver, sighing deeply.

"Billy's gone too." he said.

Lesko, his own eyes shining, appeared in the doorway.

"And where the hell's Elena?" he demanded.

Sumner Dommerich had fallen asleep.

When he woke, to banging doors and flashing lights, he thought he had been caught. Two police cars blocked him in. He almost screamed. He wasn't ready yet.

But his head cleared and he saw that they were there with an ambulance. Two men with blood on them were helped out of it. One onto a Guerney, the other able to walk but wearing handcuffs. He heard *"bar fight"* and *"stab wounds"* and *"one more dead at the scene."* Normal emergency room stuff.

Lesko came out. He had the pizza box in his hand. He took another slice out of it and gave the rest to one of the cops. It seemed, to Dommerich, like something only another policeman would do. And he wasn't bothered by the blood. He said, "Hang in there," then he walked to the Ford and climbed in.

Dommerich had been right about the Ford. But it didn't help now. He couldn't get out. All he could do was sit low until Lesko pulled away and then ask one of the cops to move his car.

That's what he did. But this other cop saw his pizza hat and asked him if he had any more. Dommerich gave him the sausage pizza that Lesko didn't want. It was almost cold. Dommerich would have thrown it out anyway.

From what he could see, the Ford had turned north on Vermont. Dommerich raced after him. He caught up with one car, then another, but neither was the Ford. There wasn't much traffic. All he could see up ahead were trucks. He knew that Lesko must have turned off.

In a way it was just as well. You can't go zooming up behind people at night and expect them not to notice. Especially one who might be a cop.

Dommerich was tempted to go home. He had almost no chance of finding the Ford. It could have gone anywhere.

His one slim hope was that Lesko might be headed for the Beverly Hills Hotel. He realized that it was almost no hope at all but it was all he could think of to try. Anyway, maybe Carla would be back there by now and he wouldn't need Lesko to find her. Dommerich made a U-turn, then went west on Beverly Boulevard.

The Ford wasn't there. Neither was Carla. Bungalow 6 was still dark except for the bathroom and he could see a corner of the note he'd left under the door. Dommerich decided that he would try to use his psychic powers.

He knew he had some. Lots of times, they would speak to him. Like when he knew which girls were rotten even if they didn't laugh at him. Like when they said, yesterday, that he should go watch Lisa's apartment. Like when they told him to go to Queen of Angels in the first place. They wouldn't have bothered, he realized, if all they were going to do was show him Lesko and then let Lesko get away without leading him to Carla.

He listened for a voice.

He heard lots of them.

That was the trouble with voices. One said go look for her up in Benedict Canyon, probably just because her name is Benedict. A stupid one said go to a movie.

But one said maybe she went home.

And maybe she did.

Her father sounded like he wanted her to. He probably left the back door open. *Tell her to come the back way*, is what he said.

It wouldn't hurt to go look. Except he was really tired.

He'd find some coffee on the way.

All Carla had intended was to take a walk.

She'd slept poorly, dreaming of her sister. In the

dream that woke her, Lisa was afraid. She was running from someone. Carla ran after her, calling to her, but Lisa wouldn't stop. Suddenly there was her father. He caught Lisa. He held her until Carla could reach them. And Lisa cringed.

"She won't hurt you," her father said. "She wouldn't hurt you for the world."

Then Carla saw her sister's face and she realized that Lisa was running from her. She was pointing at Carla's hand. Carla looked down. The hand held a kitchen knife. Carla woke up crying.

She realized that the dream made no sense. That Lisa was never, for a minute, afraid of her. Her father's part, confirming that, made no sense either. Carla remembered his face. He was actually taking her side. And she had never, except once, used a kitchen knife.

The dream wouldn't fade. The tears kept coming. She thought of waking Molly but decided against it. Molly would want to stay up with her, rub her back or something, and remind her of all those things Lisa had told her computer about her wonderful sister. That would only make it worse.

She had dressed quietly and slipped into the corridor. She passed Lesko and Elena's room, then hesitated. Through the door she could hear the sound of the television, turned low. She knocked softly, not really knowing why, and instantly regretted it. But there was no answer. She continued down the corridor, almost reaching the stairs when Elena softly called her name.

Elena couldn't sleep either. Jet lag. Lesko was still out. She saw Carla's swollen eyes and asked that she come and sit. Carla entered the room and pretended not to notice as Elena lowered the hammer of her Browning to half-cock and slipped the pistol back under her pillow. Elena had clearly heard the knock.

Carla was in no mood for television. She needed to talk. She needed some air. Elena insisted on joining her, going first to her closet for a comfortable pair of shoes.

Even the parking lot seemed confining. Carla steered

Elena toward Wilshire Boulevard, then turned in the direction of the UCLA campus. They had walked only a few yards, mostly in silence, when a car exited the parking lot behind them, blinked its headlights, and pulled to the curb in their path. Elena stiffened. Carla touched her arm. It's all right, she said. She recognized John Waldo. She explained his role, sort of a guardian angel with an Ingram. Wants to make sure she's not planning a solo visit to this Sur La Mer place.

"Are you?"

"Not at the moment."

Waldo saw the swelling of Carla's eyes and he saw Elena nod in agreement when she promised that they would not go far. Just girl talk. She needed it. No reason to wake Paul.

Waldo was not reassured. He'd known Carla too long. "Are you armed?" he asked.

She shook her head, then gestured toward his trunk. "Maybe I should be," she said.

"Better I wake up Billy," he told her. "Better he tags along."

Carla knew that it was useless to argue. And she didn't mind Billy. He would hang back, following in a car, although she couldn't help wondering what a passing police cruiser would think if they saw Bannerman's monster keeping pace behind two small women at night. She agreed to wait inside the lobby doors until she saw Billy follow him outside.

"You are not to be given a weapon?" Elena asked her.

"When I need one. Sure."

Elena smiled. "I have one. Is it still under my pillow?"

Carla hesitated, then sighed. She shook her head.

Elena opened the clasp of her purse. She left it that way, saying nothing, watching the street, until she felt the weight of the Browning. She closed the purse over it.

They strolled, Billy following, for twenty minutes.

"Tell me about her," Elena had urged.

And Carla did. She told her about the dream and how it lied. She told of her father and how he had turned his back on her. They reached the UCLA campus. Carla welcomed a change of subject. She began naming the buildings.

"I went to school here," she said. "For two years, anyway."

"A lovely campus," Elena acknowledged.

"It's also free. My first choice was Berkeley. That's where the action was. But old George wouldn't spring for the tuition."

Elena glanced at her surroundings. "It does not seem that you were deprived."

"Yeah," Carla said distantly. "I found the action, all right."

It was not what Elena meant. "You should try to make peace with your father," she said, aware that she was intruding. "For your own sake, if not for his."

Carla snorted. "And say what? No hard feelings?"

"If that will make a beginning."

"He doesn't even like me, Elena."

"Perhaps. But now he will need you."

Carla closed her eyes. "Your line was supposed to be, '*Like* you? He *loves* you. How could any father not love his daughter?'"

"I am not so naive, Carla."

"It wouldn't kill you to fake it."

Elena took her arm. "You are . . . difficult to like. But so was I once."

"What? You mean by Lesko?"

"He despised me."

Carla laughed. "Shows how fucking much you know."

"I was mistaken?"

"Lesko hated Lesko. Most of all because you popped his partner and he still couldn't stop thinking about you."

"Then perhaps you are also . . ."

"I'm not."

"Would you like me to call on him? Speak to him?"

"No. Anyway, what's this to you?"

"The truth? You believe that without your sister you have nothing. This is a dangerous state of mind. It is why you have no weapon."

"And because I don't hate Claude, right? If you talked to the poor son of a bitch, you wouldn't . . ."

"Where is your home? Is it far?"

"It's four in the morning, Elena."

"Ah. Yes. He is probably sedated."

"George Benedict? He likes suffering too much."

"Call him, then. Tell him he is in your thoughts."

"He'll hang up on me. He wouldn't have let me in the house if I hadn't brought Molly."

"Call him. This time you will bring me."

39

Harry Bunce, Felix driving, had made his second pass of the Benedict house. He thought he saw some curtains move. He slid lower in his seat.

"Take the next right," he told the Mexican. "Check out the back streets." With luck, thought Bunce, he might see something that would force them to back off.

Felix grumbled but he obeyed.

The Mexican was excited. He liked night work. He even had a special black outfit, a long Jap knife, and this dumb Ninja hat that covered everything but his eyes. Bunce had made him take it off. They were supposed to look like cops, for Christ's sake.

He had also tried to talk Marek out of this.

With Marek, arguing was the wrong approach. The way to change Marek's mind was to agree with him. Then he'd listen to your reasons and tell you how dumb they are. But sometimes they'd make him think.

Instead, Bunce had tried to tell him why snatching the girl's father was a bad idea. For openers, what's the point? Even if it messes up the head of the one who sliced Hickey, there's still the KGB, God knows where and how many, and why would they give a shit? Second, you'd have to kill the guy because once you let him go, his psycho daughter and her friends would be more pissed off than ever. Third, kidnapping is a federal crime. You don't have to cross a state line. Even thinking about it is a conspiracy and that's enough to bring in the FBI.

This last argument is what convinced Marek that he couldn't lose. Marek owned an FBI agent like he owned a couple of judges. Bunce never knew which one except that he must have had some time in grade. He would put himself in charge of the investigation, says Marek, and his office would end up leaking that the KGB did it.

Bunce saw nothing on the back streets. No sign of a surveillance.

Nor could he see the Benedict house from the rear. There was a grade school in back of it, and then some trees in between. He could make out a path through the trees but there was no telling where it led.

Might as well get this over with, he decided. The best way was the simplest. Pull into the driveway, ring the bell, say he's police, and smack the guy before his eyes can focus. The car belonged to Felix but the plates were off another car back in the airport parking lot. The backseat, this time, had been covered with a tarp from Felix's garage. Bunce fished a blackjack from his pocket and readied a roll of packing tape. "Let's do it," he told the Mexican.

But now there were lights in the Benedict house. And blinds were being drawn, all across the front. He told Felix to keep going.

"We don't have all night," the Mexican groused.

"Just hold your water."

It was almost five. The black sky had begun fading into gray. And Felix was right. Soon other lights would be turning on. Newspaper and milk deliveries would start. People walking dogs and jogging. He should get this done now. But the pulling of those blinds had bothered him. It was done, he thought, a bit too quickly. And who pulls the blinds on every room?

"Shut off your lights," he said. "Turn around." Bunce pointed to a spot deep in the shadow of several large trees. "Park over there."

He handed Felix his cigarette lighter and told him he could go play Ninja now. Check out the house on foot. Try to look in, listen at windows, make sure the father is alone, then flash the lighter if it's clear.

Felix was happy again. He pulled the hat from under his sweater and, first switching off the roof light, slid quietly from the car.

Bunce moved to the driver's seat, stifling a yawn. In that moment he lost sight of Felix. Then a hedge near the Benedict house appeared to bulge slightly and a shadow separated from it. No sound. He had to admit that the Mexican wasn't bad. He'd cut at least one throat for Marek already. Probably yelling *Banzai!* as he ripped. Silly shit like that.

Headlights appeared in Bunce's rearview mirror. They approached slowly, haltingly. Bunce lowered himself. The car was a small one, too small to be official, and it had something tied to its roof. It paused at the intersection directly behind him and the driver flicked on his high-beams as if trying to read the street signs. It came forward, passing him, he saw the triangular pizza sign and then . . .

Shit!

It was backing up.

Billy McHugh had agreed to drive them.

Carla told him, after she called, that her father was overcome with grief. That he was talking suicide. Elena thought the lie unnecessary, and facile, but she did not contradict it. The point, she assumed, was to get there before she changed her mind. Or to keep Billy from pausing to check with Bannerman.

Billy had taken them to a phone where Elena dialed the number of the Benedict house. George Benedict answered. He needed no softening. He was more than willing, even anxious, to hear his daughter's voice and to know that she was safe.

Yes, Carla told him, the man in Burbank had apparently killed Lisa. But no, she assured him, she did not kill Hickey.

"Oh," was his response. "I see."

Carla blinked. He did not seem relieved to hear it. An awkward silence.

"Well," she had asked, "how are you holding up?"

"I've been . . . your friends have been . . . worried about you."

"What friends?"

"Molly. The one you brought. She called a while ago."

Damn. "Who else?"

"Someone named Claude, a friend of Lisa's, actually. But he asked for you."

"Did he . . . ah . . . say anything else?"

"Only that he'd help you. I . . . gave him a message for you. I told him if you should . . . choose to come here, you should come the back way."

"How does it look now. Outside, I mean?"

"The FBI was out there earlier. They've gone now."

"I'll come by around noon. Are we still on for lunch?"

"Er . . . sure."

They reached Sherman Oaks in thirty minutes.

George Benedict realized that the business about lunch was a ruse but he was still not sure that she was coming directly. He unlocked the sliding glass door that led to his backyard and sat in darkness waiting.

A car passed the house. He only glimpsed its shape. Minutes later, it came again, or one much like it. This time he parted the curtains. Two figures inside. They seemed small enough. He felt sure that it was Carla and the woman named Elena.

He returned to the sliding doors and stood watching the break in the stand of trees that separated his yard from the school property. It seemed that only seconds had passed when he saw movement. One slender form, and then another in a skirt. He knew Carla at once. She moved like a cat. Always had.

He switched on a lamp so that she could see her way. In a wink, Carla was gone. The other woman, not as quick, faded back into the trees. Benedict thought he understood. He moved to the front and began drawing blinds. He had closed the last of them when the light flicked off behind him.

"Carla?" he called softly. Then his heart quickened.

A shadow, twice his size, was passing through the sliding doors. Going out. He'd been inside.

"It's okay." He heard Carla's voice. "He's with me."

He could see her now. She was at the door, waving the other woman forward. "Where are the curtains?" she asked.

"Uh . . . being cleaned."

"Let's talk in the kitchen."

"Sir?"

The driver had reached to roll his window down.

Bunce groaned inwardly. Some kid. Another dumb hat. Headlights shining toward the Benedict house. But at least Felix was out of sight.

"Is this Hayworth Avenue?"

"Haywood. Not Hayworth."

"Do you know where Hayworth is?"

"Next left. Two miles. You can't miss it." Bunce had no idea. But he wanted those headlights gone.

"Oh. Thank you." Dommerich shifted into drive.

"Um . . . hey, kid." Bunce had begun to wonder.

"Yes sir?"

"Who orders pizza this time of night?"

Dommerich glanced at his order pad and shrugged. "I don't know. Pizza's good any time."

"Yeah. Never mind."

"You want a coupon?"

"A what?"

"Three dollars off."

"Just beat it, okay? I'm trying to sleep here."

"Sorry."

The Volkswagen rolled forward, hesitated, then cut toward the curb and stopped. Bunce snarled through his teeth. But at least the kid shut off his headlights. Now he had a little flashlight. He was reaching into the back, rummaging for something.

Christ. He was getting out of the car.

"Look . . . kid . . ."

"Could you just show me?" Dommerich held a large Hagstrom map, one hand underneath it, the other pointing to the streets of Sherman Oaks.

"Just get the fuck out of . . ."

Bunce's words ended in a squawk. His hands, too late, rose to protect his throat. He felt the wetness, and the pain, and he tried to shout for Felix. Bubbles of air blew through his fingers.

He saw the knife. Again, too late. He saw it flash between his elbows and he felt a paralyzing coldness in his chest. He saw a hand, in a clear plastic glove, his chest spitting blood onto it as it pried at his ribs. He tried to grab the hand. It was too slippery. The knife withdrew and struck again, piercing his own hand, pinning it to his chest. Bunce flailed with the other, first at the knife and then at the horn on his steering wheel but the hand seemed to have no will.

The knife pulled free. It made a sucking sound. He felt a hand at his shoulder, pushing him sideways. The door to the backseat opened. The kid was coming in that way. A part of Bunce's brain wondered why but now he felt the plastic tarp being thrown over his chest and head and the kid was climbing on top of it.

A light blinded him. That flashlight. It moved from

one eye to the other and then to his throat. Like a doctor would do. The kid seemed satisfied.

"You know who I am?" Bunce heard him ask.

40

"Hold on a minute," Scholl said to Theodore Marek. "She's getting another call."

As Marek waited, seething, on the other end of the line, Scholl brought the headphone to his ear. He was alone with the equipment. He had sent his technician for coffee.

"*Miss Fenerty?*" Male voice. Deep. Trace of accent.
"*This is she.*" Voice sleepy.

Scholl's readout showed a Pasadena exchange.

"*I called last evening. You've had no difficulty, I take it.*"

"*Except for no sleep. Who are you, anyway?*"

"*I'm a friend. Truly. Do you know where the ladies can be reached? Say yes or no. No more.*"

"*Maybe.*"

"*Can you get a message to them?*"

"*Maybe.*"

"*Please write down these names.*"

Scholl listened, in considerable surprise, as the caller gave essentially the same information contained in the call he'd just played for Theodore Marek. Even the details of Marek's past life, which were news to Scholl and which Marek, not convincingly, ridiculed. All that was missing was the charge that it was Marek who ordered the death of Lisa Benedict.

"*They . . . already know this.*"
A pause. "*May I ask how?*"

"Hey . . . look. You're a voice on the telephone. Why should I . . ."

"I am Axel Streicher." He spelled it.

A silence.

"Your two friends will know the name. Tell that I said not to waste their time on Sur La Mer. Shall I spell that?"

"I've heard of it. What if they ask why?"

"The man who strangled Lisa Benedict is dead. Before she died, Lisa took his left eye. Before this man died, my wife took his right eye. No one who so much as touched her is still alive. Tell Carla that she has my word on it."

Sounds of weeping. Sobbing. Then a choked, *"I'm sorry."*

"I know that she was your friend."

"Why?" Regaining control. *"I mean, why Lisa?"*

"A stupid man did a stupid thing. That is the long and the short of it. Tell Carla that she will find no motive beyond what I have said."

"The other man said she died because she found out Marek was Ordynsky."

A hesitation. *"What other man?"*

"Listen . . . I don't think I . . ."

"Never mind. I can guess."

A pause. Then, her voice stronger, *"Sur La Mer. That's where she died, isn't it."*

"Yes."

"And you were there."

"Not as she died. I would have stopped it."

A longer silence. Then, *"Nellie Dameon."* Just that. A name.

"Hmmpf." A sound of . . . surprise? More like approval. *"What about her, Miss Fenerty?"*

"She can speak, can't she."

"Can and does, Miss Fenerty. Nellie Dameon speaks very well indeed."

41

___

"Do you?"

Bunce tried to suck air. His head heaved with the effort. Dommerich took it to mean *no*.

"I know you, though," he said.

What struck Harry Bunce, even through his pain, was the flatness, the lifelessness of the voice.

But the pain was unbearable. The kid was not very big but his full weight, knees and all, was on Bunce's chest, now filling up with blood. Bunce couldn't speak.

"I saw you leave Hickey's. You thought Carla cut him, didn't you."

A rush of bubbles.

"So now you're here to hurt her."

Bunce tried to shake his head. The knife punctured his chin, stopping it. He went rigid. In his head he saw Hickey, ginning up at him. And those eyes. The look of a man who died insane. And Bunce understood. This kid was saying that he did it.

Dommerich saw that he knew. "Uh-huh. It was me."

Bunce tried again to shake his head, denying not the truth of it but the knowledge that it was happening to him as well. His brain screamed. This kid. The real Campus Killer? How the fuck could that be?

He knew that he was finished. He almost welcomed death, if only it came quickly so that the pain would stop. But it wasn't right. He had gone to kill Hickey himself. And he wasn't after this Carla. He didn't even want to be here. He wanted to say these things so this kid would not cut him again.

Sweet Jesus.

Please. He didn't want to be done like Hickey.

His arms were pinned against his chest but his fingers, still clutching his throat, were free. Bunce made the sign of the cross. Then he stretched his fingers to the sides of his mouth. They traced the cuts which he knew were coming. His lips formed the words *Please* . . . and *don't*. He begged with his eyes.

They dulled, mercifully, before the knife moved again.

Felix heard muffled voices inside. And he heard the clink of dishes from what must have been the kitchen.

He moved to the window. The last two slats of the blinds were slightly askew. He could see into the room. Two heads, both women, their backs to him. A man stood near the stove pouring hot water into mugs. Felix saw that the window was not locked. He tested it with the blade of his tanto knife. It rose, silently, unseen, half an inch.

The younger of the two women, reddish hair, was unzipping the front of a windbreaker. The scene suggested that the women had just arrived. Felix wondered where they'd come from.

"My manners . . ." said the man with the tea, uncomfortably. "I'm George Benedict. Carla's, um . . . father."

"I am Elena Brugg." She extended her hand.

"You're one of Carla's . . . ? I mean, you don't seem like . . ."

"I am not. But I'm Carla's friend. I've come from Zürich to be what comfort I can."

Felix smiled under his mask. Carla was the redhead. She was the one who had Mr. Marek so spooked. Elena must be the other one.

He could take them both. Finish it here. Mr. Marek would be happy, Bunce would be happy, they could go home.

"That man in Burbank . . ." Benedict was talking

to the daughter but looking at the floor. "There's no doubt he's the one?"

"He had her things."

Benedict set a mug in front of her. His hand was trembling. "But it was not you who . . . avenged her?"

"A friend did. Has anyone else called, by the way?"

"No."

"Nothing from Claude? That friend of Lisa's?"

He shook his head absently. "I would have killed that man myself," said the father, softly. "I really think I could have."

"It must run in the family," the daughter said. The other woman glared at her. The daughter changed the subject. "It's been quiet outside? No cars cruising by?"

"No. Only yours."

The daughter's mug passed short of her lips. "When was this?"

"Ten minutes. Just before you came in through the . . ." He straightened. He seemed confused. "Two people in it," he said, blinking. "Not three. It drove by twice."

The woman, Elena, shifted her purse.

Felix thought he understood. That school. They must have hid their car behind·it and used that path he saw. Must have just missed each other.

He tried to puzzle out what the father meant by *three*. Maybe the two women had a driver, still with the car.

"The lights," said the daughter. Elena reached for the switch. The kitchen went dark.

Sumner Dommerich had found the school. And he saw the path.

Tell her to come the back way, her father had said. This had to be it. There was a car hidden back by the dumpster. Its hood was still warm to the touch.

He knew this was crazy. He could be five miles away by now, looking for a public phone, calling Carla to tell her about the man down the street.

But he wasn't even sure Carla was there. And what if that man wasn't alone? He wasn't alone at Hickey's. Also, how come he's not driving the Lexus this time? Not that Dommerich cared except that the Lexus had a car phone. He could have called from there.

No, that's stupid.

He didn't even know if you dialed them like regular phones. Besides, lights were going on in too many houses. And that man was still making bubbles.

He'd driven away slowly, no headlights, coasting by Carla's father's house, noting that the lights were on there as well. It looked peaceful enough. But a voice told him to make sure. Go look for the back way.

Having found it, he parked his Volkswagen on a street just down from the school and took the sign from his roof. He checked himself for blood stains. Not much. Just on his cuffs. He made his way to the path.

Felix had stayed at the window of the darkened kitchen, listening. "Get down on the floor," he heard the daughter say. "I'll be right back."

"You'll stay where you are," the father demanded. "I'll go look myself."

Footsteps. The light snapped back on. Angry whispers. Felix put his eye to the window.

The father had left the kitchen. He moved toward the front door. The other woman, Elena, was following, a gun in her hand, pointed down, as if ready to cover him. Carla doused the light again. She hurried through the house, dousing others. Felix crept toward the front.

The father was outside, on the front walk, peering in both directions. Felix understood. The father was thinking police. He had nothing to fear from them.

The father spotted the car, some five houses down. Felix could see Bunce's head. The father stood for a long moment, hands on his hips, then walked toward it.

Felix saw an opportunity. Both women would be watching the father. Their backs would be to him if he came in through the rear. The sky was almost the color of cigarette ashes but the house, blinds drawn, was dark enough for the work he was good at.

Billy McHugh saw the figure in black.

He had watched, not moving, from a spot several feet into the path, deeply shaded by foliage. He had settled there after seeing the women through the patio door. He could watch them from there, he could see passing cars, he could protect their rear. And afterward, he would put Carla over his knee. There was nothing wrong with her father.

But that thought left him when he saw a shadow move. It broke off from a hedge on the property line and blended into another at the side of the house. He eased a pistol from his belt and lowered himself to one knee.

A sliver of light gashed the shadow's head. Light from inside. Must have opened the window a crack. Was looking through it.

That wasn't smart, thought Billy. You lose your night vision. He was tempted to move on him but the shadow was a good sixty feet away across open lawn. He wished that John Waldo had come instead. Waldo could have done it. Waldo could walk through tin cans and not be heard.

The sliver winked off. Then on again. New lights. Carla's father moving through the house, turning them on, Elena behind him, with a gun out, Carla flipping the lights off again. The front door opened and closed.

The shadow eased toward the street, watching whatever was happening there. Billy braced himself to move forward, cut the distance, but now the shadow was coming back. He waited, watching, as it flowed to the rear of the house and flattened against the stucco, one arm held out, a knife in it. It now moved toward the patio door. *Good*, he thought. *Go right in*. He raised himself to follow.

Almost too late, a part of his brain sensed movement behind him. His momentum was already forward but he managed a sidestep and a dip. Something flashed where his throat had been. Billy crossed his arms as he struggled for balance. The knife flashed again, backhanded. The blade missed but its spiked pommel smashed the wrist of his gun hand. The hand went numb. The pistol dangled, hooked on one finger. He was falling.

But his mind was fully focused on the knife and on killing the man who held it. He slammed to the packed dirt of the path, face up, hands and feet ready, willing to take a cut if it would bring his attacker within reach. But the attacker hesitated. Now he was scrambling, crablike, from side to side as if looking for an opening but fearful of taking it. He backed away, making odd noises through his nose. Whining sounds. He snatched a broken piece of vine and flailed at Billy's shoes with it as if in panic. Then he threw it, harmlessly. He began backing away. Billy rolled to his feet. Now he had him. He would catch him in that path.

A distant shout. More like a wail.

It came from behind Billy. Loud but far away.

"Oh, Jesus, God . . . Oh, Jesus."

It was coming from up the street. Then a loud crash. Much closer. Billy's attacker squealed in rage. Then he turned and ran. Billy could not give chase. That crash had come from the house. The shadow was inside.

Elena had reached George Benedict.

He was on his knees, gripping the bumper of the car he'd approached, losing what little was in his stomach.

She had to ignore him. Her pistol low but ready in both hands, she kept her attention on the figure inside the car. She approached it from the passenger side window. She saw the man, now upright behind the wheel. It seemed that the lower third of his face had been cut away. His eyes stared ahead. The passenger seat was awash in blood not yet congealed. Keys still in the ignition. She heard George Benedict gagging, too loudly.

"Be still," she hissed. "Get home."

He began to groan again. "Jesus, God."

Elena knew that he must be seeing his daughter.

But there was no time to indulge him. She stepped to the front of the car and slapped him.

"Get home," she ordered as he blinked up at her. "Walk quietly. Do not run. Open your garage."

The Mexican made no sound as he entered. He stepped quickly to one side, then crouched, waiting as his eyes adjusted. He could see one of the women clearly. The one called Elena. She was lit by the small glass panes that framed the front door. He searched the darkness for the other one, and listened.

The noise came from behind him. A whipping of branches. Grunts. High-pitched. The daughter, he thought, must have gone out the back. He peered into the trees but could see nothing.

"Looking for me, fuck face?"

He spun, the tanto ready, but the blow had already arched up from the floor. It struck his elbow, shattering it. The knife tumbled through the air. He staggered backward into a plant stand. A large ceramic pot crashed to the carpet. Agony, white hot, seared through his brain. He gulped air for a scream. A scream came, but from a distance.

He saw the daughter now. She held, in both hands, a heavy Spanish candlestick, readying a blow that was aimed at his face. But she hesitated, her eyes suddenly questioning.

Carla had heard her father's voice. The front door had opened. Elena was rushing to the sound.

The Mexican kicked at her, catching her full in the chest. She tumbled backward and rolled. He lunged for the sliding door and jumped onto the patio, stepping into a webbed aluminum lounge chair and tumbling with it, tangled. He scrambled to his feet to see a man, very large, coming fast from the trees.

"Kill him," the woman said. "No noise."

The man had a gun. He was belting it. Felix seized the chance. He measured the distance and aimed a spinning kick. The big man dodged it, almost casually, pushing the foot as it passed his face. The push sent Felix tumbling. He recovered and, with a karate shout, tried a flying kick. The big man stepped inside it. One hand gripped his throat, the other his crotch. He was high in the air. He pumped his legs, searching for leverage. It did no good. The man carried him, easily, to the sharp edge of the patio brick work, then paused.

"You sure?" he whispered toward the house.

"Wait." Carla heard the sound of the garage door opening. A car engine, racing. Her father stumbled through the kitchen door, hands to his face. "No," she said, "We'll talk to that one."

Billy dropped him into a choke hold. The Mexican kicked once, feebly, then went limp. Billy noticed the flaccid elbow. A knee, he decided, would be all the better. He stretched one black leg across the bricks.

Elena, gritting her teeth against her own revulsion, had pushed Harry Bunce back onto his side and driven his car to the Benedict garage. Carla backed her father's car out to make room.

There had been too much noise. She could only hope that no neighbor had called the police. But if they had, the police might now come and go. There would be no circus of lights and cameras.

Ten minutes later, no police had come. There was only a call from a neighbor asking if George Benedict was all right. He had gathered himself somewhat. And Carla had coached him. He said that he'd been behaving badly, apologized for the noise, he was better now, he had family with him. Carla urged that he wait in the kitchen. He did not object.

Elena was not surprised to see a second man, dressed in black, being carried into the garage across the shoulder of Billy McHugh. Carla had anticipated him. She had stayed to deal with him.

Carla stood now, flashlight in hand, examining the man who was once one Harold J. Bunce. His wallet lay open on the hood. The man in black, unconscious on the concrete floor, carried no identification.

Carla's lips were drawn tight. It was clear to Elena that she, too, was struggling to crowd the image of her sister from her mind. Elena had seen no compassion for the dead man. No revulsion. Carla was too far beyond such feelings. But Elena did see a sense of wonder. A slow shaking of the head.

"Did your friend do this, you think?" asked Elena.

Carla could only shrug.

"That guy," Billy asked, "is he a fruit? About so big?" He held a hand to the level of his chest.

"I've never seen him. And don't call him a fruit."

Billy grunted. He sucked at his wrist where the spiked pommel had punctured it.

The truth dawned on Carla. "You saw him? Here?"

Billy displayed the wrist and gestured toward Harry Bunce. "Tried to do me like that. Back in that path. Started jumping around like some girl when he missed."

"I'm a fucking girl, Billy."

Elena looked skyward. Perhaps, she thought aloud, the issues of sexism and homophobia might be saved for another time.

"A twinkletoes and a Mexican Ninja." Billy couldn't let it go. "It's a first for me."

"So is being taken by a fruit, you asshole. You couldn't even . . ."

Elena clapped her hands sharply. Carla folded her arms.

"The question," said Elena, "is who sent these two and why."

"I'll ask him." He pried back the Mexican's eyelid. "A few more minutes. Meantime, we ought to call Paul."

Carla reached into the car. She grabbed Bunce's shoulder and pulled him upright. "Stick him in here," she told Billy. "Let him wake up to a smile."

Elena could only sigh.

The telephone rang in the kitchen. She heard George Benedict's footsteps on the tile. Moments later he came to the door. He called for Carla without looking in.

"It's that young man, Claude," he said. "He seems very upset."

42

"Nellie? Were you using the phone?"

Weinberg, returning to the room with Barbara, saw the directory open on the bed.

"Yes. Why didn't you, by the way?"

"Because some phones are safer than others. Whom did you call?"

"Young Dr. Feldman. I was worried about Harland. He has a big mouth, you know. I asked Dr. Mike to look in on the members."

Weinberg groaned inwardly. He tried to remember what he'd read under that name. Ah, yes. Father, Marcus, a psychiatrist. Genuine, though corrupt. Son, apparently from the baby farm but a decent sort, according to Nellie.

"Did you tell him where you are?"

"He didn't even believe *who* I am. He's never heard me speak. It took a lot of convincing."

"Please answer me, Nellie," he pressed. "Does Dr. Feldman know that you're here with us?"

"I'm crazy, Alan. Not stupid."

"Forgive me."

"But he already knew. That I left with you, I mean."

"How?"

"Young Carleton told him. He seemed to think that Carleton has flown the coop as well."

"But why would he call Dr. Feldman?"

"Same as me. To make sure the members are cared for. Dr. Mike said he's going to get all of them. Take them someplace nicer."

"How will he do that?"

"Ambulances, I suppose. Perhaps a bus."

"Yes, but, wouldn't the guards prevent it?"

"I asked. He said, 'Not this time, Nellie. It's over.'"

"She's fine. Don't worry."

Lesko heard Katz in his head.

"I'd know if she was dead. I think."

Swell.

Katz, who won't even admit *he's* dead is all of a sudden wired into who is and who isn't. That's very comforting. Shit head.

Bannerman, for the third time now, is listening to Molly's tape of her call from this DiDi Fenerty. The third time does not look like it's making him any smarter. Well, maybe a little. Lesko had never seen Bannerman look dumber than when he heard, *"I am Axel Streicher. S-t-r-e-i-c-h-e-r."*

Lesko had asked Molly who he is. She said, after Bannerman nodded okay, that this Streicher *"is like Paul, sort of."* And the wife he mentioned is like Carla, *"only . . . um, tall."*

Sheds a lot of light.

"She took a walk, Lesko." Katz again. *"You never just went for a walk?"*

Leave me alone.

"The sneaky guy . . . Waldo? He even sent Bannerman's Doberman to baby-sit. McHugh's worse than you. Guy eats people's noses."

Ears.

"What?"

He ate an ear once.

"Whatever."

Bannerman had switched off the recorder. Lesko switched off Katz.

"That phone," Bannerman said to Molly. "I have to know if it's wired."

She frowned. "I didn't pack for that."

He gestured toward the yellow pages. "Pick a store. Tell John what you need. When he gets it, go down there by taxi."

Nice, thought Lesko as she scribbled her list. Midnight shopping. Your local Radio Shack. There was a time when he'd have been making an arrest right about now.

Bannerman seemed to read his mind. "Lesko? I'll be making some decisions. You may not want to know."

"I'll stick for a while."

"So will I," said Susan.

Bannerman shook his head. "I want you out of here. No arguments."

"No way," she raised her chin. "Not this time."

"You'll be safer at the Beverly Hills Hotel. Take Molly's key."

Suddenly, Lesko noticed, she folds.

"I need someone there to take calls. Help us coordinate."

Not a word.

Another thing Lesko noticed was that every time Susan moved, her purse went with her. Usually women plopped them someplace. Not a big thing. He just noticed.

Any other time, it would have been him, not Bannerman, keeping her out of this. But Susan was right here, safe, and Elena wasn't. Maybe Elena was right. Maybe she did fill his plate.

"This Streicher," Lesko tried to keep his mind busy. "You believe him?"

"Yes."

"What about that first guy who called? That was who?"

"He might be a man named Dunville. Anyway, the information he gave was the same except for who murdered Lisa and why."

"What's the same is that they both want you to hit this guy, Marek."

"The first man certainly does. Streicher knows I have to."

"What's *have* to?"

"I can't just react. You know that."

"Except meanwhile you got half of Washington saying you shouldn't do shit, especially about Sur La Mer, when you weren't going near there in the first place. Not to mention the FBI on our asses, Huff or no Huff."

Bannerman nodded distantly.

"I had this little cousin when I was a kid," said Lesko. "I'd go to her house and she'd say don't take any cookies. They're up on that shelf. I didn't even know the damned cookies were there but she knew I'd take some. It was all so she could rat on me."

A thoughtful stare. Then a smile. From Molly, too.

They were, Lesko realized, trying to imagine him as a kid, getting his ass smacked. So much for parables. Lesko was about to try a more direct approach—such as *Bannerman, you schmuck, don't you smell just a tiny bit of a set-up here?*—but the telephone rang.

Bannerman said, "Yes," and listened.

He mouthed the name *Elena.*

Theodore Marek needed to calm himself.

Under other circumstances, a visit to his vault would have done it. In the vault there was no night or day. There was only life and beauty. The treasures of centuries. Paintings, rare clocks, and tapestries that once graced the finest homes of prewar Europe. Jeweled daggers once worn by princes. Exquisite chalices and reliquaries from the cathedrals of Minsk and Riga. His wine collection. His coins.

This morning, his vault was a trap.

He could feel it. Something in Scholl's voice when Scholl suggested he bar the door and stay there. Scholl, normally sullen, had seemed entirely too smug.

He had as much as sniffed, recalled Marek, at the denial that he was Tadeusz Ordynsky. Given time, he'll probably start sniffing in earnest. Finding old photographs. Doing computer matchups and the like. Seeking an advantage.

Well . . . he has less time than he thinks.

Oh, and Carleton Dunville.

That was his voice on the telephone. No doubt in the world.

Young Carleton might live longer than Scholl. But he'll spend that time begging for death. He'll be given to Felix. Peeled an inch at a time.

The treachery of it.

Worse, the injustice. Laying that girl's murder on the doorstep of an innocent man. Naming Harry and Peter in that other business. Naming *Peter*, for God's sake. His own flesh and blood. More than likely.

Marek had called Sur La Mer at once. Had spoken to Darby. Told him to wake young Carleton, club him to his knees, then strap him to the table alongside Henry's and wait for Felix to arrive.

But young Carleton was gone. Borrowed Darby's car. The moron gave it to him. Off, he said, for a damage control meeting in Malibu. With Mr. Marek. Another lie. And another arrow pointing to this house.

The call, according to Scholl, came from the airport. The international terminal. A false trail, probably. Scholl's people will track him. Police in six states will be looking for Darby's car, now reported stolen.

And that woman, probably the one named Farrell, had called from the lobby of a Holiday Inn in Brentwood. Scholl seemed doubtful that she was actually staying there. Marek had sent two men to check all the same. Perhaps the two women were staying nearby. Perhaps they'll use that phone again.

He wished Harry would call.

So that he could leave here. Knowing that they had the father.

He'd been tempted to take the Fenerty girl as well.

Get her to tell what she knows. At least shut her up. But she seemed to be guarded. And it was better to leave her in place to see who else, for Christ's sake, decides to use her as a conduit to those damned women. Fenerty would keep.

The Streicher call, in some ways, was even more troubling than Carleton's. Streicher is clearly this Weinberg who so reduced the Dunville family. But why would he make that call? It was obvious that he's not in league with this Bannerman crowd after all. And, yet, they do know each other. What did Streicher have to gain? An act of professional courtesy? Absurd.

And most troubling of all, how did he know that Theodore Marek was once Tadeusz Ordynsky? Carleton, the bastard, must have told him. But if so, why had Streicher gone out of his way to exonerate him in the killing of that woman's sister?

Streicher, it seemed, was still in the area. Not much of a run for it. Called from Pasadena. Another lobby of another Holiday Inn.

What was he to make of that?

Does the chain give group rates to assassins? Or, as Scholl suggested, might they have found a way to route their calls through the Holiday Inn reservations network?

It was all too much.

The one bright aspect of the Streicher call . . . he swore that those women would find nothing at Sur La Mer. No one left there to punish. No point to a raid.

Marek was grateful. It meant that he would be safer there. With the father as insurance. Lock up the vault and go. As soon as Harry Bunce calls.

What could be taking so long?

43

Lesko had snatched the receiver from Bannerman's hand.

But Elena knew better than to say much. Only that all were well. They were visiting the family. There had been difficulties. She asked that Paul, not Lesko, call back when he has a moment.

Bannerman returned the call, recording it, from a credit card phone two blocks away. Lesko, now armed with John Waldo's Ingram, went with him, serving as cover while Waldo shopped. Lesko was distracted to the point of uselessness. Twice, Bannerman had to tell him to keep his eyes on the street.

"Why you and not me?" he asked, walking back.

"She thinks I'm more detached."

"I'm fine, Goddamn it."

"You won't be."

Bannerman paused in the lobby to check for messages. There were none under the name he was using or under Molly's alias. He expected none. He was looking for some sign that a bored night operator had been eavesdropping on calls.

Lesko understood what he was doing. He also realized that Bannerman was taking his time, watching for cracks. Lesko was damned if he would give him the satisfaction.

"Bunce, Harold J."

They listened to Elena's voice.

"The one still alive is Felix Montoya. They work for a man named Theodore Marek."

Their identification had come late in her account of the past hour's events. She told of them in orderly sequence. Swiss efficiency, thought Bannerman. Lesko would never have let her get through the story. Bannerman had simply listened, as did Lesko now, saying little. He did not mention that he knew two of those names.

She told of the father finding Bunce, of Bunce's condition, and of the simultaneous attacks by Montoya and a third person, then unknown. Billy had defeated Montoya, waited until he could speak, then questioned him with the aid of a garden tool.

"They were sent by this Marek to take Carla's father as a hostage. Marek feared that Carla and another woman would be hunting him. When Montoya saw Carla, he decided to finish it here. Me as well. He seems to have confused me with Molly."

"Does he say that Marek had Lisa killed?"

"He claims that Marek is innocent. He says that Marek knew nothing of Lisa until after her death. Bunce, he says, told him that a man named Dunville killed her."

"Then why did Marek fear Carla?"

"Montoya does not know."

A pause. "Was it these two who shot Yuri?"

"Montoya says it was Bunce and one Peter Marek, now dead or dying. They were sent by this Dunville to kill Hickey. Montoya does not know why. He says all Hickey did was dispose of Lisa's body."

"And you're sure it was Claude who killed Bunce?"

"And very nearly Billy as well. He called later to apologize."

"I beg your pardon?"

"He called Carla, quite upset, relieved that she was unharmed. It seems that he saw Billy lurking in back of the house and assumed that Billy must have come with Bunce. He tried to cut Billy's throat. When that failed, he ran. Billy could not pursue him."

Bannerman was speechless. Then, *"Did Billy feel that this Claude had . . . special skills? Training?"*

"On the contrary, I think."

In his mind, Bannerman tried to reconcile the timid young man Carla had described with the apparently effortless butchery of two tough and wary men, to say nothing of having survived meeting Billy in the dark.

Elena read his thoughts. *"He is more impressive than you know. He told Carla that he followed Bunce and Peter Marek to Sur La Mer. This would seem to confirm what Montoya said."*

"Carla told you he said this?"

She understood. *"He did say it, Paul. I was listening."*

"What else did she say to him?"

"She . . . asked if he was well."

Bannerman frowned but said nothing.

"Paul . . . when he apologized . . . for attacking Billy . . ."

Bannerman waited.

"He seemed to think Billy was Lesko."

A thoughtful silence. *"Had Carla mentioned Lesko to Claude?"*

"She is now putting her father to bed. I will ask."

"It can wait. Is Bunce still in the garage? With his car?"

"Yes."

"Thank you, Elena. Put Billy on."

The recording ended abruptly.

Bannerman, carrying one small overnight bag, escorted Susan to the lobby of the Holiday Inn. He asked the night clerk to call for a taxi, then walked with her to the entrance, stopping inside the glass doors.

"According to Billy," he told her, "Claude is white, about five seven or eight, high-pitched voice, effeminate gestures. His hair is light, possibly blond, cut short. He's softly built, narrow shoulders, a bit thick around the middle.

Susan nodded, envisioning him.

"Elena disagreed about the voice. She said it's a soft monotone. Youthful."

"I'm sure I'll know him if he calls."

"If he does," Bannerman said firmly, "you'll give him Carla's message and no more. Don't let him think you're keeping him on the phone."

"Gotcha."

"And what's the message?"

"Carla says meet her, three o'clock, at the place where she stopped and got out of her car. Where the man following her made a U-turn and ran. She says that only Claude will know where that was."

"But you *don't* know. She wouldn't tell you."

"Bannerman . . . I get it. Where will Carla be?"

"Busy. Until three o'clock. Any more questions?"

"Yes. What did you say to Billy?"

"I asked him what Claude looked like."

"You clicked off the recorder to do that?"

"There were some odds and ends."

She nodded. "Like what to do with the bodies."

Bannerman heard her use of the plural. "Susan, this is not a . . ."

"Don't you dare." Her eyes blazed.

"Dare what?"

"Don't you fucking tell me this is not a game. Don't you ever say that to me again."

Bannerman winced. He willed a taxi to appear. None did.

"Those two men were killers, Susan. They wouldn't have thought twice about . . ."

"I know that."

"And it's not just Lisa anymore."

"I know that too. Don't patronize me."

Bannerman took a breath. He looked into her eyes. "In a few days," he said quietly, "Billy will be making cheeseburgers for you again. He looks forward to your coming in. He likes your smile and the way you touch his arm while you're talking to him."

Susan blinked.

"This morning he tortured that man, Montoya. By now, he's finished him. He will probably do additional damage to the corpse. Next, he'll hose out George Benedict's garage and then he'll drive the two bodies to the address of the man they worked for."

Susan wanted to look away. She wouldn't let herself.

"Billy will leave the bodies, parked there, to be discovered. The point of it is terror. The point of terror is advantage. Are you sure you needed to hear this said?"

She tossed her head, ambiguously. But she understood. Corpses and cheeseburgers. Torture and touches.

No, she didn't need to hear it said.

Lesko was alone.

John Waldo had returned with two plastic shopping bags. Molly dumped their contents on the bed, sorted through a pile of tools and black boxes, picked what she wanted, and left. Waldo reclaimed his Ingram. Lesko walked down to his room for the pistol Billy had given him. He'd already seen that Elena's was gone.

"Did I tell you?"

Katz. Lesko was in no mood.

"Elena's fine. She did real good, sounds like."

He pretended not to hear.

"So what's the matter?"

Nothing, he thought. Except that Elena should have talked to him, not Bannerman. Why Bannerman?

"Because she knew you'd go bullshit, that's why. One guy gets sliced like a pepperoni. The guy with him would have sliced Elena. Then this yingyang who does college girls almost gets past Bannerman's monster. Would you have talked to you?"

Pepperoni.

The word lingered in Lesko's brain. For a moment it seemed to mean something. Then he realized. That pizza he ate. He could still taste it.

"Bannerman's going to hit this Marek guy."

Lesko shrugged.

"*So? Are we in?*"

"*Let's see what he has in mind.*"

"*He's gotta hit Marek because Marek tried to hit one of Bannerman's own. The guy crossed the line. Then he's gonna hit Dunville because Dunville killed Carla's sister.*"

"Says who? The Montoya guy? Maybe he was trying to save Marek's ass."

"*Out of loyalty, right? While McHugh's turning him into a pork chop? Get real.*"

"Anyway, Molly says there are three Dunvilles."

"*Carla wouldn't give a shit if there were ten. She'll let God sort them out.*"

"Yeah, well I . . ."

Pepperoni.

The word flashed by again.

"Hey, David?"

"What?"

"The psycho. The Campus Killer. How could he think that was me out there?"

"In the dark? Why not? Same size, same build."

"It's not just how I look. He knew my name."

"Bannerman says maybe Carla mentioned it."

"And described me?"

Thoughtfully. "*I guess not.*"

"Then how else?"

"How about the cops? The whole task force has to know you're in town for the funeral. And Huff was telling stories, right? He would have told them you're big and ugly."

Lesko shook his head slowly. Katz was saying that the serial killer might be a cop. Or someone close to cops. Like a civilian auxiliary or even a janitor. Stranger things have happened. And it might help explain why the task force had zilch in the way of progress.

But he kept tasting pepperoni. And his mind went back to Queen of Angels and the kid with the pizzas. Monotone voice. Matched McHugh's description, such as it was.

"That's dumb, Lesko."

"Why?"

"For openers, nobody knew we were going there and we weren't tailed. Plus, nobody at that hospital knew your name except Belkin and he never said a word until the kid was gone."

"I said Carla's name. He could have heard it."

"Then he would have stuck around, tried to follow you home. Did he?"

"No."

"For the timing to work, he would have had to go directly from the hospital to Sherman Oaks. What would have made him do that?"

Lesko shook his head. "Nothing I said to Irwin."

"So?"

"Forget it. It's dumb."

44

John Waldo spotted the two men.

He had decided to watch the front for a while, at least until Molly left. She had, otherwise unobserved. But now, minutes later, he could see Bannerman, just inside, standing with Susan. Waldo squinted. Looked like Susan was giving him some shit.

The two men, in a red Porsche, came up Sunset headed east. What caught his eye was their brake lights. The car had slowed just as it reached the front entrance. Then it went on, turning into the parking lot at the far end. It disappeared behind the hotel. Ten seconds later it was back, now at the near end. It paused just short of the building line. The passenger got out. He had a camera. Careful not to show himself, he aimed the long lens at the main entrance.

Bannerman was out there now, helping Susan into a taxi, shutting the door behind her. The one with the camera lowered it. Bannerman was still in full view but the man seemed to have no interest in him. He returned to the Porsche, jabbing a finger toward the departing taxi. He wanted to follow. The driver seemed reluctant. He argued. The other man barked at him. No question, thought Waldo, that at least one of them was interested in Susan. Or in someone who looked like her from a distance. Like Molly, maybe.

Waldo released his clutch and moved out ahead of the Porsche. He shifted gears noisily so that Bannerman, now walking up Sunset, would notice him.

He stayed with the taxi for a quarter mile, then slowed, straddling both lanes. The Porsche quickly closed the distance, hugging the center line in readiness to pass. Waldo weaved in front of it. He could see the driver cursing, heard the blast of his horn. Waldo drifted right and the Porsche made its move.

Waldo jerked his wheel to the left and stamped on his brake pedal. He braced himself for the impact.

Dr. Michael Feldman's first thought was that Carleton Dunville had pulled into his driveway. He was more troubled than alarmed. He thought of the pistol that he carried in his medical bag.

But it could not be Dunville's Mercedes. A blond woman was driving with a smaller person, probably her child, in the seat next to her. A patient without an appointment. Not uncommon. Feldman relaxed.

"Please don't move."

Feldman went rigid. A man's voice. Behind him. A large hand now, on his shoulder.

"I'm not here to harm you. Truly. Just go to the door, please, and open it."

Feldman obeyed. He went to the door, the man following closely. His intention was to open it, throw it wide, and then run for his life.

"If you do," said Weinberg, who read his mind

through the tensing of his shoulder muscles, "you're
liable to knock poor Nellie down."

The Malibu address, provided by Felix, stood on a
bluff several hundred feet from the beach. A wall, with
mounted cameras, surrounded the property on three
sides. A high terrace faced the ocean. The only access to
the house was a heavy wooden gate facing inland. The
only approach was a steep two-lane road that curved to
the right at Marek's house and climbed still higher
before snaking back down.

Elena, driving Billy's rented car, waited at a bend
well above the Marek house. Carla had gone with her
but she returned on foot rather than have the car go by
those cameras twice. She jogged past a shuttered service
station on the main road where Billy had left Felix
Montoya's car among several others that were parked
there awaiting attention.

Bunce had slid into the foot well of the passenger
side, concealed by Felix's tarp. A cheap poncho with a
USC decal covered the driver's seat, which still oozed
blood. Carla had found it in Lisa's old room. Felix was in
the trunk.

Billy stood at a bus stop a safe distance away,
pretending to read a copy of *The Hollywood Reporter*,
which he'd found in a trash receptacle. Carla approached
him. She peered to the south as if waiting for a bus.

"The house is quiet," she said. "Elena's ready."

Billy cocked his head toward the service station.
"What's wrong with leaving them right there? We call
the guy and say go look."

"He's probably unlisted."

"We couldn't ask?"

She shook her head. "I've been thinking too," she
said. "The hell with psychology. We can finish it."

Billy closed one eye. "Like how?"

He listened as she explained about the heavy
wooden gate and the cameras. They had the Mexican's
car, she reminded him. They'd open the gate if it pulled

up and honked. Sit low, slouch, and he might pass for
Felix.

"I give you a gun, right? We go in and start
blasting."

She nodded. "Or I go over the wall, shoot whoever
I see, then let you in. We find Marek and we finish it."

Billy sighed. Calamity Carla.

"Paul says not yet," he told her. "Anyway . . ." He
made a gesture that took in their surroundings. Only one
main road in and out of town. One access road to Marek's
place, easily sealed at both ends. Three or four other
houses up near Marek's. Too many eyes and ears. "We
don't even know the guy's there," he said.

"He is. I could feel him."

"Yeah, well . . ." He raised his hand to her neck
and squeezed, not too hard. "You feel this too, right?"

"Billy . . ." She tried to pull free. He held fast.

"Any surprises, you take a nap. Okay?"

"Okay, damn it."

"You take the car up. Leave it. Walk up to Elena.
Drive down and around. I cover this end till you pick me
up."

"You want your balls cut off? Let go."

"Promise, Carla. Or say good night."

"I promise."

He turned her face toward him. Her eyes said that
she meant it. "Go," he said. "The keys are in it."

Carla walked back to the service station. She would
keep her word, she thought, because she might need
Billy again.

No.

She would have kept it anyway. No *because*.

But she couldn't help wishing that she was here
alone. No Billy. No Elena to think about. And that it was
still dark.

Or that she was here with Claude. Claude wouldn't
have been such a pussy.

She started Montoya's car. Then, letting it idle, she
stripped the tarp off Bunce's body and fed it into the rear

seat. She grabbed his hair and pried his head back toward her so that his face would grin up at whoever opened that door. The body was stiffening. He would stay that way.

Piece of shit.

Going to her house. Going to snatch her poor father. Damned near giving him a heart attack. Shooting Yuri . . . who really liked her . . . a sweet guy . . . best lay she's had since Russo.

She saw Billy watching her, taking a step toward her. His look said get on with it. She put the car in low and steered it toward the hill.

She would keep her promise, she thought. With just one little Lucky Strike extra. Bunce seemed to nod, agreeing with her, as she bounced over the curb cut.

Carla reached Marek's front wall and continued on until she could see Elena waiting. She stopped, backed into a driveway, and pointed the car down hill. She let it coast, making fine adjustments in the steering until the front end was lined up just so. Carla flipped the inside trunk latch and saw, in her mirror, that the lid had a good spring. It opened wide. She wished she had time to arrange Felix as well. Maybe bend that smashed arm up like a salute. Like he's saying "Hi." Pin the arm to his head with that Jap knife of his.

Except Billy would shit. He'd say, "That's games. Don't play games."

Okay. No more games.

She stepped from the car, one foot stretched to the brake, then she let it roll. She trotted with it for several feet, one hand on the wheel, aiming it. She stepped away.

Carla winced as the car veered. She tried body English. It seemed to work. The car recovered by a few degrees and gathered speed. She watched as it bore down on the wooden gate, Felix's head bouncing up as if to see where he'd been. The car hit the gate at its hinge. A crunching, grinding sound, surprisingly muted. It took out three feet of wall. Felix's legs flailed on impact, the broken knee at a crazy angle. Pieces of wall slammed them back down.

She stood, hands on hips, counting to ten.

Come on, guys. Come look.

She heard shouts. Two men appeared. She could not make out what they were yelling but she knew they'd found Bunce when their voices became high-pitched. The two men drew guns. They looked around, stupidly, every place but uphill.

"Yo!" she called.

They looked up.

Carla raised her arms. She moved her hips as if to music. Still dancing, she ran her fingers through her hair at her temples, fluffing it, making sure that they saw that it was red. One man started toward her. He hesitated when he saw that she was beckoning to him. He raised a snub-nosed pistol, taking aim with both hands. She laughed at him.

Carla turned and started up the hill, arms still raised, hips swaying to music only she could hear.

She grinned for the first time in weeks.

John Waldo dabbed at his mouth where the driver of the red Porsche had slapped him. Called him a stupid fuck.

Waldo, feigning drunkenness, had tried to exchange license and insurance information with him. The driver, young and Hispanic, heavily jeweled, was furious. He raged at the damage done to his headlight and front bumper. He snatched Waldo's wallet from his hand, then slapped him in the face with it. He kicked at Waldo's taillight, the one still unbroken, shattering the amber plastic.

"Forget it," the other one called. "Let's get back."

The driver aimed another kick at Waldo as he bent to pick up his wallet. The kick grazed Waldo's ribs and soiled his shirt. Now the driver turned his anger toward the second man, slightly older.

"Now you say forget it? Did I tell you back there it fucking wasn't her? Did I say she's too young?"

"Chulo," the other one said firmly, "shut up and let's go."

Waldo glanced in the direction Susan's taxi had gone. It had vanished into the traffic several blocks ahead.

The driver made a final menacing gesture with his fist, then stormed back to the Porsche. He climbed in, backed it into a U-turn, and drove in the direction from which he'd come. Waldo gave them a small head start, then followed.

"For God's sake, Nellie." Feldman spoke in a hoarse whisper. "What are you doing with such people?"

Nellie had asked for a few minutes alone with the young doctor. In part to put him at ease, in part to get some answers for Alan and Barbara.

"They are perfectly nice, Michael. And I'm having fun."

"They're the ones with the bandaged faces, aren't they. Nellie, do you realize that they're fugitives? Perhaps even murderers?"

"I've learned that there are worse things to be, Michael."

He listened as she told him about Lisa, the girl who had come to see her two Sundays ago. The one Mr. Bellarmine had told him about. Yes, she was really there. She told him what Henry Dunville had done to that sweet child. And how he paid for it.

The young doctor listened with an expression of profound sadness, and of guilt for having kept his silence.

"I'm going up there today, Nellie," he said. "When I leave I'm taking all the members with me."

"That's what I told Alan and Barbara. They wonder how you'll manage it."

"It's not difficult. I'm transferring them to the Motion Picture Country House. I have that authority."

"Have you always?"

"Not . . . exactly."

She took his hand, patting it softly. "I know about the files, Michael. I know they've blackmailed you."

"It was more than blackmail. They swore they'd . . ." His eyes narrowed. "You've seen my file, Nellie?"

"No, but Alan has. He took stacks of them when we absconded."

"What . . . um, is he going to do with them?"

"Help me find my other children. I've had four, you know."

"Ah . . . no, I didn't know."

She saw in his lowered eyes that he didn't believe her. But the eyes came up again and she saw that he had begun to wonder.

"Nellie? Do you know who my mother was? And . . . how ill she was?"

"I'm sorry, Michael. I don't."

"But you were there. And my father always said that my real mother was a movie star."

"I'll . . . try to remember," she promised.

But she already knew the truth. Or part of it.

It had occurred to her, riding here in the car, that Michael might ask about his mother. So she went away, back to that year. She promised Barbara that she wouldn't be long.

Soon, Nellie was standing in the little nursery in the basement of Sur La Mer. She used to go there often, late at night. They never caught her. This time, she even brought Harland. They were both looking down at the baby, trying to make him smile, Harland testing the baby's grip with his finger. Little Michael was three . . . perhaps four months old. He'd been there for less than a week. He was one of the stolen ones.

For the longest time, she could not bring herself to believe that the Dunvilles were stealing children. Even though Harland said they were. But she knew that Michael had not been born to a member.

She could have told him that, she supposed. But it would not be a kindness. He might decide to spend years going through police records and newspaper files trying to narrow the list of all those distraught young women who had allowed themselves to be distracted in some public park only to turn and find their infants gone. His mother could be anyone, anywhere, in one of a dozen states.

Nellie was tempted to make up a lie. Nadia Taylor had been at Sur La Mer then. She arrived in a coma. Motorcycle accident. She could well have been pregnant at the time. Died a year or so later. Nadia had been a dancer. Made several good films. Very bright, pretty, unmarried. Michael might have been proud to have such a talented mother. Nellie had even asked Barbara's opinion.

Barbara thought it wasn't such a good idea. For the time being, she said, let's not let anyone else know you can do that. Going back in time, that is, and remembering things so vividly. Not everyone would be pleased.

"Nellie . . ." Dr. Feldman asked, . . . you do know that Henry Dunville is dead? And Carleton the elder?"

She nodded slowly. She knew of the one. Suspected the other.

"Young Carleton called me during the night. He has also . . . absconded. Said he was going far away. Would never return. He promised he'd destroy the file on my family if I promised to see to the members."

Nellie nodded. Alan had thought as much.

"I would have anyway."

"I know that, Michael."

"Nellie, did you know that I have children of my own?"

"No. But I'm glad."

"Two little girls. And a wife who is the best thing in my life. They're staying with her mother until this is done."

"You'd . . . like me to get your file from Alan."

"I guess. Yes. It's just that I . . ."

"You don't want them to know that your real mother died a lunatic. If that's the case."

Feldman brought his hands to his mouth. "It sounds crappy, doesn't it. Said straight out."

"It's not so crappy. Your wife would worry about the girls."

"I do already. And my wife wants to try for a son."

"Alan will give me your file. If I tell you that your mother was not insane, will that be enough for you?"

He did not answer immediately. He asked, "How could you have stayed there, Nellie? You're no crazier than I am."

"Oh, I was crazy once. Later, it seemed safest to pretend."

"You're not safe with those two. Stay here. Go to the Country House with your friends."

"My friends are all old, Michael. I've decided to be young for a while."

Feldman smiled. He let it fade. "You really think they'll give you that file?"

"They've said that they will. But they might ask a favor of you in return."

The smiled returned, although rueful this time. "I bet. Have you thought about what they want from you?"

"Well it certainly isn't sex."

"What, then?"

"My mind, dear. They want me for my mind."

45

Sumner Dommerich was happy.

He eased himself into his bathtub, the hot shower running. He sat back, idly sponging his wrists where blood had seeped over the plastic gloves, thinking about Carla.

The television had no news of that man in the car. Still too early, he supposed. He had left it on and wheeled it to the bathroom door just in case but its sound was already beginning to seem far away. Water pouring through steam. Such a peaceful sound.

Dommerich could not remember when he felt so good. This, he thought dreamily, was better than anything. It was even better than making those girls stop laughing.

A lot better. These feelings were staying with him. Those others never did for very long. Just for a few seconds, usually. When the light went out of their eyes. In those few seconds everything seemed so clear. He would feel so light. So free.

But it would never last. It would just sort of fade away. Like a dream you want to remember but can't.

A book in the library talked about that. It said that people like him had this tremendous blinding insight at the moment of the murder. Not that they were really murders. It wasn't like killing someone for money or because you hate them. It was more like . . .

He wasn't sure what.

Anyway, the book said that right when he's watching the lights go out, the serial killer sees, in this big flash, what made him this way. And now that he under-

stands, he can handle it. What it does—Dommerich
knew the words by heart—is "*cancel out his own suffering and establish his own power and identity.*" And it
really does. Except it doesn't last.

Until now.

And except killing didn't do it this time.

Carla did it.

He could still hear her voice on the phone. She was
so nice. All she cared about was that he shouldn't feel
bad for screwing up with Lesko. And she was really
impressed that he'd followed the Lexus all the way to
Santa Barbara without getting spotted. He almost told
her how he did that. How he could make himself
invisible.

"*Serial killers are extremely ordinary and blend in
very well.*"

That was another thing he read. No question he
could blend in really well. But he didn't think he was so
ordinary. Unless they mean average in looks. Which he
was. Pretty much.

"*Outwardly, they're often gregarious, warm, per-
sonable, and charming.*"

That one was sort of true. He was certainly polite.
And he never said anything mean.

"*But underneath, there's no depth of feeling whatsoever. No affectionate ties, no emotional pain, no sense
of blame or right or wrong, no development of con-
science.*"

That's where they weren't so smart. What about
Lisa? That wasn't an affectionate tie? And, especially,
what about Carla?

As for having no sense of right or wrong . . . what
he did to Hickey . . . wasn't that because he knew that
what Hickey did to Lisa was wrong?

And dumbest of all was that thing about not having
any emotional pain. The pain is what goes away when
they kill. Unless, maybe, they mean being sorry. He
never felt sorry. Only a little depressed. Sometimes.

"*. . . copycat killing . . . Malibu home of . . .*"

The words penetrated from the TV.

". . . *thought to be this man, Harold J. Bunce, a former Los Angeles . . .*"

They were showing an old photograph. It was that guy.

". . . *second man, unidentified, appeared to be . . .*"

Dommerich grabbed for a towel.

". . . *exclusive videotape, taken by a neighbor at the scene. Police responding to the neighbor's call found . . .*"

The picture, wobbly, amateurish, now showed a car, all smashed, trunk open, half inside a broken wall. A man moving up the hill toward the camera, waving it off. Other men trying to bend back the gate because another car was trying to get out.

Dommerich didn't understand. But it *was* that man. He was sure of it.

This was wild.

There was a second man after all. Carla must have got him. Or Lesko. And then they took these two all the way out to Malibu to dump them. But why?

Then Dommerich understood.

Carla, he bet, made the second man tell who sent them. And then she sent them back. Maybe she went into the house first, looking for him, and he wasn't there. So she left him a message.

He missed the name of the man whose house that was. Something about art. Maybe it would be on another channel. Dommerich climbed out of the tub.

Carla would be looking for that man. The first place she'd look is probably that Sur La Mer place. But he knows what Carla looks like. He would see her coming.

Wouldn't it be great, thought Dommerich, if he could find him before Carla did. Except they'd never let him through the gates. And there were all those guards.

Maybe they could work together. Make a plan.

But first he had to find her again.

*   *   *

Bannerman would not have noticed the Porsche.

He looked up at the sound of John Waldo's tires and the grinding of his gears. Waldo tossed his head toward his rear and Bannerman saw it.

He was more curious than alarmed. A Porsche, bright red, seemed an unlikely vehicle for surveillance. Nor could he imagine why its occupants would be following Susan. Or even know that she existed. Waldo, in any case, would look after her.

In the meantime, he had one more call to make. He walked the two blocks to the public phone he'd used before and tapped out the number of Queen of Angels Hospital. He asked that Mr. Leo Belkin be paged. He was drumming his fingers to a Musak interlude when he saw the red Porsche, its bumper and one headlight newly crushed, coming back in his direction. He knew at once that Susan was clear.

As the Porsche went by, the man in the passenger seat glanced in his direction. Bannerman saw recognition—the man who'd put Susan into a taxi—but no great interest in him. He watched as the driver signaled a turn into the Holiday Inn. Bannerman looked back in the direction Susan had taken and saw John Waldo's car approaching. He raised a hand and waved it to the curb.

"Any idea who they are?" he asked as Waldo neared the public phone.

"They wouldn't show me." He cocked his head toward the hotel. "I'll go ask again where it's quiet."

"Could they be detectives?"

"All that gold? No way. They're pimps or dealers."

"Why would they have followed Susan?"

"My guess . . . one guy thought maybe she was Molly. Other guy knew Molly was older."

Bannerman blinked. "You heard him say that?"

"More or less."

Leo Belkin said his name. Bannerman asked him to wait. He covered the mouthpiece. "Get Lesko," he said. "Tell him what you told me. Then the two of you go ask."

"You checking out soon?"

"Very soon. Why?"

"Okay we leave them in the parking lot?"

"The parking lot will be fine."

"What if Lesko won't?"

"Won't what?"

"Leave them dead."

Bannerman chewed his lip. He considered letting Waldo go alone, unburdened by Lesko's fine distinction between people who are killers and people who have killed. But going alone meant twice the risk.

"It's enough to leave them useless," he said.

Leo Belkin listened as Bannerman told him of the phone calls and the events in Sherman Oaks. He was distracted. Yuri had just been returned to surgery. Internal bleeding was suspected.

The news of this Claude, his part in it, hovering about like some demented fairy godmother, did not help his concentration. He could not begin to understand such a thing. He chose not to deal with it. The appearance of Axel Streicher out of nowhere was confounding enough.

"He claims that everyone involved in Lisa's death is dead," Bannerman was saying. "I'm inclined to take him at his word."

"Which means," Belkin replied, "that you are disinclined to visit Sur La Mer. Is this not what Streicher hopes?"

"It seems to be what a lot of people hope."

"Among them Roger Clew?"

A pause. "How would you know that, Leo?"

"He called here not ten minutes ago. From an airplane, by the sound of it. He hoped to reach you through me."

"What else did he say?"

"Some inconsequential bluster about my possible detainment. The sense of it was that I can avoid that inconvenience by helping to neutralize you."

"Did you agree to cooperate?"

"Of course. In return for the name of the man responsible for Yuri. But now I have that name. I owe Roger nothing."

A weary sigh. "Marek's yours if you want him. Otherwise, I have to give him to Carla."

"I want him, Paul. But next week or next month will do for me. You, I think, do not have that luxury."

"Well . . . we do if we cancel Lisa's service and leave town now. But I don't want to leave this hanging. The time to hit is when everyone else is as confused as I am."

"About Sur La Mer."

"To say nothing of Claude."

Belkin grunted, dismissing that subject. "You have no thoughts about Sur La Mer?"

Another pause. "Probably the same ones you're having."

"That it's a safe house of some kind."

"Given Roger's interest. And the fact that the Streicher's turned up there. Very possibly."

"And yet Mama's Boy has no interest."

"If it doesn't affect me? None."

"And yet you have shown an interest. And you appear to be here in force. I believe you, Paul. But who else will."

"I know." Irwin Kaplan had asked the same question. "I need a favor, Leo."

"A safe house of your own?"

"One of yours. Room for eight or ten. I need it right now."

"That is a considerable favor."

"I know it is."

"I will give you a number. Wait two minutes. I will call it first."

The owner of the red Porsche, Chulo, was still seething.

He had better things to do than sit here. Like make

some money. This favor was costing him enough already without getting his goddamned car banged up plus going through the bullshit of getting it fixed right.

Where the hell is Kiki?

Kiki, his brother, had gone inside to see who's at breakfast. Also to give the desk clerk some story about meeting this little redhead last night in the bar, said her name was Carla, was with a tall brunette, and he'd pay $50 just for her room number so he could send roses.

Probably a waste of time. The brunette had used a phone here. That was all. She could be in Vegas now for all anybody knew.

Chulo sat, his engine idling, where he could see all exits from the hotel to the rear parking lot. A few suits, probably salesmen, walking to their cars. One big guy, mean face, walking up and down trying to remember where he parked. A guy looks like that, thought Chulo, and you think he sells car crushers or wrestling equipment . . . shit like that. It always turns out they sell ladies underwear. Or maybe Bibles.

Anyway, enough was enough.

Chulo picked up his mobile phone and punched out Marek's number. Three rings. Six rings. Then, "Yeah?"

"This is Chulo. I gotta talk to Marek."

"Chulo, not now, man. We got some heavy shit here."

"Wait a second. What?"

A breath. "Bunce and Felix are dead. That redhead cunt chopped the shit out of them and sent their car right through the gate here."

"Oh, man. Oh, fuck. By herself?"

"She had a car. The other one must have been with her."

"Oh, man. Where's Marek?"

"He took off before the cops came. He went up north. You understand?"

"Yeah." Chulo gathered himself. "So anyway, I'm wasting my time here, right?"

"I guess. You want to make some money, go see

him. The redhead and the tall one are worth a hundred K."

"No shit? Let me talk to Kiki."

"Gotta go, man."

"Yeah. Watch yourself."

Chulo snapped the mobile phone into its cradle. He looked up, hoping to see his brother coming, and he did. But a car eased into his view, blocking it, blocking him. He reached for his horn, then stopped as he recognized the driver.

"Oh, Christ . . ."

It was that drunken old fart, climbing out, pen and paper in his hands, stopping now to try to write down his plate number except he could hardly stand up. Son of a bitch. Shit-faced at this hour. This time, Chulo would slap him silly.

The old drunk approached his door. Chulo opened it. He had one leg out when the old man suddenly pivoted sideways and ducked, as if to turn and run. Suddenly Chulo felt the door slam back at him. It smashed into his chest, driving him back, stunning him. The door bounced open. The drunk, pivoting again, shot another sideways kick. The door slammed, this time against Chulo's leg, snapping it above the ankle.

He sucked air for a scream. But now a hand was at his throat, stopping it. The old drunk was leaning through his window, pressing against the door. Chulo's leg was still outside. Through a blur of tears he looked for his brother. Instead, he saw the Bible salesman. The big guy. Coming toward him. Dragging something. Chulo realized it was Kiki.

"Who you looking for?" the old man asked.

Chulo arched his body in a show of pain. In the same motion, he slid the fingers of his right hand under his jacket, feeling for the gun in the small of his back.

"Hey," said Waldo quietly. "You see this?"

Chulo looked down to see what was tapping at the underside of his nose. He recognized the shape of a silencer. His right hand found his pistol, then froze.

"Tell me all at once," Waldo sighted the barrel down across Chulo's chest. It was aimed at his right knee. "Who you looking for, who sent you, who'd you just call?"

Chulo squealed. Figures appeared at the passenger door. He saw Kiki's face, swelling as if inflated, his tongue out, a forearm across his throat. The face slipped out of view as the big man reached in and felt for the gun behind Chulo's back, crushing his fingers against it.

"The man asked you a question," Lesko told him.

"I don't . . . I don't . . ."

Waldo adjusted his aim. His gun spat. Chulo felt a hammer blow against the flesh inside his thigh. His world turned to pain.

He was aware of the passenger door opening, of his brother being heaved into the seat, legs last, one at a time. He heard the big man say, "Ahhh, shit."

John Waldo peered past Chulo's face. The other one's eyes were slits. He saw no life in them. Lesko was feeling his neck for a pulse, finding none. Waldo grumbled. "Not that I mind," he asked, "but this is your idea of . . ."

"Don't give me any crap," said Lesko, embarrassed. Waldo shrugged.

He reached in farther and laid the maw of the silencer against Chulo's knee. "Nobody ever told you to respect your elders?"

Chulo made a wailing sound.

"Do you remember my question?"

Chulo managed a nod.

"Next bad answer, I spray your kneecap all over the dashboard."

46

In the vault of the Century Bank on Wilshire Boulevard, Ashley B. Hammett, the former Carleton Dunville, kissed the thick envelope that contained his new life.

He wasted no affection on the thick bundles of cash and bearer bonds or on the envelope containing his former life. These he crammed into a leather shoulder bag that he'd found under the desk of Luisa Ruiz. Mr. Weinberg had taken his own briefcase. Luisa, sadly, would not miss hers.

The files came next. These, unlike the copies Weinberg had taken from the office safe, were on computer disks. He counted them, returned them to their protective pouch, and slipped them into his pocket.

The safety deposit box was now empty. He was tempted to drop his wallet into the box as a sort of symbolic burial but decided against it. He was not out of town yet. There was still the long drive to the Mexican border, leaving Darby's car, doubling back to San Diego by bus, buying new clothes, and beginning his journey to Hilton Head.

Ashley Beauregard Hammett.

A good southern name, that. He would have time to work on the accent.

Carleton signed his true name to the vault log, perhaps for the very last time. Not that the Dunville name didn't have its uses. Such as getting a bank officer to open up early for him. But it would soon be a burden well rid of. Marek, if he was still alive, would be clawing at the gates of Sur La Mer about now, demanding sanctuary or revenge, depending on his wits. That's if the Fenerty girl got his message into the proper hands.

Dunville shouldered the bag and made his way to parking garage elevator, also unlocked just for him. He waved good-bye to the officer and guard as the doors closed over him. He felt like whistling. So he did. He whistled *Dixie*.

He was so at peace with himself, so almost weightless, that he nearly got into the wrong car. It was a Mercedes, the twin of several kept at Sur La Mer. A thin old woman was sitting in the back seat. He was glancing around for Darby's car when his mind did a double-take. That old woman looked remarkably like Nellie Dameon.

"Ohhh," he sighed aloud.

And the man walking toward him from the rear . . . the woman walking toward from the ramp, one in shadow, the other in silhouette . . .

"Oh, no."

"No-no-no-no-no."

The lobby of the Beverly Hills Hotel was bustling with guests checking out, others en route to breakfast or the pool, bellhops stacking luggage by the main entrance, a reporter and cameraman waiting for some celebrity or other.

Susan, key in hand, approached the most harried-looking clerk and asked for mail and messages for Bungalow 6. He groped for several telephone slips plus one large envelope bearing the return address of a construction firm and handed them to her. She took a seat in the lobby and went through them, taking her time, watching for anything furtive in the behavior of the clerk. She saw nothing, no sign that he'd been given instructions.

Nor did the large envelope show any evidence of tampering. She knew what it contained. Blueprints of Sur La Mer from the Fenerty girl's father. She left it sealed. The slips were all old messages. One for Molly, three for Carla. The first was from her father, the others were from Claude. Just seeing his name gave her a chill.

On Paul's advice, she walked down the stairs to the basement coffee shop, down a narrow hallway, then doubled back. No one had followed her down. She doubled back once again and exited by the gift shop, turned left, and followed the signs to the bungalow. She passed number 6, seeing no one idling in the bungalow area, no gardeners working. Once more, she doubled back, She placed her key in the lock and saw the note as she opened the door.

The writing was in longhand, the letters cramped and tiny, the lines crooked. Susan felt the chill again. It read:

> Dear Carla:
>
> Lisa's things are in a hanky behind the berry bush right by the door. It's all I found. I wish I asked if I could keep just an earring to remember her by.
>
> Two men were here hiding but they went. Where are you? Are you okay? I'll call you after ten so you can sleep. Your friend (Claude)

Susan leaned over the bush and probed with her fingers. She found the handkerchief, then stepped inside and locked the door before unfolding it. It held several chains and bracelets, a miniature gold bar from Credit Suisse, three pairs of earrings and studs.

A wave of melancholy came over Susan. She knew that they were all gifts from Carla, given at Christmas and birthdays over the years. Last year, in Zürich during all that trouble, Carla had probably found time to shop for the gold bar. Susan put them in her purse.

Then, while she thought of it, she removed the Beretta from her purse and checked its mechanism, the spring of the firing pin, and the barrel for obstructions as Billy had taught her. Chambering one round, she walked through the bungalow checking all places of possible concealment, all window latches.

She sat on the edge of the bed that was made up, certainly Molly's, and set the Beretta down. She pulled Claude's note from her shirt pocket and read it again.

It was written on an order pad of the type used by lunch counters. The kind that said "Thank You" across the top except that the top of this one had been torn away. There was a tiny lot number at the bottom. Possibly custom printed. Her father would know, or would know how to find out.

She looked at the handwriting. More strange emotions.

The cramped, tortured letters, for all she knew, were the warning sign of a tortured mind. She wondered if all serial killers had such handwriting. Just looking at it made her uneasy.

But not the words.

As much as she loathed this young man for the sick, terrible things he had done to all those girls, the words had an undeniable . . . sweetness to them. There seemed no question that he mourned Lisa. And cared about Carla. Lonely, brittle Carla. For the first time, perhaps, Susan could understand why Carla had responded to him.

She checked her watch. A quarter to nine.

A little more then an hour until that phone rings and she hears his voice. More people from Westport should start arriving by then. Plenty of time for them to get into position on Rodeo Drive. If Carla goes for it.

Susan doubted more than ever that she would.

Carleton Dunville sat glumly in the rear of Darby's car, his head turned toward the window. Weinberg had asked that he keep his eyes averted and avoid, for his own sake, a close look at Weinberg's new face.

But Dunville could hear. He heard Weinberg rifling through the leather case, handling documents, running his thumb over stacks of them. He could hear Nellie, in the front seat, trying to comfort him. Barbara Weinberg had stayed near the ramp, covering them.

"It was the key envelope, wasn't it?" he asked.

"I beg your pardon?"

"The key to my safe deposit box. You saw it in my briefcase."

"I'm afraid so, yes."

"How did you know which branch?"

"The branch number was on the little yellow envelope. The phone book showed where it was."

Dunville gritted his teeth. "Then why, for God's sake, couldn't you have waited until nine? Banks open at nine."

"Relax, Carleton. It's not that bad." Weinberg found the envelope for Hilton Head. "What does the 'B' stand for?"

"What?"

"Ashley B. Hammett."

"It's Beauregard."

"That's certainly southern," said Nellie.

". . . Thank you."

"Do you have a big house in Hilton Head?"

"It's . . . comfortable, yes."

"You should give it a southern name as well. Like Twelve Oaks or The Willows."

Dunville grumbled something unintelligible.

Weinberg had found his second identity. A French name this time. Excellent papers. The deed to a townhouse in New Orleans. Dunville stole a glance.

"Why do they interest you? You could never use them."

"No, but I might want to stay in touch. Where are the Sur La Mer files?"

"I don't have them."

Weinberg reached to pat his chest. He felt the padded envelope. "I'll tell you what," he said. "If that bulge is what I think it is, and you give it to me, I'll give you all this."

Dunville blinked in disbelief.

"Just trying to keep it friendly, Carleton. You can even have your Mercedes."

"You'd let me go? With the money?"

"Nellie? Tell him."

"He's really very nice, Carleton."

"There you have it." Weinberg held out his hand.

Dunville sighed deeply. He reached into his pocket and produced the set of disks. Weinberg took them. He zipped the leather case and moved it onto Dunville's lap.

"What will you do with those?" asked Dunville.

"Same as you, I think. Keep them as insurance. Or in case I ever need a favor from one of these people."

"And help me find my children," Nellie added.

"Yes, that will come first. May I assume that there is no other set of these?"

"You may." To Weinberg's stare he added, "That happens to be the truth. I would never have left them behind."

"There's no record elsewhere of what I might look like?"

"If there were, I'd have taken it with me. Do I gather that you're going to stay as Alan Weinberg?"

"Either that or George Bancroft."

Nellie chuckled. Then, "I'm sorry. Private joke."

"Carleton," Weinberg asked, "who else knows that I have the files?"

"I've warned a few people. They would have called others."

"But what was the point of warning them? What could they do?"

Dunville shrugged. "Prepare themselves, I suppose. Or try to find you first."

"I take it that Theodore Marek knows."

Dunville shook his head. "Marek has . . . concluded that you're in league with those women . . . and this Bannerman. But he knows nothing about the files. I despise the man."

"Is that why you blamed him for the death of Lisa Benedict? Or was it to leave a bit of confusion in your wake?"

Weinberg gave him a moment to recover from his surprise.

"Both, I suppose."

"And, to that end, I presume you told Marek that Carla would be coming for him?"

Another shrug.

Weinberg rubbed his new chin, thoughtfully. He did not blame Carleton. Weinberg might have done the same in his place. Safety in confusion. But he did not like the thought of Carla stalking Marek, perhaps getting herself killed, over a lie. Or of Marek stalking Carla. She had family here. That made her vulnerable.

He had corrected the lie, although he wasn't sure why he bothered. Perhaps he felt that he owed that much to Lisa. For failing to have anticipated Henry; failing to have saved her. Corrected it, that is, if the Fenerty girl had passed his message on.

"Nellie . . ." Dunville was speaking to her. "I'm very sorry. I really am."

She nodded slowly. "You have decent instincts, Carleton. You should try to nourish them."

"I . . . hope to."

Weinberg grunted. "I know you have to run," he said. "He held out the keys to the Mercedes.

Dunville took them, then hesitated. He looked up toward the figure of Barbara Weinberg, not quite able to believe that she would let him drive past her. At last, he gripped the door handle.

"Good-bye, Nellie," he said. "Stay beautiful."

Weinberg gave him a gentle push.

"Good-bye, Mr. Ashley Hammett," he said. "Stay alive."

47

Theodore Marek, Darby and two new bodyguards with him, stood at the window of Carleton Dunville's office, pounding a fist against his palm, watching the road that snaked up through the morning mist.

It was well after nine. Marek's faint hope that Dunville still might appear, thinking he was dead or in hiding, was fading rapidly. But Marek clung to it, unwilling to abandon the scene he had envisioned since escaping from his home. Of seeing Dunville's face when he found him there. Of hearing his fumbling denials. Of then having him strapped to that basement table.

Poor Felix. He would have enjoyed that so. Perhaps, thought Marek, he would do it himself. Wear one of those rubber aprons. But, no. Better to stand and watch. Make suggestions. Before Carleton was allowed to die, he would feel everything that Harry Bunce and Felix must have felt.

". . . is back. Messed up. Not too bad."

That was Darby. Saying something. Marek barely heard because he was seeing Harry Bunce and he was hearing Carleton's voice, speaking to that Fenerty girl, blithely claiming that he, Theodore Marek, had murdered the sister of the redheaded butcher.

Somehow, she'd been waiting for poor Harry. Caught both of them. And then sent them back. Standing up on that hill. Daring his people to come after her. But he wasn't fooled. An obvious trap. His people would rush out and be slaughtered. Then she would come for him.

But I am innocent, he screamed in his mind.

Scholl.

Where was Scholl all this time?

Carleton's telephone rang. Marek stared at it for a moment, then flicked a finger at Darby, telling him to answer.

Whoever it was, it was not Scholl, not Carleton. Doctor someone or other. Darby was arguing with him. He pressed the "hold" button.

"It's Dr. Feldman," he told Marek. "Says he wants to move all the members this morning—take them down to the Country House. Says he's got authorization."

"Tell him . . . not until your boss says so."

Darby spoke into the phone. "Mr. Marek says . . ."

Marek waved furiously. "Not me, you ass. Dunville."

Darby flushed. "Mr. *Dunville*," he corrected himself, "has to give the okay. He'll call you when he gets in."

Darby listened. He pressed the "hold" button again.

"He's saying it was Mr. Dunville's idea. He says he has written authorization from the Motion Picture and Television Fund and wants to know if he needs to bring the cops."

"Say you'll call him back."

Darby hesitated. "I don't know, Mr. Marek. He sounds . . ."

Marek raised a staying hand. He considered the situation. That bastard, Dunville. What's his game? Certainly not a last act of humanitarian concern for the members. Probably wants to prevent their use as hostages. And what has made Dr. Feldman so defiant all at once? Didn't the Dunvilles have some hold on him? Yes, they did. Those files. Feldman's sudden bravado might mean that Dunville had destroyed them.

Yes. He very well might have. Burning all bridges. Marek seized the hope that Dr. Feldman would know if he had. Has probably been in league with him all along.

"Tell him to come," he said to Darby. "The police will not be necessary."

Insolent young pup.

We'll strap him to a table instead.

* * *

Molly Farrell had paid her driver at Twenty-ninth and Vermont, then walked to the Menlo Avenue house of DiDi Fenerty.

She saw no suspicious cars or utility workers. Several joggers moved up and down the residential streets but all of them seemed of college age. To her surprise, DiDi's friend Kevin was still on the porch. Awake. Doing squats. He saw her coming and rapped on the door. It opened as Molly approached.

DiDi looked tired but was excited to see her. She introduced her three bodyguards. They were men in their forties, all armed with hunting rifles, no concealed weapons, hard faces, sullen eyes. Molly guessed, correctly, that they were parolees. They studied her face as well, respectfully enough. One seemed awed. DiDi must have passed the night telling stories.

It took her ten minutes to check out the circuitry of DiDi's phones. She found nothing. She rummaged through her shopping bag to find the wherewithal for a different test. When ready, she asked DiDi to place a call, on any reasonable pretext, using a house mate's phone. Molly measured the amperage. It held steady. She asked DiDi to make another call, this time on her own line. The amperage dropped sharply. She let nothing show on her face until DiDi broke the connection.

"What do you think?" DiDi replaced the phone.

"That one's okay. Someone listened on yours."

"How about Kevin's?"

"It's probably clean. I'll check before I go."

Molly held up a hand to stay further questions as she dialed, using the house mate's phone, the number Paul had given her. He answered on the first ring.

"You were right," she told him.

"I know. Don't come back here. We're checked out."

"Where, then?"

"Sit tight, but don't get trapped in that house. Can you stay where the other phone is?"

He means Kevin's. "I guess so. Sure."

"Any ideas on who set the wire?"

"Could be the Sur La Mer crowd, reacting to DiDi's call. But my money's on the FBI."

"Why?"

A shrug. "They have the means. They were the only other people who talked to DiDi. And they wouldn't have believed that we came up empty here, especially when they saw the bodyguards."

"I was afraid of that." Bannerman took a breath. "Whoever tapped that phone knew that you called from this hotel. He passed that information to Theodore Marek."

Molly groaned. "I screwed up. I'm sorry."

"Forget that. We had a problem but we've dealt with it. Do you still have the keys to your rental car?"

The blue Chevrolet. "Yes."

"Lesko's coming to get them. Warn those body-guards so they don't shoot him on sight."

"That car has a tracker on it, Paul."

"I know it does. In two minutes I'll call you on DiDi's line. I'll ask you where the explosives are. You answer that they're in the spare tire of that Chevrolet and then tell me where you left it."

"Um . . . won't they be all over him?"

"That's the point. Two minutes." Bannerman broke the connection.

Molly stared at the phone as if for some clue to what Bannerman had in mind. It did not surprise her, on reflection, that Paul would look for a way to use the knowledge that the car was rigged. The most obvious use was as a decoy. Having John Waldo, for example, take it on a joy ride to tie up several FBI surveillance teams while their people were busy someplace else.

But he didn't need the phone call to do that. And that business about explosives was almost certain to get Lesko detained. A search of the spare tire, of course, would confirm that the FBI had wired DiDi, but so what? They still wouldn't know which agent was passing information to Marek.

Maybe, she thought, Paul just wants Lesko out of the way. Except Lesko would see through that in a minute.

The other phone rang. Molly gestured that DiDi should answer. DiDi picked it up.

"This is she," she answered. Her eyes widened. She raised one finger to stay Molly's outstretched hand. "Oh. Um . . . hi."

She turned toward Molly, jabbing at the handset with her finger.

"Yes," DiDi nodded. "I told her everything you said." To Molly, she mouthed the name *Streicher*.

Molly hesitated, then held out her hand once more.

Elena, at the wheel of Billy's Ford, struggled to keep her mind on the road. The pounding from the trunk, the muffled screams of rage, made driving difficult.

Five minutes out of Malibu, with Carla happily describing the destruction of Theodore Marek's wall and gate, Billy had asked her to stop behind a road stand that was not yet open. Elena assumed that he needed to relieve himself. Two minutes later, Carla, stunned and bound, was in the trunk. Her head cleared as Elena slowed for the Sunset Boulevard exit of the Pacific Coast Highway. Billy could see that the noise was unnerving her.

"You have to put your foot down sometimes," he said.

He advised Carla that they were now on Sunset, that the noise could be problem, and that he would put her back to sleep if she made another sound. She answered with a string of inventive curses but became silent when Billy asked Elena to pull over again.

Billy waved her on. The threats resumed but at a lower pitch. The pounding stopped entirely.

A few streets short of the Brentwood Holiday Inn, a car drew close behind her and tapped its horn.

"It's Waldo," said Billy. "Give him room."

She allowed him by, then followed as he drove past the Holiday Inn's entrance, giving a thumb's down signal as he did so. Billy caught a glimpse of a police cruiser, lights strobing, in the rear of the parking lot. Elena saw two more coming from the opposite direction.

Two blocks farther, Waldo gestured toward the far side of Sunset and pulled to the curb. Elena saw Paul where Waldo had pointed. He was speaking on a public phone, watching their arrival. He straightened as he appeared to notice that Carla was not in sight. Billy made a "calm-down" gesture that seemed to reassure him.

"Looks like we moved out," said Billy.

Bannerman, surprised that Molly had not kept that phone free, used the time to check in with Anton Zivic. Several men and women would be arriving soon from Westport. He needed to be sure that they knew where to go. He gave Zivic an approximate address. They were to rent cars and cruise the area until intercepted.

"They are to call me on arrival in any case," Zivic told him. "Paul, why don't you all simply leave?"

Bannerman watched as an ambulance passed and headed for the Holiday Inn. "It's tempting, but that won't end it. I'm afraid it's gone too far."

He told Zivic of Carla's latest episode as recounted by the man named Chulo. That Chulo's boss, Marek, had apparently fled to Sur La Mer. Of Axel Streicher coming back from the dead and of his involvement with Sur La Mer. Of the fact that information from a probable FBI wiretap on the Fenerty girl's phone had been promptly passed on to Theodore Marek.

Zivic smacked his lips. "All this and a benevolent serial killer. Do you still intend trying to take him?"

"We'll see how the day develops. We may not have

that luxury and, anyway, I don't think it will help us at this point."

"Tell me that you do not intend going to Sur La Mer in force."

"I'm not suicidal, Anton. But we'll have to see to Marek."

Zivic's grunt said that he was somewhat relieved. Not in force and certainly not in daylight. Unfamiliar ground, probably well guarded, no time to prepare and rehearse. Possible interference from Roger Clew. If it were Zivic's decision, he would blacken John Waldo's face and send him in alone, at night, and by morning it would probably be done.

"If Marek is indeed Ordynsky, I have some interesting information. Do you want it now?"

"Thank you. Yes."

Bannerman listened to a brief biography. Polish born, studied art at Leipzig, recruited into the Nazi Einsatzgruppen in 1942, assigned to Group A—the Baltic area—special assistant for art to General Franz Stahlecker. Looted Soviet treasures during the retreat from Leningrad. Stahlecker was either killed by Estonian partisans or else murdered by Ordynsky—take your choice. Ordynsky surfaced throughout Europe several times, selling stolen art. He vanished permanently in the mid-1950s, with the KGB hot on his trail, and, until now, was thought to have been caught and executed by them.

"Anton, could Leo already know this?"

"Not likely. Unless you told him that Marek was Ordynsky."

"I didn't."

"However, the fact that I made inquiries might soon get back to the KGB. They would want this man very badly. They would like to recover that stolen art even more. Also, they will want to know why Mama's Boy is interested."

Bannerman shrugged it off. Too remote. He had enough on his mind. Lesko was already on his way to the

Fenerty house and he needed to make that call. Then he
needed Waldo to pick up those Sur La Mer plans from
Susan. And look in on her.

He thanked Anton again and broke the connection.
He tapped out DiDi Fenerty's number. DiDi answered,
not Molly.

"Is my friend there, please?"

"Is this . . . ?"

"Yes."

"Oh . . . wow . . . she's . . . ah, on the other
line." The she blurted, "The dynamite's in the trunk of
the blue Chevrolet. It's parked outside 2800 Victory
Boulevard in Burbank."

Bannerman, startled, heard Molly's whispered voice
correcting her. "Semtex. In the spare tire."

"I heard," he said. "Thank you. Please hang up the
phone and get out of there."

"Well . . . she really wants you to call back.
She's . . . um, you know when you go bowling? And
what unions do sometimes?"

"I'll call back. But not there." He broke that connection as well.

Bowling. Unions. Strikes. Streicher.

Bannerman couldn't help but smile.

48

Susan's heart jumped when the telephone rang.

Now that it had, she was afraid to touch it. She
gathered herself, then picked it up and said hello,
grimacing at the catch in her throat.

The line was silent. Hollow.

"Is someone there?" she said, more strongly.

No answer. Then a click.

She held the phone to her ear, to no purpose, and felt her legs go weak. She sat down on the bed, feeling the hardness of the Beretta under her.

Damn.

It could have been almost anyone, she told herself. A simple wrong number. But she knew better. She could feel him in the hollowness, the emptiness, of the line.

Damn. Damn. Damn.

"I have had . . . many thoughts of you, Molly. It's been . . . six years?"

"More like eight."

"Yes. Eight. I know that I should have . . ."

"Axel . . . you didn't owe me anything." *Except*, she said in her mind, *you might have told me about you and Bonnie, face-to-face*. "Except," she said aloud, "you might have let me know you were okay."

"It seemed easier this way, for all concerned."

"That phone was wired, Axel. Someone else knows you're not dead."

"Marek, you think?"

"FBI, I think. But it looks like they told Marek."

A long silence. Then, "It doesn't matter. We have a new life."

"I don't suppose you'd tell me where."

"Molly . . ."

"I understand, Axel."

"I've told Bonnie about you. About us. Her response was that I have very good taste."

"Axel . . ." A different response sprung to mind. She thought better of it. "Why did you call DiDi again?"

"To make sure that my message was passed on. There is nothing for you at Sur La Mer. Nothing for Carla."

"There's Marek, apparently. He's got people out looking for us. He's tried twice to hit us."

"And Bannerman feels he must hit back. Bannerman's law."

"Axel . . . what's your stake in this?"

"Would you believe . . . protection of the innocent?"

"I'd believe covering your trail."

"I've left no trail. Trust me on that."

"You remember Roger Clew? He doesn't want us going there either. Why, Axel?"

A surprised silence. "I . . . don't know. I can only guess that he knows what it is. I won't explain, Molly, because it is truly none of your business. But Roger, believe it or not, might be protecting the innocent as well."

"Well . . . I'll talk to Paul."

"Where can I reach him?"

"Where can he reach you, Axel?" she asked dryly.

"Very well. Ask him . . . that he take no action before noon today. He has my word that no advantage will be lost."

"I'll tell him."

"Molly . . . make him believe me."

"I said I'll tell him."

Sumner Dommerich was so tired.

He knew that he wasn't thinking properly. The voice should not have taken him by surprise. It was probably the tall one with the brown hair. Named Molly. Maybe Carla was right there.

Except that if Carla read the note, she knew he'd be calling about now. She would have answered the phone herself. Unless, maybe, she was on the toilet or something.

He was tempted to call again and ask. Like, are you Molly? But that wouldn't do any good because he didn't know Molly's voice. She could be anyone, pretending to be Molly. It could be a trap. Maybe Carla was there but she was tied to a chair and gagged. Maybe men were waiting outside in the bushes again.

No. Wait.

Don't get all upset.

Just go look, maybe.

Think of ways to get her to open the door so you can see if it's Molly.

"You know what I think?"

Katz.

Lesko tried to shake him away. His own thoughts were dancing between what might happen when this cab pulled up to that Chevrolet and Elena, and Susan, and the strange behavior of Molly Farrell.

No question she had something on her mind. Usually, she's the most laid-back of the whole bunch, very together, but now she looked like someone just slapped her.

For a minute there he thought she might have heard how he squeezed that greaseball's neck a little too long. But that wouldn't have bothered her any more than it bothered Waldo. It only bothered him.

"I think some guy dumped her."

What?

"I seen it a hundred times."

You've seen what?

"Like when a guy's wife or girl friend tells him to take a walk. I remember when you looked like that."

Lesko curled his lip. Right. With everything else going on here, shit-for-brains thinks Molly's worried about her love life.

Ahead, he saw a service station. He asked the driver to pull in while he made a quick call. He wished there was a way he could reach Elena, make sure they all got back okay, but at least he could check in with Susan, get that much off his mind.

She answered on the second ring. "Claude?"

"No, it's me. You okay?"

Heavy breathing. "I guess. Sure. Daddy, I have to keep this line open."

"You got the door bolted? The windows?"

"Yes, I've—wait . . . someone's here."

Lesko's stomach knotted.

"Daddy, it's Elena and John Waldo. I have to give them a package."

"Wait. You're sure it's them?"

"I see them. They're . . . um, checking things out."

"You don't open that door for anyone else, you understand?"

"Daddy . . ."

"Nor for the chamber maids, the bellboys, room service . . ."

"I really have to go."

"Susan!" he snapped.

Exhaled breath. "Yes?"

"No . . . pizzas, either. Don't send out for a pizza."

"Good-bye, Daddy."

Lesko listened to the dead line. He knew how dumb that must have sounded. A part of his mind dared Katz to open his mouth about it. The other part saw Elena through Susan's window. He was glad he called.

Carla, her scraped knees bleeding through her jeans, sat sullenly in the back of Waldo's car as it headed south toward Culver City on the San Diego Freeway. Bannerman sat in front of her. Billy and Elena followed in the second car. Carla saw the road signs leading to the airport.

"Are you putting me on a plane?" she asked. "I won't go."

He shook his head. "I wish I could."

"Then where are we going?"

"To an address Leo gave us. Be still, Carla."

That was the most he'd said to her.

He had left her in Billy's trunk until they were well away from the Holiday Inn. Then he stopped to call Molly again. Only after that had he freed her, taking her arm, leading her to Waldo's car as she struggled against him trying to get at Billy. She quit struggling when he appeared to be eyeing the other trunk.

She sat alone with him then, Billy covering on foot, while Waldo and Elena drove off to pick up a package from Susan. He wouldn't even tell her what it was.

She had tried to apologize, in her fashion. Or, rather, to explain: Fear is a weapon, she said. Bannerman himself had taught her that. Now Marek would be terrified. He'd care more about saving his own ass than moving against them. But Bannerman had turned the radio on, as if to drown her out. He listened to news broadcasts until Waldo and Elena returned.

He was being a prick, she thought. And he was hurting her.

Worse than not talking, worse than the anger for which she had prepared herself, was the look in his eyes. She saw mistrust, even dismissal.

She felt her throat begin to thicken and grow hot. Oh, no. She was damned if she would let him see her cry again. She tried focusing on the radio news. It was all about Claude. Did he or didn't he? That didn't help because it brought thoughts of Lisa. She tried thinking of Yuri, yesterday, in her bed, later telling her about his Maria. That was a mistake. The tears came hard.

They seemed to soften him a bit. She hated herself for it nonetheless.

"Carla . . ."

"Fuck you."

Bannerman ignored the response. He patted his pockets as if looking for a handkerchief, finding none.

"There were three Dunvilles," he told her. "One did kill Lisa. He's now dead. Another Dunville would have silenced DiDi Fenerty. He's also dead. The third Dunville appears to have been innocent. He's left town. We're not likely to see him again."

She found a tissue in her purse. "How do you know all this?

"I'll tell you. But not for a while."

"Does everybody else know?"

"Only some."

"The reliable ones."

Bannerman made a face. "As it happens," he told her, "there's been no chance to brief any of you." He made a gesture that embraced both cars.

"We're here now."

"It can wait, Carla."

"Does Susan know? Does she know more about my sister than I do?"

He chewed his lip. "Stop that. Right now."

Waldo turned onto the ramp for Culver City.

"I need new stockings," she said.

Bannerman blinked at the nonsequitur, then remembered. Her knees. "We'll get you cleaned up. Elena probably has some to spare."

"I want my own."

Bannerman, fed up, turned in his seat as Waldo coasted to a stop. He saw Carla's knife. She held it, more defensively than threatening, close to her body. With her free hand she opened the door.

"Don't make me cut you," she said.

49

"The things I do for love."

Alan Weinberg muttered this aloud as Barbara rummaged through the supply closet at Dr. Michael's office, searching for a set of whites that would fit him. She found one jacket that would do if worn unbuttoned.

Weinberg sat in a chair, Kleenex tucked into his shirt collar, as Nellie went to work with her makeup kit. She would, she had promised, give each of them a nice California tan. Age them a few years. Hide the scars. She had also gathered an assortment of props such as eyeglasses, stethoscopes, and a well-chewed pipe for Alan.

Barbara had already dressed in a nurse's uniform of sorts. A white dress and stockings. She would use her own sneakers. And she had fashioned a sort of wimple out of a pillow case.

"You're supposed to be a nun, I take it."

"It hides my hair." She paused at a mirror to check. "And it might put them at ease."

"But isn't there supposed to be a black thing that hangs down the back and sides?"

"I'll make one. Another pillow case. It will have to be white."

Weinberg grunted doubtfully. It boggled the mind. A Jewish nun. Sisters of the Holy Uzi. But, he realized, it would probably serve its purpose. He did not imagine that the personnel at Sur La Mer were familiar with the dress codes of the various religious orders.

This was all Barbara's idea initially.

Not that she'd actually proposed it. But he'd seen that half-smile grow on her face as Dr. Michael explained how he planned to pick up the members. He would drive his own station wagon, he said. He would lead a minibus to be provided by the Motion Picture Country House and driven by one of its orderlies. The minibus carried basic medical equipment, oxygen, and it had an electric lift for wheelchair patients.

"I wonder if they'd recognize us," was all she said.

Weinberg's best response, he realized too late, would have been to feign a heart attack. Anything to interrupt her train of thought.

But "I wonder," was what he answered.

And Nellie added, "Oh. I would feel so much better if you two went with Michael."

Absolutely not. Weinberg was adamant. They hadn't gone through all that surgery just to go back and show off their new faces.

"That's just the point," Barbara had argued. "No one at Sur La Mer would expect us to come back. If we dress in whites, they probably won't even look past the uniforms."

"They won't look at all because we won't be there."

"But we'll see them," she pressed. "We'll know what Marek and his shooters look like in case we ever run into them again. That could save our lives someday."

"So could minding our own business. No."

"And we'll see how they're deployed. You'll be able to tell Molly."

Weinberg hesitated. That argument, having Bannerman in their debt, had a suggestion of merit. Still, it seemed foolhardy. What if they get in and find that Marek won't let them out again? In fact, why should he let them go at all?

But Barbara had that look of hers. That half-smile. He knew that he could argue all morning and in the end she would say something like, "You're right. It's foolish for both of us to go. You wait here with Nellie."

And she would mean it. There would be no question of laying down the law. One doesn't marry Bonnie Predd and expect her to become a geisha overnight.

In the end, all he could do was what he did. Call Molly. Try to dissuade her, at least. Failing that, ask for three hours' grace.

That and try to believe his wife when she swore that she had no other motive spinning around under that wimple. No yielding to sudden impulses such as she had when taking her leave of Carleton the elder. No plan to leave Theodore Marek—that abuser of children—stitched to the wall under the "benefactors" plaque bearing his name.

She said she wouldn't dream of it.

Susan could not remember feeling so alone.

Carla's belongings, and Molly's, scattered throughout the bungalow, seemed like ghosts. She busied herself with straightening the rooms. Carla's things, in particular, affected her in that they seemed so ordinary. She could not have said why. Or what else she expected.

She heard people passing outside, chatting idly, just another day. She wanted to be with them. She had drifted to the window, watching them turn toward the lobby entrance, when she saw the bellboy step aside for them and then continue on in her direction.

He was carrying what looked to be a small bouquet of flowers and he was heading toward the door of Bungalow 6.

She was surprised more than alarmed. He was a young man but, beyond that, he bore no resemblance to Paul's description of Claude. And she had seen him in the lobby earlier.

Susan, with the Beretta in hand, answered his knock through the bolted door.

"Flowers for Miss Benedict," he said.

She asked that he leave them outside.

When he left, but while still in her sight, she quickly opened the door and snatched the flowers, then bolted the lock again. She put the Beretta back on safety and tucked it into the small of her back.

The bouquet was a small FTD assortment in a miniature brass watering can. She opened the card. It read:

> I hope you're okay.
> Your friend, Claude

The card envelope bore the address of the hotel's gift shop but the handwriting was not in the cramped, painful script of the note he'd left under the door. She realized that he must have ordered them through a florist some distance away. This handwriting, practiced and feminine, was probably that of the gift shop clerk.

It was such a tiny bouquet. Mostly carnations. A harmless little thing, and yet it made her shiver.

But what, she wondered, did it mean? That he would not be calling again? All she could do was wait.

A half-hour passed. In that time she understood anew why her father had clung to the man she'd grown up calling Uncle David. She even tried talking to him, asking him about the flowers. He didn't answer. Then a different bellboy came. With cookies this time.

Once again, she asked that he leave them outside. She waited until more people passed before unbolting the door and retrieving them. The cookies were by Famous Amos. The bag, well sealed, showed no sign of tampering. The note, again from the gift shop, read,

> These are my favorite.
> Your friend, Claude.

Something about the cookies disturbed her. More so than the flowers. She couldn't say what.

Uncle David?

Still no answer.

More time went by. Perhaps twenty minutes. It passed slowly. She had just stepped into the bathroom when she heard another knock at the door.

"Yes?" she called.

"This time it's a pizza," came the voice.

"Oh." The bellboy, she thought, must be wondering what comes next. A chocolate cake? "Just leave it, please."

"Not too long, okay? It's no good cold."

"Sure. Thank you." She heard him walk away.

Funny, she thought, that her father would tell her not to send out for pizza. She tried asking him, not David Katz, why he would say that.

"Just don't," she imagined him saying. *"Do what I tell you."*

Susan opened the door, keeping it on its chain. She looked down at the pizza box, no note this time, and it suddenly struck her what had bothered her about the cookies. They were a gift shop item. The flowers, prepaid, could have been ordered anywhere but there's no FTD for Famous Amos cookies. They must have been ordered in the gift shop itself. Claude must . . . might . . . be here.

She closed her right hand over the Beretta at her back and reached for the chain on the door.

"He's been watching you," came a voice. Her own. *"Twice you picked up the things he sent. He knows you're not Carla or Molly."*

What would Molly do? Susan wasn't sure. What she would not do was scare him off. Or blow this chance.

Swallowing hard, she threw off the chain and opened the door wide. She crouched, one arm extended as if to reach for the box. She heard a sound, then withdrew, bracing herself. A white blur appeared in the doorway at the level of her chest. Another pizza box. A figure behind it, charging at her. Pivoting, she blocked the box with her free hand and kicked under it, aiming the edge of her shoe at the leading knee. The figure squealed and stumbled. Susan gripped the rigid box, keeping it between them. She kicked again as Billy had taught her, this time at the side of the knee. A scream. She saw a flash of steel. It swiped at her under the box but the man holding the knife was already falling. He struck the table that held the cookies and the flowers and the telephone. They crashed to the floor with him.

"Drop it," she said, her chest heaving.

He was clutching his knee, his face contorted by pain. He looked up at Susan and at the pistol she held in a combat grip. His eyes darted about the room as if looking for a place to hide. They stopped at a point behind Susan, near the still open door. The eyes went wide.

"Get her," he wailed.

She knew better than to turn. "I said drop it. Drop the fucking knife."

Dommerich ignored her. He pointed the knife past her.

"She hurt me," he blubbered. "Get her."

A shadow moved across the floor. Susan spun. Her finger squeezed the trigger but the Beretta did not fire. Horrified, she remembered that the safety was on.

"Easy," came a voice from outside. "Don't shoot me."

Carla's voice. Susan's heart pounded.

She would have.

"Lesko?"

Roger Clew, sitting in Jack Scholl's car, watched in disbelief as the familiar figure climbed out of a taxi and into the blue Chevrolet. Raymond Lesko. *The* Raymond Lesko. Who hadn't even bothered to scout out the street.

"You know him?" asked Scholl.

Clew nodded, perplexed.

He had only met Scholl ten minutes earlier. Clew had called him by radio phone on his way from the airport. Patched through to Scholl's car, he learned that a surveillance had been set up around a rental car that had been traced to Carla Benedict. Scholl had reason to believe that the car was soon to be reclaimed, possibly stocked with explosive devices.

"This reason to believe," Clew asked, frowning. "Where'd it come from?"

"I can't tell you that. But it's solid."

Clew watched as Lesko pulled out into traffic. "Don't fuck with me," he said darkly.

Scholl's color rose. "We . . . might have a wire. Some local girl. They've been passing messages through her."

"A legal wire?"

Scholl answered with a shrug.

"I want to hear the tapes."

"I . . . destroyed them. The bureau could be embarrassed if . . ."

Clew looked at him, more disbelief. And then at Lesko's Chevrolet, now headed south in no particular hurry. Another FBI car had fallen in behind.

"I want to talk to Lesko," he said. "Take him right now. No guns."

"Negative." School shook his head. "He'll lead us to Bannerman. I want them all."

Clew let out a breath. "How many agents in this surveillance?"

"Eight, not including us. Four cars."

"And how many at that house where the car went through the wall?"

"Four."

Thirteen agents, thought Clew. All tied up by a diversion in Malibu and musical cars in Burbank. The LAPD, meanwhile, is neutralized because Bannerman promised them the serial killer if they'd give him room. They believed it, he supposed, because they wanted to.

Clew had no doubt of what was happening here. It was Bannerman, clearing the children off the streets. Bannerman was about to hit Sur La Mer.

He reached for Scholl's radio phone and handed it to him.

"Take him," he said, "or I'll have your ass for breakfast."

The KGB safe house in Culver City was a union hall for migrant workers.

A nice idea, thought Bannerman. A dormitory upstairs. Other quarters for staff. A steady flow of middle-class, well-dressed whites with social consciences. Hot meals provided by a nearby Catholic church. It even had a government grant. It functioned, Leo Belkin assured him, quite legitimately and quite in the interests of the migrants although the key organizers were all KGB operatives.

Belkin had joined him there, feeling the need to take a break from his vigil and also to smooth his way among nervous Soviet agents. Not the least of his reasons for coming was to remind Bannerman that a favor of this magnitude would require a substantial quid pro quo, if only to keep peace with Belkin's superiors.

"Can you spare some people," Bannerman asked, "to keep an eye on Marek's house and gallery?"

"To what purpose? You say he's fled."

"Trust me on this. It's in your interest."

Belkin was noncommittal. But Bannerman knew that he'd see to it.

Bannerman tried Susan from a secure phone. He got a busy signal. Annoyed, he told Belkin how Carla had bolted from the car. Possibly headed back to the Beverly Hills Hotel and her supply of pantyhose. More likely headed for Sur La Mer. John Waldo had gone there in hope of intercepting her. And otherwise to scout it. Billy was outside flagging new arrivals. Elena was resting.

"And if Carla gets there first?" Belkin asked.

"Then she's on her own."

"This does not . . . force your hand?"

Bannerman sighed. He shook his head slowly.

Leo Belkin saw sadness, not anger, in his manner. The words, and their tone, said that he had already reconciled himself to the loss of Carla. He would not risk other lives to save her from herself. Belkin wondered, even if she survived, would Bannerman ever allow her to return to Westport.

"What will you do, Paul?"

"I'll wait."

"But not for long, I think."

Bannerman shook his head again, distantly.

He realized that Belkin expected, even hoped for, some dramatic response. He was, after all, the famous Mama's Boy. And that was the problem.

He would not deny that the legend had its uses. But it was a burden just as often. Two winters ago he'd gone to Switzerland to ski, only to ski, and people died because they simply would not believe that. Even now, Leo Belkin could not quite accept that he had no deeper purpose in coming to California. Or that he knew as little as he did.

He had no idea what Axel Streicher wanted to protect. Or why he needed until noon. Or what Roger was afraid of. There must be dozens of people, he thought, perhaps hundreds, who were at this moment trying to find him, and, failing that, trying to anticipate his next move. Wondering what the phantom Semtex was for.

Let them.

If everything they think they know is wrong, their actions will be wrong. He had no wish to die for their mistakes either.

His next move, he now decided, would be to take a nap.

After he tried Susan again.

50

On the camera monitors at the rear of the main house, Theodore Marek watched the arrival of the small caravan. He had darkened the room, the better to see the screens.

In the lead, a Volvo station wagon, that annoying young doctor at the wheel, a nurse . . . no, a nun . . . in the passenger seat holding a clipboard. A jitney bus followed, the markings of the Motion Picture Country House on its side, a man in white driving, a pipe between his teeth. Marek watched with satisfaction as the gates swung shut behind them.

He turned to another monitor that scanned the great lawn. The members, most of them, were scattered about, some in wheelchairs, that blind old man busy with his stupid paints.

Marek had reconsidered keeping them all, including Feldman and his helpers. That other asylum would only start calling, looking for them, within a matter of hours. But he could certainly delay their departure.

Make sure all documents were checked, all members examined, and then of course fed. In the meantime, keep them in the line of fire should any other visitors decide to come calling.

The door behind him opened. A dim light spilled in from the hall. He glanced over his shoulder, seeing that it was the decanter of brandy and the sandwich he had ordered. The tray was set down at his side. A glass was poured. Retreating footsteps. The door closed again.

He checked another bank of monitors, trained where Darby had deployed the other guards. He could not see them but he knew that they were there. They were well armed and out of sight.

The cameras covering Tower Road showed no activity there. One man walking a dog. One car, his own bodyguards in it, cruising the perimeter. They had alerted him by radio of Dr. Feldman's approach.

He wished he had more of his own people out there. But he'd ordered the best of them to stay at the house and guard his possessions. Especially his vault. Keep the media away. Keep the police from penetrating any farther than had poor Felix's car.

Mr. Marek, they were to say, was out of town, incommunicado, inspecting the art collection of a famous recluse. All very hush-hush. He knows nothing of these people who came crashing through his wall.

Even at Sur La Mer, Marek would stay out of sight. Right here, watching the sweep of the monitors. Let Darby deal with Feldman in his normal bumbling, officious and time-consuming manner. When that nun with her clipboard discovers one of the members unaccounted for, it ought to keep them all in the line of fire even longer.

"Drink your brandy, Mr. Marek."

Marek jumped at the sound of the voice. A woman. He spun in his seat, instantly terrified, his eyes alternately wide and squinting as he tried to make out the dim figure standing, arms folded, her back against the door. The sister? The Benedict woman? Impossible. And yet there she was. Small. Short hair. An odd shine on her face and on her forearms.

"How did you . . . who . . . I didn't . . ." He couldn't catch his breath.

"Drink it, please." She took a step toward him.

A wave of relief flooded upward from his stomach. It was not that woman at all. It was the homely one. Luisa. Cried all the time. Played dead when he touched her. The one he'd returned.

His brain whirled but he remembered now. Darby had said something about her. That she was back. "Messed up . . . not too bad," he'd said. Marek had paid no attention. Back from where?

Her face, her arms, seemed to have been burned. They were covered with ointment. The hair wasn't short. It was simply gone but for a few tufts at the rear. He stared, transfixed, more aware of her increased ugliness than of the small pistol half hidden under one folded arm.

"Luisa," he managed. "What . . . I mean, how did you . . ."

"Drink your brandy." Her arms separated. The pistol dropped to her side. The movement caused her to wince and yet Marek saw peace, not pain, in her eyes. "Drink it. Then we'll talk."

Susan had never seen Carla so calm. Her own pulse was still racing. Carla seemed to be sleep-walking.

She watched, the Beretta ready, as Carla entered the bungalow and approached the pale young man who sat curled into a ball against the sitting room couch. One of his hands still held the knife. Both hands massaged his injured knee.

"Hello, Claude," said Carla. She lowered herself to his side. Susan noticed that her knees were hurt as well. They had bled through her jeans.

Gently, Carla took the knife. He did not resist.

"H . . . hi, Carla," he stammered. He tried to smile. She answered it.

Carla studied the fighting knife, testing its balance. "Claude? You use two knives, don't you."

He swallowed. "You could tell?"

"I could tell."

He drew one hand from his knee and touched the pocket of his windbreaker. Carla reached into it and found the black leather case that contained his skinning knife. She slid both weapons well under the couch.

"Can you walk, do you think?"

"I'll try."

"Um . . ." Susan stepped closer. "Walk where, Carla?"

Carla ignored her.

"Is she your friend?" asked Dommerich.

Carla hesitated, but she nodded.

"I didn't know. I mean, first I thought she was the older lady, Molly, but then I saw she wasn't. Then I was afraid they arrested you for what I did or maybe they had you tied up in here. Or something."

"No harm done. It's okay."

"Oh." He touched one of her knees. "You're hurt, too."

"Just scraped. I'm fine."

Dommerich's eyes wandered the room, searching. "I sent you flowers," he said.

Carla glanced where they had fallen. "They're lovely. Thank you."

"And cookies."

"I saw. Try to stand, Claude."

"Carla." Susan took another step. "He stays where he is."

She turned her head, gesturing toward the Beretta. "Put that away. You won't need it."

Susan shook her head.

"Look at him," Carla said quietly. "Does he look dangerous to you?"

Claude was wide-eyed, his jaw slack, the lower lip protruding. A sunken chest, soft at the waist. No, he did not look dangerous. None of his victims would have thought he did either.

Susan glanced around the room as if for help. She saw the fallen telephone. She wanted to rush to it and pick it up, hopeful that it would then ring and she would hear Paul's voice telling her what to do.

What would he say?

He'd be very calm. He'd tell her to keep him there. Wait for him. Maybe even call the police.

But Carla wants to take him, Paul. I think she'll let him go. She's not even asking what his real name is. Paul, I can't let her take him.

Put her on the phone.

She won't talk to you. She's helping him, right now, to his feet. She's asking if he has a car outside.

Then let her go, Susan. Don't take her on.

Paul, I have a gun.

What gun?

Mine. I mean, there were two in your bag. I might have to shoot him.

Don't. Do you hear me? Do not. You're not like us, Susan. You never can be like us.

In her mind, Susan hung up on him.

She had to. Claude was standing. Carla brought his arm around her shoulder. Susan felt for the hammer with her thumb, making sure that it was fully cocked.

"Let us by," she said. "Be careful with that."

Susan felt the beginnings of tears. "Carla . . . please don't make me." She raised the Beretta, lining the sights against the young man's chest.

Carla took a breath. "Hurt him, Susan, and I'll hurt you," she said.

Susan glanced at the ceiling, the floor. She considered a warning shot. Maybe several. Draw a crowd.

Carla saw the thought in her eyes. "I'll hurt you for that, too."

Susan heard the click of a knife springing open. It flashed in Carla's right hand. She had not even seen where it came from.

"Claude?" Susan heard herself say his name.

He turned his head. He looked at her sideways.

"Talk to her, Claude. There's no way you're walking past me."

His lips moved, indecisively. The lower one trembled. "I . . . I was trying to help, you know," he said at last.

He was suddenly six years old, she thought.

"I know," she said.

"Your name is Susan?"

She nodded.

"Those guys . . ." he cocked his head vaguely toward Burbank and toward Thousand Oaks. "They were worse than me."

She found herself wanting to reply. But she could not.

"Didn't they shoot you once? You and this lady . . ." He groped for a name. It came to him. "Elena?"

Even Carla blinked.

Susan could only shake her head. Her father flicked into her mind. Pizzas. His warning. Her mind could not finish the equation.

"Sit down, Claude." Susan set her jaw. "Tell Carla you're staying."

He seemed to consider it. Then he lowered his head. "I can't go to jail. They'll . . . I know what they'll do to me there."

He tugged Carla forward.

A tear spilled onto Susan's cheek.

She fired.

51

Lesko, spread against the roof of the blue Chevrolet, submitted to a body search.

Three cars full of suits had cut him off as he neared the Hollywood Freeway. They showed weapons, held ready, but they were not pointing them. That struck him as odd. What did not surprise him at all was that one agent, apparently in charge, had gone directly to the trunk and was unscrewing the spare tire.

"He's clean," said the one who had patted him down and was now handcuffing him. Lesko had left his pistol with Bannerman.

Another car squealed to a stop. Two men, dressed more casually than the others, climbed out. The one from the passenger side was staring at him. Lesko saw recognition on his face. LAPD, he decided. Probably Andy Huff.

"Lesko?" he asked.

"Nice to meet you." Lesko stood upright.

Huff looked at the older agent. "Scholl? What the hell is this?"

"You'll see."

Lesko heard the hiss of escaping air. Then grunts and prying sounds. Then silence.

"So?" Huff asked.

Lesko turned to look at the older agent. He saw the disappointment on his face. And confusion. The other agents had "you-win-some, you-lose-some" expressions. But not the one named Scholl. With him it was personal.

He had to hand it to Bannerman. The son of a bitch was smart. *"You'll know the one who set the wire,"* he had said. *"You'll see it in his eyes. If you don't, Katz will."*

Yeah, well, fuck you about Katz.

But suddenly Lesko wasn't so sure anymore because the passenger door of Scholl's car opened and he saw that the man climbing out was Roger Clew.

Little prick.

The one whose games got Elena shot. And Susan almost killed. He waits until the cuffs are on.

Clew nodded a tentative greeting.

"Fuck you, too," said Lesko.

Clew's expression showed no surprise at all. "Nothing, right?" he said to Scholl. "And he's unarmed?"

Scholl spread his hands.

"Where's Bannerman, Lesko? We need to talk."

"Ah . . ." Huff stepped in. "Could we discuss jurisdiction here? Maybe even what the charge is?"

"Obstruction, for openers," said Clew, showing his identification. "And it's a federal matter."

Huff looked at Lesko, questioning.

Lesko saw the gridlock caused by his interception. Obstructing traffic was more like it. "I'll tell you later," he said to Huff. "Clew's a weasel but don't get on his shit list."

Clew's color rose. Huff saw it. "I'll stick around anyway," he said.

Lesko shook his head. "Weasels need closed doors. That's where they make deals." He raised an eyebrow toward Clew as if inviting agreement.

Clew glared at him, then looked down, the equivalent of a nod.

Huff hesitated. "Bannerman's deal," he said. "Delivering the Campus Killer. Is that still on?"

Lesko grunted. "Bannerman's a different kind of prick but he's straight. Yeah, Andy. I'd say it's on."

More hesitation. "You'll be okay?"

"I'll call you. We'll have a beer."

Lesko watched him go back to his car where he snatched at a microphone, probably calling his captain. Lesko stood, largely ignoring Clew, who was already telling him how much trouble he was in. A litany of threats. Something now about murder charges for a slicing in Malibu and a crushed windpipe in a Brentwood parking lot. This was Clew's idea of a softening up.

Bannerman had known that he'd show, although maybe not this soon; he even outlined the script—threats, deal, more threats, better deal, maybe some flag-waving mixed in.

"The first offer," said Bannerman, *"will be immunity for you in return for my whereabouts. This will expand into a guaranteed safe conduct back to Westport if we all, including Belkin and Streicher, surrender immediately and if there's no hit on Sur La Mer.*

"Hear him out. But your answer is no because we can't deliver Streicher and because Roger won't keep his word in any case.

"The trick," said Bannerman, *"is to find out what he thinks we want. Without that, we have no leverage."*

"Has he gone there?" Clew was asking, his voice low, urgent. "Is he there right now?"

Lesko pretended to hesitate, then shook his head. "He doesn't need to."

At first, Clew's expression showed relief but then he stared hard. "What does that mean?"

Lesko shrugged. "Whatever he wanted there, he's got it."

"This," Bannerman had told him, *"is your key line. Watch carefully."* Lesko did. Clew was trying to show no reaction but he deflated visibly. His eyes said *Oh, shit.* This was clearly trouble. But Scholl, standing near, had a different kind of *Oh, shit.* This was more like disappointment. In one shot, he had hit two very different nerves. From here, thought Lesko, it ought to get interesting.

"Do you know?" Clew chose his words. "What he's got, I mean?"

Another shrug.

"I've got to see him," Clew said through this teeth. "I'll meet him alone but it's got to be now."

Bannerman's leverage, thought Lesko, seemed to be building nicely. Clew even jerked his head toward the agent who had cuffed him and who was coming with his key. As the cuffs came off, Lesko worked at framing his next few questions, designed to elicit a few more hints as to what the hell they were talking about. But his train of thought was interrupted by a yell from Andy Huff who was waving his arms. Lesko lifted his chin.

"Susan Lesko," Huff called. "Is she your daughter?"

His stomach tightened. "What? What happened?"

"There's been a shooting. Come on."

As if in a dream, Lesko was aware of Clew stumbling backward. An agent raised a hand to his chest and was suddenly down. Guns coming up. Clew running toward them, arms waving, men making room now. Katz, he thought, was shoving them aside. But Lesko barely saw all this because his eyes were locked on Huff's. Huff saw the question.

"That's all I know. Get in."

Carla was on the floor with him, stroking him, her head crooked at an odd angle.

He lay in a fetal position, his arms hugging the pillow that she had pressed against his abdomen. A towel, jammed under his belt, helped stanch the flow of blood from the rear.

Carla had checked the exit wound. It seemed clean enough. Copper jackets. The bullet had probably passed through his kidney but it hit no bone. She could feel him going into shock. That was good. It would ease the pain.

She reached for a couch cushion to place under his head. She managed it, but with difficulty. Her right arm was almost useless. Her neck throbbed terribly; his arm had been around her when the bullet struck, and her neck was wrenched when they fell together. It was just as well. She did not know what she might have done to Susan otherwise.

"C . . . Carla?"

"Shhh. Don't talk. Help is coming."

Susan had backed out the door. There were people passing. They'd been startled by the shot. A woman squealed at the sight of Susan's gun in one hand and a knife in the other. The knife was Carla's. She'd dropped it when her arm went numb. Susan shouted for them to call an ambulance.

"Claude's not my real name."

"I know. Shush."

"It's Sumner," he gasped. "Sumner Todd Dommerich."

"That's a good name."

"My . . . mother called me Todd. I like Sumner."

"Sumner, then."

"Toad."

". . . What?"

"That's what my father called me. Toad."

She said nothing. But she felt his hurt.

"Carla?"

She reached to brush his cheek.

"Don't be mad at Susan."

She took a breath.

"Is she nice?"

"I guess."

"As nice as you? And Lisa?"

"Claude . . . be still."

"Am I dying?"

"No."

"I think I am. I don't mind."

Carla thought again about the wound. You could never tell with a gunshot. But she didn't think it was fatal. If they stopped the bleeding in time.

"I get crazy sometimes."

She shrugged one shoulder. "Who doesn't."

He grunted, then shook his head. "Not like me. I did things . . . well . . . you know."

"You did some good things, too, Sumner. You helped your friends."

She felt a smile.

There was a flurry outside. Men coming. No guns or

uniforms. Probably hotel security. They were talking to Susan. No attempt to disarm her. Susan gesturing into the bungalow. The men seemed afraid to enter. One rushed back toward the lobby.

She heard sirens in the distance. Sumner did not react to either. He was very still.

Carla remembered his knives. She rolled onto her back, the better to use her good arm, and felt for them. She found the skinning knife and worked it free of its case.

"What are you doing?" he asked drowsily.

"Nothing. Thinking."

"If we went before . . . I mean if Susan didn't . . . where would we have gone?"

"Canada, maybe."

He murmured approval. "The north woods. We'd find a cabin."

"Maybe. Sure."

Or maybe just down to the beach, thought Carla. Stretch out in the sun. Talk. She'd rub his back, make him feel good . . . sleepy . . . like now. Then she'd slide her knife through the base of his skull. One twist. He would die with a smile.

Dommerich dozed again.

Outside, sounds of running feet. Voices. She saw Susan bending her knees, lowering her weapons to the ground. A policeman, uniformed, gun in hand, stepped into view and took them. Another dashed across the door. Susan talking to them now. Trying to calm them. Explaining.

They entered in spite of her, one high, one low, from either side. They saw the skinning knife. Its blade was pressed against Dommerich's throat, just under the jaw line. One asked her, quietly, to put it down. Carla's eyes flashed, warning him away.

Susan stepped through the door. A policeman reached for her. She shook him off. She stepped closer, and knelt, saying nothing. She listened to the sound of Dommerich's breathing. It was becoming labored.

Carla looked into Susan's eyes.

She saw that she understood.

Carla yanked the sodden towel free. They would wait together.

52

———

Barbara Weinberg blessed herself as she entered the double doors leading to the main hall. It seemed the thing to do.

Outside, her husband and Dr. Feldman were rounding up the members one by one. Darby was following, obstructing where he could, curiously taking the side of those members who were protesting this interruption of their fresh-air period. Jason Bellarmine refused to leave his canvas unfinished. Harland was close-hauled in a storm off Catalina.

Darby, in any case, gave no sign that he recognized Alan who, she assumed, would let Feldman do the talking.

Barbara walked with a limp. The cause of it was the silenced MP-5 taped to her inner thigh but she felt that the limp added to her disguise. The first real test of it was just inside the hall—the desk guard she'd disabled just last Sunday.

But he barely looked up as she asked which doors led to the Members' Wing. She reached for a light switch. He told her, rudely, to leave it alone. She wondered why the hall was being kept so dark—there was only the guard's desk map—but she was not about to make an issue of it.

She had no actual need to visit the Members' Wing except for the sake of appearances. Nellie, of course, was nowhere outside. She was back at Dr. Feldman's house, watching television. It would not do, however, to have anyone wonder why they made no effort to find a member whose name appeared on her clipboard.

A sudden clatter and a tinkling of glass startled the guard. He spun in his chair toward its source. Down the hall, thought Barbara. One of those rooms on the left. The guard, snatching a cane, rose to his feet and hobbled in that direction. Thrashing and banging sounds began. Barbara, only mildly curious, stood and watched.

The guard knocked on a door, waited, and knocked again.

"Mr. Marek?" She heard him call.

Barbara chewed her lip. No, she told herself. Don't. You as much as promised.

The guard opened the door. The room bathed him in gray light. Barbara heard a moan from inside and then a female voice. The guard seemed to stiffen but he entered. Barbara lifted her long skirt and winced as she peeled the surgical tape from her skin. Holding the MP-5 against her thigh, she eased herself along the paneled wall until she had almost reached the door.

A woman, almost hairless, skin glistening in the same gray light, backed into the hall. Her right hand, which doubtless held a gun, was still inside the room. She saw Barbara. Barbara's instinct was to shoot. But she did not. The MP-5 remained hidden within the folds of her skirt.

"Don't interfere, Sister," said the woman.

Barbara recognized the voice, and now, less readily, the face. Luisa Ruiz. Alan's thermite must have oxidized over time, lost much of its heat. Still, Ruiz was a mess.

"May I?" Barbara gestured toward the door. Ruiz hesitated. She did not say no.

Barbara saw the guard first. He was on the floor, prone, his hands clasped behind his head. Next, she saw the man whom she presumed to be Theodore Marek. He, too, was on the floor amid broken glass. He was not so much on his back as on his head and heels. The back was impossibly arched and totally rigid. An obscene grin split his face. His teeth protruded.

"Jesus, Mary, and Joseph," she murmured. She affected an Irish accent. It seemed a nun-ish thing to say.

Ruiz, watching his agony, raised a hand to stop her from entering.

"You can't help him, Sister," she said.

Barbara recognized the effects of strychnine. The dramatic arching of the spine, the facial spasms, respiratory paralysis. As she watched, the body began to relax. Another spasm would follow soon. He tried to scream but could not. He had bitten through his lower lip. His fingernails were torn and bloody where they had clawed at the carpet.

"How much did you give him?" She asked, then wished she hadn't. It was not a nun-ish question.

Ruiz appeared not to notice. "About two hundred milligrams. In brandy. Don't waste your time."

Barbara pursed her lips. Killed him three times over, she thought. A particularly nasty death. The cycle of spasms could go on for an hour. He would feel every second of it. Barbara, unaware of it, raised a hand to her mouth.

"Don't do that," Ruiz told her.

"Don't do what? . . . My child."

"Bless him."

Barbara understood. Ruiz assumed that she was beginning another sign of the cross, although with her left hand. Barbara lowered it.

"He . . . has hurt a lot of people."

"Has he hurt you, my child?"

"Yes." She became aware, suddenly, of the burns on her face and hands. "Not this. I mean . . . a long time ago. I really was . . . a child."

"This man . . . hurt a little girl?"

She nodded. Her breath caught in her throat. "Then God will forgive you."

*   *   *

The approach to the Beverly Hills Hotel was ablaze
with flashing lights. Huff's car, like the ambulance
before it, had to mount the grass. A television news van
tried to follow but it was waved off by shouting policemen. Camcorders were everywhere.

All Lesko knew, or cared about, was that the victim
did not seem to be Susan. He'd heard that much on Huff's
police radio. *"Woman with a gun . . . officers responded.
Woman disarmed . . . white male down . . . hostage
situation . . . second woman, possibly wounded, holding police at bay . . . shooting victim alleged to be the
Campus Killer."*

But the identification of Susan as the woman with
the gun was still tentative as was the identity of one
Sumner T. Dommerich and one Carla Benedict. Oral
declarations, no confirmation. The mention of the serial
killer was enough to create a circus.

Lesko had a leg out before Huff's driver stopped.
He bulled though the still-gathering crowd. Huff followed on his heels, waving his badge.

He saw her and his knees went weak.

She was sitting, handcuffed, at the base of a tree.
Her face, streaked with tears, tried to turn from whirring
cameras. He rushed to her. A policeman moved to stop
him. Only a shout from Huff saved the policeman from
harm. Lesko dropped to his knees, embracing her. She
sobbed against his chest, trying to speak. Several minutes passed before he began to make sense of what she
was saying.

Through the open door of Bungalow 6, he could
see the EMS crew working on a body. He caught a
glimpse of Carla, inside, also handcuffed. She seemed to
be wearing a cervical collar. She was staring at the floor,
oblivious to the flashes of police photographer cameras.

Andy Huff, a Motorola to his ear, was talking to the
arresting officers. A suit, probably FBI, appeared in the
doorway. He gave a thumbs-down sign to Huff. Huff
acknowledged with a nod then held up a hand as he
listened to a call. Lesko saw him make a fist and shout,

"Yes!" Huff beckoned to him, almost grinning. Lesko would not leave Susan.

More FBI arrived, Scholl leading them, Roger Clew behind. Lesko met Clew's eyes. He saw bewilderment in them, and concern for Susan that he knew was genuine. It had been a while, but he knew that the man from State liked her.

Huff led one of the uniformed officers to the tree where he knelt to remove Susan's handcuffs. Lesko took her wrist and kissed it. Her arms snaked around his neck and squeezed it with more force than he thought possible.

"We . . . ah . . . have a confirmation," said Huff quietly. "Detectives went to his apartment. They found . . . artifacts. Bracelets made out of blond hair. Other evidence. The knives. There's not much question. And it was more than six."

Lesko nodded. From inside, he heard the zipper of a body bag.

"For what it's worth," Huff touched Susan's hair, "your daughter's a hero."

"Yeah, well . . . give us a little time, okay."

"Wait." Susan's voice. "What about Carla?"

"Well," Huff rocked a hand, "we have a problem there. Whatever else this Dommerich did, they could hit her with murder one."

"Daddy?"

"Yeah, sweetheart."

"Me, too. I helped her."

Huff studied the sky to show that he didn't hear that.

"Daddy?"

"Sweetheart, shut your mouth."

"Daddy, then help her. Or get Paul."

"Okay. Shut up. Give me a second."

They were wheeling the body out. Then Carla. She was in a fog. Lesko wondered about the bloodied knees. Susan tried to look but he blocked her vision.

"Hey, Andy?"

"Yeah."

"See that guy over there?"

"The State Department guy? What's he want here?"

"His name's Roger Clew. He's a fixer. Go tell him . . . he fixes this, I give him what he wants."

The man Marek had seen walking a dog, on the Tower Road monitor, was John Waldo.

It was Waldo's practice to travel with a retractable leash. A dog could always be borrowed from someone's yard. No one ever seemed to look twice at a man walking a dog.

His basic purpose in strolling along Tower Road was not so much to spot Carla as to be seen by her. To make her think twice about going in by herself. But he really didn't think she'd show. Broad daylight, no equipment, no weapon except her dumb knife and no idea of the layout once she got here. He, at least, had studied the plans.

She's probably just cooling off someplace, he decided. But if she did turn up, she'd check out the perimeter first, starting with the gates and cameras. And it wouldn't take her five minutes to notice that one blind spot where two cameras faced in different directions.

Walking a dog is fine but you can overdo it. A dog shits or he doesn't. After the station wagon and the little bus went in, he decided he'd better sit in the blind spot for a while. He let the dog go. A young golden retriever. It sniffed around a little, then trotted off when it looked like Waldo wouldn't be much more fun. It only lived a few streets away.

Golden retrievers and yellow labs were the best when you needed a dog. They're always wandering and they never get skittish. You don't even really have to steal them. You just call them, tell them how pretty they are and they say, "Hey, you want to play?"

Waldo was half-tempted to go up and take a look. Except that his job was to watch for Carla. On the other hand, he thought, this is the way she'd come in. He turned to peer in through the pine trees. Thick woods. Plenty of cover. Idly, he picked out a route. He still had no intention of following it but then he noticed a footprint.

It was more of a scuff. Where the ground sloped sharply. Someone had dug a shoe into the carpet of pine needles to boost himself up. Or herself. Waldo grumbled inwardly. From the width, it was a very small shoe.

Nah. No way.

He tried to imagine how Carla might have beaten him here. After she took off from Bannerman she would have had to steal a car almost immediately and she'd have to have known exactly where this place is. He had needed an address and a map to find it. On the other hand, she's from California. Maybe she knows Santa Barbara.

Waldo still couldn't believe it. But the footprint bothered him. He decided to take a closer look. He stepped over the low fence and up the small slope.

He found more scuff marks and the clear imprint of a sneaker. About a size four. Carla was wearing sneakers. Waldo examined the imprint wishing he'd brought his reading glasses. Still, he could see that it was reasonably fresh. But not that fresh. Pine needles had fallen onto it. And whoever was scrambling around in here was a little bit of a klutz. Carla wouldn't have left so many tracks.

He was about to turn back when he noticed the trip wire. He examined it critically. It was poorly hidden or at least poorly maintained. Not enough tension either. he climbed a little farther and found another one, same story, except this seemed to be electrified. He also noticed that some of the rocks were greased. What for, he wondered? Sneak in here and we get your pants dirty? Whoever laid this out should be ashamed of himself.

His curiosity had gotten the better of him. He continued on. Ten minutes later he could see the eaves of the house. A big sucker. Two minutes after that he saw a row of marble benches, a hedge, and a vast lawn beyond it. There were a dozen or so old people scattered over the lawn, a couple of doctors, several guards. The guards carried rifles. He assumed that this was not usual. Must be for the Marek guy. He unzipped his jacket part way, leaving access to the Ingram slung under one arm and the silenced pistol slung under the other.

Off to his left, overlooking the ocean, Waldo saw a tall elderly man who was making a painting. He was standing at an easel slapping red paint onto a canvas. Red was also the only color on his palette. To Waldo's eye, the picture didn't look like much of anything. Must be modern art.

"Hey."

Waldo heard the voice and froze. Stupid. He'd allowed himself to get distracted. Why do people always stop to watch painters?

"You. I'm talking to you."

Waldo pretended not to hear or see. He knew it was a guard but he realized from his tone that the guard was not greatly alarmed. He would stand still. Let the guard come to him. Then Waldo would quietly put his lights out and slip back down the hill.

"You hear me? You're not allowed past the tree line."

The guard did not approach. He stood, some thirty yards to the right, now snapping his fingers.

"Anyway, get down to the bus. You're going bye-bye."

Waldo understood. The guard thought he was one of these inmates. This was annoying because he was a good twenty years younger than anyone he could see on the lawn. He only looked old. It was the hair, mostly. And this guard was a punk kid with a ring in his ear.

"Come on. Move. Wake up."

Waldo let his jaw go slack and his eyes go vacant. He would have drooled if he had enough spit. He stood there until the guard lost patience and closed the distance between them. Good. Waldo would enjoy teaching him respect. But just then the painter decided he was finished. He had closed up his case and was starting this way with his easel.

The guard was almost within reach but Waldo knew he'd better wait. Except the guard, this close, still thought he was that old. The guard came on, and tugged at his sleeve.

"Come on, Pop. Both you guys get down there."

Waldo, staring vapidly, allowed himself to be shoved into step with the painter. He could hear the guard muttering behind him. Waldo knew what he was probably saying: "If I ever get like that . . ."

Right, you little fuck. You don't know how close you came to not even making lunch.

He could see that two people were already aboard the bus. Others were walking toward it, one by one. Up at the house, another guard, this one leaning on a cane, was standing at the double doors with a tall nun looking over his shoulder. He was calling to someone else. "Captain Darby," it sounded like. A beery looking man with a cap left one of the doctors and walked up toward the terrace.

Waldo didn't feel he had much choice. It was either climb into the bus or be left standing in the open. Better to mix in with the rest of the white hair. An old woman was getting ready to board. She stopped and intercepted the painter who was about to walk past her. John now realized he was blind. The woman took his easel and case, handing the wet red painting to Waldo. Waldo's fingers smeared it. It didn't make much difference. He held the canvas until he could stick it onto a rack. Waldo took a seat in the rear. The old woman did a double-take but she was more interested in helping the painter. No one else paid much attention.

At the rate they were going, it looked as if it would take all morning to fill the bus. But then this Captain Darby turned around at the double doors, looking dazed. He cleared his throat and began shouting instructions to move things along. The two doctors seemed surprised. The bus was loaded within five minutes, wheelchair patients last. One was dressed like an Admiral. Waldo was crowded in against another old woman who wore makeup like Vampira's grandmother. She dumped a pile of scrapbooks on his lap.

Next, the guards' captain came down toward the bus. He was followed, very closely, by the nun—who walked funny—and by a small woman who had a greasy face and hardly any hair. Waldo hadn't noticed her before. The captain was more than dazed. Waldo recognized the look of a man who had a gun barrel tickling his liver. The bald woman marched him to the bus and gave him a front seat.

The nun had broken off. She walked over to the doctor with the pipe in his mouth. Guy looked familiar. Waldo couldn't place him. Whatever the nun was telling him now, he didn't seem to believe it. The nun was shaking her head, denying something, pointing to the little bald one. The doctor just threw up his hands. He asked her a question. In response, she ran a finger down her clipboard and nodded as if to say that all the patients were accounted for.

The doctor tossed his head toward the station wagon, which the younger doctor was now starting. The nun climbed in, stiffly. Once seated, she seemed to be tugging at her crotch. The doctor climbed into the driver's seat of the jitney bus and closed the door behind him. He started the engine. The bald one gave him a funny look but mostly she kept her eyes on the captain.

This was getting interesting.

Waldo had an idea that there might be a problem at the main gate but that the bald one and the nun had doped out a solution.

Just in case, he cracked his window and slid his Ingram under the top scrapbook.

He hoped that the golden was not still hanging around.

53

The first four of the reinforcements from Westport had arrived at the airport. It was a condition of using Belkin's safe house that they not be given the address over the phone. They would rent cars and drive to a certain avenue in Culver City where they would look for Billy McHugh.

When they appeared, Bannerman had the phone in hand, about to make his second attempt to reach Susan. He was already anticipating what she would say: "Relax, Bannerman, I can handle this. I'll call you when Claude calls me. Now get off the line."

And she would be right, he decided. He put the phone down. Besides, he wanted to keep it clear for Lesko's call.

He showed the four where they would be sleeping, where the weapons were, and began briefing them on the events of that morning. One of them, Janet Herzog, had been the closest of any to Carla. He asked where she thought Carla might have gone.

"She said she wanted her own pantyhose?" Janet answered. "Then she went to get her own pantyhose."

This did not strike Bannerman as an insightful response. He was about to point out, patiently, that Carla had more than underwear on her mind when the phone rang. It was Molly.

"Turn on the TV," she told him.

"Molly?"
"Hello, Axel."
Molly took the call in Kevin's house. Barbells

everywhere. DiDi and two of her father's people sat
transfixed in front of the television set. The third bodyguard was watching the front with Kevin.

"Could I ask . . . who all came to California with
you?"

"Why?"

"Indulge me. Please."

She hesitated, then decided there's no harm. "You
know about Carla and Paul. Billy's here. You wouldn't
know Ray Lesko or his daughter but they're on TV at the
moment."

"No . . . I mean just Bannerman's crowd."

"That's all for the moment."

"That's all? Doesn't he usually send an advance man
to . . ."

"Oh, yes. John Waldo. I'm sorry, Axel. I have a lot
on my mind."

A long silence. Muffled whispers.

"Axel . . ." Why the tap dance, she wondered.
Her sense was that John was the object of the probe. She
also found it odd that he showed no interest in why the
Leskos might be on television. "What's this about?"

"Ah . . . nothing, really. I thought I saw John
Waldo . . . on the highway. But that's not why I called,
actually."

She waited.

"Theodore Marek is dead. Or . . . does Paul know
that already?"

Another undertone. But no. She'd just spoken to
him. "I don't think so."

"Well, he is. My word on it. Tell him that there will
be no more mischief. Miss Fenerty can relax as well."

She said nothing.

"Molly? Did you hear me?"

"Carla's been arrested, Axel. Turn on the news."

More whispers. Molly heard a blurted audio and
the rapid switching of channels. Then news about the
serial killer. She listened and watched at the same time,
giving Streicher a full two minutes. He came back on.

"Carla knew him?"

"It's a long story."

"They should be giving her a medal. Why are they talking about Hickey?"

"They think Carla did that one. And a man named Bunce. Claude . . . I mean, Dommerich did . . . but the FBI isn't buying it."

A thoughtful pause.

"Has Roger Clew turned up?"

"I'm not sure."

"He will. Tell him to deal with it."

"Axel, we're not holding many cards. The price could be high."

She heard a chuckle. It annoyed her.

"How would you like all the aces? And a queen or two in the bargain."

"Axel . . ."

"I know. What is there to be jolly about? Tell Bannerman this. Roger, and I'm sure Barton Fuller, will do anything he asks if he says four magic words. The words are these. *I*—meaning Bannerman—*have the files.*"

"What files?"

"I think they'll know."

She shook her head. "Come on, Axel. Paul's supposed to take this on faith?"

"If not Paul, you. Don't doubt me on this, Molly."

She let out a breath. "Okay, I have the files."

"All of them. Over two hundred of them. Since 1932."

"From Sur La Mer, right?"

"Exactly."

"They'd want to see a sample."

"Good thought. Give me a fax number."

She gave him two. Mario's in Westport and in care of herself at the Beverly Hills Hotel.

"Axel . . . if this really works . . ."

"Bannerman will owe me. I know."

"I was going to say me. I'll owe you."

Another silence. Then, "I did love you, Molly."

"Is Bonnie right there?"

"She is. She knows it."

"Don't be a jerk, Axel. Go find a life."

The Weinbergs had not lingered at the Motion Picture Country House. Genuine nurses had begun helping the members off the bus. Darby, head low, mixing with them, crept away under the impression that no one had noticed.

Alan and Barbara shook hands with Dr. Michael, thanking him for the offer of his station wagon. They would call him, tell where he could retrieve it. In return, he extracted a promise that he would hear from Nellie from time to time.

It was then that Alan noticed a short, white-haired member whom he could not recall seeing at Sur La Mer and who, although his appearance showed the ravages of Alzheimer's, looked remarkably like old John Waldo. He was holding a stack of scrapbooks, being tugged along by the actress who thought she was Theda Bara. Weinburg, blinking, lost no more time in leaving.

En route to Dr. Michael's house, Barbara told him that he must have been mistaken. No, she had not taken a final head count but neither had she seen anyone who resembled John Waldo. Why, in any case, would he penetrate Sur La Mer just to ride a bus back out? Weinberg had to agree. He would ask Molly nonetheless. Find out, at least, whether Waldo is even in California.

The greater shock, on speaking to Molly, was to learn how busy Carla Benedict had been.

"The poor dear," said Nellie, watching the continued coverage. "First her sister, and now this."

"She'll get through it," said Barbara. "She's very tough."

But Barbara had her doubts. Carla had never been known for her stability but she was certainly vibrant, sharp, like the edge of her knife. Now, on the screen, she looked dead inside.

"She reminds me . . . of me," said Nellie, "when the pain became more than I could bear."

Barbara understood. After Tom died. After the drugs and the liquor stopped helping. Still, it was hard to imagine Carla being that fragile after half a lifetime of sudden death. Perhaps, she thought, none of it had ever hit so close to home before. Or perhaps there really is such a thing as one too many. If anything ever happened to Axel . . . Alan . . . that might be her own one too many.

"Nellie . . . we'd better go."

"I wish we could help her," said Nellie.

"I think Alan just did. They won't hold her very long."

"Holding is what she needs."

"Her friends will take care of her. She'll be fine."

"Could we go to the service? Just to make sure?"

"Ah . . . What service?"

"For young Lisa. It's tomorrow. The man on the television just mentioned it."

Barbara glanced at her husband. He was glaring back at her. The glare was unnecessary. She took the old woman's hand.

"Come on, Nellie. Let's go pick out our boat."

54

The headquarters of the Campus Killer task force was located in the Municipal Building in downtown Los Angeles.

Elena had reached Lesko there. She brushed aside

his threats of what he would do to Bannerman and said
that they were coming. She asked what entrance they
might use in order to avoid the press. Lesko asked Huff.
Arrangements were made.

The large squad room fell silent as Bannerman
entered, Huff and Elena with him. Huff had met them
inside the basement garage. Lesko came forward. Elena
intercepted him, a hand against his chest, warning him
with her eyes to be still.

"Where is Susan?" Bannerman asked Huff.

Lesko glared at him. "You happy now? You got
everything you want?"

Huff gestured. "My office. Straight ahead."

"And Carla?"

Huff pointed to a closed door. "Interrogation, but
she hasn't opened her mouth. I sent a lawyer in. She
won't talk to him either. There's also your friend from the
State Department. He's waiting for you down the hall.
There's a conference room."

"Thank you."

"Hold it. Right there."

A balding man in a suit pushed forward, his hand at
his hip inside his jacket.

"He gets five minutes," Huff said to Sholl.

"He gets nothing," Scholl barked, "until I say so.
And nobody sees the girl until she's booked."

Lesko stepped forward. "It's time we had a talk, shit
head."

Bannerman, ignoring this, walked to the door of
Huff's office. He rubbed his face as if to soften it, then
knocked. Susan did not answer. He opened the door and
stepped inside.

"Relax," said Lesko quietly. "I'm going to do you a
favor."

He had put an arm around the shoulder of the
special agent in charge. He led him to a quiet corner.

"You're not going to book my daughter. You don't
even want to question her."

"Why don't I?"

"Here's what you do instead. Today and tomorrow you talk to the press, you take a few bows. You're already figuring how to grab credit for this, right?"

"Take your hands off me."

Lesko squeezed him. "The day after that, you put in your papers. Go raise chickens or something."

"What? Who the hell do you . . ."

Lesko dug in his nails. "You see, Jack, I know you're dirty. Now you're going to get all out of joint, tell me I'm crazy, but in your head you're wondering how I know, right?"

Lesko watched his eyes. Scholl was wondering. Probably seeing the empty tire. Thinking back. Trying to piece it together.

"You won't figure it out, Jack. Aside from being dirty, you're stupid. I mean, that's why they gave you the shit jobs, right?"

Scholl's color rose.

"The good news is I probably can't prove it. The bad news is I don't have to. It's enough that we know. You understand what I'm saying? We're not talking due process here."

Lesko watched the color drain.

Susan was at the window, staring out at nothing, a polystyrene cup in one hand.

Bannerman could see her reflection in the glass. He knew that she could see him as well. She didn't turn.

He heard Molly's voice in his mind. Molly was saying, *"Just go to her, put your arms around her, hold her, don't talk except to say that you love her. For God's sake, don't pat her."*

What about the coffee cup?

"Bannerman . . ."

He placed a hand on her back, rubbing it, not patting. With his other hand he took the cup and set it down. He embraced her. She did not respond. She kept her arms between them. Now she pressed, pushing him away. She picked up her cup.

"I love you, Susan," he said.

A short exhaling of breath. Almost a laugh. "More than ever?" she asked.

"As much as ever. This makes no difference."

"It does to me."

"I know that."

"It's nice to be a member of the club, though. You won't have to explain me anymore."

Bannerman chewed his lip. "Susan . . . would you rather talk to your father? Or Elena? They're right outside."

She shook her head. The suggestion seemed to anger her.

But he was hearing a low-level hysteria. He'd never had to deal with it before. He thought of suggesting a policewoman. Or a police psychiatrist. He knew that there must be someone in the building who was trained in counseling officers who'd been in shootings.

"Bannerman . . . that's not what she needs."

"I know a place," he said. "Lake Arrowhead. We could rent a cabin. Just the two of us." Oh. Except the funeral is tomorrow.

"I'm not going anywhere. I killed someone, damn it."

"Well," he touched her hair. "The fact is you didn't. You punched a hole in him. It was Carla who let him bleed to death."

She hugged herself. "We both did. Me just as much."

"Okay. Why?"

"I don't know."

"Because you hated him? To get even for all his victims?"

She shook her head.

"What's left is kindness, Susan. Even the police realize that."

Susan waved a hand. Not a dismissal, exactly. A change of subject.

"Paul, I would have shot Carla, too." she said. "She was going to let him go. She was ready to knife me if I tried to stop her."

Bannerman hadn't heard that part. Carla might have cut her, he supposed, but not dangerously. And Carla certainly would not have let him go. She would have taken him someplace, put him at ease, thought it over, and then ended it. Susan, however, did not need to hear that she shot that kid for nothing.

"Where did you hit him, by the way?"

The question surprised her. But she touched herself to show him.

He nodded inwardly. Just below the belt. He knew that Susan tended to pull up and to the right. She had probably aimed for his thigh.

He understood that she would need time. The worst wounds are self-inflicted. Susan, learning to shoot, must have wondered what it would be like to kill. And whether she could do it. She had probably imagined a number of scenarios, most involving self-defense. She might even have imagined tracking down and executing someone who had harmed a friend. Himself, most likely.

But the opponents she envisioned would have been mean and dangerous, probably lunging for a weapon as she fired. She would not have envisioned a sick, pathetic creature such as Sumner Dommerich.

"Paul?"

"Yes?"

"Could you please just shut up?"

He blinked.

"Could you please just hold me?"

"Colonel Belkin?"

"Yes." He knew the voice.

"The Marek house seems to have been abandoned."

"No FBI?"

"They withdrew one hour ago. Then a man comes

by taxi. He is dressed as a security guard. Ten minutes later, the man in uniform leaves and so do five other men. They are carrying suitcases, boxes, even paint- ings."

Belkin raised an eyebrow. He pinched his nose thoughtfully.

"I am putting you on hold," he said.

He asked information for the number of Sur La Mer in Santa Barbara. He dialed that number. Six rings. Eight. There was no answer. He punched the "hold" button.

"Move in," he said. "Secure the house. Search it thoroughly. I will send two more men with tools."

"What are we looking for, Colonel?"

"Anything that reminds you of home, Lieutenant."

Lesko reached for the knob of Huff's office door. Elena slapped his hand. She told him to knock.

Bannerman answered. He saw Lesko, the anger gone, replaced by a look of discomfort.

"You two must talk," Elena said. "I will stay with Susan." She took Bannerman by the arm and eased him into the squad room. She stepped past and closed the door behind her.

"Two things," Lesko said, avoiding his eyes. "First, I don't blame you for putting Susan in that position. I had a hunch about that pizza kid. I even knew what he looked like. I didn't follow up."

Bannerman squinted. "How could you . . ."

"He was at the hospital. I'll tell you later. The thing is I tried to make a deal with Clew to get Susan off the hook."

"What did you give him?"

"I'd have given him you, maybe Belkin's place in Culver City, myself for the guy in the parking lot, and a dirty fed."

"But . . . you didn't."

He shrugged. "Susan wouldn't go along. She won't

let Carla take a fall by herself. Anyway, I could see Clew
didn't give a shit."

"Did he tell you what he wants?"

"He wants us by the balls, Bannerman. And that's
what he's got."

"Detective Huff?"

"Yeah, speaking."

"This is Molly Farrell."

"Are you coming in, Miss Farrell? There's a warrant
out."

"I'm twenty minutes away. But I need to speak to
Paul Bannerman."

"You'll still come in? No matter what?"

"No matter what."

"Hold on a second."

55

Roger Clew sat making two lists.

The first was a set of conditions. Or terms. Whatever. They were the promises he intended to extract
from Bannerman.

Foremost among them was that Bannerman fully
explain his intentions regarding Sur La Mer, and then
promise to abandon them. The next was that he and all
his people move out of Westport. Return to Europe. Go
back to work. The alternative was criminal prosecution
of Carla, Susan Lesko, Molly Farrel, Bannerman himself
under the NICO statute if nothing else, and possibly
Lesko if a drug dealer named Chulo is able to pick him
out of a lineup. Also the indefinite detainment of Leo
Belkin, Yuri Rykov, and Elena Brugg.

The second list was more of a timetable. It defied belief but there it was. Bannerman had been in California for less than a day. In that time he managed to join forces with the KGB, hook up with Axel Streicher, have at least five known thugs killed or crippled, and still have the leisure to track down and dispatch a serial killer who'd been hunted for more than a year by a force of two hundred men. Using Susan as a decoy. Susan, Clew would let off the hook.

Good that they all kept busy. Another twelve hours at this rate and Sur La Mer might be a pile of rocks.

He would rather not have it this way, getting Mama's Boy back into the fold. But the opportunity, once presented, could not be passed up. Above all, whatever Bannerman had learned about Sur La Mer, whatever his intention, he had to be stopped. Too much harm could be done, valuable assets lost. Or subverted through blackmail.

The phone rang. The receptionist. May she bring Mr. Bannerman and Mr. Lesko in?

Lesko?

Why not?

We'll put him to work as well. And throw in the Bruggs of Zürich.

"Colonel Belkin?"

"Yes."

"Do you . . . did you . . . know what is here?"

"I . . . suspected."

"We will need a truck. A big one. Also packing materials, padding. Also we should have a restoration expert so that we can remove the panels without damage."

"The panels?"

"They are solid amber. He has a book of photographs here, all about Catherine's Palace in Pushkin as it was before the war. The panels are the same as those in the book."

"Ah, yes." My God.

"Who is this Marek, Colonel?"

"We are wasting time, Lieutenant."

"Of course, yes."

"I will send the truck. Do your best without the expert."

"Colonel Belkin?"

"Yes?"

"They will name streets after you for this."

Bannerman was cool. Clew had to admire it.

He had laid out his conditions. And the alternatives. Bannerman never batted an eye although twice he had to restrain from reaching over the table.

"Well?" Clew sat back. He looked at his watch. "Do you need time to think it over?"

Bannerman shook his head. "But you might, Roger."

Crew smiled. "Tell me why."

"Marek's dead, for openers."

Clew looked at him blankly. "You mean the man whose wall Carla caved in? That Marek?"

Bannerman nodded.

"So what?" The name meant nothing to him.

Bannerman shrugged "Okay. Let's try the Dunvilles."

Clew kept his expression bland. "What about them?"

"They're dead, too. You'll find two of them at Sur La Mer. You won't find the third."

A long silence. "You hit them?"

Bannerman shook his head. "I'm just here for a funeral, Roger."

Clew stood up, pacing. He kicked a chair. "You just killed yourself, Bannerman. Nobody will help you now."

"Roger, I have the files."

Clew stared. "What files?"

"All of them. Over two hundred. Going back to 1932."

Clew blinked rapidly. "Two hundred what? People?"

"Over two hundred."

"I don't believe you."

"Molly's on her way over with a sample. Could we get some coffee in the meantime?"

Clew hesitated, then buzzed the receptionist, largely to give himself time to think. He ordered a pot and three cups.

"What do you want for them?" he asked.

"They're not for sale."

"Okay, you're going to make me ask. What do you want not to use those files? That's assuming they exist."

"Not much. Tear up your list. Clean up this mess. Leave us alone."

"Or else what?"

"I use them, Roger."

"Bannerman . . ." Lesko opened the taps of all three wash basins in the lavatory. "What the hell was all that?"

Bannerman weighed the wisdom of telling him. But Lesko had a right. His neck was out as far as anyone's.

"I should have briefed you. Thanks for going with it."

"Going with what? What files?"

Bannerman shushed him. "I have no idea. But Roger sure does."

"How did you know Marek is dead?"

"Streicher told Molly. He didn't elaborate."

"You got no files?"

"Just a sample."

"And that's enough to make Clew roll over?"

"It looks that way."

Lesko splashed water onto his face. "All that other stuff he thinks you did? You didn't do shit."

"Should we go back and tell him that?"

"No, but it's the principle. This whole thing, you hardly ever got off your ass except to make phone calls and now there's Clew thinking you're this fucking mastermind."

Bannerman winced at the language.

"You know who did more than you? That DiDi
Fenerty did more than you."

Bannerman's eyes became hooded. "I still have time
to go beat up on Roger. Would that make you happy?"

"It would be a start."

"Have you done everything people think you've
done?"

"No, but . . ."

"But you use it. So do I. Count your blessings,
Lesko."

Bannerman heard a knock at the lavatory door.

"Mr. Bannerman?"

The receptionist. "Yes?"

"There's a Miss Farrell to see you."

"Be right out. Thank you."

"Sir, there's also a call from a Leo Belkin. He's
holding."

56

The sample file Molly brought was a before and
after on Theodore Marek, ńe Tadeusz Ordynsky. Bannerman had it in hand when he took Belkin's call.

The call from an enraptured Leo Belkin was to tell
him that the use of the safe house, now apparently not
needed, had been repayed a thousandfold.

It was also to ask how Bannerman knew about the
contents of Marek's vault, and about the panels. How,
for that matter, had he known that Sur La Mer had been
abandoned and that the men at Marek's house would flee
as well.

Bannerman listened through several minutes of

gushing before it became clear that Belkin was talking about stolen Russian art. He didn't know what he meant by *panels* and he didn't ask.

In fact, he'd had no idea that there even was a vault. There was only the chance, based on Anton Zivic's briefing, that Marek had perhaps kept an icon or two for himself. Apparently, he'd kept a great deal of it. Bannerman read to Belkin from the file. Belkin was dumbstruck.

"Um . . . How is Yuri, by the way."

"Out of danger, Paul. I can't wait to tell him. This is so . . ."

"Actually, it was sort of his idea."

"I beg your pardon?"

"He . . . probably won't remember, with the head injury and all, but somehow be found out that Marek was Ordynsky. Carla told me. I did some checking with Anton."

"Yuri, you say."

"Yup."

"I am to believe this? Even if Yuri denies it?"

"As I said . . . the head injury . . ."

"Quite so."

"I would think there might be a commendation in it for him."

"At the very least. Paul? Thank you."

The next phone call, actually to Lesko, was from Irwin Kaplan, whom Bannerman liked and trusted, but who didn't like him very much.

Irwin knew nothing whatever about Sur La Mer nor did he wish to. The real purpose of his call was to ask whether Bannerman would take a call from Barton Fuller, Clew's boss, and, if so, would Bannerman level with him?

This indirect approach did not seem to promise much in the way of leveling but Bannerman said he would talk to Fuller, whom he generally respected and trusted within limits. They talked for more than an hour.

The problem with leveling was Fuller's opening premise. Fuller assumed that Bannerman had mounted a long-planned, brilliantly coordinated assault on Sur La Mer with the intention of tracking down and/or compromising certain of the Sur La Mer alumni. Bannerman chose not to correct him but he gave Fuller two assurances.

The first was that the KGB had not had, nor would it ever have, access to the files. The second was that he, Bannerman, would not use them unless provoked.

"You say there are *hundreds* of those files, Paul?"

"Over two hundred. Since 1932."

"What sort of people? I mean, would I know the names? Are they in sensitive . . ."

"All sorts, Mr. Fuller. And, yes, I imagine you'd know some of the names."

It certainly wasn't a lie. It wasn't leveling either but it was the best Bannerman could do in his near total ignorance of the contents of those files.

The most intriguing revelations from Fuller, which explained a great deal, were these. Certain people in government had become aware only five years ago, not fifty or sixty, that one individual had been completely made over at a place called Sur La Mer. Fuller didn't ask how they found that out. Possibly, an FBI background check blundered into it. Perhaps someone made a deathbed confession. Whatever.

But this one individual named several more alumni. They, in turn, were quietly investigated and some were confronted. They named others. Fuller acknowledged that there might have been a dozen in all. Not two hundred.

Certain of these had since had children and even grandchildren who were, themselves, blameless, and who had made lives of their own. One turned out to be a congressman.

It was decided that to expose these people would do more harm than good. The investigation was quashed but the alumni were monitored forevermore.

Bannerman asked why the government did not simply close Sur La Mer down.

"That would have . . . broadened the investigation. Arrests would mean trials, publicity, scandal. It could not have been done quietly."

"On the contrary, I think it just has."

"We . . . operate under certain constraints, Paul, which do not burden you. We would not, for example, have wiped out the Dunville family."

"So you protected them instead."

"I wouldn't say that . . . exactly."

Bannerman smiled. "You used them, didn't you, Mr. Fuller. You put people of your own through Sur La Mer."

"You're playing with fire, Paul."

"I thought we were leveling."

"If we did put people through, they would have been people to whom this country owed a debt. You would not have disapproved. And we would have been assured that no records had been kept by the damned Dunvilles."

And that was that.

There was one more plea, of course, that Bannerman surrender the files. He declined with regrets. And repeated assurances. If left alone.

The remaining problem was Streicher.

If Streicher decided to compromise any of the people Fuller knew about, Fuller would conclude that Paul Bannerman had broken his word. On the other hand, Streicher had as much as promised Molly that he would protect the innocent. He had even predicted, unlikely as it sounded at the time, that protection of the innocent might be in Roger's interest as well.

Still, Bannerman would have to try to find him.

Later.

Right now, his first concern was Susan. And then Carla.

*   *   *

"Lesko?"

Katz. Dumb shit. *"Don't talk to me."*

"What do you mean?"

"That pizza kid. Dommerich. I knew he was the one and you talked me out of it."

"All you had was this paranoid hunch. I gave you logic. Anyway, since when do you listen to me?"

"Yeah, well, if you kept your mouth shut I would have stayed there with Susan. I would have recognized him when he showed up with the pizza."

"Well . . . at least I was right about Scholl."

"When?"

"When they stopped your car. I knew he was the guy."

"David, you never said a word."

"I would have if you weren't sure. See? I give you credit. Try it sometime, Lesko."

Lesko grunted.

"Anyway, in this whole thing, not one person was ever a hundred percent right about anything."

"I know."

"Bannerman ends up smelling like a rose and he never had a clue."

"I know."

"In fact, the only one who knew what he was doing was that Dommerich kid. And things only made sense to him because he was nuts."

This was another thing that bothered Lesko. A part of him had been rooting for that kid. Another part felt sorry for him. *"David? How did he get away with it? For so long, I mean."*

"Now you're asking my opinion?"

"Forget it."

"The answer is who looks at pizza deliverers? If you see a stranger out in the hall, you wonder. If he's wearing a pizza hat, you don't."

"I guess. Yeah."

"Even if the cops warn you, watch out for strang-

ers, who'd worry about a pizza kid if he stopped and
asked for directions?"

"Yeah. Right."

"In college towns, lots of girls hitch rides back to the
campus with pizza kids because they know that's where
they're headed."

This had never occurred to Lesko. He hated it when
that happened. "David, damn it, how would you know
that?"

"It just figures. Or the pizza kid pulls up to some
girl and tells her she shouldn't be out walking alone with
this nut on the loose. He's only a pizza kid, right? So she
gets in."

"Yeah." It made sense. "And all she sees is that hat.
Two minutes later, she probably couldn't tell you what
he looked like."

"Yeah."

And the kid knew it, thought Lesko. Poor sick
bastard. People probably looked right through him all
his life. With the hat on, they probably never even saw
him.

Lesko wondered if he'd ever feel the same about
ordering a pizza.

57

Carla gave the eulogy.

She stood before a packed church, one arm around
her father. Yesterday, he'd rushed to her side. Today he
couldn't talk. He just clinged to her.

Carla held together reasonably well but she was
taking care not to look at the closed white casket in the
center aisle.

She told what Lisa meant to her, how Lisa had embodied almost all that was good and decent and loving in her life. George Benedict began to cry. Carla actually kissed his hand.

There must have been three hundred people in the church. About half were students from USC. Kevin the weightlifter in a stretched-out suit. DiDi Fenerty came with her parents but she sat with Molly. The bodyguards were there. They weren't needed. They just wanted to come.

The other half consisted of neighbors, friends from out of town, two carloads of Russians, probably all KGB, and the contingent from Westport, which had grown to fourteen. Andy Huff came with several detectives. He sat with Lesko and Elena. Roger Clew arrived late and stood, uncomfortably, in the rear until Bannerman welcomed him with a nod and motioned him to a pew. John Waldo wandered outside, looking in through the doors occasionally.

DiDi had tried to say a few words. She couldn't finish. Molly had to go up and read the rest from DiDi's notes.

Susan, her expression glazed, wept quietly throughout. Bannerman held her hand. He knew that not all the tears were for Lisa.

The service aside, she seemed much better today. A long talk with Elena had helped. Then he'd taken her to the Venice beach so that she could feel life and warmth all around her. He made her eat something and urged her not to watch the news. She did anyway.

One program said that a journal had been found. It recorded the six college girl murders and a total of ten others, including several men, over a five-year period, his parents being the first. The final entry had been made on the last day of his life. It mentioned Hickey by name. It described Harry Bunce.

Hearing all this helped Susan after all. It helped her come to terms with having put him out of his misery.

They all, except Carla, spent the night at Belkin's safe house where no reporter could find them. Carla stayed at her father's house.

Carla would not be coming back, she told Bannerman. Not right away. She would stay with her father for a while. He'd told her that Yuri was welcome there as well, after he was discharged from the hospital, to convalesce until he was able to travel.

Then, she thought, she would take him home. Back to Bern, where he was stationed. Leo Belkin had already given permission. She said there was a girl, named Maria, who lived in Zürich. She played the cello. Yuri was in love with her. Carla said she wanted to go and visit her, try to help things along. Elena seemed to think she knew the girl. Or of her. A young widow, husband killed in a training accident, left with an infant daughter. Elena was sure she had seen her play. She would arrange an introduction, perhaps lunch at her villa, where Carla would stay when she comes to Zürich.

John Waldo slipped into the church during the singing of a hymn. The last pew on the right was empty. He found himself standing directly behind Roger Clew.

This gave him dark thoughts. He moved farther to his right. He could also see better now, because he was standing behind a little old lady. She heard him fumbling with the hymnal. She dabbed her cheeks with a handkerchief, then turned to show him the correct page. She smiled. Nice lady, he thought. Nice face.

The couple sitting with her glanced back, first the man, then the woman. Waldo might not have noticed except that the man, big guy, had nudged the woman.

The man looked familiar.

Oh, yeah.

The last time Waldo saw him, he was a doctor. Wore glasses. Pipe in his mouth. Except he looked familiar then, too. Waldo noticed a fairly recent scar behind his ear. Another one under the jawline.

The hymn ended and they sat. The priest was

getting communion ready. People started whispering to each other. It must be, thought Waldo, that you don't have to be quiet now. He leaned forward.

"Hi," he said.

The man smiled and nodded, keeping his eyes on the alter.

"You remind me of someone," said Waldo.

"George Bancroft," said the old lady, turning.

"Who?"

"George Bancroft," she said softly. "The actor."

"Oh, yeah," he whispered. "Ganster movies. Years ago."

The old lady reminded him of someone, too. She was probably on that bus where they thought he was one of the patients. That still bothered him. He leaned forward again toward the lady.

"Do I look real old to you?" he asked.

She pursed her lips. "Not so very."

"How old? Make a guess."

Nellie studied him. "Not more than eighty, I think. More like seventy-five?"

Waldo grunted. He was nowhere near that.

Not real near.

That did it, he thought. He knew what he was going to do. He was going to get a face-lift.

They could laugh at him if they wanted. But lots of men do it. This big guy did it, and now he looks like an actor.

He would tell Bannerman that he wants to stick around for a while. Get it done here, because Los Angeles is probably where all the best cutters are. Maybe talk Billy into doing it, too. McHugh's not getting any prettier.

Outside, after church, he would ask this guy for the name of his cutter and how much it costs. Maybe he'd bring Bannerman over. Get this guy to help him tell Bannerman why it's a good idea.

Yes.

That's exactly what he'd do.

From the author:

For the record, there really is a Mario's in Westport. Right across from the train station. Readers from as far away as Saudi Arabia have visited the place and stolen menus. They all ask for Bannerman's private table and they ask to meet Billy.

Yes, he's really there. You can't miss him. So am I, as often as not. And John Waldo lives five minutes away. There's even an Elena. She actually does live in Zürich—in the villa described in *The Bannerman Effect*—but she won't let me use her real surname. As for Lesko, about ten different women have told me they'd like to take him home with them. I don't understand that at all.

You don't want to know Carla Benedict. Fact is, I thought she was going to get killed off in *Bannerman's Law,* but she's too mean and, besides, people complained.

Elena, by the way, is pregnant. She's about to marry Lesko. Leo Belkin has offered them a visit to the Soviet Union as a wedding present. You'd think the Russians have enough trouble already, but things get worse. Read these next few pages. You'll get the idea.

Stop by if you're in the neighborhood.

Regards,

Nearly an hour passed before the general returned his call. The Armenian had lapsed into an exhausted stupor. As the telephone rang, Kerensky told his brothers to revive the man, slap his face, give him peppered vodka.

The voice on the telephone gave no name or greeting, but it was unmistakable. It was very soft, somewhat high pitched, almost fatherly in tone. Stalin's voice was like this. Kerensky had often wondered whether the resemblance was deliberate.

Kerensky repeated the instructions given by Major Podolsk, first assuring the general that he did not doubt that they were authorized. It was only that they seemed lacking in specifics. If the general could give him some better idea of what he was looking for . . .

"Where they go," Borovik interrupted him, "who they see, what they talk about. The specifics are implicit, Kerensky."

"Yes. Of course they are."

"What else, then?"

"Comrade General . . . it is only that . . . in the course of watching them I will surely learn more about them. Would it not be better if I knew more at the outset?"

"Such as?"

"Well . . . Belkin. The diplomat. It has entered my mind that he might be KGB. If that is so . . ."

"I am all the KGB that need concern you, Kerensky."

His heart sank. He liked the feel of this even less.

"Is there anything else?"

"No. Only . . . that I had hoped to see you."

"It was not necessary."

"I mean, for the thief. The Armenian who stole from you. But . . . I will release him now, as Major Podolsk ordered."

A hollow silence. "You still have him? In that vat?"

"Yes."

"De . . . describe him. Tell me what y . . . you see."

The stammer. The faint tremor in the voice. It was what Kerensky was hoping to hear. He began relating how they lured the man to the sausage room, overpowered him, bound him in entrails, gagged him with the snout of a pig. This last was not accurate, but a pig snout was easier to envision than tripe. He added details that Major Podolsk would not have known, such as the plan to feed part of this man to his cousin and such as watching the Armenian try to flop on the surface like a fish whenever they approached the red button.

"Press it again," said the general. His voice was now a croak. "Tell me what he does."

Kerensky signaled his brother, Feodor. Feodor pressed the button. The Armenian squealed and thrashed. Kerensky described what he saw. The level was dropping quickly. The Armenian had no hope now of gripping the rim. Kerensky had to stand on a chair to see. The man's feet seemed dangerously close to the grinding gears. Kerensky said this to Borovik.

"Shall I stop it?" he asked.

The reply, amid heavy breathing, was an impatient grunt. Kerensky understood. He was to keep talking. He turned the phone from his mouth so that it could capture the Armenian's shrieks. Suddenly, the man began to vibrate. Shaking violently, as if electrocuted. The shrieks became gasps. The eyes popped wide and the mouth opened into what seemed a frozen grin. There, in a blink, the mind was gone. Both legs to the hips, as well.

Borovik's breath came more rapidly. Kerensky had no doubt that he was masturbating.

"Comrade General?"

Kerensky had given him time to gather himself.

"Yes . . . yes." The voice sounded tired but content. A man lost in reverie.

"What will I tell Major Podolsk? He ordered me to release that man."

A small sigh. "You did. He went into hiding. Left Moscow. That's the end of it."

"This other thing you have asked of me . . . is it . . . a sensitive matter?"

"What? Oh. You mean the tourists."

"Is it dangerous, General?"

"No."

"Could I ask why a KGB officer is traveling with an American policeman?"

A pause. "This is what I wish to know, Kerensky."

Kerensky grunted. No evasion this time. Leonid Belkin was definitely KGB. But Borovik's tone had become impatient. Kerensky had hoped that lifting his spirits would make him more communicative.

"Comrade General, I ask these questions only so that I might choose the proper people. Might it come to pass that I would be asked to . . . take strong measures?"

"One must always remain flexible, Comrade."

"I see."

"Choose well, Kerensky. But see to this personally. Also quickly. Their flight has already landed."

"Immediately. Yes."

"Do this for me, Comrade, and the next service I ask of you will take you to America."

The sausage maker blinked. Borovik knew well that this had been his dream.

"To New York, Kerensky. And to Miami."

Drugs, he realized. It must involve drugs. But he thought about meat as well. In America, he had heard, meat like this was reserved for dogs. And not just pork from old pigs. In America, the dogs get beef. Even liver. Whole sections of supermarkets have food only for dogs and this much space is given also for cats. One may even buy toys for them so that they are not left unamused while their owners work.

"Kerensky?"

America has meat-packing plants, they say, where dogs are brought in and allowed to choose what they like best. This, then, is what goes to the supermarkets. Kerensky found this very hard to believe, but everyone who has been to America says it's true. They claim that trained dogs and cats are even put on television and are shown expressing their preferences. This, it seemed to him, was a demand economy gone mad.

"Kerensky!!"

"Yes . . . yes, Comrade General."

"When you bring the sausage to the cousin, you will watch him eat it?"

"My brother will."

"No. You. And do it where there is a telephone."

Kerensky understood. He rolled his eyes.

General Borovik broke the connection. The grinding machine groaned and shook. Feodor kicked it. The machine shuddered to a stop. Feodor cursed.

Well, Kerensky decided, his brothers would have to dismantle it themselves. He must get to the Savoy, make arrangements, see the faces from those photographs while they were still fresh in his mind. Stop thinking about America. It was making him giddy.

Miami.

Not so far from Miami was also Walt Disney World.

"Moscow is what, eight hours ahead of us?"

Susan Lesko's voice came from the kitchen, where

she was fixing breakfast. He heard the crackle of frying bacon.

Bannerman, still in his robe, sat on the patio of his Beachside Commons home sorting through several envelopes of wedding snapshots.

"Nine, this time of year," he answered. "They should be on the ground by now."

While he showered Susan had set two places for breakfast on the umbrella table outside. Too pretty a morning to waste, she said. At his place she had left a fresh mug of coffee, a glass of cranberry juice, which he had just poured into the shrubbery, and a second juice glass containing an assortment of about twenty vitamin pills. He had given up trying to persuade her that the coffee at his elbow was all he ever wanted for breakfast. She also left the snapshots and a pencil. She asked that he go through them, matching names of some of the less familiar faces. She would then put an album together.

"Paul? Have you ever been there?"

"Not to Moscow, no."

"But you've been to Russia."

Bannerman hesitated. "Only to Leningrad once. Just in and out."

He heard a long silence broken only by the rattle of utensils. He knew that she was deciding whether or not to probe further. It probably meant that she had heard a story from Billy McHugh or John Waldo, both of whom had gone in with him.

"Could you ever go back?" she asked. "As a tourist, I mean?"

"I suppose so. Sure."

That's if he didn't mind being watched and bugged every second of every day that he was in the country. If he didn't mind half of the world's intelligence services, to say nothing of the KGB, wondering what he was *really* up to. They would, no doubt, be wondering the same thing about Lesko's visit. As they had about the wedding.

Their interest had come as no surprise. Bannerman had lived too long in a world where almost nothing was taken at face value. In the United States alone, four different agencies had already wondered aloud why *else* so many of his people had gathered in Zürich last week.

He had gone out of his way to calm them. There was no *else*. The ten who flew over from Westport were those who were especially close to Lesko and Elena. Actually, twice that number had been invited. He had to disappoint the other half. As peaceful as the past year had been, he would not risk leaving Westport undefended.

Then, once in Zürich, a new round of assurances became necessary, because other contract agents began showing up from all over Europe. Some thirty in all. They had not been invited, but they were not entirely unexpected. Word gets around. They came by to say hello. No, Mama's Boy is not back in business. It was not a hiring hall. Put that out of your heads. It's a wedding celebration, pure and simple.

He could not blame them for wondering, he supposed. After all, each of these men and women had worked for him, at one time or another, when he was Mama's Boy. Many had worked for Mama before him. But that was then and this is now.

He sorted through several snapshots of the ushers and bridesmaids. These were taken at the rehearsal by one of Elena's cousins using Susan's camera while Susan gathered the wedding party and made them pose. Bannerman was in most of these. As the camera clicked away, he remembered seeing Roger Clew, from the State Department, standing out of range bemusedly shaking his head.

"You wonder why people get curious?" Clew said to him afterward.

"It's just a wedding, Roger. Like any other."

"No, no. My *parents*' wedding was like any other. My parents didn't have a wedding party consisting of you, two KGB officers, a former GRU colonel, and an official of the Drug Enforcement Administration."

"I'm sure it was very nice all the same."

"And that's just the men." Clew pressed his fingers to his temples as if to contain a headache. "We also have bridesmaids . . . all very pretty, very virginal, by the way . . . who include Carla Benedict, who works with a knife, Molly Farrell, who makes bombs, and Janet Herzog, who favors a knitting needle. Not to mention Susan Lesko, who has now been blooded as well."

This last bothered him somewhat. The various intelligence services had probably begun building a file on Susan during the first month of their acquaintance. Roger's certainly had. That, he supposed, was to be expected. But, at a more visceral level, he didn't like hearing her name lumped in with Carla and the others. She was not like them. Blooded or not.

"And here they are, people who spent most of their lives trying not to be photographed, all posing with shit-eating grins like this was the junior prom."

Bannerman shrugged. "Shouldn't that tell you something, Roger?"

"I know. You're retired. It still makes me crazy."

"Roger . . . don't start."

Bannerman was surprised at first to learn that Clew had been invited. Elena knew that he and Roger had once been close, but that Roger had hatched one cute scheme too many aimed at getting him and his people back to work. Water under the bridge, she said. A wedding was a time to mend fences.

That, he supposed, might have been one motive. Gratitude might have been another. It was Roger who had quashed two outstanding indictments against her a couple of years back, without which she could never have returned to the United States. She might also have decided that having Roger as a witness was better than having him plant operatives among the waiters and microphones among floral arrangements.

Bannerman heard the sound of vegetables being chopped. It meant that Susan was making one of her western omelets. He stood up from the table and walked to the sliding door, intending to persuade her that the bacon and an English muffin would be plenty. Her omelets were delicious, but if he ate one he would either have to forgo lunch or run two miles this evening.

Instead, he stood watching her. She was at the counter, her back to him, wearing one of his shirts and not much else. She owned several robes, but she seldom wore them in the morning, mostly, he suspected, because she knew perfectly well what wearing that shirt did to him. No designer of lingerie has ever come up with anything remotely as sexy as a man's shirt on a beautiful woman in the morning.

She half turned while he was watching, using one of those long straight legs to kick a cabinet shut. The same motion pulled the shirt tight against one breast and, being worn open to about the fifth button, partially exposed the other. She was pretending not to notice that he was standing there. She yawned, or pretended to yawn. The yawn turned into a catlike stretch, an arching of her back that caused her breasts to rise as her cheeks rolled languidly across her shoulders. A toss of her long brown hair revealed more of her face. Now he saw the tiny contented smile tugging, just barely, at one corner of her mouth. He knew the look. He also knew that there was no use in protesting the western omelet. She would only suggest that there was more than one way to work off a hearty breakfast.

Bannerman turned away from the patio door without speaking. No use in rewarding smugness. He took his seat at the umbrella table, which Susan had purchased the summer before. She'd chosen the rest of the patio furniture as well, plus the several hanging plants on wrought-iron poles and all of the azaleas and dwarf rhododendrons that bordered the area. His own contribution had been a plum tree that, according to Susan, would not bear fruit for another two seasons. He could wait. In the meantime, he was quite proud of it. It was the first tree, the first *anything*, he'd ever planted. He'd bought two books that showed him how to care for it, unwilling to trust a single source. Typical, Susan had smirked. But it seemed to be doing very well. A week ago it was covered with about a million pinkish blossoms, and now the long, purple leaves were pushing through.

The deck had been bare before Susan entered his life. Sometimes, at night, before Susan, he would wander out here with a Scotch and sit against the railing. Being careful to stay in deep shadow. All house lights turned off. Even then, he didn't make a habit of it. Habits kill. He would not have dreamed that one day soon he'd think nothing of lolling around out here in his bathrobe, in broad daylight.

His first-ever breakfast on the patio came the day after the umbrella table and chairs were delivered. Susan took his mug and his Sunday *New York Times* from his hands and told him to get out there and enjoy the morning. That time he'd stalled for about thirty minutes, long enough to get two of his people to come and check out the area, being careful not to let Susan see them. She found out later. Hit the ceiling. Said it was a crummy way to live. He had not thought of it in those terms. Over the years, caution had become such a part of his nature that there was barely any thought process to it at all. He likened it to the buckling of a seat belt, but Susan dismissed that analogy. You don't wear a seat belt, she said, just to warm up the car and you don't call in a SWAT team every time you feel like getting some air. He could offer no argument that did not sound paranoid.

By the fourth or fifth Sunday, he had even stopped slipping a pistol into the folds of his newspaper.

Colonel General Gennadi Borovik's mood had darkened again. He stood at the window of his office overlooking Dzerzhinsky Square, the pleasure of Kerensky's Armenian all but forgotten. Before him, across the square, was the Savoy Hotel, where Belkin and his companions would be staying.

Why, he asked himself, of all the hotels in Moscow, had Leo Belkin chosen the Savoy. Why a hotel for foreigners? Why the one hotel that stands directly opposite KGB Headquarters? The choice could only have been deliberate. An insult. A thumbing of the nose.

Each of their rooms had of course been prepared. Belkin would expect nothing less. He would caution the American and the Swiss to guard their words. But the American would probably forget. Americans, even policemen, are children about such things.

Off to his right, on a corner outside the Detsky Mir department store, Borovik spied an old woman, a *babushka*, aiming a camera in his direction. Now he saw the reason for it. A small group stood in the square, waiting for a lull in traffic so that they could pose for a souvenir photograph with Moscow Central in the background. The old mother was clearly ill at ease.

From her gestures, Borovik knew that she was telling the others to arrange themselves quickly so that she could be done with it. They obeyed. The old mother quickly lowered the camera, concealing it, and blessed herself. Ten years ago, even five, few would have dared to take such a photograph.

Ten years ago, Borovik reflected, few Muscovites would have even walked along the sidewalk in front of the building. Every Russian claimed to know of someone who did so and heard screams coming from many of the barred ground-floor windows. Some said the hair of this man or this woman turned while in just one day. Others say that this foolish person stopped to listen at one of the windows and was seized and beaten to death by guards. Or torn to pieces by their dogs. Or dragged inside to join the chorus of screams. Never seen again. Not his wife or husband either. His grandparents soon vanished as well.

Even for two years after Gorbachev foreign tourists would ride past in their buses and if one of them should ask, "What was the big mustard-yellow building back there?" the Intourist guide would pretend not to hear. Or she would say that it was just an office building. An insurance company. Which it was before Lenin. She would never say that this was KGB Headquarters. That behind the gray stone of those first two floors are the basement cells of Lubyanka Prison.

But these days, he thought disgustedly, we have guided tours of the building. In every group there is a bumpkin who says, "Tell me confidentially. Is Wallenberg, the Swede, still down below?" or, "Can I see my father's old cell? Perhaps he left a forwarding address."

We have a KGB museum where children can touch pieces of the American U-2 and where young people can buy KGB T-shirts, which they wear not with respect but with impudence. We have a KGB chairman who appears on television talk shows and must smile as he is asked the most impertinent questions.

Borovik could not imagine exposing himself to such nonsense. Not that he was ever asked. The chairman would not allow it in any case. Television is not for you, Gennadi Mikhailovich. It is only for handsome officers who look European and have good teeth. Perhaps this is not exactly what he said but it is what he meant. No short, squat officers with Tartar blood. No brutish faces with Neanderthal brows. Only those who fit the new and benevolent image of the KGB. You would embarrass us, Gennadi. You would scare the children.

So, thought Borovik, we endure the insults. We

smile. We wait. Meanwhile, we write down the names. We write down all their names.

"General Borovik? Sir?"

Major Podolsk's voice. Borovik had not heard his knock. He raised a hand to show that he was deep in contemplation. Let the young major cool his heels a while.

He was a good enough officer, Borovik supposed. Another of the new breed but more pragmatic than most. Did not mind picking up a few rubles on the side. Drinks daiquiris, however. What Russian drinks daiquiris and reads Agatha Christie? He is probably homosexual.

"What do you have, Major?" Borovik still did not turn from the window.

"A list of the guests. Profiles on most of them. Our computers are searching out the rest."

"Any surprises?"

"A great many, General. The American State Department was represented by the undersecretary for foreign affairs. The Drug Enforcement Administration by its deputy chief of operations. This was no ordinary wedding."

Borovik spat. "Very perceptive, Comrade." Also Mama's Boy with a small army of his criminals, the Bruggs with all their millions, and two KGB officers. "What have you learned from Yasenevo?"

The Yasenevo complex—headquarters of First Chief Directorate on Moscow's outer Ring Road.

"They . . . say it is none of our affair."

Borovik sneered. "Not while these three remained in Zürich, perhaps. But now they are in Moscow. In Moscow, they are mine."

"Sir, it remains possible that they have truly come as tourists."

Borovik did not bother to reply. "We had how many at the wedding? Two?"

"One, actually. The one called Cassius. The other saw that he would be recognized. He had to withdraw, but will continue electronic surveillance."

"One, then. Has he reported?"

"He is . . . withholding his report. He wants more money."

Borovik turned at last. "Payment was agreed upon, no?" In his mind, he saw Kerensky's mixing bat.

"Cassius acknowledged this. But he asks what is it worth if he can penetrate Paul Bannerman's inner circle? The question, however, is rhetorical. What he wants is a contract to broker all heroin shipments through—"

Borovik waved him off. "He can do this? Penetrate Bannerman?"

"He believes so. Yes."

"And this other business. Does he know why General Belkin has come to this country with an American policeman and a former drug trafficker?"

"He says only that you will be surprised."

The shorter man grunted. Nothing would surprise him. "Promise him what you must," he said. "Bargain first, but make the agreement."

The major looked at his watch. "He should be calling in. He is late, actually."

Borovik turned once more toward the Savoy Hotel, this time to conceal his excitement. "And Kerensky's people are in place?"

"Yes, General."

He felt a swelling. The excitement grew. "Go and wait for the call," he said. He tossed a hand, dismissing Podolsk. He did not exhale until the door clicked shut. He stepped to his desk and pulled a bottle of peppered vodka from the drawer. He drank deeply.

The vodka would slow the swelling. But soon he would need relief. There was once a house nearby where women could be bound and beaten but it had closed its doors. The women all left to work the tourist hotels where the Japanese in particular pay ten times as much and do not even make them scream.

Perhaps he would go down to the basement. There, if one concentrates, the screams can still be heard.

(John R. Maxim's next Bannerman novel will be available in October 1992.)

THRILLERS

Gripping suspense...explosive action...dynamic characters...international settings...these are the elements that make for great thrillers. Books guaranteed to keep you riveted to your seat.

Robert Ludlum:

☐	26256-4	THE AQUITAINE PROGRESSION	$5.95
☐	26011-1	THE BOURNE IDENTITY	$5.95
☐	26322-6	THE BOURNE SUPREMACY	$5.95
☐	28773-7	THE BOURNE ULTIMATUM	$5.95
☐	26094-4	THE CHANCELLOR MANUSCRIPT	$5.95
☐	28209-3	THE GEMINI CONTENDERS	$5.95
☐	26019-7	THE HOLCROFT COVENANT	$5.95
☐	27800-2	THE ICARUS AGENDA	$5.95
☐	25899-0	THE MATARESE CIRCLE	$5.95
☐	27960-2	THE MATLOCK PAPER	$5.95
☐	26430-3	THE OSTERMAN WEEKEND	$5.95
☐	25270-4	THE PARSIFAL MOSAIC	$5.95
☐	28063-5	THE RHINEMANN EXCHANGE	$5.95
☐	27109-1	THE ROAD TO GANDOLOFO	$5.95
☐	27146-6	THE SCARLATTI INHERITANCE	$5.95
☐	28179-8	TREVAYNE	$5.95

Frederick Forsyth:

☐	28393-6	THE NEGOTIATOR	$5.95
☐	26630-6	DAY OF THE JACKAL	$5.95
☐	26490-7	THE DEVIL'S ALTERNATIVE	$5.95
☐	26846-5	THE DOGS OF WAR	$5.95
☐	25113-9	THE FOURTH PROTOCOL	$5.95
☐	27673-5	NO COMEBACKS	$5.95
☐	27198-9	THE ODESSA FILE	$5.95